Praise for Monica Burns' *Mirage*

"With sexual tension as scorching as the desert the novel is set in, MIRAGE is the kind of historical romantic adventure I cut my teeth on and have been missing for years. Ms. Burns has written a cinematic, compelling, and highly recommended treat!"

~ *Sylvia Day, Nationally Bestselling author*

Rating: Top Pick 4.5 Stars "A strong storyline, engaging characters and seductive love scenes make this a must-read."

~ *Romantic Times BOOKreviews*

"The love scenes are emotion-filled and wonderfully erotic and Altair's responses are enough to make your toes curl...her descriptions of the sight, sound and smell of Egypt transports the reader there, masterfully conveying the beauty of the culture and its people. I adored Mirage from beginning to end."

~ *Two Lips Reviews*

"Mirage kept me up half the night as I raced to the finish of this action-adventure romance... If you're a fan...[of] authors like Betina Krahn, you'll enjoy Mirage."

~ *Romance Reader At Heart*

Look for these titles by
Monica Burns

Now Available:

Dangerous

Mirage

Monica Burns

A SAMHAIN PUBLISHING, LTD. publication.

Samhain Publishing, Ltd.
577 Mulberry Street, Suite 1520
Macon, GA 31201
www.samhainpublishing.com

Mirage
Copyright © 2009 by Monica Burns
Print ISBN: 978-1-59998-831-3
Digital ISBN: 1-59998-615-9

Editing by Imogen Howson
Cover by Anne Cain

First Samhain Publishing, Ltd. electronic publication: October 2007
First Samhain Publishing, Ltd. print publication: June 2009

Dedication

For Steve and Doug, two wonderful brothers-in-law, who unknowingly inspired me to pick up the pen again. Their simple observations about my writing inspired me to push on. If two guys who know nothing about romance books believed in me, then how could I help but believe in myself. Thanks and love to you both.

And for Aunt Min; she believed it would happen from the first word she read.

Acknowledgements

A big thank you to D'Ann Dunham from the Romance Writers Community Yahoo group for her expertise in the equine field. Your feedback made for a strong scene.

Chapter One

London, 1880

"Good Heavens, you're a *woman*."

Alexandra Talbot bit back the tart reply threatening to spring from her mouth. The man might resemble a toad, but at least he wasn't blind. He'd realized right away she was a woman. She tightened her jaw before she forced a smile to her lips.

"Could you please tell Lord Merrick I'm here? He's expecting me."

"But he's expecting *Alex* Talbot."

"I'm Alex Talbot."

"Well, I...there must be some mistake. Lord Merrick is *definitely* not expecting a female."

"I'm sorry, Mr.— What did you say your name was?"

"Stevens, miss."

She nodded. "Mr. Stevens, his Lordship agreed to see me, and unless English manners have gone the way of so many other ancient civilizations, I'm certain he'll honor our appointment."

The clerk rose from his wooden chair, wearing an affronted look. "I must protest, Miss Talbot. This is highly unusual."

"I've no doubt it is, but I'd be grateful if you would inform Lord Merrick that I'm here."

The short, apple-shaped man scurried away to an office door down one of the British Museum's austere hallways. As he disappeared from view, Alex heaved a sigh of frustration. She was far better at debating Egyptology issues than she was at charming men into doing what she wanted.

Perhaps she should have brought Jane with her. Men seemed to fall all over themselves when it came to helping her friend. She frowned. No. She'd made the right decision in coming here alone. Peeling off her black gloves, she shoved them into the beaded bag Jane had insisted she buy. Men weren't the only ones susceptible to Jane's charm. Her friend had persuaded her to purchase more feminine trappings than she could ever want or need. She'd protested the selection of every article of clothing before they left New York, but she'd lost each argument.

Restless, Alex paced the floor, and the train of her green satin gown was a soft whisper on the marble tiles. Her hand brushed against the swag of material hugging her hips. She'd managed to keep the fripperies and ruffles on her gowns to a minimum, but the bustle at the back of her dress was a fashion trend she could have done without.

Brushing a stray lock of hair off her cheek, she frowned. She would much rather be wearing her work clothes. They were far more comfortable. Of course, if she'd tried to stroll into the British Museum wearing trousers, she never would have gotten this far.

All of this would have been so much easier if she were a man, and a British one at that. Her American accent and forthright manner were enough to earn her plenty of arched eyebrows. She could only imagine what people would think if they were to see her in her work clothes bent over a selection of dusty books and papyri.

Work. The thought of it made her long for home. New York seemed so far away. Even more so since she'd discovered the Rosetta Stone had been taken off display for preservation and study. She grimaced. In fact, the discovery had almost convinced her all the plans she'd made would disintegrate like an ancient papyrus. Then, as if her father's spirit had been in the hotel room looking out for her, Lord Merrick's letter had fallen out of the stack of papers she'd brought with her to London.

As the Dean of Ancient Civilizations at New York University, her father had been a longtime correspondent with the Museum's Egyptology Director, Lord Merrick. It had been a simple matter to use her nickname instead of her full name and request an appointment.

Still, her deception might prove to be a terrible miscalculation if the museum clerk had his way. If she could just see the Stone, it would allow her to verify the translations she and Father had worked so hard on. Then she'd be able to honor his last wish and achieve her own dream.

Footsteps echoed in the hall, and she looked up to see Mr. Stevens headed toward her. Retrieving her portfolio from the chair beside the man's desk, she studied his expression with a sinking heart. The man's smug look made it clear her gambit hadn't paid off.

"I'm sorry, Miss Talbot, but his Lordship has had a sudden change of plans and is unable to see you at this time."

"I see, and when might Lord Merrick have another appointment available?"

"I'm afraid his schedule is quite full at the moment, and I don't see how I can possibly squeeze you in before the end of next month."

Alex struggled to keep from glaring at the man as he resumed his seat and went back to work. The rough edge of the portfolio bit into her palms as she considered bashing the pompous clerk over the head with the leather case. Obviously, he believed ignoring her was the easiest way to be rid of her. She stood there for a moment, trying to decide what to do. To come so far, only to be turned away. No, she couldn't accept failure. Not now.

With a swish of her gown's short train, she swept around the desk and strode determinedly down the hall to the door she'd seen the clerk enter. She was more than halfway to her destination before the man realized where she was headed and raced after her.

Ignoring his outraged command to stop, she knocked sharply on the glass pane that bore the gold-lettered title, Director of Egyptology. At the brusque invitation to enter, she sailed through the door with her underskirts rustling a soft imitation of her annoyance.

The office was crammed with a large assortment of artifacts, and the musty smell was similar to her father's office at the university. It comforted her. All her life she'd spent happy hours in rooms similar to this. It reminded her of a time and life she could never experience again.

"What the devil?" The portly man seated at the desk came to his feet quickly. Pasting a polite smile on her face, she moved forward with her hand outstretched.

"Lord Merrick? I'm so glad you agreed to see me. I felt certain Mr. Stevens had misunderstood you." She tried to make her smile as warm as possible. As much as she hated playing the charming coquette, she needed to convince this man to give her access to the Rosetta Stone.

One hand swiping through his bushy white hair, Lord Merrick peered at her over his spectacles. Wide sideburns lined his heavy jowls, and his unforgiving expression would have done a stern reverend justice. Behind her, Stevens burst into the room muttering his apologies. Lord Merrick waved the man away and came around the desk to clasp her hand. A touch of anger lit his limpid blue gaze, but he politely brushed her fingers with a kiss.

"Well, young lady, I think you know full well I was expecting a different Alex Talbot."

She lifted her chin and met his gaze with a forthright look. "What I know is that you were extremely interested in my father's theories about Per-Ramesses."

"So why didn't Professor Talbot come himself?"

"My father died unexpectedly last fall from influenza." Alex swallowed the grief rising in her throat.

Lord Merrick's cold expression dissolved into sympathy as he guided her to a chair facing his desk. "You have my sympathies, Miss Talbot. Your father was one of the world's foremost Egyptologists. Our correspondences were highly valued by me."

"And that's why I've come to you, Lord Merrick. My father's last wish was for me to complete his life's work." The bustle forced her to perch on the edge of the seat, and she silently cursed the uncomfortable fashion she wore.

Skepticism arched the man's snowy eyebrows as he returned to his chair and shook his head. "My dear, I understand your desire to grant your father's last wish, but please believe me when I tell you that even if you have all your father's notes, without his knowledge...well, it's impossible."

Alex leaned forward, her hands tightening on her portfolio. She mustn't fail now. She had his attention. She needed to guard her words carefully. "My lord, I began working with my father at the age of fifteen, and I worked at his side until his death. I studied his notes, questioned him relentlessly. I'm confident I know as much as he did about Per-Ramesses."

"And you want access to the Rosetta Stone, is that it?"

"Yes, my lord. I need to ensure the translations my father and I made are accurate. It's critical to finding the location of Per-Ramesses."

"*Finding it?*" Lord Merrick exclaimed. "Young lady, what the devil makes you think you can find Per-Ramesses when England's chief Egyptologists haven't done so?"

"Because those gentlemen didn't have what I do—my father's notes and my father's knowledge. It had been his intention to come, but his death prevented it. I'm here now, and I intend to honor his memory by proving his theories and mine correct."

Sitting stiff and straight in the leather wing-backed chair, she recognized the look of disbelief on Lord Merrick's face. Jane had worn a similar expression when Alex had laid out her plans. The difference was her friend hadn't hesitated to call her insane. Lord Merrick just didn't know how to do so politely. His face bore the same benign condescension she'd seen far too often on the faces of most university faculty in New York. They believed her inferior simply because of her sex.

There had been the exceptions. Men who had found her intelligence a refreshing change, but they'd been few and far between. And it was doubtful even those forward-thinking men would have agreed to a wife working at their side. Only her father and Uncle Jeffrey had truly encouraged her pursuit of archeology. Every other man was suspect as to his real intentions where she was concerned.

Merrick leaned forward, his hands clasped and resting on his desk. "Miss Talbot, the desert is difficult enough for an Englishman, and it's definitely not a place for a woman. I cannot sanction this in any way."

"Forgive me, my lord, but I'm simply asking you to give me access to the Stone so I can corroborate our translations."

"I'm sorry, my dear, *but* in all good conscience, I can't do

13

that."

Hands clenched, she kept her voice even with difficulty. "And if I were a man?"

"Naturally, things would be different."

"Naturally," she mimicked in a bitter tone.

"Why don't you let her look at the Stone, Merrick?"

Alex twisted around in her seat to stare at the man sitting in the corner of the room. She'd been so preoccupied with her desire to persuade Lord Merrick to her way of thinking, she'd failed to realize there was someone else present. As he rose to his feet, she drew in a quick breath at the sheer height of the man. He was easily more than six feet tall. She was far from short, but if she were standing, he would tower over her by several inches. It wasn't like her to pay too much attention to the men she met, but this man was impossible to ignore. Well-built, his lean figure sported a dark blue coat, which fell open to reveal a dove gray waistcoat and matching trousers. As he moved forward, the grace and regal bearing of his step reflected a primeval power. This was a man accustomed to prevailing in whatever matter he undertook. Her heart skipped a beat.

Silky waves of dark brown hair caressed the collar of his coat in a length that was almost barbaric. On any other man, the style would have looked ridiculous, but on him it was devastating. It suited the rich brown of his sun-kissed skin. A wave of heat washed over her. Dear Lord, no man she'd ever met had affected her like this. Deep brown eyes studied her closely, and she suppressed a tremor of excitement as she met his probing gaze. Dark eyebrows arched over incredible eyes, and the merest hint of a smile touched his full, sensual lips.

He reminded her of a sleek leopard, content to watch its prey before pouncing at just the right moment. The sudden image of him dressed as a pharaoh holding the collar of such a large cat caused her palms to grow damp. Where on earth had that come from? Appalled, she jerked her gaze away and turned back to Lord Merrick, who frowned at the other man.

"The devil take it, Blakeney. You can't be serious."

"Why not? What harm will it do?" The stranger shrugged as Lord Merrick stared at him in appalled horror.

"But she's...she's..."

Merrick was as blind as that little toad Stevens. The man was making his decision solely based upon her sex, and not her capabilities, which she'd outlined so clearly. All her life, her father had treated her with the respect of first a student and then a colleague. He'd accepted her as fully capable of acquiring the same knowledge as himself. No doubt, the possibility of a woman finding the lost city of Per-Ramesses without male assistance was incomprehensible to this man.

Her stomach tightened with concealed anger. If she didn't get out of here quickly, she'd forget what little presence of mind she had and confirm the notion that women were temperamental, hysterical and unfit for working in an academic setting. Determined to remain charming to the end, she rose to her feet and forced herself to smile.

"Gentlemen." She gave both men a sharp nod of dismissal. "I'm sorry you're not interested in my work or my father's. I had hoped to convince you otherwise. However, I can assure you, I'll find Per-Ramesses—with or without the Museum's help."

Wheeling about on her heel, Alex rushed blindly to the door lest they see the tears of frustration threatening to spill down her cheeks. She grasped the brass doorknob and turned it. Large, sun-drenched fingers touched her light-deprived skin and stopped her. Fiery warmth streaked up her arm until it spread its way through every inch of her body. Startled by her reaction, she yanked her hand away and lifted her gaze up to meet his. When he smiled, her heart slammed against the wall of her chest. Lord, the man's smile was as potent as his touch.

"Miss Talbot is it?"

"I'm sorry, sir, you have me at a disadvantage."

"Forgive me." He offered her a small bow. "Viscount Blakeney at your service. I'm liaison to the Museum's Foreign Office of Antiquities."

"Another of the Museum's minions?" She could have bitten her tongue off at the sarcasm in her voice.

His eyes narrowed and his features resembled an ancient stone statue. The look he pinned on her sent a shiver down her spine. Even Ramesses could not have intimidated or excited her more. The fanciful thought made her frown. She wasn't here to find a modern-day pharaoh, especially one condescending to help her.

Once more, she reached out to open the door, but his firm grip on her wrist stopped her again. The touch made her mouth go dry as his fingers sent a shock of sensation up her arm. Again her heart skipped a beat, and a spark of awareness flashed in the depths of his brown eyes.

She inhaled a sharp breath as his thumb caressed her pulse with gentle pressure. The touch made every nerve in her body scream at the way his presence was assaulting her senses. As he leaned toward her, the whiff of a tantalizing spice spiraled between them. The scent was familiar, but it was difficult to think with him so close.

"Do not discount me, Miss Talbot. If you wish to see the Stone, I'm willing to escort you to its present location." The stern note in his voice helped her regain her faculties.

"And do not discount me, my lord. I do not suffer fools gladly, nor do I look fondly on those who think me a fool." This time she kept her tone even, yet firm. She could be polite, but she had no intention of letting this man, or any other for that matter, manipulate her.

A brilliant smile curved his mouth, and she wanted to bask in the warmth of it. Heavens, but the man was mesmerizing. She needed to control this urge to simper like an addle-brained simpleton in his presence.

"I seriously doubt you're a fool, Miss Talbot. Although it remains to be seen if you are foolish." Releasing her from his grip, he opened the door and swept his hand toward the corridor. "Shall we?"

"Right now?"

"I thought you wanted to see the Stone?" There was more than a hint of amusement in his voice. For the first time, she heard the melodious accent beneath the proper English. The sound was so familiar and yet so foreign.

"Well yes, but I'll need at least an hour or more to study the markings."

"Then you'll have it."

Behind them, Lord Merrick came to life. "I say, Blakeney. It's just not done. She's likely to wreak havoc in the workroom. The scholars will be quite distracted by her presence."

The anger bubbling just beneath her calm surface exploded

as she turned to face the protesting director. *"x one aay aza mn name zapa oyhh eanno."*

"I *say!* Did she just speak Coptic?" Merrick sputtered.

A glimmer of respect and assessment sparkled in the dark brown eyes studying her face. "She did, *and* with impeccable clarity."

Alex flushed at the amusement she saw tugging at his mouth. It was obvious Lord Merrick didn't understand the language, but Lord Blakeney's knowledge was clearly far superior to the older man's. Oh God. The man would never take her to the Stone now. Whatever had possessed her to speak in such an unladylike manner? The director really was a pompous jackass, unfit for the duties of his office, but she should have realized one, if not both men, might be fluent in the language of the pharaohs. When was she going to learn to think before acting?

"Well, what the devil did she say?"

She held her breath as Lord Blakeney arched a regal eyebrow at her in only the way a British male could. Well, there was nothing for it now. She lifted her chin up in a stubborn gesture, ready to translate her words.

"The young lady thinks you perform your duties like the hardiest of mules."

Alex started with surprise. He'd not given her away. Why had he translated her insult in such a positive light? Her surprise evolved into suspicion. What did he want?

"Harrumph. Does she now." Merrick eyed her with skepticism. "Well, Blakeney, if you're compelled to show her the Stone, do so, but if the scholars protest, it's on your head."

With a slight nod, Lord Blakeney grasped her arm and ushered her out into the corridor, closing the door behind them. As they walked in silence, Alex finally recognized the tantalizing smell of cedarwood mixed with another spice she couldn't identify. It cultivated her earlier image of him in Pharaoh's garb, his legs sleek and powerful beneath a short loincloth. She could even visualize her fingers gliding over the hard sinews of his golden arms and chest. Would his bared body be as muscular as his clothing hinted?

The decadent thoughts horrified her. Heavens, she'd been around Jane too long. Her widowed friend's constant consideration of men's physical attributes had finally rubbed off on her. Quickly she thrust the images aside. But it was difficult to do so given the way her body reacted to his.

Several corridors later, she knew she'd never be able to find her way back to the exit without her escort. A slight shiver skated down her spine. She knew nothing about the man accompanying her. But her body did. Her skin had not stopped tingling since the first time he'd touched her. She tried to suppress the sensations. For all she knew he could be the worst kind of rake—the kind her friends had warned her about before she left New York.

A moment later, Lord Blakeney ushered her into a well-lit room. Worktables lined the walls, where several men were immersed in their study of various documents and books. In the center of the room, on a waist-high pedestal, stood the object she'd come to see.

Her fingers tightened on the portfolio she carried and she sucked in her breath as she drew near the Stone. Reverently, she stretched out her hand then stopped. Was it being treated with a solution her fingers might disturb? She turned back toward him.

"May I?"

"By all means." A small smile curved his mouth. Feet planted slightly apart, he folded his arms across his chest. For a moment she forgot the misshapen basalt slab as she pictured him in the hot Egyptian climate, his rippling chest muscles glistening with oil her hands applied. The heady image stole her breath away, and she saw his eyes darken with a dangerous invitation.

Gathering her wits, Alex sucked in a ragged breath and turned her attention back to the Stone. Her hand caressed the cool surface of the ancient rock, the carved indentions rough beneath the pads of her fingers. Her throat tightened. This would have meant so much to her father. Touching the Stone would have been the culmination of his lifelong dream. Now it was her dream. Her chance to prove that a woman was just as capable as a man when it came to finding an ancient city.

She peered closely at the artifact's surface, noting several hieroglyphs identical to ones in the notes she carried. Without thinking, she quickly opened the portfolio in her arms and sifted through the papers. It took a moment, but she finally extracted the page she sought. She examined it for a moment then looked closer at the Stone. The glyphs on her page were slightly different from the black basalt slab's markings.

Pulling her pencil out, she sketched a mark from the Stone onto her paper. The difference in the mark was small, but significant. She inhaled a sharp breath of excitement. Her father had been right. Per-Ramesses was at Khatana-Qantir, and she was going to find it. She scribbled another correction onto her paper as her gaze shifted between the Stone and her work.

There, another glyph that didn't match. She pulled another sheet of paper from the folder and scanned the symbols. The significance made all the difference in the translation. She smiled. Her persistence had paid off. With these final corrections, Per-Ramesses and his beloved Nourbese would soon see the light of day after more than three thousand years.

She pulled one page after another from her portfolio, intent on verifying the work she'd brought with her. Eventually, half her portfolio lay spread out at her feet as she continued to confirm and correct her notes. Time held no meaning as she studied the markings. The light changed as she worked, and she frowned as shadows hovered over the black basalt, making it difficult to read the symbols. Throwing her head back, she looked up at the skylight. She'd been so absorbed in her work she'd not even noticed the sun was setting. With a quick glance at the workstations that circled the room, she saw most of the scholars had left. She didn't even see Viscount Blakeney.

She rolled her head around to stretch her neck muscles before stooping to pick up several stacks of paper she'd placed on the floor. The sudden frisson rippling over her skin made her suck in a quick breath. She swallowed hard as a golden-skinned hand picked up some papers and offered them to her.

As she looked up into Lord Blakeney's dark brown eyes, the warmth of his gaze heated her body to a fevered pitch. It was like being taken from the coolness of a cave out into the heat of a desert sun. The sudden awareness of him spiraled a cord of tension through her. Disturbed by the wild sensation, she accepted the papers with a sharp nod of her head. Standing upright, she quickly jostled her portfolio closed as she tried to ignore his presence. Impossible.

"Please forgive me, my lord. I didn't mean to inconvenience you by working so late. I've imposed on your kindness."

"There's nothing to forgive. It's obvious you have a passion for your work."

She glanced back at the Rosetta Stone. "Yes, it's been my life for a very long time."

"And did you find what you were looking for?"

Excited, she smiled as she bobbed her head. "Yes, and I know I'll be successful now. I only wish…"

"You wish your father were here to share the triumph." His firm lips curved in an understanding smile.

"Yes, both he and my uncle would have been elated, and it would have been difficult not to be carried away by their euphoria."

"Your uncle?"

The memory of their recent deaths made her throat constrict. In less than a year, she'd lost the two most important men in her life. She controlled her sorrow and nodded. "Uncle Jeffrey is the one who first tempted my father with the idea of finding Per-Ramesses."

"Was your uncle an Egyptologist as well?"

"Oh, no, Uncle Jeffrey was a member of the spiritualist movement."

Skepticism arched the man's eyebrows at her statement, and Alex cringed as she realized her mistake. Everyone had believed her uncle a madman, but he'd provided too many clues about Per-Ramesses for her or her father to discount him as such. The man's arbitrary dismissal of her uncle disappointed her for some strange reason.

"Come, I'll see you home. Where are you staying?"

"At the Clarendon, but your escort is unnecessary. I'll have a hackney take me to the hotel."

A stern expression hardened his rugged features as he grasped her elbow and ushered her out of the workroom. "I think not. London after dusk is no place for a lady unescorted. I cannot leave you to such a fate."

Swallowing hard, she protested. "I appreciate your kindness, my lord, but I'm quite accustomed to taking care of myself. The streets of London are hardly any more treacherous than those of New York."

"Perhaps, but I'll escort you safely to your destination nonetheless."

The set of his jaw indicated she would not sway him in the matter. With a quiet sigh, she acquiesced to his stubborn insistence. The gloomy corridors of early afternoon were now almost dark. Had she really been working for so long? It seemed like just a few moments ago that she'd first touched the basalt's cool surface. The last of the sun's light barely lit their way as they entered a large exhibition hall filled with Egyptian artifacts.

Above their heads, a balcony encircled the room with more exhibits, while the various sarcophagi they passed threw eerie shadows across their path. Glancing upward, she frowned. Had something actually moved on the balcony? She scoffed at the notion, but a shiver scraped its way down her back. It was impossible to shake the disturbing sensation of being watched.

She glanced up at her escort. Lord Blakeney appeared quite unconcerned as he guided her across the large room. With a slight shrug, she discounted the inner warning. As usual, her imagination was out of control. Yet, despite her best intentions, the sensation refused to go away.

By the time they reached the middle of the room, the hair on the back of her neck had spiked with apprehension. Something was wrong, but she couldn't pinpoint exactly what. Ahead of them, two giant statues of Anubis provided an arch over the doorway leading into another gallery. Guardians of the tomb, the jackal-headed figures presented an ominous picture as they approached the entryway.

Foreboding tensed her muscles as she shot a quick glance at her companion. There wasn't a hint of concern or wariness on the man's face. Lord, she was acting like a muddleheaded goose. As they drew close to the statues, she looked up with awe at the massive monuments.

They were magnificent. Would she find similar treasures at Per-Ramesses? Out of the corner of her eye, a shadow flitted along the wall of the balcony encircling the room. Just as quickly the vague form disappeared. She frowned. She was almost as bad as Uncle Jeffrey—seeing things that weren't even there. A scraping sound made her stop abruptly. Lord Blakeney

21

paused as well and eyed her with curiosity.

"Is something wrong, Miss Talbot?"

"I'm not sure." She shook her head. "I thought I heard something."

Arching an eyebrow, he glanced over his shoulder to search the dark recesses of the room's corners. The scraping noise came again, this time louder and she looked up to see a large stone plummeting toward her. Inhaling a breath of terror, she froze. In the next moment, a strong arm snapped around her waist and jerked her to safety. The sandstone shattered on the floor behind her. Buried in the warmth of Lord Blakeney's embrace, Alex shuddered.

Alive. She was still *alive.*

She'd been too terrified to move. In the distance, shouts sounded through the hall. Trembling, she struggled to remain calm as the voices grew in strength.

Pushing her away from him, Lord Blakeney's hand brushed over her brow and cheek as he studied her with a look of concern. "Are you hurt?"

Unable to speak, she shook her head. He glanced back at the disintegrated sandstone on the marble floor before looking upward. She followed the direction of his gaze and saw the hole in the balcony. It must have been a loose stone, just waiting to fall. A man slid to a halt just outside the Egyptian room.

"My lord, are you and the young lady all right?"

"Yes, Martin, we've escaped injury. Miss Talbot, however, is quite shaken from her narrow escape. Get several of the men to help you clean up this mess, and tomorrow I want the balcony and wall inspected for other loose stones."

His strong arm still wrapped around her in a protective gesture, he guided her around the pieces of broken sandstone. As they passed beneath the somber statues of Anubis, she shivered. Had she really seen a shadow up on the balcony or had her intuition been trying to warn her of impending disaster?

More importantly, had Uncle Jeffrey been right? Was there really a curse on those who searched for Per-Ramesses and Nourbese's tomb?

Chapter Two

Sheikh Altair Mazir sank back into the plush leather cushions of his carriage. Seated opposite him, Alex Talbot sat quietly, her face pale in the gaslight shining through the window. She was amazing. No tears, no hysteria. If it weren't for her pallor and the way her hands were trembling, no one looking at her would be able to tell she'd almost been killed a few moments ago.

"I'm sorry your visit to the museum was so frightening."

She lifted her gaze to his, and his gut clenched at his physical reaction to her. Damn, but those hazel eyes of hers were nothing short of incredible. Large and round in her face, they flashed with whatever emotion she was feeling at a particular moment in time.

"I admit it wasn't exactly what I expected." A wry smile tipped the corner of her mouth. Then a look of mortification spread across her face. "Forgive me, my lord. I failed to thank you for saving my life. If you'd not pulled me away from where I was standing..."

"Don't dwell on it. You're safe now."

"But you saved my life. I shall always be in your debt."

Her gratitude was discomfiting given his connection to her. He needed to explain who he was, but he couldn't find the words. Instead, he watched her through the shadows, remembering the way her soft curves had pressed into him when he'd pulled her out of harm's way. His groin tightened at the memory. Her body had been soft and luxuriant against his. Lush and sensual.

Unable to help himself, his gaze slid down to the round

fullness of her breasts. The images dancing through his head teased his senses and his imagination. Would her nipples be as inviting and pink as her generous mouth? Or perhaps they would be dark against that creamy complexion. The thought singed his skin with fire.

At that moment, her gaze met his. From where he sat he could see the way her eyes darkened with the awareness he'd seen earlier. Her enticing mouth parted slightly, and he swallowed hard at the urge to pull her into his arms again. Christ, he was acting like a stallion determined to mount a mare. The thought prompted an image of her on top of him with her golden-chestnut hair tumbling down over her creamy shoulders. It hardened his cock immediately.

Dragging his gaze away from her, he peered out the window of the coach. Traffic was heavy tonight, and it was taking longer to get to the Clarendon than usual. If they continued at this slow pace, his groin was going to be in agony by the time they reached the hotel. He turned his head and caught her watching him. Her cheeks darkened in the muted light as their eyes met. There was curiosity and something else shining out of those mysterious hazel depths.

"You seem puzzled by something, Miss Talbot."

"Yes." She nodded her head then quickly denied her response. "I mean no...I'm sorry, it was rude of me to stare. I...it's just that you don't look like the other English noblemen I've met."

The comment made him stiffen, and he was thrown back to a different time when another woman had said the same thing. Even after ten years the thought of Caroline cut deep. He closed the door on the painful memory. The past was behind him. He'd paid dearly for Caroline's betrayal. It wouldn't happen again.

"And how do you think an English nobleman *should* look?" he said in an icy tone.

"I'm sorry. You must think me terribly rude. It's just that your skin tone and profile remind me of the Egyptian pharaohs I've seen in different texts."

Biting the inside of his cheek, he wasn't sure how to interpret her comment. Accustomed to society's contempt for his mixed blood, he didn't care what people thought of him. But something about this woman made him care, and he didn't like the sensation. And he especially didn't like the way his body reacted to her soft shape.

"I'll take that as a compliment," he said with a bit more irony than he intended.

"Oh, but it was. A compliment I mean. I'm terribly sorry. I have this habit of speaking without thinking first. My friend Jane warns me all the time to guard my tongue, but I can't seem to help myself."

He folded his arms across his chest, studying her contrite expression. At this stage in his life, he found it easy to ignore the prejudice and scorn most of London society flung his way. But this woman posed a conundrum. For some unfathomable reason, he hesitated telling her who he was. What he was.

Confused by the notion, he frowned. She'd given him no reason to think she would be appalled by his confession, and yet it was a risk he didn't want to take. Eventually, he'd have to tell her the truth, but for the moment—for the moment he was content to let her think of him as Lord Blakeney.

Clearing his throat, he smiled. "I hope your scare tonight doesn't make you hesitant to return to the Museum."

"Oh no, not at all. I'm sure it was an accident." She frowned for a moment, staring off into space. The idea that it hadn't been an accident nudged at her. It was rather odd how that stone had fallen just at that precise moment. And what about that shadow she'd seen? She'd thought her imagination had been playing tricks on her, but now she was convinced that wasn't true. She'd seen someone up on the balcony.

"So when do you plan on returning?" His deep voice drew her attention back to him.

"Actually, I don't need to. It's hard to believe, but I answered all my questions this afternoon."

"*All* of them?" The doubt in his voice made her smile.

"Yes, I didn't expect to finish so quickly, but my translations were much more accurate than I expected. Although I did find a couple of odd references in my notes the Stone didn't account for, but I'm sure I'll be able to decipher those points in a day or two."

"I see, and when do you intend to leave for Egypt?"

"I would imagine by the end of next week." She mentally

ticked off some of the items she still needed to purchase before setting sail.

"Next *week*?"

"Well, I've already made some arrangements, but there are still a large number of supplies to purchase. I'd love to leave tomorrow, but it's not possible."

"And how thoroughly have you thought through this adventure?" The censorious note in his voice pulled her gaze toward his stern one.

It sounded almost as if he was worried about her. The thought astounded her, but even more unsettling was the pleasure it gave her when she considered the possibility. Still, the last thing she wanted was anyone interfering with her plans. She'd given her word to her father she would find Per-Ramesses, and she intended to keep her vow.

Her father had believed in her abilities. She would not fail him at this stage of the game. She'd also made a promise to herself. All her life she'd studied and worked hard to make this journey. Finding Per-Ramesses would prove to the academic world that a woman could be just as good an archeologist as a man.

"This trip has been in the planning for more than two years. My father and I considered every detail."

"*Every* detail? What about a guide into the desert?"

"My father had been corresponding with Sheikh Mazir, a Bedouin, who offered to serve as his guide to Khatana-Qantir."

Tension hardened his jaw line as he eyed her with his piercing gaze. "And how reliable is this man? For all you know, he's a barbarous savage who'd just as soon slit the throat of another infidel as serve as a desert guide."

The bloody image made her stomach flip unpleasantly. Few things made her blanch, but the mere reference to blood made her queasy. No doubt, a phobia left over from childhood when she'd cut her foot. The blood streaming across the floor had been nothing compared to the doctor's visit and subsequent suturing. Shaking off the vivid memory, she struggled to ease the nausea churning in her stomach.

"My father had every confidence in Sheikh Mazir. He told me quite often that the Sheikh was a very special man."

"Indeed."

"Yes, indeed." She sent him an arched look, irritated by his pessimistic tone. "I'm certain Sheikh Mazir will respect the agreement. After all, Bedouin law decrees he honor the covenant."

"Even if the Sheikh does keep his word, I find myself agreeing with Lord Merrick about your expedition. The desert is a harsh, unforgiving land." His mouth was tight with disapproval as his forbidding gaze settled on her.

"I'm aware of what I'm up against, my lord. My father and I discussed our trip and its hardships countless times. I'm not afraid."

"You should be, Alex. You should be very afraid."

The sound of her given name rolling off his tongue pulled a sharp breath from her. As her eyes met his, the predatory expression on his handsome features sent her heart careening out of control. The look reinforced her earlier image of him as an ancient Egyptian ruler. Stern, strong and master of his domain. He would rule a woman's heart with simply the crook of his finger. The wickedly seductive images from their first meeting flitted through her head as her gaze focused on his mouth. What would it be like to kiss him?

Appalled by her wanton thoughts, she looked out the carriage window at the gaslights lining the street. What was wrong with her? Her interests had always been centered on her studies and working with her father. She'd been kissed before, but those caresses had been fumbling attempts at best from would-be-suitors.

No man had ever captured her attention the way this man did. In her studies, she'd learned about the sexual practices of the ancient Egyptians. Her view of their activities had always been of a scientific nature. But now—now she understood some of the erotic poetry she'd translated without her father's knowledge.

Curiosity had driven her to learn more, but she had never understood the emotions a physical attraction could arouse until now. The intensity of her attraction to him was disturbing, not to mention inconvenient. A man would only be a hindrance in her determination to find Per-Ramesses and fulfill her father's last wish.

She darted a glance in his direction to find him watching her. In an instant, every thought in her head was swept aside. The look in his eyes was dark and dangerous. Her mouth went dry at the sight. Oh this man was trouble, plain and simple. The sooner she fled his presence, the quicker she could control the way her body was responding to him.

A fraction of a second later the carriage rocked violently to a halt, and the jolt propelled her forward into his arms. Outside there were shouts of anger and blame, but inside the carriage the silence hung thick and heavy.

Heat flushed her skin at the close contact as the scent of him rushed at her senses with heady abandon. The woody fragrance of cedarwood tantalized her nose, and she finally recognized the scent of sweet fennel. The mixture was earthy, fresh and wholly masculine. It suited him.

Hot tension made every nerve-ending in her body grow taut as she realized how close his mouth was. It would only take a small movement and his lips would be covering hers. The thought pulled a sharp gasp from her. Oh, this was not good. Not good at all.

"Has anyone ever told you how lovely your mouth is?"

The dark seduction in his whispered question released more than a dozen butterflies in her stomach as she struggled to control her heartbeat. Even if she'd been able to do so, she didn't have time to give him an answer as his hard mouth covered hers.

This was nothing like the fumbling kisses she'd experienced before. His mouth was bold and confident on hers. It startled her with its raw intensity, but more surprising was how much she was enjoying his touch. Her blood slid hot and heavy through her veins. She'd been right. The man was definitely dangerous, but at the moment she didn't care.

The gentle nip of his teeth on her lower lip caused her to gasp, and he took the opportunity to sweep his tongue past her lips to the inner recesses of her mouth. The hedonistic rush that surged through her settled in the pit of her stomach. It boiled there in a hot vessel ready to overflow.

Without thought, she responded to his kiss, her tongue dancing with his as a soft moan trembled deep in her throat. Strong fingers trailed along her cheek before sliding down her throat. His lips captured hers again as he pulled her tightly against him.

Bloody hell, but the woman was a fiery temptation. She tasted like forbidden fruit. Lush, ripe and sensuous. With just a kiss, his cock had become hard as iron. It pressed against him in a lustful cry for satisfaction. Her tongue swirled around his in a seductive move, and he suppressed a groan of need.

He had to touch more of her. Gently, he feathered her cheek with kisses until he reached the lobe of her ear. As he nibbled on her, his fingers made short work of the buttons running down the front of her dress. The silky smoothness of her skin caressed his fingers and a soft cry escaped her lips as his hand glided across the base of her throat and down to the top of her full breasts.

God almighty. He wanted to bed the woman right here in the carriage. Small pants of excitement blew past her lips as he drew back from her. Her hazel eyes had turned green with passion, and her full mouth had a sensual curve to it.

She was hot heat in his hands. He had only to press his advantage and he'd be inside her, satisfying the cravings of his cock. His finger lined a path from the base of her throat to the shadowed valley between her luxuriant breasts. God, he wanted to suck on her. A shudder broke through her at his touch, and he paused. What the hell was he doing?

This was Alexander Talbot's daughter. A man he'd admired a great deal. How could he possibly take advantage of her like this? The sound of Caroline's voice echoed in his head. *Because you're a savage. A heathen who will never be accepted by London society.* The memory of that day made him grow still. No. He wasn't a savage. But making love to Alex in the carriage certainly didn't qualify him as a gentleman.

With a quick movement, he picked her up and plopped her back into her seat. His groin protested angrily, but he ignored the pain. Her mouth formed a soft *moue* of surprise, and it beckoned to him like a Sahara mirage. Tempting and tantalizing in its beauty. He swallowed the desire threatening to rule his senses. For the first time he realized the carriage was moving again.

"I took advantage of you."

"I don't recall protesting *too* loudly," she said with a wry note in her voice.

The matter-of-fact response caused him to stare at her in surprise. A flush crested over her cheeks and she quickly looked away. He'd never met anyone like her before. Impulsive, stubborn, intelligent and forthright. Did she take after her father? The thought of the professor made him frown as he looked out at the shadowed streets.

She was Talbot's daughter and as such she deserved respect, not this cavalier treatment. Out of the corner of his eye, he watched her button up her dress. As the creamy complexion of her throat disappeared beneath the green satin dress she wore, his hand itched to reach out and stop her.

What the devil had Talbot been thinking when he'd burdened her with this quest for Per-Ramesses? It was a difficult and risky journey. Merrick was rarely right about anything, but there was one thing they both agreed upon. The desert was no place for a woman of society. It was a harsh existence without the modern comforts women were accustomed to.

Glancing in her direction, he saw her smoothing out the wrinkles in her gown. She looked delicious enough to eat. The image of her straddling him returned to haunt him, and he clenched his fists. Determined to push the tempting image from his thoughts, he closed his eyes for a moment. When he opened them, his gaze met hers. There was no rancor in her eyes. In fact, he was certain a flicker of excitement still gleamed in her gaze. Crushing his desire, he looked away.

It was best to ignore the fact he'd even kissed her. Unfortunately, that was difficult to do given how succulent and sweet she'd tasted on his lips. The base need stirring in his body sent a jolt of tension through him. Christ Jesus, he'd not felt this ruttish in years. The Clarendon's well-lit driveway illuminated the inside of the carriage, and he expelled a sigh of relief.

"It seems we've reached our destination."

"Yes." The single word was a forlorn sound. It twisted his insides. She'd almost lost her life tonight, and he'd taken advantage of that vulnerability to satisfy his own needs. He was a bastard. If he'd gone back to the desert where he belonged, none of this would have ever happened. At least there, he didn't feel quite so alone. His mother's people had always accepted him as one of their own.

He cursed himself again for giving his oath to a dying man. He should never have agreed to his grandfather's pleas, even if he'd done so out of love. Adamant the Blakeney line not die out, the old Viscount had begged him not to give up his title or holdings. Now he was trapped like a fox between the hounds and freedom.

Each year his agreement to spend half the year in England and the remainder in the desert was growing more burdensome. No doubt his grandfather had thought it easier for him to find a suitable wife among London's nobility. He'd known the futility of that exercise before the old Viscount had died, but it hadn't saved him from the inevitable task of honoring his word.

The carriage rolled to a halt. Exiting the vehicle, he turned to offer his assistance. She slid her hand into his, and the light touch warmed his body. He grimaced at the effect she had on him. One would think him a schoolboy the way his body was reacting to the woman. Taking her arm, he guided her up the steps of the hotel.

As they entered the lobby, a young woman standing near the concierge's desk hurried toward them with a relieved smile on her face.

"Oh, Alex, there you are! I've been half sick with worry. I was beginning to think something terrible had happened." The woman kissed Alex's cheek then stepped back. "Heavens, you look completely washed out."

"I'm fine. Jane, this is Lord Blakeney. He helped me get access to the Rosetta Stone. My lord, this is my friend and traveling companion, Mrs. Jane Beacon."

Altair stiffened. Explaining why he'd not mentioned his identity before now was not going to be easy. He was far from ashamed of his Bedouin blood, but he didn't like the possibility of seeing her look at him with disgust. For just a bit longer he wanted her to know him as Lord Blakeney, not a half-breed who was the subject of scorn and ridicule.

He shoved his thoughts aside, fully aware he had to convince her she was undertaking a foolish errand. While he was honor bound to follow through on his agreement with her father, he had to convince her it was in her best interest to give up this foolish venture.

"Do I understand that you're going with Miss Talbot on this dangerous expedition?" He eyed the woman with disapproval.

The question immediately earned him Alex's scorching glare. Turning his head, he met her scowl with one of his own. The harsh condemnation on his face made her clench her hands with frustration.

What was it about this man that intensified every emotion in her body? Moments ago his touch had almost blinded her with passion, now his disapproval incited her bull-headedness. She knew perfectly well it was a dangerous expedition, but she wasn't about to admit it to him.

"It is *not* a dangerous expedition," she retorted.

"It bloody well is," he snarled in a low voice.

Alex shuddered. She wasn't sure if it was from the fury in his voice or the reference to blood that disturbed her. Why did the English feel it necessary to constantly associate blood with their curses?

"I have the situation well in hand, my lord."

"Do you? I wonder. What if Sheikh Mazir doesn't speak English? Venturing out into the desert, *even with* a Bedouin guide, is a serious undertaking for any man. For two women it's twice as treacherous."

Alex flinched at his brutal tone. He was right. She knew it. But if she agreed with him, it would be the same as admitting that Lord Merrick was right, and she was determined to prove the old goat and all the other naysayers wrong. Frowning with determination, she shook her head.

"I think you exaggerate, my lord. I am confident Sheik Mazir will ensure our safety."

"Then at least allow me to find someone reputable to accompany you on your journey. Someone you can count on if you run into trouble."

Alex opened her mouth to reject the offer, but the touch of Jane's hand on her arm stopped her. With a shake of her dark head, the other woman sighed. "Perhaps he's right, Alex. I know you and the professor planned for every contingency, but there's a difference between being adventurous and foolhardy. I doubt your father would have approved of us going to Egypt on our own."

The gentle remonstration made her tighten her lips. Irritated more by the fact that the man was correct as opposed to his insistence on meddling in her affairs, she shrugged with disgust.

"Oh, all right, we accept your offer to find us an escort," she muttered before she raised her index finger in an imitation of a schoolmarm. "But I'll not tolerate any interference from this person you're determined to foist upon us. This is my expedition, and I'm going to do things my way. Is that understood?"

With a nod of his head, his lips curled slightly at the corners as if amused by a private joke. "Your wishes are quite clear, *anide emîra.*"

The Bedouin phrase caught her off guard, and it took her a moment to translate. Glaring at him, she remained silent in the face of his clear amusement. Stubborn princess, indeed.

✧

His body taut with angry frustration, Altair charged down the steps of the Clarendon toward his carriage. The woman was the most obstinate little mule he'd ever met. She knew full well how dangerous this journey of hers was. He'd seen her acknowledgment of the fact in her eyes. But the way her mouth had thinned to a stubborn line had clearly indicated her refusal to admit she was wrong.

With a sharp command to the driver, he threw himself against the leather cushions of the vehicle. He should have told her who he was from the beginning. At least his words would have held some weight then. She would have taken Sheikh Mazir's words of caution more seriously than those of Lord Blakeney. The irony of the situation wasn't lost on him.

A bitter laugh broke past his lips. Hardly anyone in the Marlborough Set would take the word of a sheikh over an Englishman. But in this instance, he was certain Alex Talbot would have respected the opinion of Sheikh Mazir.

Now he had a decision to make. Continue along his present course until forced to tell her the truth or reveal his identity at the next opportunity. Even on such short acquaintance, he knew her well enough to know she'd be furious with him when he confessed his deception. It would make it difficult for her to trust him, something that was essential when one was in the desert.

His fist slammed into the leather seat. Damnation, what had he been thinking? He'd never hidden behind his English ancestry before, why had he done so now? The vision of a sultry mouth flashed before his eyes. Because she intrigued him. Excited him. The taste of her singed his lips again as he recalled their passionate exchange. Kissing her had been a mistake. It had only intensified his attraction for her.

With a sigh, he closed his eyes and leaned his head against the seat's cushion. Never had his English heritage ever felt like such a yoke as it did now. And all because he'd denied his Bedouin blood. A sudden longing for the freedom of his *gambaz* swelled through him.

The flowing garment enhanced one's ability to move so much easier than the form-fitting fashions of London society. It wasn't just the freedom of movement he missed. There was an unfettered liberty he enjoyed under his Bedouin title. In the Sahara he had license to be himself.

Always torn between two countries and cultures, he knew more about prejudice than most people. It was one of the reasons why he refused to marry. Even if a woman were willing to look past his bloodline, his lifestyle was a difficult one. Living on the edge of polite society for half a year and the other in the beautiful, but harsh desert would be a difficult existence for a woman used to the comforts of the civilized world.

A sudden desire to be free of his English birthright surged through him. If he hadn't given his word to his grandfather, he'd have discarded the responsibilities and title of Viscount Blakeney long ago. His oath was the only thing that kept him here. Since the age of ten, he'd spent six or more months in England each year. First Eton, then Cambridge had occupied his time, then he'd spent successive winters working at the British Museum.

But it was when he returned home to the Sahara that he experienced true happiness. As a member of one of the Sahara's oldest Bedouin tribes, his knowledge of the desert, its people and past made him a valuable resource to the British Museum. He couldn't count the number of times his work with the Museum had saved him from the tedium he found London society to be.

Unfortunately, even that haven was no longer sacrosanct. Merrick was becoming tedious and disagreeable in their working relationship. The man was so firmly entrenched in rules and regulations he threatened the Museum's expansion into the area of Egyptology.

The carriage came to a halt, and Altair stepped out of the vehicle with no clear decision as to what he should do where Alex was concerned. Entering Blakeney house, he went to the study and poured himself a stiff drink. The liquid burned the back of his throat.

A quiet cough behind him announced his butler, Marshall. "Forgive me, my lord, but a message was delivered for you earlier."

Turning around, Altair picked up the note from the salver Marshall held. With a nod of dismissal, he broke the wax seal and unfolded the parchment. The message was short, but succinct. Merrick wanted to know if there was any credence to Alex's theories. Damnation, the bastard was going to try to steal the discovery out from underneath her.

The paper crackled as he balled it up in his fist. Merrick was a fool to allow his prejudices to color his perspective. If Alex did know how to find Per-Ramesses, the Museum would do well to look past her gender because the results might well be the find of the century.

A smile curved his mouth. It had been entertaining to see her storm Merrick's castle in an attempt to persuade the man to her way of thinking. She'd been polite and forthright despite the man's condescension, but like most people, even she had a limit. When she'd bluntly insulted the man in Coptic, he'd found her audacious response amusing and interesting. Coptic was a difficult language to master, and she knew it well.

The memory made him grin before he frowned. He still hadn't made up his mind what to tell her. Decisions were never difficult for him, and he found his indecisive behavior annoying. Well, whatever he decided didn't change the necessity of honoring his agreement to lead her out to Khatana-Qantir. He might have agreed to the arrangement thinking he was dealing with the professor, but he'd given his word. There was no going back. But it was the excitement charging through him that made him uneasy. Almost as uneasy as the thought of Alex Talbot's lush, sensuous body.

Chapter Three

The fetid smell of London's docks assaulted Altair's nostrils as he stepped from his carriage. In front of him, the wharf was a frenzy of activity. His muscles tensed with excitement. He was going home. Sheikh Altair Mazir was going home.

No more playing the role of Lord Blakeney for another six months. No, that wasn't true. Unless he told Alex the truth, he'd still have to play the role for her benefit. Blast, why couldn't he make a decision about this?

The reasons were far more complicated than he cared to delve into. At the moment, not telling her seemed the lesser of two evils. Especially given his interference in her travel plans this past week. She'd be livid if she figured out he was responsible for the change in her transportation arrangements. Learning Lord Blakeney and Sheikh Mazir were one and the same would only make matters worse.

His gaze focused on the *Moroccan Wind*. The sleek, three-mast schooner looked swift and sturdy. The sight of her pleased him. He'd purchased the ship specifically to handle his small trade expeditions to and from Cairo, as well as Morocco.

From where he stood, he saw Alex's softly rounded figure pacing the ship's deck. His body stirred in response to the sight of her. Damnation. What was wrong with him? He'd seen attractive women before—Alex Talbot was no different.

But she was. His body tensed and tightened every time he got near her. Even in his dreams, he lusted after her. Those dreams had turned his desire into a constant physical ache. Watching her now, he recalled some of the things he'd done with her luscious body in his dreams. The hedonistic memory hardened his cock immediately.

Shoving his erotic fantasies of her into the back of his head, he frowned. Lust wasn't the only thing that drew him to Alex. She'd aroused his primal instincts as well. His friendship with the professor was a compelling reason for him to protect her. But it was more than that.

The need to protect her from harm went deeper. It touched a primeval part of him he'd never experienced before. Instinct, not logic, dictated his actions where she was concerned. Even the possibility of her scorn hadn't made a difference in his determination to watch over her.

Scowling, he studied Alex with narrowed eyes. The ethnic slurs society had always directed at him no longer cut deep as they once had. It had been years since he'd allowed himself to feel anything about the opinions of others. Caroline had taught him that hard, but important lesson. The way she'd left him had made him realize his mixed blood was an insurmountable barrier. He could never trust a woman to love him for who he was, not what he was. A half-breed.

Even if Alex didn't bear any prejudices, keeping her at arm's length was the best thing to do. But that would be far from easy. He growled a noise of frustration. He should never have given his word to guide the professor and his party to Khatana-Qantir in search of Per-Ramesses. It's what had gotten him into this mess in the first place.

Content to study her from afar for just a bit longer, he folded his arms across his chest and watched as she directed the loading of her luggage onto the ship. A bundle of energy, she'd led him on a merry dance this past week as he'd tracked her movements. It hadn't been an easy task getting her passage switched from the *Corinthian* to his own ship.

The *Corinthian*'s captain had balked fiercely at parting with two passengers and their supplies. The man's resistance had forced him to trade a profitable Calcutta cargo for an agreement to transfer Alex and her friend to the *Moroccan Wind*. Then again, he could honestly say the man had more than earned his fee considering Alex's reaction to losing her passage.

Tucked away in a darkened doorway across from the *Corinthian*'s berth, he'd seen Alex's fury when the captain informed her of the change in plans. Although he'd been too far away to hear what she was saying, her body language had been easy enough to read. God help him if she discovered he'd arranged the switch. She would definitely not take kindly to his attempts to keep her safe and out of trouble.

Shrugging slightly at the thought, he wondered if Professor Talbot had ever considered his daughter headstrong. He could imagine the headaches the man must have experienced if that were the case. Obstinate, independent and forthright, the woman didn't hesitate to make her wishes known.

She was also determined to succeed in her quest. Her thoroughness in arranging her trip convinced him that she and her father had considered as many contingencies as possible for their journey, except for one. The professor's death.

The fact that he would never have the honor of meeting Alexander Talbot in person saddened him. Their correspondence had been a pleasant one, and he'd readily agreed to guide the man's archeological party to Khatana-Qantir. When he'd confirmed his agreement last month, he'd done so thinking the letter writer was the professor, not his daughter. Knowing he'd agreed to lead this expedition without knowing the man was dead was a source of irritation. Bedouin hospitality and his sense of honor decreed he had no choice but to abide by his commitment. And something told him Alex Talbot knew that and had counted on it.

Like a feather stroking his skin, the strange accent of her voice filtered its way into his senses. His mouth went dry as her American inflection tantalized and excited him. Grimacing, he shook his head.

He needed to end this fascination he had for the woman. The last time he'd experienced a similar stirring of emotion, he'd paid dearly. Even if he were foolish enough to let a woman into his life, she'd find his nomadic lifestyle taxing. Living on the fringe of English society was almost as difficult as the challenges of his desert existence.

Any woman who cared for him would have to suffer both. He could easily give up England, but love of family and home would never allow him to give up the desert. It didn't matter anyway. He'd yet to meet a woman willing to accept him for who he was and not his heritage. From aboard ship, Alex's odd-sounding accent stroked his senses again as she chastised one of the sailors.

"No, no. Those trunks are to go in my cabin. I don't want them in the hold where water might get at them."

"But miss, there's no more room in your cabin. Where will you sleep?" The raspy voice of one of the sailors was a direct contrast to Alex's silky one.

"Surely there's another cabin on board I can use."

"No, miss. It's best we put the trunks below."

Altair sensed a battle brewing and crossed the quay to stride up the gangplank intent on suppressing a mutiny. "It's all right, Sully. Put the trunk in Miss Talbot's cabin."

"Aye, my lord." The sailor nodded respectfully and moved away.

Spinning around to face him, Alex brushed a stray lock of golden-brown hair out of her face, tucking it behind her ear. From where he'd stood on the dock, she'd only been visible from the shoulders up. Now, seeing her up close, his body reacted immediately to her appearance.

Good God, had the woman taken leave of her senses?

She wore her male garments with an easy-going confidence that astounded him. A beige pair of trousers, tucked into black riding boots, hugged her shapely legs to the point of distraction. It was clear she wasn't wearing a corset, and the white lawn shirt she wore sent his mind reeling.

Perspiration molded the material to her skin, the shirt clinging to the voluptuous curves of her breasts. His initial reaction was a desire to pull her close and cup the round softness of her. Taking his time, he'd unbutton her shirt until he'd freed her lush breasts and could suckle her. The thought of doing so tugged at his groin, and it was only through sheer willpower that he didn't reach for her at that very moment. Even more amazing was how she was unaware of the havoc her appearance was wreaking on his body.

Were all Americans this mad? If Lord Merrick were to see her now, the man would see to it that anything she found at Khatana-Qantir would never see the light of day. Credibility for a woman in the archeology field was almost impossible to achieve, but it called for decorum, not blatant defiance of social standards.

Not a single board member of the British Museum would take her work seriously if they saw her dressed like this. Not to mention what the crew must be thinking. He watched a grizzly sailor walk by her with a leering grin on his face. The man needed to keep his eyes front.

"You there," he snarled at the sailor. "Keep your eyes and your head on your business."

Blanching from the scathing order, the sailor bobbed his head. "Aye, my lord."

The man scuttled off, leaving Altair to glare after him. He'd have to instruct Balfour to make sure the men knew they weren't to go near Alex. As for him, he needed to stay as far away from this woman as he could. And that was going to be far easier said than done.

His gaze flashed back to her face, which was flushed with exertion. Hazel eyes sparkled with excitement and her full lips beckoned him like forbidden fruit. It was a lovely mouth. Tempting him to taste her. She looked delicious enough to eat, and the thought of doing so made his groin tighten with lust. Crimson suddenly crested high on her cheeks, and he allowed a small smile to curve his lips.

"Lord Blakeney, this is a surprise. Have you come to see us off?"

"Not exactly." He shook his head at her puzzled frown. "I told you I'd find someone to escort you to Egypt, and I have."

"Well, where is he?"

"Right here." He folded his arms and quirked an eyebrow as he waited for her reaction.

"*You?*"

"I could think of no one else better suited to help you succeed in your search for Per-Ramesses."

"But I...you can't possibly be serious." Consternation furrowed her forehead.

"Does this mean you're refusing my services? If so, I'll ask the crew to start removing your luggage and supplies."

"What are you talking about?" She narrowed her gaze at him, fingers splayed over her hips as she rested her hands on her waist. The movement jutted her full breasts out toward him, and he swallowed hard.

"The *Moroccan Wind* is my ship, and it's the only one headed for Egypt in the next four weeks. If you wait for another ship, you'll find the desert all the more treacherous at the beginning of summer."

Amusement forced him to bite the inside of his cheek as she glared up at him. Manipulation wasn't a pleasurable pastime for Alex Talbot. He would need to be more subtle in the future or he would likely have a miniature sirocco on his hands. The idea of taming that storm shot a bolt of anticipation through him. He immediately crushed the thought.

"How many dialects of Arabic do you speak, my lord? Sheikh Mazir is a Berber, how do I know you can communicate with him?"

Not for the first time, the irony of the situation wasn't lost on him. The only communication problems Alex Talbot would have with Sheikh Mazir would be if she didn't do as he instructed. He'd made a mistake not telling her who he was in the beginning, but the bridges were in flames behind him. What alarmed him was his desire to avoid earning her anger and contempt. Disturbed by the knowledge, he narrowed his gaze.

"I'm fluent in a number of different Arabic dialects and more than capable of conversing with your Sheikh," he snapped as he sent her a cold look. "So unless you're ready to give up this quest of yours, I suggest you hold your tongue."

A stunned expression clouded her face as she stared up at him, her eyes wide. Without saying a word, she turned and walked away. Her silent response made him grimace. The hurt in her wide gaze made him believe she was far more vulnerable than he'd realized. About to follow her, he drew up short when he sensed someone approach him from behind.

"My lord, we should be done loading the cargo within the next hour, shall I give the word to set sail?"

Turning to the captain, he nodded. "That will be satisfactory, Captain Balfour. I'm eager to see whether we can beat the *Bint-el-Nil's* eight-day record."

"Aye, my lord." The captain grinned. "I was hoping you'd ask me to test this lady's capabilities. I look forward to doing so."

"Then what do you say to a wager? A bottle of my finest brandy if you make it to Cairo in seven days."

"And if I make it in six, my lord?" The older man grinned again.

Laughing, he clapped the master sailor on the shoulder. "Then you'll have earned a case of the prized drink."

"Done." The captain shook his hand then strode away with the rolling jaunt so typical of mariners.

Alone again, Altair instinctively turned his head and searched for Alex. Disappointed when she didn't materialize in his line of sight, he sighed and headed toward his cabin. Alex Talbot didn't care what he thought. The woman had one goal in mind and that was to discover Per-Ramesses. He rubbed his neck muscles in a weary gesture. Something told him the journey he was undertaking would be far more difficult than he could ever imagine.

✧

"I couldn't believe it. He just stood there and calmly informed me he was going to be our escort to Cairo," Alex exclaimed.

The heels of her shoes echoed her aggravation as she paced the floor of the cabin that doubled as the ship's salon and dining room. Even more annoying was the sound of the pink silk evening gown she wore at Jane's insistence. Glancing down at the simplicity of her dress, she emitted a disgruntled sigh. At least she'd been able to convince the dressmaker to take off all the ruffles and fripperies that had originally covered the gown. When they set out for Per-Ramesses she was foregoing any type of dress whatsoever.

Why couldn't she be brazen and wear men's clothing all the time? *Because you know how that behavior would be viewed, Alexandra Talbot.* It was difficult to forget the appalled look in Lord Blakeney's eyes this morning when he'd seen her dressed as a man. But there had been another expression on his face too. Desire.

The memory of his hot gaze skimming over her sent a frisson of excitement dancing across her skin. The way he'd looked at her on deck had sent hundreds of tiny wings fluttering inside her stomach. And she'd liked it even more when he'd kissed her. The thought of his kiss heated her body. He would be a masterful lover, confident and sure in his ability to please a woman. The image of him naked made her ears burn as dismay shot through her.

She didn't want to like how Lord Blakeney looked at her, and she certainly didn't want or need his protection. After all, she and Father had meticulously planned every detail of this trip. She wasn't some silly girl in need of a strong man's guidance. And she most definitely wasn't about to let the man tell her what she could and couldn't do.

"I don't know why you're so upset. The man is simply trying to be helpful." Jane sat at the table. Shaking out her napkin in a dainty motion, she laid it in her lap.

Alex sighed with frustration. "I know that, but you weren't there last week when Lord Merrick was treating me like some simpleton, incapable of one clear thought."

"Well that doesn't mean Lord Blakeney feels that way."

"That's just my point, Jane. I don't know anything about the man. He works at the British Museum, and in the *Egyptology* department, for heaven's sake. For all I know, the man is coming along simply to report back to Merrick. I can't trust him. I don't want to trust him."

"Really, Alex, I think you're over exaggerating. Lord Blakeney is a gentleman, I'm sure his intentions are nothing but honorable."

"Perhaps, but the last thing I want is Blakeney, or any man, watching my every move on this trip."

"Come, sit down." Jane pointed at the seat across from her at the dining table. "All this pacing of yours is making me weary. I don't know where you get all your energy."

"It's excitement. I just wish Father and Uncle Jeffrey were here." Alex bent her head to contemplate the tips of her pink kid shoes peeking out from under her gown. Her father and uncle would have made this trip not only exciting, but exceedingly amusing as well.

"Oh, Alex. I know how hard this is for you." Jane sighed. "Losing someone is always painful, but we both know they wouldn't have wanted you to grieve so."

Her friend's soft reply made her start. Jane had suffered

loss in the past as well. She quickly rounded the table and gave her friend a hug.

"I'm sorry. Will it make you feel better if I say I'll make a distinct effort to seek out Lord Blakeney's good points?"

Her question provoked Jane's laughter. "Why, Alexandra Talbot, if I didn't know better, I'd say you were interested in the man."

Appalled, Alex stepped away from her friend. "Don't be *ridiculous!*"

"If you ask me, the fact that he's charming and handsome will make the voyage pass that much more quickly."

Alex took her seat across from her friend and released an unladylike snort of disgust. "I might have known you'd pick up *that* particular refrain."

"Are you telling me you're completely impervious to our host's considerable charms?"

The teasing note in her friend's voice made Alex grimace. She wasn't about to let her friend know just how disturbing Lord Blakeney was to her senses. "I have no use for a man intent on charming me. I'm quite content with my life as it is. Give me a statue of Ramesses or Anubis any day over the affections of a man."

"Statues are a cold substitute for the warmth of a lover," said the source of her misery as he entered the medium-sized cabin.

Alex jerked her head around in his direction and sent him an askance look. Her reward was a small smile curving his mouth, while the dancing light of laughter in his eyes twisted her insides in too many directions. The man obviously took pleasure in goading her. Well, she refused to play his game.

Jane, the traitor, smiled a welcome as the man bowed over an extended hand. "Good evening, Lord Blakeney."

"Good evening, Mrs. Beacon. Welcome aboard the *Moroccan Wind.*"

"You must forgive Alex, she's usually quite charming, but I'm afraid her desire to reach our destination has made her a touch edgy."

"Indeed." The smooth one-word observation made her feel as if he'd given her a lengthy lecture. "Good evening, Miss

Talbot."

"Good evening," she mumbled before ducking her head to avoid his gaze. He took a seat at the end of the short table. One hand resting on the white damask tablecloth, he toyed with the stem of his wineglass that a porter had filled the moment he entered the room.

Out of the corner of her eye, Alex eyed his fingers as they caressed the crystal. The memory of his fingers caressing the tops of her breasts made her suck in a sharp breath. Heat spread its way over her skin as her nipples grew taut, pushing against the restraint of her corset. Her gaze flitted toward him, and her mouth went dry as she found him watching her. Ducking her head, she struggled to control her body's reaction to him.

The porter held a platter of roast beef in front of her, and she gratefully took a helping. Anything to avoid the unsettling gaze that so easily triggered a hundred different wanton thoughts and needs inside of her. Determined to eat and escape to her cabin, Alex ate in silence, barely following the conversation between her friend and Lord Blakeney. She'd almost finished her meal when Jane smiled at her.

"Isn't that right, Alex?"

Caught with food in her mouth, she quickly swallowed the bite-size potato as she shook her head. "What?"

"I said all this started with your Uncle Jeffrey."

"What did?" She frowned for an instant. "Oh, you mean the search for Per-Ramesses. Yes, it all started with Uncle Jeffrey."

"The one who was a spiritualist?" The deep note of his voice caressed every inch of her body, and a tremor raced down her back. Dear Lord, the man's voice was enough to make her mouth water. The memory of his seductive voice telling her how beautiful her mouth was teased its way through her head. Flustered, she tried to focus on the conversation.

"Yes, Uncle Jeffrey told Father all about the city and where to find Nourbese's tomb."

A sudden snapping sound rent the air, and Alex stared in astonishment as the crystal glass in Lord Blakeney's hand shattered beneath the force of his grip.

"Blast," he growled.

The sight of blood dripping from his hand made Alex's stomach lurch with a sickening thud, and she could feel the color draining from her face. Across from her, Jane hastily sprang to her feet.

"Oh no you don't, Alexandra Talbot. You are not going to faint. His Lordship is fine." Reaching her side, Jane quickly fanned the air in front of Alex. Closing her eyes, she could feel the room spinning around her. Oh, God, she didn't want him to see her this weak. This helpless. Despite her best intentions, she sank into a dark oblivion.

Chapter Four

Murmurs echoed over Alex's head as her eyes fluttered open. The dark brown gaze of the man bent over her sent a warm pulse of pleasure circulating through her veins. Disoriented, she shifted her attention away from him and realized she was lying on the couch that sectioned off the salon portion of the cabin from the dining area. Jane peered down at her from over Lord Blakeney's shoulder. A look of merriment gleamed in her violet eyes.

"Well, now. You look much better than you did a few moments ago. At least you have a little color in your face." Jane winked at her. Her friend obviously found her situation vastly amusing.

"How are you feeling?" The quiet concern in his voice wrapped Alex in a warm cloak of protection. She enjoyed the sensation, and a wave of color warmed her cheeks at the knowledge.

"Much better, thank you." She pushed herself up into a sitting position, her arm exploding with heat as his hand cupped her elbow to assist.

Remembering the reason for her faint, she swallowed and took a quick peek at his hand. White cloth bound two of his fingers. "And you?"

"A few scratches, nothing serious."

He stood upright, and stepped back to allow her to rise. When she was on her feet again, Jane eyed her with skepticism. "Are you sure you're all right?"

Although the room reeled in front of her, Alex nodded. She refused to faint again. "I'll be fine. What I need is some fresh air.

If you'll excuse me, I think I'll go up on deck."

"Not me, I'm going to stay here and study that Coptic dictionary you gave me." Jane strolled over to a small reading-table and picked up a thin volume. "Something tells me it's going to come in very handy in the near future."

"I'll join you." The husky timbre of his voice told Alex not to argue with him.

She slid a sidelong glance in his direction before nodding. Jane had already sunk down into a comfortable chair near the gaslight, and Alex sent her friend a glare of reproof before walking out into the night. The salty tang in the air filled her lungs and told her they were well out to sea. With a sigh of appreciation, she looked up at the beauty of the night sky.

"It's beautiful, isn't it?"

With a nod at his observation, she moved forward across the open deck, her eyes pinned on the sky. Still a bit woozy from her recent faint, she stumbled forward as the ship encountered a large swell and lurched over the wave.

Strong arms prevented her from falling as he pulled her into his side, and fire enveloped her with the speed of a hawk in its dive. Disconcerted by the wanton sensations racing through her, she arched away from him. Beneath her fingers, his muscles tensed under the lightweight material of his jacket. In an instant, she was free of his embrace. No sooner had she put distance between them than she craved to be back in his arms.

"Thank you," she murmured. "It seems I've been saying that a great deal to you since we first met."

"Your gratitude is unnecessary."

His flat response troubled her. The moonlight cast his dark features into relief, his eyes staring at something beyond the bow of the ship. His stern demeanor made her think she'd offended him somehow.

"Perhaps not, but you have my thanks nonetheless."

His reply was a sharp nod. With a brisk flick of his wrist, he gestured for them to continue forward along the deck. Strolling across the wood flooring, they reached the ship's rail. The sculpted wood was slightly damp from the ocean mist as she grasped the chest-high barrier. Below, dark waters parted to make way for the ship as white foam and spray threw itself against the sides of the vessel. Once more, she stared up at the night sky, her body throbbing with an unexplained awareness of the man standing next to her.

"What will you do if you find Per-Ramesses?" His unexpected question surprised her.

"I'm not sure what you mean."

"If you find the ancient city, what will you do? Excavate the entire site or allow someone else to do it?"

"Someone like the British Museum, you mean?" It was impossible to restrain her bitterness.

He glanced down at her, his gaze unreadable in the dark. "I'm sure the Museum will be more than happy to look at your findings."

"And take the credit for my work as well," she said coolly.

"If you do know where Per-Ramesses is, then you're about to make history, and no one can take that away from you."

"Perhaps, but it won't stop the Museum from trying. The idea of a woman archeologist is heresy."

"I've not noticed that it's stopped you so far." There was a thin layer of humor in his deep voice as a small smile curved his lips.

Silence drifted between them, and Alex leaned on the ship's raised banister. Staring out over the water, she watched the moonlight dance across the restless waves. The man puzzled her. He acted as if it was quite natural for her, a woman, to start out on a quest to find Ramesses' lost city. His reaction made her nervous. Why was he so eager to help her?

First, he'd arranged for her to have access to the Rosetta Stone. Then he'd appointed himself the task of escorting her to Egypt. When the *Corinthian* revoked her passage, she'd been annoyed, but put it down to coincidence until this morning when he'd come on board. His blithe announcement that the *Moroccan Wind* belonged to him had stunned her.

She didn't know how, but he was responsible for her losing her berth on the *Corinthian*. Her intuition told her that. Somehow he'd maneuvered her into traveling on his ship, and it irritated her. She had no need of a protector, especially one as disturbing and dangerously attractive as Lord Blakeney.

Beside her, he shifted slightly, his arm brushing against

hers. The instant fluttering of her heart made her swallow hard. Maybe she did need a protector. Someone to help her guard against these feelings he aroused in her. Despite her best efforts, every time the man came near her, her body erupted with fire and heat.

But could she trust him? The only thing she knew about him was that he worked for the British Museum. That, in and of itself, was enough to make her want to keep him at arm's length. Still, as much as it displeased her to admit it, his presence wasn't completely unwelcome. He did make her feel safe, especially since she was certain someone had been following her for the past week.

She'd tried to put it down to her imagination, but that was difficult to do when the same man kept turning up everywhere she went gathering supplies for the trip. Much to her chagrin, the man's presence had unnerved her, making her think back to the recent deaths of her uncle and father. Their deaths had seemed natural, but the man following her had simply raised more doubts. Uncle Jeffrey had warned them they'd be met with resistance, but he'd never explained. His warning had taken on new meaning now.

Could their deaths have been murder? But how? She wouldn't even question their deaths if it weren't for the fact they'd both died of the same illness six months apart. That could not be a coincidence. But she was at a loss to understand how or, more importantly, why.

And what about her narrow escape in the Museum? That could have easily been an accident, but her instincts told her differently. Then there was Lord Blakeney's obvious interference. With all that had happened she was wary about his motives. Still, despite her distrust of him, his sincerity seemed genuine, and something about him reassured her, comforted her.

Her father would have liked him. They seemed to have similar temperaments. Uncle Jeffrey would have simply relaxed and enjoyed the pleasure of having two potential victims for his rapier wit. Beside her, she heard him clear his throat.

"You mentioned Nourbese's tomb earlier. It's unusual for anyone outside the desert to know that name."

"Uncle Jeffrey is the one who introduced us to Nourbese."

Alex grinned at the memory. "Although Father and I were ready to have him declared insane."

"Why?"

"Because the first time he mentioned her, he claimed he was the reincarnation of Ramesses and that Nourbese had been his wife."

He sucked in a quick breath. She laughed at the restraint of his reaction. Her father's response had been a bit more explosive. Lord Blakeney obviously found the idea difficult to accept as well.

"Your reaction isn't quite the same one Father and I had. I can still remember Father storming out of the library the day Uncle Jeffrey asked us to find Nourbese's tomb. It wasn't until he produced some clear evidence that we realized there might be some truth to his vision."

"Vision?"

"Uncle Jeffrey described it as that. He'd been working in the garden when he said he was transported back to another place and time. His descriptions of the images were quite vivid. Naturally, we were quite skeptical, but when he drew several hieroglyphic symbols he'd seen on one of the monuments in his dream, Father and I were convinced he'd indeed had a vision."

"Why would the drawings convince you?"

Alex turned back to stare out at the ocean. A chill skated over her skin as she remembered translating the symbols. *Trust not the Mazir who lies for he intends only death and destruction to those in his path.* Whoever that person was he was dangerous, and she, for one, intended to keep her distance.

"Uncle Jeffrey was the quintessential businessman and he amassed a fortune expanding the family business. The man could tell you to the penny how much his quarterly statements were, but he wouldn't have known the difference between the Coptic alphabet or a hieroglyph to save that fortune."

"And the hieroglyphs he drew, what was the translation?" There was an intense note of curiosity in his voice, and Alex stiffened. An inquisitive nature was one thing, but his interest made her wary.

"Oh, a tribute to Nourbese and references to several landmarks near Per-Ramesses."

Lying always made her uneasy, especially when the translation was a warning. She didn't look at him, but she immediately sensed the tension in him abating. The way he was acting made her think he knew more about Nourbese than he had admitted. Did he know the entire story about the doomed priestess?

The first time she'd read Nourbese's story it had astonished her. Her father had found an obscure text with the woman's story in it, and it had taken four or five readings to ensure her translation was correct. Legend said that Ramesses had fallen in love with the young woman and married her.

Politics had come into play because Nourbese had not been of royal blood. A member of the Mazir tribe, her place in the Pharaoh's house had been a precarious one. So precarious she'd been murdered shortly after the birth of her son. The politicians had insisted Nourbese's tomb be hidden from view as she wasn't royalty.

Ramesses had disregarded the demand, which resulted in the robbery and desecration of his wife's tomb. Devastated, he'd built another tomb for his beloved wife in a secluded location. The storytellers said that only the rib of Ramesses would identify Nourbese's current resting place, but they never described the rib itself.

She was fairly certain the rib was an artifact of some sort, but couldn't be sure. Did Blakeney know any of this? If so, why didn't he tell her? The thought that he might actually be working for the Museum sent a note of disappointment sailing through her. She shivered.

"You're cold." He immediately slipped out of his jacket and draped it over her exposed shoulders.

The heat of his body still permeated the coat, his scent lingering in the air. Her senses tingled at the spicy aroma. Standing in the shadow of his warmth, she trembled again as his hawk-eyed gaze scanned her face. Once more the image of a pharaoh entered her head as she looked at him.

A long finger trailed over her cheek, making her throat tighten with a knot of anticipation. The light touch tensed every muscle in her body as she saw his eyes darken. What was it about this man that made her want to forget everything but the potency of his touch?

Mesmerized, she couldn't move, and her pulse rate jumped to more than twice its normal speed.

His gaze never left hers as his fingers glided across the base of her throat down to the low vee of her gown. The caress made her inhale sharply, and her breasts pushed against her undergarments with a painful awareness. The achy sensation skimmed its way through her limbs until it peaked just below her belly.

Hard hands encircled her arms as his jacket slipped off her shoulders and fell to the deck. She didn't care because her body was on fire. Beneath his fingers, the thin slips of material that served as her sleeves slid downward. The action made her bodice drop to the edge of her corset and she drew in a sharp breath.

Lord but she wanted him to kiss her again. She needed to feel his mouth dancing across hers. In some deep portion of her brain, a warning rang out against this dangerous attraction, but she did nothing to stop the inexorable motion of his body pulling her against him.

Each one of her nerve endings was tuned to a feverish pitch as she trembled in his grasp. Her hands splayed across his wide chest as she looked up at him. Muscles tense with expectation, she didn't protest as he embraced her fully in his arms. Instead she reveled in the wanton sensations bombarding her body as he held her close.

The sound of the sea enveloped them as Altair drank in the crisp scent of sea mist on her skin. The soft, delicious smell of honey drifted up from her hair. It suited her. It reflected her strength and vulnerability, but most of all it whispered a seductive invitation as powerful as the Nile itself.

Her small tongue darted out to wet her upper lip, and his cock stirred to life at the sight. The feel of her in his arms made him grow hard, and the image of her lying beneath him on a bed of silk cushions made him lower his head toward the fullness of her mouth. He knew it was insane, but he wanted one more taste of her. Perhaps it was the only way to drive her out of his head. Get these maddening images of her out of his thoughts.

"My lord." The intrusive sound of Sully's voice pulled a groan from Altair's lips. Damn it to hell. Could the man have not timed his intrusion better? He quickly released Alex.

"What is it, Sully?"

"Captain said to tell you a storm's brewing from the southwest, and that you might want to encourage the ladies to stay in their cabins." Altair looked in the direction the sailor had stated. A dark mass of clouds had erupted into the night sky with surprising suddenness.

"Thank you, Sully. I'll see Miss Talbot to her cabin. Please attend to Mrs. Beacon."

"Aye, my lord."

He turned to Alex, only to find her gone, his discarded jacket on the deck the only evidence of her recent presence. Cursing softly, he retrieved the coat and shrugged back into it. Insane, that's what he was. Insane. What had made him think to even attempt kissing her? The answer stirred in his trousers again.

"Bloody hell," he snarled. Reaching out for the ship's railing, he gripped it tight beneath his fingers.

He needed to stay as far away from Alex Talbot as possible or he'd surely suffer the torment of the damned. She was intoxicating, but he needed to put her out of reach. The dull ache in his fingers reminded him of the cuts he'd suffered from the broken crystal. It was a rare occasion when someone could startle him, but Alex had done just that when she'd mentioned Nourbese's name. Myths were many among the Mazir tribe, but of all of them, Pharaoh's first wife was the most treasured and revered of all names.

Lightning flashed out over the water, accompanied by a clap of thunder. The waves crashing against the *Moroccan Wind's* hull muffled the storm's roar. From the way the wind had picked up, Altair knew they would soon be in the midst of heavy rain. He breathed in the fresh tang of the mist blowing into his face as his thoughts turned back to Nourbese.

Since her death, descendants of Nourbese and Pharaoh had led the Mazir tribe. Even he, despite his own half-breed existence, carried their blood in him. Her name had disappeared from ancient texts and monuments long ago, but her story lived on in the fireside tales of the Mazir storytellers. Throughout his childhood, he'd listened with fascination to the legend of his beautiful ancestor.

The temple priests in Thebes, afraid of Nourbese's influence over Ramesses, had murdered the tribeswoman after the birth of her son. Pharaoh had just come to power, and a political struggle had prompted the heinous crime. Only the quick thinking of Nourbese's maidservant had saved Pharaoh's son from the same fate as his mother. With the child safely delivered to the Mazir tribe, Nourbese's father, the Sheik el Mazir, kept his grandson hidden fearing for the child's life.

Mad with grief at the loss of his wife and uncertain as to the fate of his son, Ramesses built an elaborate tomb for his beloved, burying her with the great ceremony befitting a queen. Not satisfied with their evil deeds, the priests broke into Nourbese's tomb and stole her canopic jars, intent on condemning her soul to wander the void between Egypt and the afterlife.

In return, Ramesses wiped out all existence of the priest sect responsible for the atrocity, along with their temples and families. Recovering his beloved's canopic jars and sarcophagus, Ramesses moved his government to Per-Ramesses, carrying Nourbese's remains with him. He interred her in a cloistered location, marking her tomb with the rib of Ramesses—a sign only the woman crowned with hawk feathers would recognize.

A large drop of rain splattered across Altair's hand. More raindrops pelted his cheeks as he turned his face up to the sky. Above him, another bolt of lightning lit the dark, illuminating the masts and unfurled sails. Captain Balfour stood on the bridge, shouting directions at crewmembers scrambling to comply with his orders. Something about the man's stance told Altair they were in for some rough seas.

The wind had already increased its intensity in the past few minutes alone. Striding over to the stairs leading to the bridge, he reached the captain's side in a matter of seconds.

"How bad?" he shouted over the howling gale.

"Bad enough, my lord." Balfour pointed toward the bow of the ship and the black, starless sky ready to engulf them. "We can't go round it. We'll have to pass through the heart of the beast."

Nodding, Altair barely kept his balance as a large wave crashed into the bow, roughly rolling the ship to one side.

Aware he could do nothing but get in the captain's way, he descended to the main deck and entered the dimly lit corridor leading to the main cabins. Rivulets of rain streaked down his back as he braced his hands on either wall of the corridor, waiting for the ship to recover from its roll.

A loud crash sounded in the cabin behind him, and a muffled scream tensed his muscles. Spinning around, he moved quickly to the cabin door. With his balled fist, he pounded on the wooden barrier.

"*Alex*, are you all right?"

Not hearing an answer, he tried to open the door. It cracked only slightly. No light came from inside the cabin, and dread scraped a bony finger over his spine. "Damn it to hell, Alex! Answer me."

"I'm here." The faint sound of her voice eased some of his fear.

"Are you all right?"

"Yes, but I'm stuck."

Altair threw his shoulder against the door and pushed with all his strength. This time the wood barrier gave way enough for him to peer into the dark cabin. From the corridor's gaslights, he could make out trunks stacked from floor to ceiling. "*JahīMī JinnīYa*," he growled in disgust.

"I am *not* an angel from hell, my lord, and I'll thank you to remember that."

"It was an expression of irritation, Alex. And to ensure I don't use the phrase again within your hearing, these trunks are going into the hold tomorrow morning."

"We'll see about that," she muttered.

Silently cursing her for her stubbornness, Altair pushed on the door again so he could slide into the cabin. In the dim light, he could make out the trunk blocking the door. He shoved it out of the way then turned to see Alex pinned against the wall by a large steamer trunk.

"Are you hurt?" he asked as he set her free.

"No, I'm fine, just a little shaken."

Once again, the ship rolled roughly to one side. Losing his balance, he stumbled forward, pinning Alex between him and the wall. With his hands pressed against the wall, her body molded itself into his hard figure. She fit him perfectly. With great effort he tried to swallow the knot of desire swelling in his throat. Reluctant to withdraw, he slowly pushed away from her.

The soft gaslight from the corridor revealed the sheerest of nightgowns covering her sensual curves, and her golden-brown hair curled riotously down onto her shoulders. His mouth went dry at the enticing sight. Even in the dim light, he could make out the dusky nipples cresting against the transparent material covering her creamy skin. They were taut buds beneath the sheer cloth. He ached to lower his head and suck on her. Without realizing his intentions, his hand touched her side, slowly moving up to just below one tempting breast.

Her gasp of surprise blew warm air across his cheek, but she didn't resist as his thumb gently stroked her. Gold lights sparkled in her hazel eyes, and her breasts rose and fell rapidly, encouraging him to continue. With a slow caress, he slid his thumb over the swollen nipple that beckoned so invitingly through the fine silk of her sleepwear.

Again, she gasped, but it was a sound of delight. He lowered his head to the side of her soft neck, breathing in her delicious honeyed scent. She trembled against him as he kissed her creamy skin. The soft moan parting her lips captured his attention, and slanting his mouth over hers, he drank in the sweet taste of her. The heady sensation of his lips against hers shook him to the core.

She tasted even more delectable than he remembered. He cupped her fullness with his hands, his thumbs tracing circles around the hard pebbles on each breast. As she leaned into him, his cock swelled in his trousers to a hard length. Damn if she wasn't the most tempting creature he'd caressed in a long time. She was like a desert flower, sweet smelling yet exotic to the point of distraction.

Need surged through him and he impatiently sought the heat inside her mouth. As his tongue mated with hers, triumph whetted his hunger at her tentative response. She wanted him. It delighted him that she didn't try to pull away. Instead, she arched her body closer to him, a tiny mewl whispering from her throat.

God, but she felt good in his arms. Eager, supple and fiery, she pressed her body to him. With her body snug against his, he couldn't help but wonder how tight she would be around his cock. The image of plunging into her made his ballocks draw up with need. At the excruciating pleasure the image gave him, he shuddered against her, almost losing his seed.

Sanity lashed out at him as his cock demanded satisfaction. What the hell was he doing? He wasn't some barbarian willing to take his pleasure of her in this manner. He was supposed to be keeping her safe from harm, but instead, he was indulging himself and his craving for her.

His body protested violently as he struggled to bring his raging desire under control. Damnation, but he wanted to take her here and now. Wanted to feel her hot passage clenching around his cock as he slid inside her. Shaken by the intensity of his emotions, he roughly pushed himself away from her. With a sharp shake of his head he tried to clear the lustful thoughts threatening to overwhelm his self-control.

"Bloody hell," he growled. "Where's your robe?"

"On...on the bed." Her voice throbbed with passion, and he fought the urge to pull her back into his arms.

He glanced over his shoulder and saw her filmy robe lying beneath a trunk that had fallen onto the bed. The ship rolled again and he watched the trunks teeter in their precarious positions. With a quick move, he lifted one corner of the trunk and retrieved the robe. Extending his arm in an abrupt gesture, he handed the garment to her.

"Put this on before I do more than just kiss you, woman."

She didn't hesitate to follow his orders. When she was completely covered, he grabbed her elbow and pulled her out into the corridor. The rolling ship threw her into his side, and his body groaned with a need he'd not assuaged in months. He'd disposed of his last mistress more than four months ago and not replaced her. Now the tempting figure clinging to his side was testing the very limits of his self-control.

He wanted nothing more than to pick her up and carry her to his cabin. Plunging into her heated silk depths would be like absorbing the warmth of a desert morning sun. He growled with self-disgust and dragged her down the narrow passageway to the cabin he knew Jane Beacon occupied.

His fist slammed into the wood with a knock that echoed the thunder bellowing outside. "Mrs. Beacon, it's Lord

Blakeney."

Moments later, Alex's friend opened the door, her forehead creased with worry. Not waiting for the woman to ask any questions, he thrust Alex forward. "Miss Talbot's room is full of trunks, and the rough seas make it far too dangerous for her to sleep in there. If I hadn't heard her scream, she might have been seriously injured or worse. She only just narrowly escaped harm."

He didn't look at Alex, but his fingers felt her stiffen in his tight grasp. The ship rolled again, but his firmly planted feet kept him balanced. Releasing Alex, he made to turn away. Her hand touched his sleeve halting his departure.

"Thank you, my lord."

"You're welcome," he said gruffly. "Tomorrow those trunks are going into the hold."

"But I can't risk—"

"Tomorrow, *Alex.*"

Without waiting for her to argue, he strode away.

Chapter Five

As Altair stalked away down the corridor, he heard Jane Beacon's door snap shut. Growling with frustration, he plunged into his cabin and slammed the door behind him. The woman was far too tempting a morsel to have on board his ship.

Removing his damp coat, he tossed the garment aside before he stripped his shirt off his back. It landed on top of the jacket. A large bay of windows ran the width of his stateroom, situated at the stern of the ship. From where he stood, he saw lightning snake through the sky.

The storm resembled his chaotic thoughts, but the antics of the tempest outside were no worse than the gale assaulting his inner soul. He frowned as he dimmed the gaslight attached to the wall. Damnation, he'd been a fool to agree to help Talbot with his archeological expedition. And damn the professor for putting the thought of Per-Ramesses into Alex's head.

Why couldn't he keep his hands off the woman? Christ, he really was the heathen the English believed him to be. He'd almost carried her in here just to satisfy his own lust. The memory of her hard nipple under his thumb sent a hot wave curling up his hand and into his arm.

Throwing himself onto the mattress, he stared up into the dark, trying to ignore the ache between his thighs. He could still feel the warmth of her body against his. Her body had felt like the morning rays of the desert sun, sultry yet echoing with a hot promise.

Another groan slipped from his mouth. Never had he experienced such a demand for release before. Usually he could control his desire, but the memory of Alex in his arms scorched his skin. He burned with need. A need he had to satisfy.

With quick movements, he freed his erection, his mind flowing with images of Alex's voluptuous curves as he grasped his needy cock in his hand. Stroking himself, he imagined cupping her breasts as he slid his hard length between the lush mounds. At the same time, his thumbs would rub over her stiff nipples. As the silky skin of her breasts caressed his cock he could see her tongue flicking out to lick him. A harsh groan rolled out of his mouth at the thought. He could actually see her pink tongue swirling around the tip of him as he slid his cock between her breasts toward her mouth. A shudder rocked him as a new fantasy took hold in his mind.

She knelt at his feet and circled the edge of his staff with her tongue. Her touch light, she caressed his hardness with her fingers before moving to fondle his ballocks. The touch tightened the tension inside him. God, she was driving him mad. He wanted her mouth on him. Sucking him hard and fast. As if realizing the power she had over him, her hot tongue slid slowly along his engorged cock, teasing him, torturing him as he anticipated her mouth closing around him.

He groaned. Slowly she drew him into her mouth, her gaze meeting his as she slid her lips over him. There was an expression of womanly confidence in her beautiful eyes. She knew. She understood how much he wanted this. Wanted her. An instant later her mouth and throat engulfed him. The moment her silky lips clamped down on him, he cried out. Christ Jesus, where had she learned that little trick? As she rocked her mouth over his cock, her dusky nipples grazed his thigh.

Unable to help himself, he reached for one breast. Beneath his thumb, the nipple was hard, but the flesh surrounding it dimpled at his touch. When she finished sucking on him, he wanted to suck on her. He jerked as her mouth slid up and down his hard cock with more speed. The heat, the friction was driving him mad.

And then she moaned.

Christ Jesus. He closed his eyes at the hedonistic gratification engulfing him. She repeated the moan, and the sound sent vibrations rippling across his cock. A second later, her mouth tightened around him. As she sucked on him, her tongue flicked over the engorged vein just below the cap of his cock. The touch of her tongue on that spot was enough to make him give her anything she wanted. He groaned at the images flying through his head as his ballocks tightened beneath his erection.

Faster and faster her mouth flew over his iron length. The friction built to an intense heat until he exploded white hot in her mouth. A guttural cry rolled out of him as his cock throbbed its release. In that split second, the vivid image of Alex left him, leaving only the cold harshness of reality.

He was alone.

Uttering a low growl of frustration, he reached for a cloth to clean himself. Rolling out of bed, he removed the rest of his clothing, down to his bare skin. Somehow, he needed to put Alex out of his head. She wasn't for him. It wasn't just the harsh realities of the life he led that helped him form that opinion.

He was who he was—a half-breed—nothing would ever change that fact. A long time ago, he'd believed it was possible for a woman to care for him despite what he was. But Caroline had shown him the flaws of such an expectation. He now knew it was unrealistic to think any woman would see beyond his mixed blood to the man he really was. Even if a woman were to try, he could never trust her enough to believe his heritage was of no consequence.

Padding over to the large window overlooking the ship's wake, he watched the lightning slash at the cresting waves. The sooner they reached Cairo, the better. At least there he'd have a buffer between him and Alex, in the form of his cousin.

Raised together, he and Medjuel had been inseparable as children. It had forged a special bond that lasted to this day. His cousin was more brother than anything else. Grandfather had instructed both of them how to lead the tribe, although Altair had always known Medjuel would be selected by the tribal elders to be Sheikh el Mazir upon their grandfather's death.

A pure Bedouin, Medjuel was of royal blood, while the blood of an Englishman flowed through Altair's veins. Still, his cousin and his desert family had never shunned him because of his English blood. He held the honorary title of Sheikh and served as Medjuel's agent in all matters related to the tribe.

What would Medjuel think about Alex and her search for Nourbese? The thought made him inhale a deep breath. He wheeled away from the window. The coolness of the wood planks felt good against his bare feet as he paced the floor. Despite his time in England, he'd never lost his sense of superstition and beliefs in the occult. Growing up, he'd heard the familiar oracle so often he knew it by heart.

From the new world, a woman crowned in hawk feathers will come to find Pharaoh's wife. She will return the jars of life to Nourbese enabling her spirit to join Ramesses in the afterlife. In return, Pharaoh's beloved will bestow a wealth of ancient knowledge and treasure on her deliverer, which will benefit all the Mazir.

Was the prophecy about to come true? Would Alex discover Nourbese's tomb? What would it mean to the Mazir tribe? Then there were the Museum's expectations. The British Museum paid him to act as a liaison between archeologists and the Egyptology department. If Alex did discover Per-Ramesses, the Museum would do everything in its power to have a part in the excavation.

He threw himself back onto the bed. With one arm draped over his eyes, he contemplated his predicament. If Alex found Per-Ramesses, he would have to notify the Museum. He had no doubt about her feelings on that issue. The questions and indecision he experienced when it came to Alex were frustrating. In all his twenty-nine years, he'd never allowed anyone to throw him into such a quandary as this woman had done. Not even Caroline had succeeded quite so well.

The memory tightened his jaw. He'd not been more than eighteen when he'd first laid eyes on Lady Caroline Spencer. Accustomed to racial slurs and prejudices, he'd expected her to reject outright his attentions. To his surprise, she'd not turned him away. If anything, she seemed more than eager to let him court her.

Even when he'd broached the subject of his heritage, she'd been adamant that she would never scorn him because of his mixed blood. Infatuated, he'd proposed marriage, never dreaming she would ever stop loving him.

Indulged since childhood, Caroline had convinced her

parents to let them marry, and their engagement had taken London by surprise. At first there were only the slight snubs, the snide remarks and the chilly silence when they appeared at a social engagement. Then the invitations dwindled.

With each passing day, he'd watched Caroline withdraw from him as the life she was accustomed to slowly disappeared. On the fringes of polite society, they were excluded to the point that she had finally turned on him. Denouncing him as a filthy Saracen in the main lobby of the St. James's Theatre, she'd dissolved their engagement at the same time. The pain of that public humiliation was something he'd never forgotten.

But despite that humiliation, here he was enthralled with another woman. While it was true Alex wasn't Caroline, she was still a threat because she made him wish things were different. That alone made her all the more dangerous to him. The farther away from Alex he stayed, the better. Tonight he'd almost succumbed completely to her charms. What would he do when they were deep in the desert with only a wool tent flap between them?

✦

Alex listened to the storm slowly fade as the ship moved into calmer waters. Next to her, Jane's quiet breathing indicated her friend was asleep. She closed her eyes, feeling her breasts grow heavy as she remembered the touch of Lord Blakeney's hand on her.

When his thumb had rubbed over her hardened nipple, a slick heat had filled the apex of her thighs. She'd ached there, wanting the fulfillment of that need. She'd often wondered what that need might feel like, and now she knew.

More than a year ago, she'd found a book her father had hidden from her. Based on the Erotic Papyrus of Turin, the translated text had displayed twelve different drawings of an explicit nature. Each drawing displayed followers of the Egyptian goddess Hathor engaged in different coitus positions. Shocked by the explicit pictures, she'd turned to Jane for answers.

Her friend had insisted on seeing the drawings and pointed out that some of the acts depicted were often quite pleasurable.

What her friend had never expanded on was how a single touch could evoke such lustful sensations in her body.

Why had she allowed him touch her so intimately? She should have protested, but the fact was she'd enjoyed the way his touch made her feel. The tip of her tongue wet her dry lips, and she remembered the fiery way his mouth had possessed hers. Her nipples grew taut as she ran her fingers across her breasts. She wished it were Lord Blakeney's hand running over her, once more stroking her until she ached for more.

The rigid length of him pressed against her leg had excited her more than she'd ever believed possible. Memories of the pictures from the papyrus had flashed through her mind, making her wonder what it would feel like to experience one of those positions with Lord Blakeney. The moral outrage warring with her wicked thoughts had been easily silenced by the heat of his mouth on hers.

Her hand slid across her breast and down her stomach to the warm ache between her thighs. What would she have done if he hadn't stopped touching her? Would she have behaved in the manner of an ancient Egyptian priestess willingly offering herself to Pharaoh? The thought excited her. Every time he came near her, she visualized him as an Egyptian ruler. Sleek and well-oiled by handmaidens in preparation for some ancient rite of sexuality to honor the Goddess Hathor. Her muscles tensed at the image.

But something else about him attracted her. There was a mysterious quality about him. It was as if he carried some great burden. The elusive nature of his emotion intrigued her. She sighed into the dark, irritated by her inability to think of anything else but Blakeney.

Concentrating on her expedition would keep her mind off the man. She had to make her father's last request her primary focus. She couldn't allow anything to get in the way of finding Per-Ramesses, nothing at all. Not even Lord Blakeney himself. She'd just have to block him out of her thoughts.

Another sigh of frustration parted her lips as she rolled over in bed. Not thinking about the man was going to be difficult given the fact she wasn't the least bit drowsy. In fact, as hard as she tried not to, images of Lord Blakeney continued to fill her head. And the images of what he was doing to her were shocking, but thrilling. Her fingers dug into her pillow as she pulled it over her head in hopes of achieving oblivion.

It wasn't until a ray of sunshine from the cabin's small window warmed her cheek that she stirred from a sleep she had not expected to materialize. From across the cabin, Jane greeted her with a smile.

"Well, I must say this adventure is proving to be everything you said it would be."

Rising up on one elbow, Alex pushed a tousled mass of hair out of her face. "What are you talking about? Has something happened while I was asleep?"

"Nothing I'm aware of—I'm simply referring to the way Lord Blakeney showed up at my door last night with you in tow."

Alex could feel the blush creeping into her face as she climbed out of bed and retrieved her robe from the chair. As she shrugged into the wrapper, she shook her head. "His Lordship seems to find himself with the unenviable chore of keeping me out of harm's way."

"Oh, I don't think he minds."

"Well, I'm quite certain he does."

Jane crossed the floor and pulled out a dress from the trunk beside the bed. As she met Alex's wary gaze, she arched her eyebrows. "Alex, you have a lot to learn. If there's one thing I know, it's men, and Lord Blakeney is completely enthralled with you."

Appalled by her friend's observation, Alex felt her jaw sag in astonishment. "That's absurd."

"Well, explain to me why the man looked like he wanted to carry you off to his cabin and have his way with you throughout the night."

The image Jane ignited in Alex's mind made her cheeks burn hotter. She whirled away from her friend and stalked to the door. "Don't be ridiculous. Lord Blakeney had just rescued me from my own stupidity. If anything, the man was furious with me."

"Where are you going?" Jane exclaimed.

"To my room. I need to dress."

"Alex, you can't go out of here dressed like that."

Ignoring Jane's admonishment, Alex threw open the door. The moment she entered the corridor, she saw Lord Blakeney's tall figure outside the door of her cabin. His back to her, she admired the width of his strong shoulders and the way his silky brown hair was pulled neatly back in a queue with a dark blue ribbon. As she moved toward him, she remembered how his hair had hung loose the day they'd met at the British Museum. He'd not worn it that way since. Butterflies stirred in her stomach as she realized how much she wanted to see him that way again. There had been a beautiful untamed quality about him that had thrilled her.

She frowned. The man occupied her thoughts far too often. The sooner she controlled the impulse to think about him, the better.

She was only a couple steps away from him when a sailor emerged from her cabin carrying one of her trunks. The man's glance in her direction widened to one of surprise. Immediately, Blakeney spun around. For a moment, he stood thunderstruck as he stared at her.

"Get that trunk down to the hold, Jensen," he growled without looking at the man. Striding toward her, he pushed her back down the passageway. The expression on his face was one of furious anger. As they halted in front of Jane's door, he planted himself in front of her to shield her from the prying eyes of the sailors entering and leaving her cabin.

"Have you lost your mind?" he snapped in a low voice. "Do you have any idea what sort of invitation you're sending to those men?"

"I was simply returning to my cabin to dress. I wasn't issuing any invitation. I'm quite suitably covered."

"Any woman who looks like she's just spent the night in her lover's arms, dressed in a robe that fails to hide her sensuous curves, is an invitation few men can ignore."

Alex stared up into the darkness of his glittering brown eyes. She didn't know whether to be irritated or pleased by his words. Irritation won. "I don't recall issuing an invitation to you last night, but that didn't stop you from trying to take advantage of me."

Tension froze his body and she immediately regretted her words. That had been unfair of her. He'd touched her, yes—but she'd offered up no resistance. In fact, she'd been more than eager for his touch. He'd been a gentleman. It would have been easy for him to push his advantage where she was concerned, but he hadn't. He was an honorable man.

His magnificent features suddenly resembled a statue from an ancient Egyptian monument, and ice could not have been colder than the expression in his eyes.

"I apologize for acting like a heathen last night, Miss Talbot. It won't happen again. Now return to Mrs. Beacon's cabin before I have the captain turn this ship around."

His resolute demeanor left her thoroughly chastened, and she quickly opened Jane's door and slid into the room. Resting her back against the door, she closed her eyes. A soft chuckle echoed close by, forcing Alex to send her friend an arched look. "What?"

"Any man who can describe a woman in the manner that Lord Blakeney just described you is definitely infatuated."

"You were eavesdropping!" Alex glared at the dark-haired widow.

"It was difficult not to. The man's voice carried right through the door. Although I must admit my curiosity as to what really transpired between the two of you last night."

Amusement lit the violet eyes watching her closely, and Alex grimaced. "For heaven's sake, just go and get me some clothes."

Jane laughed as she gently pushed Alex away from the door. "As you wish, but I'll eventually have the complete story from you."

The moment her friend left the cabin, Alex sank down into a nearby chair. Heavens but the man was an enigma. He'd been furious with her, but there had been something else in his eyes as he'd scanned her figure a few moments ago. Could Jane be right? Her friend had good instincts when it came to men. She nibbled at her bottom lip with her teeth. Even if Jane was correct, she refused to give in to her own attraction for the man. Better to think that Blakeney found her annoying rather than attractive. To think anything else would be far too dangerous.

She didn't want Blakeney or any other man hampering her expedition. This was her project now. Father and Uncle Jeffrey had been her colleagues. They'd valued her expertise; and their support of her in pursuing a career in archeology had been highly unusual. In many ways, their treatment of her had served as a measuring stick against which to compare other men. No one had ever reached Father's or Uncle Jeffrey's mark on that stick. No, a man would only complicate matters. Especially a man who could pass for an ancient ruler of Egypt.

✧

Overhead, a starry night waged battle with the pink dawn for control of the sky. Staring out over the bow of the ship, Altair could see the faint firelight that glowed along the shoreline. Cairo. A rush of relief surged through him. The past five days had proven far more stressful than he expected. Alex had stayed as far away from him as she could, but it had been impossible for him not to know when she was near. Even if he were blind, he'd recognize her soft scent of honey and the sound of her tread.

His lust for her had continued to grow over the past few days, despite his best efforts to destroy the feelings. Images of her voluptuous body filled his nights, while his dreams displayed her naked curves poised over him. He reassured himself those dreams would soon fade. Soon his first mistress would consume him, replacing Alex Talbot. The Sahara would claim him as she always did. Her strange beauty would envelop him, bringing him the peace he longed for.

The sails of the *Moroccan Wind* billowed and snapped in the fresh wind. He inhaled the air deeply. The heat of the desert wafted beneath his nose, and his body tingled with the sense of homecoming he felt. Hands braced on the ship's rail, Altair watched as the soft colors of dawn filtered across the sky to illuminate the Pyramids towering over Cairo.

They rose up from the shifting sand with the same grace they'd had for more than four thousand years. Sunshine danced off their peaks, showering them with pink and yellow rays of brilliant light. With each passing minute, the sun embraced more of the massive monuments until the glorious display of nature caressed the man-made structures like a lover's kiss. The sight never ceased to take his breath away. Something about sunrise in this ancient land elicited an awe and respect that he'd yet to experience elsewhere in the world.

Instinct told him Alex was nearby. He turned his head and saw her at the railing several feet away. Excitement and expectation brightened her expressive features as the sun revealed the Pyramids in all their glory. He recognized in her face the same joy he experienced every time he saw the magnificent creations. Content to watch her in silence, he noticed every change in her expression, interpreting each nuance as it crested her face.

Today she wore a blue taffeta gown that hugged her curves as a glove might a hand. Like all her dresses, it was devoid of bows, lace or other trappings. The high neck hid the beauty of her throat, but the gown highlighted the fullness of her breasts.

He closed his eyes, visualizing her as she'd appeared that night in her cabin. He could still feel the hard pebbles of her nipples on the pads of his thumbs. The familiar stirrings of desire tightened his body, and he grimaced. Why the hell couldn't he stop thinking about bedding her? His eyes flew open as more potent images flooded his head.

Up on the bridge, the captain called out to him. "My lord, I believe you owe me a case of your finest brandy."

Alex started at the sound of the captain's voice, and Altair's gaze met hers as she turned her head sharply. Pleasure still touched her skin, and he wondered if she would take on such a glow after a night of lovemaking. Burying the thought with a grunt of annoyance, he looked up at the captain.

"I believe you're correct, Balfour. How soon before we dock?"

"Within the half hour, my lord."

His stomach growling, Altair headed toward the dining room for breakfast. He'd need a hearty meal to keep him going until later in the day. As he entered the room, he sensed Alex's tread close behind.

"My lord, might I have a word with you?"

The fresh tangy smell of citrus drifted through the air as he turned toward her. "What may I do for you, Miss Talbot?"

"I'd...I wanted..." Hesitating, she bit her lip.

Some mischievous part of him enjoyed seeing her at a loss for words. He folded his arms and stared down at her. "I'm quite hungry, Miss Talbot. Might I suggest we discuss whatever's on your mind over breakfast?"

With a sharp nod of her golden-brown head, she swept past him and took a seat at the table. Joining her, he picked up a napkin and snapped it in the air before laying it in his lap. He hid a smile when she jumped at the cracking noise the white linen square made. As the porter set a steaming bowl of porridge in front of him, Altair reached for the crock of honey in the middle of the table. He poured a steady stream of the golden liquid into the bowl before picking up his spoon. Keeping his gaze on his meal, he stirred the first course of his breakfast.

"Now, then, there was something you wanted to ask me."

While she hesitated, he tested a spoonful of the hot gruel in front of him. Out of the corner of his eye, he saw her toy with her place setting.

"My lord, I know I can be stubborn, illogical and on occasion not consider the ramifications of my actions. However, if there's one thing I do know it's this—I'm going to find Per-Ramesses. I'm going to achieve what my father never had the opportunity to do, and I need your help to accomplish that."

"You've already secured my assistance, Miss Talbot. I'm not sure what you're asking of me."

"We're about to undertake a momentous expedition, and I feel that we've somehow gotten off on the wrong foot. I'd like to clear the air between us."

He coughed as his porridge went down the wrong way. Quickly reaching for his drink, he took a large draught of the cold milk. Good God, did the woman not realize how difficult it was to keep his hands off her? Did she think he disliked her?

Lifting his head, he eyed her with curiosity. "Am I to understand you think we're enemies?"

Nervously, she fingered the tablecloth. "Well, I don't think enemy is the word I'd use. Rather I think we've come to regard each other as wary adversaries. I'd like to change that."

Alarms went off in his head as he studied her carefully. What was she up to? She'd avoided him like the plague since their first night at sea, a fact for which he was grateful—but now she wanted to be friends? God help him. Friendship wasn't what came to mind when he thought of her. He wanted a much more intimate relationship with Alex than the one she was proposing. Friendship with Alex Talbot would play havoc with his libido and they were about to embark on a dangerous journey. Respect for his authority was called for in this situation, not friendship and definitely not intimacy of the nature *he* was considering.

"And what exactly is it about our acquaintance you want to change?"

"You're enjoying this aren't you?" Her brow furrowed in frustration as she frowned at him. "All I'm trying to do is establish the basis for a pleasant working relationship. Without your help, it will be extremely difficult for me to succeed in realizing my dream and my father's."

There was a note of fear in her voice, and regret pricked him like his morning razor. He leaned back in his chair and frowned. "I take it you have some ground rules for this working relationship?"

"I do." She leaned forward, an earnest expression lighting up her features. "I think we should treat each other as colleagues. Perhaps it might even help if you thought of me as one of your men so to speak."

Coughing violently to cover his laughter, he waved away the glass of milk she offered him. Did the woman really think he would ever think of her as just another male? The memory of dusky nipples embraced by white silk taunted him, and he swallowed hard. Caution urged him to ignore her plea, but he remembered his agreement with her father.

After all, he couldn't very well leave her to her own devices in Cairo or the desert for that matter. Someone needed to look after her. Otherwise, she was bound to hire the services of some reprehensible guide. At least she'd be safe with him. This last thought made him wince. He'd like to think she'd be safe from him, but would he be safe from her? Shoving the thought into the back of his mind, he cleared his throat.

"I find it highly unlikely that I could ever consider you, how did you put it? One of my *men*? That said—I believe we can at least maintain a civil and professional relationship with a few conditions."

"What sort of conditions?" A wary spark gleamed in her hazel eyes.

"Well, to start with, it's important that you accept my word as law when we're in the desert. It's an inhospitable environment, and to disregard my instructions could well lead to your death."

"I understand, but I thought Sheikh Mazir was going to be our guide."

"He will, but as I understand it, you don't speak the Berber dialect."

She sighed with exasperation. "Oh, all right. What else?"

"We will have set hours for the search and excavation of any site. Working during the hottest part of the day is suicidal, unless you're accustomed to the heat."

"Agreed."

"Finally, if anything seems odd or out of place to you, I expect you to report it to me immediately."

"What do you mean?"

"There are warring factions in the desert that are quite dangerous. If you see someone or something that seems out of place, I want to hear about it."

"Fine, I'm willing to agree to your conditions. Now here are mine." She tipped her head at him in a regal manner. "You'll respect my knowledge, and when I say we need to go to a particular spot, we'll go there, no matter how ludicrous the direction might be."

"Agreed."

"I expect you to treat me with the respect and courtesy you would afford any of your male colleagues."

"Understood." He nodded his agreement to her demand, noting the gold flecks sparkling in her eyes.

"And you're not to notify the Museum if we find Per-Ramesses. I don't want any interference from Lord Merrick or that stodgy board of his."

The demand took him by surprise. He'd expected something different. He didn't know what, just not this. Studying her closely for a long moment, he remained silent, before leaning forward to resume eating his breakfast.

"My lord, did you not understand my last condition?"

"I did." He didn't look at her, but continued to eat his porridge.

"Then I take it you agree to it as you did my other requirements."

The movements he made were distinct and deliberate as he pressed his napkin against his lips. From the corner of his eye, he caught her look of bewildered annoyance. He leaned back into his chair and beckoned the porter to take away his almost empty bowl. As the servant left the dining room, Altair arched an eyebrow at her.

"No, I do not agree, Alex."

She stared at him in dismay, her hazel eyes darkening with irritation and a trace of fear. "I see. I suppose there's nothing I can do to change your mind?"

"I'm afraid not. You're asking me to neglect my duties, and that's something I won't do."

"Very well." With a quiet sigh, she rose to her feet and left the cabin. The quiet manner in which she retreated astounded him. Bewildered, he watched her leave. Well, that was a surprise. Where the devil was that indomitable spirit of hers? With a baffled grunt, he shook his head. A plate of eggs with bacon was set in front of him, and he returned to his meal.

The woman continued to amaze him. He'd expected her to rant and rave at him for having the audacity to deny her request. Well, perhaps she'd realized her condition was too difficult for him to agree to. At least she'd taken his refusal well. When they docked, he'd arrange for a trip out to the Pyramids. She'd enjoy that.

He might even witness the same excitement and expectation he'd seen on her face earlier. The image lingered in his mind as he continued with his breakfast. He'd just swallowed the last bite of his toast when he heard the familiar scraping of the ship's hull against dock pilings. He was *home*.

Chapter Six

Out on deck, he caught the pungent aroma of oriental spices on the breeze. Captain Balfour called out a number of orders and sailors scrambled to do his bidding. Altair inhaled a deep breath of air. The familiar scents allowed a warm peace to settle into his limbs.

Striding to the ship's rail, he looked out onto the dock. The colorful sight of Medjuel and other tribe members in their native dark blue *gambazes* made him grin. He thrust his hand up in a gesture of greeting. Immediately, a roar rent the air in an enthusiastic reception. Rifles lifted above their heads, the fifty or more men on foot and horseback shouted their welcome as they waited for the ship to finish docking. Across their faces, they wore the henna markings of their tribe, ancient symbols of the royalty from which they'd descended.

The moment the gangplank was set into place, he walked down to where Medjuel stood waiting for him. The grin on his cousin's face echoed the one Altair wore. He halted in front of the Bedouin. A moment later, the shorter man embraced him in a warm, enthusiastic hug. Again, another cry of jubilance swelled up into the air.

"God, be praised! You've come home at last," Medjuel exclaimed in the native tongue of their Berber tribe. The sound of the Mazir language was a soothing balm to Altair's soul. He hadn't realized how much he'd missed hearing the rhythmic sound, and it was easy to lapse back into the ancient language.

"I take it you missed me?"

"Missed you?" Medjuel laughed with a shake of his head. "Occasionally, but just when I lacked decent competition for a camel or horse race."

"Now that I'm back, you'll no longer remain undefeated." He grinned before asking the most important question of all. "My mother?"

"Gameela is well and eagerly awaits your return." Medjuel engulfed him in another brotherly hug. "By God, it is wonderful to see you. Each time you leave, I fear we'll never see you again."

Elation at being home pulled a deep laugh from his throat. A moment later it died, as he breathed in the lemony scent Alex wore.

"Sheikh Mazir, I'm Alexandra Talbot. You corresponded with my father, Professor Talbot."

Medjuel's eyes scanned her with appreciation, and a spark of possessiveness danced across Altair's spine at the look. Seeing his cousin was about to reply, he squeezed the man's shoulder as he used their native tongue.

"Have care, cousin. Let's see what she's up to."

With a wink, Medjuel nodded and remained silent. Altair turned around, his eyes taking in Alex's determined expression. He waited patiently beside his cousin for her to continue. The confusion in her eyes made him want to reassure her, but he remained silent. She raised her chin slightly as she directed her gaze at Medjuel.

"My father asked you to take him to Khatana-Qantir. I've come in his place, and I hope you will honor your agreement."

Altair folded his arms as he sent her a look of admiration. "Your Arabic is quite good, Alex, but what makes you think the Sheikh understands you?"

"Very well, since the Sheikh doesn't understand Arabic, tell him I no longer require his services."

Something about the mutinous tilt of her head bothered him. Despite their short acquaintance, he could tell she had a plan in mind. Altair narrowed his eyes at her. "So, just like that you're giving up, going home?"

"Oh no, my lord. Far from it. I simply intend to find someone else to serve as my guide. Someone who speaks Arabic, which means I'll no longer have need of your services either."

Alex watched the shock quickly evaporate from the handsome features of the man towering over her. Harsh anger slowly darkened his face. Beside him, Sheikh Mazir stared at her in horrified amazement. The Sheikh's expression confirmed what she had already suspected—the man had known all along what she was saying.

She scowled at Lord Blakeney. "I thought you said the Sheikh didn't speak Arabic."

"No. I merely asked what made you think he understood the language."

His stoic response infuriated her. The man knew full well how she would interpret his comments. "Well, obviously the man understood me, because his face tells me he thinks I'm crazy."

"You are! Where the devil do you think you're going to find a reliable escort out to Khatana-Qantir? There are plenty of brigands in this city happy to lead you into the desert. And they're the same villains who'll slit your beautiful throat and return to Cairo with your money, where none would be the wiser."

She searched his eyes and knew he spoke the brutal truth. Fear slithered down her spine and a shiver cascaded through her. Still, she refused to have him accompany her into the desert. His refusal to agree to all her conditions illustrated she couldn't trust him. She refused to let anyone from the Museum have access to her work.

Desperate, she turned and looked at the short Bedouin watching the exchange with interest. For the first time in her life, she wished she had the ability to charm a man into doing what she wanted him to do. Instead, she settled for a heartfelt plea.

"Sheikh Mazir, please, I must go to Khatana-Qantir. You agreed to take my father there, and I ask that you honor his request."

As if considering the request spoken in Arabic, the Sheikh raised one hand to stroke the short-cropped beard on his chin. A moment later, he lifted his head to converse in his native tongue with Lord Blakeney. The two of them argued heatedly before the Sheikh turned to face her.

"I shall honor your father's request, but only if Altair

accompanies us. He is well loved by my people and me. I refuse to enter into a bargain where he is not included."

"Altair?" She stared at the Sheikh in confusion. Who was the man talking about? His translator? A guide? Not even the fact that the Sheikh had spoken in flawless Arabic punctured her bewilderment. What on earth was the man talking about?

"I'm Altair." Lord Blakeney's quiet words made her frown. He was the most vexing man she'd ever met. Why on earth would he claim to be this Altair the Sheikh wanted to bring with him? She raised a hand to her forehead and rubbed her temple, thoroughly confused.

"I don't understand."

"I told you I'm no stranger to the desert. I visit the Sheikh's camp regularly and use the Arabic name given to me, which is Altair."

The Mazir had given him a name that meant soaring eagle. An image of the majestic bird filled her head. The name suited him. His arrogance and demeanor were worthy of the majestic bird, almost as much as her images of him as ruler of Egypt. Irritated with the way her musings distracted her from the current situation, she frowned.

Lord Blakeney was Altair, and the Sheikh refused to be her guide unless Altair accompanied them. The idea of spending more time in his company made her nervous. The man was far too dangerous. He aroused her senses to the point that she longed to agree to the Sheikh's demand. But how could she trust him? He couldn't possibly understand what it was like to covet the respect of one's peers. As she teetered on the brink of refusing, Altair leaned toward her.

"Think long and hard, *ana anide emîra*. I would hate to see that pretty neck of yours nicked by the cruel blade of a less than honorable man."

Images of a bloody death immediately made her stomach churn. Flinching at the uncomfortable sensation, she met his watchful gaze. She saw a calculated flicker of amusement in his eyes. The devil was enjoying himself, and at her expense. Incorrigible, that's what he was. Incorrigible and maddening. What made him think she enjoyed being called *his* stubborn princess? But she did enjoy it.

She winced. Well, her attraction to the man didn't mean

she enjoyed how he always managed to manipulate her. She wouldn't do it. She wouldn't give in to his coercion. She refused to have the Museum interfering with her work, and that meant not having Lord Blakeney accompany her. Without a word, she spun about and stalked up the gangway. She needed to think. Somehow, she needed to find another way to Khatana-Qantir.

As she reached the ship's deck, a strong hand grasped her arm. Pulled to an abrupt stop, she looked up at Altair. Annoyed by the fact she was already thinking about him in terms of his Bedouin name, she scowled.

"Unhand me."

"Why do I get the feeling you're not going to accept the Sheikh's offer?" he asked between clenched teeth.

"Why should I? I'm certain I can find some other desert sheikh perfectly willing to take me to Khatana-Qantir and still keep my head."

"You little fool! You've no idea what you're up against here. Why are you so adamant against me serving as translator and guide?"

Yanking her arm out of his grasp, she glared up at him. "Because the moment I find Per-Ramesses, you'll contact the Museum. The next thing I'll see is Lord Merrick's narrow-minded contingent of male Egyptologists arriving to take over my excavation, shutting me out completely."

"That's *it*? That's why you're not going to accept the Sheikh's offer?"

"I think that's a very good reason."

"*Damm gahannam.*" He spat out the curse with the ferocity of an enraged lion. She frowned. Did he really have to retain the ridiculous English habit of saying bloody hell, even when speaking in the Bedouin tongue? Glaring at him, she folded her arms across her chest and remained silent.

Abruptly he wheeled away from her, his long legs eating up the deck with furious repetitive strides. After a moment of pacing, he halted in front of her. "If I give you my word not to contact the Museum, will you agree to Sheikh el Mazir's condition?"

Fury etched its harsh and forbidding lines across the dark planes of his rugged features. What had prompted him to make such a sacrifice? For it was nothing less. In giving his word, he would not be able to contact the Museum without dishonoring himself.

"I have your word?" She watched him snap his head in a sharp bow. She extended her hand. "Then I agree to your conditions and the Sheikh's."

Altair almost crushed her hand in his large, strong grip. "Take care you heed my instructions well from this point forward, *ana anide emíra*. If you don't, I'll extract my vengeance in a manner that will no doubt shock you."

For a second time, he'd referred to her as *his* stubborn princess. The possessive nature of his tone sent a tiny thread of excitement spinning its way through her body. There was something vital and sensuous resting beneath his words. The rakish expression in his gaze as it swept over her made her heart jump.

She'd seen that look in his eyes the night he'd touched her so intimately. Alarmed, she tugged her hand out of his firm grip. She took a quick step away from him, her heart slamming into her chest as heat swelled inside her. His gaze narrowed, and her breathing accelerated as he seemed to stare into her soul.

With an unintelligible expletive, he turned away and strode off the ship. Moving to the ship's railing, she watched him become embroiled in a passionate discussion with the Sheikh. Odd how he'd referred to the Bedouin as Sheikh el Mazir and not Sheikh Mazir.

In all her father's correspondence with the man, the Sheikh had never signed his name as leader of the entire Mazir tribe. She furrowed her brow at the thought then shrugged the matter aside. The discussion between Altair and the Sheikh had grown very heated, and the el Mazir's men viewed their argument with laughter. Both Altair and the Sheikh ignored the loud amusement as they continued their debate.

"Good morning."

She turned her head quickly at the sound of Jane's ▸rful greeting and glared at her friend. "Where have *you*

▸, you sound like you didn't get enough sleep last ▸s sleeping peacefully until I heard this outrageous racket of male shouting."

"That would have been Sheikh el Mazir's men. They're apparently quite fond of Altair."

"Altair?"

Alex grimaced as she realized she'd referred to Lord Blakeney by his Bedouin name. Without looking at her friend, she gave a toss of her head in the direction of the two men arguing on the gangplank. "Lord Blakeney is apparently much friendlier with the Sheikh and his tribe than we were led to believe. They call him Altair."

"Oh, I see."

"You see what?" Alex gripped the ship railing, prepared for her friend to say something shocking.

"It explains why, for an Englishman, he argues with the same abandon as the Bedouin," Jane murmured as she leaned against the rail beside Alex. "I wonder if his lovemaking would be equally passionate."

Rolling her eyes, Alex shook her head in disgust. "If you were a man, I could understand your obsession with the idea of passion and lovemaking. But you're not."

"No, I'm not a man, but I do know that what transpires between a man and woman can be a beautiful and exciting experience. It's nothing to be ashamed of—rather it should be celebrated with enthusiasm." A smile of wisdom curved Jane's mouth, while a touch of sadness darkened her violet eyes.

When Alex didn't respond, her friend tipped her head toward the two men who stood on the gangplank exchanging heated words. "Is the Bedouin, Sheikh Mazir?"

"Yes, although Altair refers to him as Sheikh el Mazir."

"I don't understand the difference." Jane frowned in puzzlement.

"Sheikh Mazir is an honorary title. It's given to a trusted family member who serves the Sheikh el Mazir, who is the leader of *all* the tribe."

"Hmmm, an interesting nuance for just one tiny sound. I wonder if I could start calling myself Jane el Beacon. Jane, leader of all the Beacons in New York."

The amusement in her friend's voice pulled a reluctant smile to Alex's mouth. "You're definitely a leader, but I doubt seriously that your mother-in-law would welcome your use of the title."

A pained grimace contorted Jane's mouth. "Did you really have to remind me about Gladys? As far as she's concerned, I was the one who betrayed Michael, not the other way around."

"I'm sure she doesn't. How could she?"

"Because Michael was her only child and for that reason alone, he could do no wrong. It didn't matter that he died in his mistress's arms." Jane bobbed her head in the direction of the men on the gangway. "So what are those two fighting about?"

"I haven't the faintest idea."

"Whatever it is, it's a topic of great importance to them both." Jane rested her arms on the railing as she leaned forward. "I thought you knew Arabic."

"I do, but they're using a native dialect, and I can only catch a word here and there that I recognize."

"They must be excellent friends to argue so vehemently."

Alex nodded at Jane's observation, but she kept her eyes trained on the two men. Although Altair's skin wasn't quite as dark as the Berber's, it would require very little for him to blend in with the Sheikh's men. All he would need to do was loosen his hair, add the traditional facial markings and wrap himself in a dark blue *gambaz* like the Berber tribesmen. He would be magnificent. Alex clenched her fists in self-recrimination. She was thinking about the man far too often, and in the most inappropriate terms.

"Do you suppose we'll be able to disembark soon? I'd love to enjoy a warm bath at the hotel," Jane asked.

Thankful for the opportunity to focus on something other than thoughts of Altair, she turned away from the scene on the ship's gangway. "I would imagine we could go ashore anytime we'd like. I'm sure Captain Balfour will send our luggage to the hotel."

"I don't know why you insisted on bringing so many trunks with you."

"I needed all of Father's papers and books. Leaving them at home meant I would have somehow left part of him behind. Having his work with me makes me think he's here as well. I'll just have to hire a few extra camels to carry them."

"If you're referring to those trunks of yours, they're staying behind." The deep voice behind her made Alex jump. She whirled around to find Altair's dark eyes studying her with a tinge of irritation.

"I must have my father's papers and books. You can't possibly expect me to find Per-Ramesses otherwise."

"Take only the most important articles. I'm willing to let you take three trunks, no more, and that includes clothing as well."

"You're willing?" Alex stiffened at the autocratic note in his voice. "*Am I,* or am I *not,* paying for this expedition?"

"You are—however, you gave me your word you'd follow the conditions I laid out for this journey. Have you changed your mind?"

She clenched her fists together in irritation as she shook her head and remained silent. With a sharp nod, he accepted her mute agreement. In the next moment, a poisonous arrow of jealousy shot through her as he turned and smiled pleasantly at Jane.

"Good morning, Mrs. Beacon. I trust you slept well?"

"I did indeed. How soon will we be able to go ashore? I'm longing for a hot bath." Jane's smile made Alex grit her teeth. Her friend was suddenly quite cozy with the man. Exasperated, she turned away, intent on returning to her cabin to gather a few things.

"Let me settle some last minute details with Captain Balfour, and I'll take you there." Altair's response halted her in her tracks.

For some reason the idea of his escorting them to the hotel angered her. It was as if he'd taken on parental duties where she was concerned. She turned around slowly, determined to remain calm and serene, despite wanting to explode with frustration at his autocratic behavior.

"My lord—"

"Lord Blakeney doesn't exist here," he interrupted in a quiet voice. "Here I'm called Altair. I answer to no other name."

Her anger cooling somewhat at his somber tone, she nodded. "As you wish. I simply wanted to point out that it's not necessary for you to accompany us to the hotel. We'll be fine on our own."

"I believe it is necessary. You're in a strange country with customs completely different from your own. Sheikh el Mazir has charged me with your safekeeping, and I intend to ensure your safety at all times."

Alex glared at him for a long moment before expelling a breath of frustration. Without another word, she stalked off to her cabin. The man was impossible. His behavior reminded her of several of Father's colleagues. Sympathetic and kind, they'd tried to make her believe they had her best interests at heart too. What they really wanted was to bring her to heel like a well-trained dog. Well, the man needed to realize she wouldn't accept his authority with the meekness of some English miss.

A niggling voice of doubt chided her for such a churlish attitude. Comparing Altair to Father's colleagues was somewhat unfair. In truth, he'd acted as if her search for Per-Ramesses was an acceptable occupation for a woman. None of Father's associates had ever accepted her abilities so openly. They'd always looked for some discrepancy in her knowledge or expertise in the field of Egyptology. Nonetheless, the man was still manipulating her, and she didn't like it. Not one bit.

The door to her cabin slammed open and she smiled with grim satisfaction at the sound. Gathering up her portfolio of notes, she straightened and turned toward the door. Her sharp movement was met with a loud hiss from the corner of the cabin. The hideous sound made her go rigid as terror slithered and coiled its way through her. The bulbous head of the cobra was unmistakable, its body poised in striking position on the floor. Scream. She wanted to scream, but something deep inside told her not to. Desperately, her mind tried to grasp at any information her father might have shared about the dreaded creatures.

Jane's voice echoed in the passageway. The sound tugged her body in the direction of the doorway. It was the smallest of movements, but it made the snake sway menacingly. Panic sailed through her as her friend appeared in the doorway. She had to ensure Jane didn't enter the room. As her friend paused on the cabin's threshold, Alex remained perfectly still.

"Stay out," she breathed.

"What on earth are you whispering for?" A puzzled expression crossed Jane's face, but she didn't enter the room.

Alex's gaze flitted back to the corner of the cabin, where the snake still wove back and forth in a pernicious motion.

"Cobra."

"Oh, dear God." Jane's whisper barely reached Alex.

From where Jane stood in the open doorway, two large trunks blocked her view of the snake. More importantly, it prevented the cobra from seeing Jane. In spite of the fear crushing her breathing, Alex was thankful she'd resisted having all her trunks removed from the cabin. Hysteria welled up inside her. Perhaps Altair was right. She was stubborn, but then that trait had saved Jane's life.

The question now was how she could save her own life. Out of the corner of her eye, she saw Jane back slowly away from the door. The screams inside her head reverberated with painful intensity throughout her body as her friend disappeared from view. No! How could Jane just leave her like that? If she was going to die, she didn't want to die *alone*.

A moment later, she heard Jane's shoes clicking against the wooden planks of the corridor as she raced away. The vibration made the viper move its body in an insidious, mesmerizing dance. Alex barely breathed as she struggled to remain motionless. She was going to die without even having set one foot on Egyptian soil. The cobra swayed again, the hissing noise it made breaking through the icy paralysis holding her in place. The instinct to run was difficult to control, but remaining rooted in place was the only reason she was still alive. What was it Father had said? Snakes didn't have auditory abilities. They only reacted to air currents, vibrations and movement.

The sound of a quiet voice in the doorway broke through the darkness threatening to swallow her whole. "Alex, I'm here."

Her gaze jerked toward Altair's solid figure in the doorway. The sight of his grim features made her want to run to him. Run to the safety of his arms. Her desire to race toward him must have revealed itself in her expression. With an authoritative wave of his hand, he silently ordered her to stay where she was.

"Everything's going to be all right, Alex." Soft and soothing, his voice eased some of her tension. "I want you to remain perfectly still. It won't hurt you unless you move. Now, I want you to slow your breathing."

The screams of panic inside her continued to rise, threatening to overtake rational thought, and it took every ounce of her willpower to stave off her fear and retain her rigid position. She started to slide her gaze back to the viper.

"*No.* Look at me. I want you to look at me." The rough command drifted softly through the air, and her gaze locked with his. "That's it—now I want you to slow your breathing. It will help you keep your balance. Good, nice and slow. That's it."

The comforting sound of his voice eased some of her fear as she stared into his reassuring gaze. Concern had carved tense white lines at the corners of his mouth, and she knew he'd do whatever necessary to protect her. She knew it as sure as she knew she would find the ruins of Per-Ramesses at Khatana-Qantir.

The loud explosion of a rifle shot reverberated from the cabin's porthole. In that split second, a bullet pierced the snake's body and slammed it against the cabin wall. It slowly slid down to lie still on the floor.

When a warm hand touched her arm, she screamed in reaction and violently struck out at Altair's hand. She slapped his hands away in a panicked response to her ordeal. Tremors shuddered through her as she struggled to escape the strong arms wrapping themselves around her body. Enveloped in his tight embrace, her body released her terror in the form of heartrending sobs she couldn't control.

Unable to stop the shudders seizing her body, her teeth chattered as she heard him issuing commands in the Mazir tongue. Terror took a long time releasing her from its grip. Through it all, he simply held her close and murmured soothing sounds to ease her trembling. She gulped back the last of her sobs as he lifted her chin with cool, tapered fingers.

"You were incredibly brave, Alex. Braver than most men I know."

Still deeply shaken, she shuddered again. "I don't feel brave at all."

"Perhaps not, but you not only saved yourself, but Jane as well. She could have easily been killed if you hadn't warned her."

Another set of tears welled up in her eyes, and she brushed

them away with the back of her hand. Jane could have died, and it would have been her fault. She was responsible for her friend coming on this trip. She'd convinced Jane it would be an adventure. What if they encountered more of the deadly snakes?

A new bolt of fear shot through her as Altair slowly released her from his arms. Someone wanted her dead, she was certain of it. It was the only explanation for how the cobra—she shuddered again at the horrifying image—had gotten into her cabin. Her fear created a distinct edge to her nerves, and she jumped as Sheikh el Mazir appeared in the cabin doorway.

"How are you feeling, *shagi emîra*?" he asked. A concerned look darkened his eyes as he smiled at her. The man had the same warm eyes as Altair.

"I'm hardly a princess, let alone a brave one. I owe my life to the man who killed that vile thing."

The Sheikh touched his heart, lips and forehead with his fingers, rolling his hand out toward her as he bowed slightly. "I am honored to have been of service, *emîra*."

Gratitude welled up inside her, and Alex moved toward him. Clasping his hand in hers, she bowed her head in his direction. "Whatever you ask of me, it will never be enough to repay my debt to you."

A strange look gleamed in his liquid brown eyes as his dark gaze locked with hers. It was a look of assessment, and she wasn't sure what to make of it. He shifted his gaze to Altair. Speaking in the Mazir tongue, the Sheikh smiled. Although she couldn't translate the entire statement, she recognized the words *worthy* and *princess*. She glanced over her shoulder at Altair. From his dark frown, whatever the Sheikh had said, the words had not been to his liking.

Chapter Seven

Alex stepped into the warmth of the morning sun, squinting against the bright light. In front of her, Jane hurried forward and clasped her in a tight hug.

"Oh, thank God."

Jane drew back, her hands still gripping Alex's arms. Guilt swept through her at her friend's worried expression. She should never have convinced Jane to come with her. She'd almost gotten her friend killed. If that had happened, she'd never have been able to live with herself.

"I'm so sorry, Jane."

"Whatever for?" Puzzlement eased the look of worry on her friend's face.

"You could have been killed. I should never have talked you into coming on this trip with me." She shuddered at the memory of Jane in the doorway of her cabin and the look of horrified fear on her friend's face.

"Don't be ridiculous, you didn't talk me into anything." Jane gave her a slight shake before hugging her one more time. "Besides, you were the one in danger, not me. I'm just thankful the Sheikh managed to kill that horrible thing."

Alex cringed as she recalled the terrible moment Jane had rushed away. She'd actually believed her friend had deserted her. How could she have thought such a thing? Jane was not the type of person to desert friends in need. No, all of this was her fault. She should never have considered coming to Egypt.

"Perhaps Altair was right. Maybe I don't have any business being here." Biting back tears, she didn't know how to deal with the depth of the despair assaulting her.

"What kind of talk is that? It's not like you to quit when the odds seem against you."

"This is different. Someone other than me could have been hurt. I don't want that kind of responsibility."

"Now you listen to me, Alexandra Talbot. This wasn't just your father's dream. It's yours as well. Are you going to quit at the first sign of trouble?"

"I'm not quitting, I'm just thinking maybe this entire expedition wasn't a good idea."

Jane arched an eyebrow. "Well, it sounds like you're quitting to me. And that's the one thing I never thought I'd see."

Alex closed her eyes and shook her head. Jane didn't understand. How could she? She didn't want to quit, but she didn't want anyone to get hurt because of her. Someone was trying to keep her from reaching Khatana-Qantir. First, there was the incident at the Museum, the stranger following her in London and now this.

A snake didn't just slither onto a ship without someone seeing it. And since England didn't have cobras, the only assumption left to make was the deliberate release of the viper into her cabin sometime while she was on deck.

She heaved a sigh. A lethargic sensation filled her limbs, and she moved slowly toward the rail of the ship. Leaning against the wood, she stared down at the busy wharf. Dozens of blue-covered Berbers swarmed the dock, working to dispose of the cargo coming off the *Moroccan Wind*. She watched the activity with detachment.

What was she going to do? Should she just give up and go home? What would Father have done? She'd always been so strong. Not afraid of anything. Well, almost anything—blood obviously was still her Achilles' heel.

Beside her, Jane rested her hands on the ship's railing. "Look out there, Alex. Do you see those Pyramids? That's four thousand years of rich history. Per-Ramesses is the same way, only no one's discovered it yet. That's a dream worth fighting for, don't you think?"

The quiet depth of passion in her friend's voice surprised her. Did Jane have a dream she'd not told her about? For all her straightforward manner, Jane still could surprise her. No, her friend was right. Per-Ramesses was an aspiration worth fighting for, and achieving her dream meant she had to stay.

"Yes—it's a dream worth fighting for." She smiled at her friend. An unexpected noise sounded behind her, and she wheeled about in fear. The sight of Altair's tall figure forced a sigh of relief from her lungs.

"I didn't mean to frighten you." The regret in his voice warmed her heart.

"It's all right. I'm just a tad jumpy. It will pass."

He nodded his head, but his eyes remained dark with an emotion she couldn't decipher. "If you and Mrs. Beacon are ready to leave, I can escort you to the hotel. I've arranged for all of your things to be unpacked and repacked to ensure your safety."

"Thank you. Although I think it unlikely you'll find anything."

"I agree, but I prefer to remain cautious." The assessing glance he directed toward her made Alex conclude that he too believed someone had deliberately released the deadly snake into her cabin.

She flinched as he stretched out his arm toward the gangway. The understanding look on his handsome face bolstered her courage, and she forced a smile to her lips. Jane, assuming a motherly air, wrapped her arm around Alex's waist as they left the ship.

Despite her ordeal, she found her tension dissipating as their landau rolled toward the hotel. Jane commented on their mode of travel, and Altair indicated the hotel prided itself on providing every European comfort possible for its guests. Alex was delighted with the open vehicle. It allowed her to see everything all around her.

Towering above it all were the Giza Pyramids. They had stolen her breath away as sunrise had slowly revealed them to her from the deck of the ship. Golden symbols of an era long dead to the rest of the world, they spoke an ancient language all their own. With each layer of stone, their symmetrical, triangular shapes reached toward the heavens, reminding her how small humankind really was.

Oddly enough, she didn't feel as if she was viewing them for the first time. It was a strange feeling. She'd never been to Egypt before, and yet it was as if she'd finally returned home after a long absence. Everything seemed so unusual and strange, yet so familiar.

The pungent odor of the dock quickly evaporated, replaced with fresher, more aromatic smells. As the carriage moved through the narrow streets, she inhaled the exotic scents of first one spice then another. One moment the mildly sweet and spicy scent of coriander teased her nostrils before the strong perfume of saffron replaced it. Suddenly the sweet fragrance of fennel drifted its way past her nose, and she immediately looked at Altair.

The unusual assortment of oils he used for his personal scent included fennel. Were his ties to Egypt and the desert the reason he used such an unusual mixture for his toiletries? She breathed in the licorice-like aroma, remembering how the fragrance blended with the cedarwood on his skin to create a decidedly masculine aroma.

With great effort, she tried to ignore the pleasure the smell gave her, but she failed. The scent grew stronger—assailing her senses in the same way the shouts of every merchant did. The musical language of Arabia filled the air, a perfume for the ears. On either side of the streets, merchants spilled their wares out onto the stoops that adjoined their shops. Beguiling and seductive, the vendors shouted out their encouragement to stop and buy something. Several times, she had to force herself not to plead for the carriage to stop.

Women, garbed from head to toe in beautiful silks, walked past them. The only parts of their body showing were their hands, feet and eyes. Their eyes were beautiful. Kohl darkened the dusky color of their eyelids, giving them an exotic look. She wondered if Altair liked his women to wear kohl around their eyes.

An erotic image filled her head. What would it be like to stand before him, dressed in colorful silks with kohl on her eyes and a veil covering her face? Her heart hammered at the notion. She darted a quick look in his direction only to find him watching her. Heat burned her cheeks, and she quickly pulled her gaze away from his. Thank goodness the man couldn't read her mind.

Beside her, Jane pointed out the Pyramids rising into the sky as the carriage rolled out into a wide avenue lined with sycamore and palm trees.

"Aren't they magnificent? It's unbelievable that man created something that's withstood time for more than four thousand years."

Seated across from them, Altair smiled. "I thought I would arrange for a trip to the Pyramids tomorrow. It would allow you time to relax before we set off for Khatana-Qantir."

"That would be lovely, my lord—" Jane paused and smiled apologetically. "I'm sorry, you prefer Altair, don't you?"

"I do. The men of the Mazir tribe are my brothers, and I'm proud to bear a name that makes me one with them."

"Then if we are to call you Altair, I insist you call me Jane," she said with a smile. "Tell me, how did you meet the Sheikh?"

"My father knew Medjuel's grandfather."

"Medjuel?" Jane shrugged in puzzlement.

"The Sheikh el Mazir. He is Medjuel to those closest to him."

Half-heartedly listening to their conversation, Alex tensed. It still puzzled her that Altair referred to Sheikh Mazir as leader of the tribe. Her father would never have made the mistake of not knowing the difference. Perhaps she'd simply misunderstood him. She shrugged to herself. It really didn't matter. She had an escort into the desert, and that was the important thing. Her reverie ended as the carriage came to a halt in front of a lovely hotel.

"Oh my word! Isn't it beautiful, Alex?" Jane's surprised delight echoed Alex's pleasure as she stared up at the picturesque building.

The building's front was an intricate pattern of spiked archways and decorative slits, while a dome of glass served as a roof. Flowering plants adorned the pristine, white façade and its surrounding grounds. A large palm tree filled the center of the hotel's circular driveway, while baskets of jasmine hung from the walkway encircling the building. Several short myrtle trees lined the front of the hotel. In full bloom, their branches were laden with lavender blossoms. The delicious fragrance of the flowers soothed her senses, and Alex sighed softly.

"I take it the hotel meets with your approval?" Altair's quiet question sent her nerve ends skidding into one another. The sensual note in his deep voice stroked her skin with a heat that made her nipples harden and push against her corset. Oh God, the man had just asked a simple question, and yet the reaction of her body implied he'd done much more.

"It's beautiful." She choked out her words, aware her answer possessed a breathless quality.

The door to the carriage opened, and Jane accepted the hand of the porter who had hurried to meet their vehicle. Altair quickly followed, then turned to assist Alex from the carriage. The warmth of his touch sank through her skin to heat her blood, and she trembled at the smile he sent her.

His hand at her elbow, he ushered her and Jane into the bright, airy hotel. Inside the large entryway, a fountain bubbled cheerfully in one corner, while a small aviary in the center of the lobby provided a musical serenade of bird songs. Above them, the glass roof allowed light to filter down through the palm fronds that towered over the hotel, providing natural shading for the crystal roof. The hotel manager, a small, wiry man, hurried forward to meet them, a cordial smile on his dark-skinned features.

"Welcome, welcome. We're delighted to welcome the guests of Sheikh Mazir to the *Billôr Sarâya*."

Altair stepped forward in a quick move, a look of tension on his features. "Hakim, the Sheikh has requested the royal suites for Miss Talbot and Mrs. Beacon. Their luggage will be arriving shortly."

"But of course, Excellency. The suites are ready—"

"Thank you, Hakim. I'm certain you've seen to everything, you always do. Please arrange baths for the Sheikh's guests immediately."

"Of course, Excellency. It is an honor to serve you. The *Billôr Sarâya* is always happy to welcome you and—"

"That will be all, Hakim. Bring me the room keys, and I'll escort the ladies upstairs."

Puzzlement furrowed the small man's dark brow, and Alex glanced up at Altair's face. His jaw was taut with tension as he glared at the manager. She narrowed her eyes. Why was the hotel manager treating Altair as if he were royalty? If the man had greeted her and Jane in the same manner, it would be understandable. But the dark-skinned manager seemed only concerned with Altair's wishes and commands. The two men stared at each other for a long moment before the hotel manager bowed in an obsequious manner. "Of course, Excellency."

The man scurried away as if Altair's mere presence had served to intimidate him. Alex frowned. Something mysterious floated beneath the surface of their conversation. It raised the specter of doubt as to Altair's true motives. He worked for the Museum, making it hard for her to trust him. It was a nagging suspicion that was difficult to shrug aside.

"*Billôr Sarâya.* What a lyrical-sounding name. What does it mean?" Jane's voice broke through the uneasy silence.

"Crystal Palace." Alex spoke at the same time Altair did, and she turned her head away when Jane arched her eyebrow in amusement.

Blast! She should never have agreed to Altair's bargain. The man set her nerves on edge. His cryptic mannerisms made it impossible not to think he was hiding something from her. But what? Biting her lip, she studied his haughty profile.

As if aware of her probing look, he turned his head and arched an eyebrow at her in a silent question. Flustered, she quickly looked away, all too aware of how a mere glance from him made her body vibrate and tingle with sensation. Everything Altair had done could easily be explained away. She was letting her imagination run amuck where he was concerned. Although she was certain someone was trying to kill her, she couldn't possibly consider him a suspect. He'd saved her life twice now. A murderer wouldn't save the person they were trying to kill.

Hakim returned and halted in front of Altair. He bowed in a humble manner and offered the keys without looking up. Tension and annoyance played across Altair's face as he accepted the skeleton keys. She was about to comment on the hotel manager's servile manner, when a man strode into the hotel lobby.

The man swiped off his wide-brimmed hat before he slapped it against his leg and dust flew off the brim. Lean and muscular, the man stood almost as tall as Altair, and his skin was tanned a deep golden-brown. The light from the glass ceiling danced across his brown hair bleached almost blond by the sun-drenched environment. He looked around the lobby until he saw Altair. A wide grin on his face, the man strolled forward.

"Altair! I came as soon as I heard you were back."

Wheeling about, Altair grinned widely. For a brief instant, Alex wished she could bring such an expression of pleasure to his face. Dismayed by the thought, she immediately pushed it aside. Little good would come from considering the effect the man's smile had on her—let alone wishing she could produce a similar response on his part. It would only get in the way of her efforts to fulfill her promise to her father and herself.

"Leighton, it's wonderful to see you." With a hearty handshake and one hand on the stranger's shoulder, Altair greeted the man.

"And you. How long has it been? A year and a half?"

"At least that." Altair turned toward Alex and Jane. "Leighton, let me introduce you to Miss Alexandra Talbot and Mrs. Jane Beacon. Ladies, may I present Leighton Marlowe, Earl of Tunbridge."

"Ladies." The earl nodded in their direction, his gaze briefly pausing over Jane's face for a fraction longer than necessary before turning back to Altair. "So, what the devil are you doing in Cairo? I would have thought you'd be out in the desert this time of year."

Beside her, Jane stiffened. Surprise shot through Alex as she watched her friend's face cloud with irritation. It was the first time she'd ever seen her friend completely ignored by a man. From Jane's expression, it was apparent she wasn't accustomed to such disregard either.

She lightly touched Jane's arm, but her friend simply shook her head as an undefinable expression pulled her mouth into a tight line. It was unlike Jane to act like a spoilt child. But given the earl's good looks, she could understand why her friend was peeved at being ignored. Suppressing a smile, Alex returned her attention to the men and their conversation.

"Will you be heading out to the camp anytime soon? I'm sure Gameela is eager to see you."

Without meaning to, every muscle in Alex's body tightened into a coil of tension. Who was Gameela? Did he have a mistress here? The notion sent her heart plummeting toward her stomach before righting itself.

"Actually, I'm not sure when I'll be going to the Sheikh's camp. I'm helping Sheikh el Mazir lead an expedition out into the desert, up near Khatana-Qantir."

"What do you expect to find out there? It's just a small village—nothing of any consequence."

A puzzled expression crossed the earl's face, alerting her to Altair's rigid posture. As he glanced over his shoulder, she grew still at the evasive look on his sharply carved features.

"Perhaps, but Miss Talbot here thinks otherwise."

"Hmm, possibly. I recall that American professor you corresponded with claimed Per-Ramesses existed out there."

Her stomach lurched at the comment. The earl had to be talking about her father. Why hadn't Altair told her about corresponding with her father? What possible reason would he have for keeping such information a secret? Once again, distrust about his true intentions reared its head.

"Actually, I only translated and prepared the correspondence between the Sheikh and the professor." Altair gave a nonchalant shrug of his shoulders, but his tension was evident in his rigid pose.

"But I—"

"Speaking of the Sheikh, he's actually here in Cairo for the next couple of days. I'm sure he'd welcome seeing you at the villa."

Puzzlement vanished as the earl's features became unreadable. He arched his eyebrows at Altair before nodding his head. "I'll make sure to stop in to see him before I head out to Luxor. No doubt, he'll have some interesting tales to relate. It was good seeing you, Altair. Ladies."

The two men shook hands, and with a brief nod in their direction, the earl strode away. Jane emitted a disgruntled sniff of anger, her gaze locked on the earl's departing back. If she hadn't been so disturbed by Altair's deception, Alex would have marveled at the icy fury on Jane's face. Instead, she ignored her friend's fit of pique and pinned her gaze on the man beside her. He frowned as she glared at him.

"Shall we proceed to your accommodations, ladies? The Sheikh's men should deliver your trunks from the ship soon, and Hakim will no doubt have your baths ready in short order. I've some arrangements to make for our trip to the Pyramids, so once I've seen you to your rooms, I'll be on my way."

"Will you join us for dinner, Altair?" Jane's voice held just an edge of sharpness to it. "And perhaps you'd convince the earl to join us. I'd love to learn more about Luxor."

Curiosity glinted in Altair's eyes as he bowed in Jane's direction. "It might take some doing, but I'm sure I can convince Leighton to join us. He's a bit rough around the edges, but he can be quite charming when he chooses to be."

"Indeed," Jane snapped. As her friend walked away toward the hotel's main stairway, Alex turned sharply to face Altair.

"The earl might be rough around the edges, but he gives me the impression he has nothing to hide. You, on the other hand, my lord, seem to have more secrets than anyone I've ever met."

Tension tightened his mouth into a firm line. "As I've said before, Lord Blakeney doesn't exist here. And exactly what secrets are you referring to, Alex?"

The way he said her name made her heart skip a beat. With difficulty, she fought to keep her mind focused on discovering the truth. "Why didn't you tell me you were corresponding with my father?"

"You never asked."

His elusive answer sent outrage surging through her. "I shouldn't have to ask," she snapped. "You knew who my father was. Why didn't you just tell me you knew Sheikh el Mazir? Why didn't you tell me you were his translator?"

"I didn't think it important."

"Of course it was important."

"I don't see how it would have made a difference."

She stared at him for a long moment, her thoughts spinning and careening into one another. Fists clenched, she glared at him. "The difference would have been my ability to trust you."

Ignoring the grim expression on his features, she wheeled about and stalked away from him. Behind her, she heard his soft curse before his footsteps sounded quietly against the marble floor of the hotel foyer. When he reached her side, he grasped her elbow. As discreetly as possible, she tried to withdraw her arm from his clutch, but he merely tightened his grip.

The pace he set easily allowed them to catch up with Jane. With a grim smile, he gestured toward the stairs. The three of them mounted the steps to the second floor where Altair guided them to a set of adjoining rooms.

As they stopped outside the first door, he raised his hand in a commanding gesture. "Wait here, I'd like to ensure the room is safe."

He quietly opened the door and entered the room. After a few moments, he returned to the hallway. "I believe you'll find the room spacious and quite safe, Mrs. Beacon."

Jane, her earlier irritation seemingly dissipated, smiled and nodded. "Thank you. I'll look forward to seeing you at dinner this evening."

With a quick squeeze of Alex's hand, Jane entered her room and closed the door. Altair didn't look at her as he moved to the next door and inserted the key into the lock. As he disappeared through the doorway, Alex followed him into the room. In silence, she watched him search the suite. When he disappeared into the adjoining bath, she took in her surroundings. Spacious in size, the room held a large bed draped with white mosquito netting, while a small dresser rested against the opposite wall.

A light breeze from the open window caused the sheer curtains bordering the casement to billow out into the room. As she moved to take in the view, the door behind her thudded shut. Jumping with fright, she whirled about as Altair charged out of the bath. Instantly, she realized the breeze must have caused the door to shut on its own, and she sighed with relief.

Across the room, their eyes met, and she trembled slightly at the brooding expression on his face. Folding his arms across his broad chest, he studied her in silence. Tension charged the air as that tingling sensation he always aroused in her edged its way across her skin.

"You're to remain in the hotel for the rest of the day." His soft command made Alex tighten her mouth in rebellion.

"I did not come all this way to hide out in a hotel room."

"Nevertheless, you'll do as you're told."

Infuriated, Alex glared at him and braced her hands against her hips. "Or what? You'll refuse to take me to Khatana-Qantir?"

In an explosive movement, he unfolded his arms and strode across the floor. Towering over her, his large hands grasped her arms as he gave her a slight shake.

"No, I'll not refuse you that," he said through clenched teeth. "However, here is a demonstration of what to expect if you disobey my orders."

With a resolute movement, he enveloped her in his arms, and she uttered a small gasp. The heat of him swallowed her whole, and despite the knowledge that she should protest his actions, she couldn't. In truth, she didn't want to do anything except feel the touch of his mouth against hers once more.

One strong hand slid behind her neck. His thumb circled over her skin, skimming her earlobe. The sensual touch only emphasized the impact he had on her senses. This was not the way she'd planned things for her trip into the desert. She'd not counted on meeting a man so mysterious and devastatingly handsome that she was willing to offer herself up like a sacrificial lamb on the altar of the Egyptian goddess Hathor. Unable to drag her gaze away, her eyes locked with his and her breathing grew rapid as he lowered his head. In the next instant, his mouth singed hers, pulling a soft moan from her throat.

Part of her knew she should be pushing him away, but something stronger held her fluid in his arms. Hard lips demanded a response, and she pressed her body into his to answer the summons. As his tongue swept into her mouth, the bittersweet taste of hazelnut coffee mixed with the unique flavor of him and teased her senses. Her heart spiraling out of control, she responded with an intimate, probing stroke in return.

His deep groan warmed her mouth like a fiery oven. Strong fingers stroked across the top of her breasts through the thin cotton of her dress as she pressed her body into his. Delight shivered through her. Sweet heaven, she didn't want anything between them. She wanted to feel his hard muscular body beneath her fingertips—against her skin.

Blind desire made her push at the jacket he wore, and he obliged her by sliding out of the garment and quickly unbuttoning his shirt. Trembling, she stared at the bronzed muscles of his chest before she reached out to glide her fingertips across his sculpted body.

He was beautiful—just as she'd imagined. No pharaoh could ever have been as devastating. The sun had drenched his hard, sinewy body until it was a golden hue. Her fingertips grew hot as she touched him. Her thumb scraped over a nipple, and he drew in a sharp breath. The sound told her she'd pleased him. She loved touching him and his unsteady breaths provoked her to do more than just touch him with her hands. Slowly, she leaned into him, pressing her lips to the hardness of his body. A shudder tore through him, and she marveled at his solid warmth. Her tongue flicked out to taste him. A faint trace of licorice tantalized her taste buds. He tasted hot—spicy. She inhaled the exotic aroma of cedarwood and sweet fennel. It heightened his powerful, masculine scent.

Beneath her hands, his muscles rippled. Lost in the pleasure singing through her veins, she offered no protest as his hands slid from her shoulders to her back where he undid the buttons of her dress. Instead, she continued her exploration of his upper body, her mouth and fingers recording every rough edge of him.

Seconds later, the laces of her corset were undone, the offensive undergarment removed. She stiffened, aware that she was close to the point of no return. Then the burning touch of his hand brushed across her breast and she was lost. Delight sped through her, washing away any protests her mind tried to offer up. As she arched away from him slightly, her breasts rode higher on his chest. The sensation of his skin scraping across her nipples hitched her breath. When his mouth took possession of one nipple, a wild tremor shook her. His hot tongue swirled around the rigid peak in a torturous motion as intense gratification held her in its grip.

A pulsing need grew inside her, clenching her muscles with an unwavering need for release. She should be protesting, ending this wild, passionate encounter. But she didn't. She couldn't have even if she wanted to.

The need curling through her was in total control as a delicious ache settled near the apex of her thighs. She sensed movement, but the pleasure weaving its spell over her didn't allow her to comprehend anything until she felt the bed pressing against the back of her legs.

She fell backwards onto the soft mattress and stared up at him. He towered over her, his dark eyes coveting her naked flesh. The white lawn of his shirt, splayed open almost to his waist, revealed a hard, muscular chest. From the middle of his torso, a dark line of hair dove toward his navel. Down to where his arousal swelled beneath his trousers.

He stared down at her, drinking in the creamy smoothness of her skin. She was even more voluptuous in the sunlight. He'd never seen such full, succulent breasts. Slowly, he reached out to trace the darkened areola surrounding her nipple. Her eyelids fluttered at the light touch, and the skin around her hard peak dimpled.

Another moan parted her lips as his thumb rolled over the taut nipple. The sound stiffened his cock until it ached with a relentless demand for satisfaction. He was playing with fire where she was concerned, but at the moment he didn't care.

Chapter Eight

An explosive need pulsated its way through Altair's limbs. Inside his trousers, his cock throbbed its demand for satisfaction as she stroked him through the material. Her bold move intoxicated him.

His thumb circled the tip of her again. Another soft mewl of pleasure escaped her lips. The sound encouraged him to cup a full breast in the palm of his hand. The milky white globe was a sharp contrast against his brown skin, while small goosebumps puckered the dusky-colored skin of her areolae. Hard and swollen, her nipples uttered a silent invitation.

He leaned forward to suckle her. Milk and honey danced inside his mouth, while a citrus scent wafted from her hair into his nostrils. With each flick of his tongue across her hard nipple, a tiny shudder vibrated through her. The poignancy of her response increased the level of his desire. Her skin was aglow with passion, just as he'd envisioned it earlier today.

Beneath long, silky eyelashes, her hazel eyes glowed with a fire he knew his own gaze echoed. He wanted to see all of her. To press his mouth against every inch of her silky skin. Would the curls between her legs be the same golden-brown as her hair or darker? More importantly, would she be wet with liquid heat, ready for his cock to slide into her, filling her? Would she be as tight around his cock as he thought?

The thoughts racing through his head made him harder than he ever believed possible. The excruciating need to plunge into her drove all sense of reason from his head. Bracing his hands on either side of her, he teased first one breast, then the other with his mouth and tongue. Gently, his lips clamped onto a nipple and tugged it. The action pulled a husky cry of delight from her throat.

As he suckled the sweetness of her, the hard bulge of his cock pressed into the softness of her thigh. He swallowed the gasp of pleasure parting her lips with a deep kiss. The fresh tang of her tongue against his reminded him of the ocean, while the sweet smell of her honeyed skin tantalized his senses almost as much as the feel of her did.

His hand gathered a handful of her skirt and slid it up her leg. Fire engulfed his fingers as they traveled up her firm calf to the fullness of her thigh. She was soft and pliant beneath his hand. God, he needed her. Needed to bury his cock in her and feel her body gripping him.

The garter holding up her stocking gave way easily under his quick movements. His breaths came hard and fast. Never had he craved a woman the way he did her. He wanted to see his dark legs entwined with hers as he took her from one height of pleasure to another. The feel of her, the scent of her, the taste, they all rolled together to pull him into a whirlpool of lost reason.

The smoothness of her thigh made his fingers itch to ride higher and explore the nest of curls he knew existed at the apex of her legs. As his hand slid across her mound, she bucked against him. Damn, but she was ready. He could smell her heat, the musky scent of her. It was intoxicating. His fingers parted her folds, needing to feel the creamy heat of her desire.

Reality crashed through him as a loud knock sounded on the door. Shock washed over her face at the noise, before a deep crimson flooded her cheeks. Berating himself for losing control, he straightened upright, pulling her with him. Quickly, he helped her adjust her clothing. With a gentle touch, he brushed aside her trembling fingers to button her dress for her.

"Tell them to wait a moment," he whispered as he passed the buttons through their slits. She did as he instructed, and the husky sound of her voice tightened the desire coiling inside his cock. Tendrils of hair had escaped the knot at the back of her head, while her cheeks were flushed with pink. She looked ripe and sensuous. The look suited her, and he ached with the need to release his physical tension inside her. With difficulty, he swallowed the urge to order her visitor away.

Her slender hand reached up to smooth the front of her dress, and his eyes focused on the hard nipples pushing through the thin material of her gown. Suppressing a groan of desire at the enticing sight, he pushed her corset under the bed with his foot. When was the last time he'd lost control like that? His fingers slipped slightly on the buttons of his shirt. He couldn't remember. Bending over, he picked up his jacket and shrugged into it. He glanced in Alex's direction as he crossed the floor to answer the door. She'd moved to the window and she didn't turn around as two women entered the room with hot water and towels. The women disappeared into the bath leaving him alone with Alex once more.

She turned around to face him, a lost look in her eyes. The confusion furrowing her brow made him wince. For a long moment, he studied the bewildered expression on her face. What could he say or do to explain how he'd lost control? He took a step toward her, but stopped as she recoiled from him in dismay.

Without realizing it, he clenched his hands into fists, the muscles in his body tightening at her reaction. Did she think he was about to ravish her? Of course she did—hadn't he nearly accomplished that very thing? Even if her ultimate safety was his goal, using a kiss to coerce her into obeying his orders had been a mistake.

The kiss had escalated into something far more intense than he'd expected. He needed to keep his distance from Alex Talbot. She had a way of making him lose control, and losing control would only lead to trouble where she was concerned. Furious with himself at the misstep, he bit the inside of his cheek.

"Stay in the hotel," he ground out through clenched teeth. "My advances are not nearly as dangerous as the hazards outside the *Billôr Sarâya*."

Not waiting for her response, he strode angrily from the room. As his long stride ate up the distance to the stairs, he berated himself for his behavior. He'd taken advantage of her. Caroline had been right all along. He was a savage. No gentleman would have acted with such disrespect.

Only a barbarian would succumb to his desire so easily. Once again, he'd played on her vulnerability. He'd sunk to a level of uncivilized behavior that sickened him. Reaching the hotel lobby, he saw Hakim hurrying toward him.

With a disgusted sigh, he halted as the smaller man bowed in front of him. "Excellency, the ladies' trunks have arrived. Miss Talbot has far more luggage than will fit comfortably in her room."

"Miss Talbot is used to working in tight spaces, Hakim. If necessary, line the damn walls of her room with the bloody things."

Not waiting for a response, he strode out of the hotel all too aware of the man's look of astonishment. Damn it to hell, the woman had tied him into knots. If he didn't take care to keep his distance from her, he'd find himself in a worse state altogether when she discovered it was him and not Medjuel who had agreed to take her out into the desert. There was no doubt in his mind that she'd be furious. She'd made it quite clear she didn't like someone lying to her.

The forbidding thought shot tension through each of his muscles. Why the devil didn't he just tell her who he was? What he was? No. He needed her to trust him if he was to keep her safe in the desert. Telling her now would destroy what little confidence she had in him.

A small voice in his head scoffed at his excuse. His continued deception wasn't just about maintaining her trust. He immediately silenced his innermost thoughts. Whatever the reason was that kept him spinning this web of lies and deceit— he didn't want to examine it too closely. Instinct told him the answer would rock him to his very core.

Half aware of the floral scents mingling in the dry air, he walked back toward the docks. His stride long and swift, he tried to outdistance his morose thoughts, but failed. They pursued him with all the zeal of an outraged Englishman determined to humiliate him at all costs.

The tight coil of regret inside him pulled a harsh breath out of him. He'd grown used to the idea of being a man without a country, but Alex was a potent reminder of what he craved and yet could never have. If he'd told her the truth from the beginning, he wouldn't need to worry about her trusting him. Her father's confidence in him would have been good enough for Alex.

Ahead of him, he caught sight of a familiar dark blue *gambaz* only worn by the Mazir. To his amazement, the blue-robed figure stopped in front of a tavern that was a stronghold of the Hoggar, an enemy tribe of the Mazir. Astonishment turned to anger as the tribesman glanced furtively about before darting into the tavern.

Who would dare betray the tribe? Unable to see the man's features from where he stood, Altair hurried down the street and entered a shop across from the Hoggar tavern. The traitor would come out soon enough, and he would find out who had dared to consort with Sheikh Tarih, leader of the Hoggar.

Inside the shop, he moved away from the door and examined a number of different beautifully woven rugs. Every few seconds, his gaze scanned the street in front of the tavern. The shop owner approached him, and Altair gestured to the first rug he saw.

"How much?"

"For you, Excellency, ten thousand piastres."

The old man's response told Altair the shopkeeper knew who he was. Arching an eyebrow, he shook his head. "Ten thousand piastres? This rug is lovely but worth no more than two thousand piastres."

"But look closely at the weave, Excellency. It is unparalleled in Egypt. Nowhere else will you find such beautiful craftsmanship. Surely it is worth at least seven thousand piastres to a man of your wealth and position."

Altair shook his head and glanced out the window toward the establishment across the street. Returning his attention to the shopkeeper, he folded his arms across his chest. "Spoken like a man who knows more than he reveals. I'll give you three thousand piastres for the rug."

"Ah, Excellency, you wound me. How could I possibly part with such a beautiful rug for less than five thousand piastres?" Laughter sparkled in the limpid gaze of the old man, and Altair found himself smiling back.

"Four thousand piastres, and no more."

"Done!" the shopkeeper exclaimed with satisfaction. "Shall I have it sent to Sheikh el Mazir's villa, Excellency?"

The question made Altair send the man a probing glance.

"So you know me."

"Yes, Excellency, Sheikh el Mazir was kind enough to back the establishment of my shop. You are well known to me, Excellency."

Studying the man's laughing gaze for a moment, Altair remembered a letter from his cousin more than six months before that discussed several business ventures. It appeared this shop was one of those investments.

"Your name?"

"Sahir Mabur, Excellency."

"Well, Sahir, I believe your suggestion to deliver this lovely rug to the Sheikh's villa is an excellent one."

He turned his head to peruse the storefront across the street. As he did so, Sahir clucked his tongue. "Tch, tch, tch, Excellency. The man you saw go into the tavern will not be out for some time."

"How do you know that?" Altair tensed with suspicion.

The shopkeeper smiled patiently and bowed. "It is not the first time I've noticed your tribesman going into the tavern."

"Do you know who the man is?"

"Alas, I don't, Excellency. But I did send word to Sheikh el Mazir of the man's activities. It is a bad thing to betray one's people."

Altair nodded as his gaze drifted back to the front of the establishment across the street. "I'd like to wait here until the man comes out."

"Of course, Excellency, you honor me with your presence in my shop. May I offer you a cup of coffee?"

"Thank you."

The merchant disappeared into the back of his shop, while Altair moved to a spot along the wall that afforded him a clear view of the tavern opposite the rug shop. A few moments later, Sahir returned with a small cup of coffee. Altair accepted the drink with a smile of gratitude. The aromatic scent of cardamom filled his nostrils as he took a small taste of the brew. Strong and sweet, the coffee reminded him he was home.

While the merchant returned to his duties, Altair leaned against the cool stone wall, savoring his drink. His gaze returned to the tavern. Who was the tribesman who'd gone into the Hoggar stronghold and why? What would make a man betray his tribe? More importantly, what sort of betrayal was the man planning? Had Medjuel investigated the man? Did his cousin even know the man's identity?

One question after another bombarded him. He sipped at the thick coffee in his cup as he pondered the questions filling his head. Then there was Alex. Twice now, someone had attempted to kill her. The stone falling from the balcony at the Museum had not been an accident. According to workers, someone had deliberately dislodged the stone.

Then there was the snake. A viper as deadly as a cobra could never get aboard a ship like the *Moroccan Wind* on its own. Someone had been going up and down the gangplank from the moment the ship docked. It would have been easy for someone to move about unnoticed. No, someone had intentionally put the snake in Alex's cabin.

He grimaced at the memory of seeing her terrorized, struggling to keep from leaping toward him. Bravery was not a trait limited to men, but she had exceeded even the courage of some men in battle. Why would someone want Alex dead? It didn't make sense.

Frowning, he sipped at the thick drink in his cup. Nothing had made much sense to him since he'd met Alex. In little more than two weeks, the woman had managed to turn him inside out with anger, desire and amusement. Medjuel was right—she was a woman worthy enough to stand at the side of Pharaoh or a mere sheikh.

But he wasn't Pharaoh, and while he might be a mere sheikh, his blood and lifestyle would always stand between him and any possibility of loving a woman like Alexandra Talbot. Even if Caroline hadn't betrayed his trust, she would never have been able to survive in the desert. With unexpected fervor, his inner voice suggested that Alex was different. She had strength and courage. Two essential qualities for surviving the harsh Bedouin lifestyle. He shoved the thought aside. It didn't matter what he thought or believed. Alex's safety was in his hands, and he needed all of his wits to protect her.

The sun was almost directly overhead when his quarry emerged from the Hoggar tavern. From where he stood, Altair could see the man's face plainly. The Mazir looked furtively around him before heading off toward the docks. Swallowing the last of his coffee, he called for Sahir. When the merchant emerged from the back of the shop, Altair handed him the empty cup.

"Thank you for your hospitality, Sahir. I shall tell Sheikh el Mazir he made a wise decision to invest in your business."

"You humble me, Excellency."

Nodding, he said goodbye and strode out into the street. The sun now pushed high into the sky, and Altair took mental note of the heat his European clothes generated. The moment he reached the villa, he'd talk with Medjuel and then change into his *gambaz*. He'd be much more comfortable.

But his comfort would only be a physical relief from the heat. With mixed emotions, he headed toward the family villa. Each stride he took pounded out his anger against the street's hard surface. Why hadn't Medjuel told him about this treachery? What the devil was going on? There was a traitor in their midst, and it unsettled him.

The fierce pace he set ate up the distance to the family villa in minutes. Entering the inner courtyard, he followed a stone path through wild splashes of floral color. As he passed the small fountain in the center of the open-air court he heard the soft cooing of a pair of Namqua doves. The courtyard was one of his favorite places, and he'd spent many a moonlit night here, simply enjoying the night sky.

This time he paid little heed to the beauty around him. Instead, he charged into the house and headed toward the study his cousin used whenever the tribe was in Cairo. Barreling into the room, he saw his cousin's mouth curl with amusement.

"What has the lovely Miss Talbot done now to make you so furious, Altair?"

"Alex's done nothing. I just came from Sahir Mabur's shop where I witnessed a Mazir entering the Hoggar tavern. We have a traitor in our midst."

Medjuel's face took on a troubled expression, as he rose to his feet and moved to the window overlooking the courtyard. Despite an outward appearance of serenity, his cousin's knuckles were white with tension as he gripped the frame of the window to stare out at the tranquil scene.

"I know."

"You know!" Altair snapped. "Why haven't you done something about it?"

"Because I'm waiting for the right moment to confront Mohammed. There's been word that some of our wells have been taken by Tarih's men. If Mohammed is helping them, I need to know what he's been telling the Hoggar. If I approach him too soon, it's quite possible I won't find out what Sheikh Tarih is up to."

Medjuel turned slowly to face him. His cousin was obviously troubled, yet he seemed almost resigned to the betrayal of their tribesman. Altair shook his head and frowned. Why hadn't Medjuel written to him about Mohammed? As his cousin's advisor, he needed to know about these things.

Why had his cousin remained silent on an issue that affected the entire tribe? Was there some question as to his commitment to the tribe? The family? He'd always served Medjuel with more loyalty and love than any other tribesman. Surely his cousin knew that.

"It's unlike you to not confront someone. What if Mohammed tells Tarih about the three new water sources we found last spring? If Tarih can't use them, he's malicious enough to contaminate them simply to keep us from using them. We can't afford to lose any of our water sources."

A cold expression crossed his cousin's face. "Are you questioning my leadership?"

"No, of course not." Altair stared at his cousin in puzzlement. "I'm simply offering you counsel as your advisor."

"And you've told me." Medjuel grimaced. "I've had Mohammed watched for several weeks now. When the time is right, I shall deal with the traitor."

"Medjuel, you know you can count on me to help with anything that might be troubling you, don't you?"

"Of course I do, Altair."

Altair watched his cousin turn away to stare out the window again. He had been gone too long. It was his responsibility to support his cousin in leading the Mazir. He'd failed Medjuel in that respect. While his cousin was dealing with life and death issues here, he'd been in London doing very little.

"I'm sorry. I should have come home sooner."

"Your presence would not have made a difference." Medjuel turned around to eye him closely for a moment, then with a smile his cousin strode toward him and grasped Altair by the arms. "But you're home now, and that is all that matters."

From the study doorway, a loud, joyous voice cried out Altair's name, and he whirled around to see his stepbrother racing toward him.

"Kahlil," he exclaimed with a delighted laugh as he embraced the young man in a tight hug. He released his brother and took a step back. His hands settled on Kahlil's shoulders before he gave a gentle tug to the goatee the younger man wore. "Look at you, little brother. I go away for a few months and you finally manage to grow a beard."

"And you need to grow yours back." Kahlil grinned.

Altair squeezed his brother's shoulder as he saw their mother entering the study. Her beauty still visible, despite the strands of silver filtering through her coal-black hair, Gameela Mazir was every inch the Bedouin princess. Even her name meant beauty and grace. It was easy to see why his father had been so enamored with her. Stepping forward, he opened his arms, and she hurried into his embrace.

He held her tight for a long moment before stepping back away from her. With a kiss to her brow, he smiled. "You are well?"

"Yes, and so happy to have you home again." Gameela beamed at him.

"And Jemal?"

"You know your stepfather. The spring lambs have arrived, and you know how important they are to him."

That he did. Jemal had married his mother shortly after he'd turned twelve. He'd resented his stepfather, and not made things easy for the man. But Jemal had been patient. Patient and wise. Instead of trying to win his approval, his stepfather had made him responsible for the care of an orphaned lamb. He'd known nothing about how to care for a lamb, and when the animal wouldn't eat, he'd gone to Jemal. His stepfather had solemnly looked back at him, and pointed out that not all orphans were willing to take to a new parent. But that love, kindness and patience would serve both well. He'd gone back to his lamb—finally getting it to eat. Still, he'd not missed the parallel between him and Jemal. It had been the beginning of the end of all their differences. His stepfather was a good man, and had become a close friend.

"Are you staying for dinner, Altair?" Kahlil's question jerked him back to the present.

His brother's request made him wince with regret. "Actually, I agreed to dine with Miss Talbot and Mrs. Beacon."

"But you'll be staying here?" Gameela's voice held the slightest trace of entreaty.

Capturing his mother's hands, he leaned forward and kissed her cheek. "Yes, I'll be staying here. At least until the day after tomorrow."

"So soon?" Kahlil protested.

"I'm afraid so. Miss Talbot is in a hurry to get to Khatana-Qantir. She thinks it's where Per-Ramesses is as well as Nourbese's tomb."

Silence filled the study, and Altair looked over his shoulder at Medjuel. A strange expression crossed his cousin's face, but he couldn't decipher it. Their eyes met, and the look vanished. Altair dismissed Medjuel's expression as one of surprise. They both knew how unusual it was for anyone outside of the tribe to know Nourbese's story. Beside him, Kahlil broke the quiet.

"If she finds Nourbese's tomb, that means the tribe will be granted riches beyond our wildest dreams."

Gameela shook her head as she arched her brow. "You've been listening to too many folk tales, young man."

Altair met his mother's curious look. "I think Miss Talbot might actually find Nourbese's tomb, Mother. She's a bright and remarkable woman."

"And brave. A woman worthy of you, cousin." Medjuel's laughing words arched Gameela's brow higher. "I have no doubt that you find her quite lovely."

"I think I should like to meet this woman, Altair."

His mother's firm voice made him groan. "Not this time, Mother. When we come back from Khatana-Qantir, I'll arrange for Miss Talbot to join us for dinner."

Medjuel burst out into laughter, and Altair glared at his cousin. His glower simply made his cousin laugh all the harder. The mirth rolling from his cousin almost made him forget how tense Medjuel had been earlier. He would do whatever he could to help his cousin. Nevertheless, it didn't stop him from wondering if Medjuel's course of action was in the best interest of the tribe. He'd stayed away too long. Far too long.

Chapter Nine

Alex stretched her limbs as her eyes slowly opened to take in the netting surrounding her canopied bed. Last night's dinner had been a pleasant evening, despite the tension between her and Altair. Jane had gone out of her way to charm Lord Tunbridge. She had seemed determined to make the man enamored with her.

Sitting up in bed, Alex smiled. It had been amusing to watch her friend match wits with the earl. Jane had been irritated by the man's dismissive behavior in the lobby yesterday, particularly when she was unaccustomed to being ignored. Her friend would have considered it a challenge to bring the man to his knees and make him adore her.

As she'd watched her friend engage in a duel of words and witticisms with the earl last night it had provided a small buffer against the emotions Altair had aroused in her. The sight of him entering the dining room of the *Billôr Sarâya* had only rekindled the fire he'd ignited in her earlier on this very bed. The memory of his touch on her skin made her heart race.

With a sharp movement, she flung the covers off her and scrambled out of bed. *Stop it, Alex—the man is a rake. His behavior was a way to control you.* She strode to the dresser, which had a scalloped mirror attached to the back. Hands braced against the wooden surface of the furniture, she scowled at her reflection.

"Admit it, you enjoyed every minute of it, Alex Talbot," she whispered at the image in the glass.

The woman looking back at her shook her head as if trying to deny the accusation. Her eyes fluttered shut at the memory of Altair's heated gaze on her last night. It had been difficult to forget that only a few short hours earlier his hands and mouth had been exploring her body in a way that drove the breath from her lungs.

Staring at her reflection once more, she slowly slid her nightgown off her shoulders to study her body in the mirror. Just thinking about the man had already hardened her nipples, and her breasts felt heavy. Her fingers glided over her rigid nipples, as she remembered the way he'd suckled her.

She cupped each of her breasts, her thumbs strumming each nipple. Her eyes closed, she remembered how Altair's tongue had teased and nipped at her. She ached with the need to feel his touch once more. She wanted him to tempt her again. Her mouth grew dry at the memories, and she inhaled a ragged breath. She wanted more. She wanted to feel his hands on her skin again.

Her eyes flew open to stare at her reflection in horror. No— no, how could she want that? How could she crave the kisses of a man she couldn't trust? She needed to learn more control. She was here to find Per-Ramesses and Nourbese's tomb, not to act like a wanton *harîm* girl.

With a disgusted sniff at the image in front of her, she turned away from the mirror. Whether Altair liked it or not, she intended to enjoy her brief stay in Cairo. Nothing he could do would spoil her enjoyment of the city. In the desert, she'd have to do his bidding, but here in town, tolerating his over-protective behavior was a different matter.

She'd just finished dressing when an authoritarian knock sounded on her door. Startled, she turned her head toward the noise. Her heart instantly skipped a beat. It was a distinctive knock. She visualized Altair on the other side of the wooden barrier. When she hesitated, the knock came again. Insistent and impatient. It was him.

She hurried to the door to answer the commanding raps. His tall figure filled the doorway as she flung the door open. She fought to keep breathing. There was only one word to describe him. Magnificent. Unable to take her eyes off him, she struggled to calm her erratic heartbeat. Somewhere in the back of her mind, curiosity made her question why he was dressed like one of the natives. The thought was a fleeting one as she fought to keep her senses from responding to his commanding presence.

Dressed in the dark blue, flowing garment of the Mazir, he looked as if he had been born to wear the desert clothing. No longer the English lord, he was as lean and predatory as a leopard. A utility belt filled with rifle cartridges crossed his chest, while a pistol was tucked into a belt around his waist.

His entire appearance emanated a sense of danger and excitement. Beneath his eyes, Mazir tribal symbols stained his brown cheeks. His wavy brown hair, no longer restrained by a ribbon, tumbled down over his shoulders. The image of spiking her fingers through the dark, glossy curls sent a stream of liquid fire through her.

Good lord, she barely knew the man, and yet here she was ready to offer herself to him. She drew in a sharp breath, as she looked up into the warmth of his brown eyes.

"Good morning," he murmured. Alarm bells went off in her head at the sound of his husky greeting. If she were to open her mouth, she was certain more than a dozen butterflies would flee their captivity in her stomach.

"Good...morning." The breathless quality of her voice dismayed her. Oh God, she sounded as flustered as she felt. The sudden glint of satisfaction in his eyes made the fluttering wings in her stomach stir restlessly. Her voice had revealed far too much about the effect he had on her. Desperate to regain control of her senses, she swallowed the sensual urges threatening to take control.

"I...you...you look so different. Not like yourself at all."

"And how do you think I should look, Alex?" His eyes narrowed slightly as he studied her intently.

The dark, disturbing expression in his gaze sent her heart slamming into her chest. Tiny frissons caressed her skin as his gaze slid over her. Aroused by the mysteriously hungry look in his eyes, she shook her head as if doing so would help clear her thoughts as well as the desire curling inside her.

"It's just that you surprised me. I wasn't expecting to see you dressed like a Mazir."

"I find the *gambaz* cooler and more comfortable than my English clothes."

She nodded at his explanation. Oddly enough, he did look

comfortable. Far more so than when he was wearing the starched shirt and tie he usually wore. The *gambaz* enhanced the dangerous edge of his darkly handsome features.

Did the man have any idea how devastating he was dressed like a Bedouin? There was a wicked savagery about him that tantalized her senses and made her breath hitch. Trying to suppress the urge to reach out and touch him, she inhaled a deep breath.

"Is something wrong, Alex?" The gleam in his eye made the palms of her hands damp.

"No, not at all." She forced the words past her lips, alarmed by the need building inside her.

A brown finger traced the outline of her lips as he leaned toward her. Cedarwood and sweet fennel tempted her senses. "Liar," he whispered, as a smile of satisfaction curved his mouth. "Your heart is beating as if you were a jerboa caught in the claws of a leopard."

His analogy was ironic given she'd likened him to a leopard earlier. Especially when she really did feel just like a mouse trapped beneath his masterful gaze. The dark brown eyes holding her gaze hostage glittered with a dangerous light. Drinking in the masculine scent of him, her lungs tugged in a sharp breath of need. She wanted him to kiss her. Appalled, she tried to find a footing on the slippery path she was treading. Diversion. That's what was called for—a diversion.

"I...I...why do you wear the Mazir marks on your cheeks?" She almost blew out a whoosh of air as she asked the question with great relief. That would help lessen this tension between them.

"They reflect the sunlight and protect my eyes. But they're also a sign of my respect for the Mazir." He arched an eyebrow at her as his finger trailed along the edge of her jaw in a slow, seductive stroke. The touch singed every nerve in his path. "But that's not what you really wanted to ask me, is it?"

"I don't know what you're talking about." She took a quick step back from him.

"Ah, so you didn't want to ask when we were to visit the Pyramids. As you wish." As he turned away from her, she sprang forward. The man was tormenting her by making her think he wouldn't take her to the Pyramids. Determined to halt his departure, she clutched at his arm. How soft the material of his robe was beneath her fingers.

"Don't you dare tease me like that!"

A quick flame came to life in his dark eyes as he turned and looked down into her face. The slight smile curving his lips made her heart race. The man was far too attractive for his own good.

"How would you like me tease you, Alex?"

She took a quick step backward at the surprising question. With an abrupt shake of her head, she pressed her hand against his chest as he followed her.

"I don't...I meant...I want to visit the Pyramids."

"I see. So you weren't hoping I'd find some other way to tease you?"

"I don't know what you're talking about," she spluttered.

His dark hand reached out to caress her cheek. No. If he kissed her again, she wouldn't be able to control the desire shooting through every part of her body. She took another step back. Once again, he followed her. Now the space between them was almost nonexistent. He lowered his head. Dear Lord, he smelled wonderful. He had an earthy male scent that tormented her senses. A shiver pulsed through her as the warmth of his breath stirred the wisps of hair at her ear.

"Don't you? That's disappointing because I'm finding it increasingly difficult to get the image of your luscious body out of my head."

She gasped at the seductive heat of his words. He nipped at her ear lobe and reason slipped out of her head.

"Do you know what I dreamed about last night, Alex? I dreamed I was sucking on those beautiful, dusky nipples of yours."

"Oh, God," she whispered, unable to say anything else.

"Can you imagine what else I dreamed about? Shall I tell you?"

Don't moan, Alex. Whatever you do, don't moan. She swayed into him, her fingers splayed across the upper part of his chest.

No.

No. This wasn't good at all. Looking up at him, she knew he

was going to kiss her. She wanted him to. The shivers of delight skimming through her told her just how eager her body really was for him to kiss her. She should have been shocked. Instead, she simply offered her mouth for the taking.

The deep growl that rolled from his throat sent excitement skimming through her, and her eyes fluttered closed in anticipation of his kiss. At that precise moment, Jane's cry of panic echoed in the hall.

"Let her go!"

Her groan didn't pass her lips. The heat warming her body vanished as Altair stepped away from her and into the hall to face Jane.

"Good morning, Jane."

"Dear Lord! Altair! I...Your appearance... I...I didn't realize..." Jane's voice trailed to a halt as she tried to control her embarrassment.

"My apologies. I should have warned both of you about my habit of wearing Bedouin clothing while in the Sahara. I was just explaining to Alex that I find it much cooler and more comfortable than what I would wear in England."

With an understanding nod, Jane smiled. "Of course. So is Alex proving difficult this morning?"

"No more than usual. I was merely trying to reassure her that our trip to the Pyramids would be quite safe."

"Well, if she's protesting too much, we can always leave her here. I, for one, am determined to see those Pyramids with or without her."

Alex glared at her friend as she stepped into the corridor, closing the door behind her. "I am *not* protesting nor am I being difficult. If you wish to leave me here, then do so. I'll find someone else to take me. Perhaps Lord Tunbridge?"

Pink flushed through Jane's cheeks at the comment. So the man's lack of interest *had* pricked her friend's ego. Alex smiled with satisfaction. No one would ever be able to say she couldn't best Jane Beacon in a verbal duel. Beside her, Altair cleared his throat. The sound was more like a growl, and when she looked up at him, she saw a glint of dark emotion in his gaze. Her heart skipped a beat. While she wanted to believe it was fear that sent her heart pounding, she knew better. The man excited her, and his possessive look sent a shiver of anticipation streaking down her spine.

"Ladies, shall we proceed downstairs for breakfast? The Pyramids await us." With an abrupt gesture, he swept his arm out before him to urge them forward.

One glance at Jane's expression spoke volumes. Her friend had seen the possessive gleam in Altair's eyes. With a pointed look at Altair's face, a sly smile curved her friend's mouth. The wink Jane sent her made her heart sink. *Blast her hide!* First, she interrupts just when Altair is about to kiss her, and now she was acting as if it were all part of some grandiose plan of hers. Expelling a puff of air in aggravation, Alex scowled.

Inviting Jane to accompany her to Khatana-Qantir might not have been a good idea after all. Her friend wouldn't hesitate to create mischief where she and Altair were concerned. Well, she refused to let any devilry on Jane's part distract her from the task at hand. Work would occupy most of her time, and the rest—well, the rest of the time she would just keep her distance from Altair. How difficult could that be? She glanced up at the man walking beside her and nearly tripped as his gaze met hers. From the look in his eyes, it might be much more difficult than she imagined.

✧

The sun blazed high overhead, and Alex had to admit Jane had been right about the parasols. She might hate the silk frippery, but it did help to lessen the heat somewhat by blocking the intense sunlight. Ahead of them loomed the Pyramids.

Not quite a hundred years ago, Napoleon had passed this way. Erroneous decisions might have won and lost his empire, but he'd been right about these magnificent monuments. From the summits of the Pyramids, forty centuries did indeed have their eyes fixed on all who walked in their shadow.

If they were this imposing from here, up close they would only reinforce how small she was in comparison. As the landau rolled to a stop in front of a large corral of camels, Altair climbed out of the vehicle. He turned and assisted first Jane, then Alex from the carriage.

"From here we shall ride *Ata Allah.*" As he pointed to the camels, Jane's face paled slightly.

"What?"

Laughing, Alex patted her friend's arm. "It means gift from God. Bedouins believe camels are gifts from God to help them survive the harshness of the desert. Although they've a reputation for nasty temperaments, Father told me camels are really quite gentle. So you've nothing to fear."

"Fine, but I want the oldest one of the bunch. That way it won't take off at a gallop or whatever it's called when they run."

"As you wish, but as Alex has already pointed out, there's nothing to fear." The low, seductive chuckle drifting over Alex's shoulder made her tingle. Mesmerizing. It was the only word she could think of to describe his voice. Even a quietly spoken hello was enough to shoot bolts of delicious tension through her limbs.

Jane nodded sharply, but it was obvious her friend didn't believe a word either of them said. They did look intimidating though. Jane didn't like horses very much, so getting on one of these large ships of the desert wasn't going to be to her friend's liking at all.

With a laugh, Altair turned away and walked over to a short, wiry man wearing a dust-covered robe and turban. Close by, Alex saw three children playing in the dirt. They looked just as impoverished as the children they'd seen playing in the streets of Cairo yesterday and today. Her heart went out to them. Simply by circumstance of their birth, they were forced to live a harsh existence.

For their height, she guessed they were at least eight or nine years old, but they were so thin. Not one of them could weigh more than forty pounds. Dressed in rags, they jostled each other as they watched her. She smiled. They might be shy, but they were definitely curious.

Reaching into her skirt pocket, she pulled out several coins. Hand outstretched, she stepped toward them. The moment they retreated from her, she stopped. Well, being wary of a stranger wasn't a bad thing. Perhaps the last tourist to pass this way had been far from pleasant. As unfortunate as it was, humankind rarely had sympathy for those less fortunate.

While she'd not grown up poor, humility had been a firm

lesson her father insisted she learn. Humility and compassion for others. Not wishing to frighten the children any further, she tossed the coins down into the dirt at their feet. As they scrambled to pick up the money, she turned around to see Altair watching her with cold anger.

The icy glare wasn't just disturbing—it intimidated her. Whatever her crime, he seemed willing to wait before he took her to task. With a quiet word of encouragement, he guided Jane to the camel he'd selected for her. With Jane comfortably situated on her mount, Altair turned toward Alex.

Her eyes narrowed as he walked toward her. From the look of his angry expression, she wasn't going to receive the same type of solicitous care Jane had. Not speaking to her, he grasped her elbow in a tight grip and dragged her toward one of the camels. She tripped over her feet as he pulled her along.

If he was angry with her— If? All right, he *was* angry. But the least he could do was to tell her why he was so incensed. Her elbow ached from where his fingers bit into her flesh. As they halted at the side of a kneeling camel, Alex tugged her arm free of his tight grip.

"You're hurting me," she snapped.

"Get on the camel, Alex."

The rough edge of his voice made her think of a razor. Oh, he wasn't just angry, he was furious. But why? Glaring at him, she did as he ordered. His movements were sharp and rough as he adjusted the umbrella shade over her head. When he finished, he leaned down toward her. Once again, his fingers bit into her flesh, but this time he captured her chin and forced her to look at him.

"If I ever see you tossing coins about like that again, I'll make you wish you'd never left America."

"I was only trying—"

"I know what you were trying to do," he bit out in a harsh whisper. "You were thinking those filthy little savages might dirty your clothes, and throwing them a few coins would keep them away. Well, they don't need pity from someone too afraid to go near them. These are proud people, and I won't have you insult them. Is that clear?"

"Of all the—"

"Is that clear?"

Staring up into the fury tightening his dark features, she gulped down her fear. He looked every inch the barbarian. That was why he was furious? Because she'd tossed some money at the children? They'd been afraid of her, and she'd simply wanted to help. The last thing she'd meant to do was insult someone. Holding her tongue, she nodded. She wanted to explain, but in his current mood, he wasn't about to let her finish a sentence.

At her nod, he wheeled away from her and stalked off toward his camel. Watching him go, a knot settled in her throat. Did he really think she was some prim, snobbish English miss who believed those children beneath her?

Well, if he thought that, he was wrong. Completely wrong. Her camel lurched to its feet, and she clung to the pommel of the saddle. The animal's ungainly gait was like being on the *Moroccan Wind* in rough seas. Her gaze settled on Altair's back.

How could he think so harshly of her? He hardly knew anything about her or her upbringing. Respect for other cultures was a lesson she'd learned well. How else could one be a true scholar if one didn't value the differences in others?

Altair's camel led the way with Alex drawing up the rear of their small column. With the camels walking in tandem, it prevented any of them from having a normal conversation. She was glad of it. The last thing she wanted at the moment was to talk with anyone. Anyone at all. Not even if the Pharaoh Khufu himself were to walk up and say hello would she be interested in holding a conversation.

Huge sand drifts rose and fell all around the landscape that surrounded the Sphinx and Pyramids. Its massive body entrenched in the sand, the Sphinx's colossal head rose majestically to the sky. The monument cast its large shadow over the trail they followed, and she held her breath for a moment.

In the shadow of this chiseled stone creature, pharaohs and queens had walked where she now walked. She wished her father were here to experience this moment with her. Despite its enormous size, the half lion, half man monument found itself dwarfed by Khufu's great pyramid tomb.

In front of her, Jane turned in her seat and waved at the

large stone structure.

"Magnificent, isn't it?" she called.

Forcing a smile to her lips, Alex nodded. It should have been everything she'd dreamed it would be, but it wasn't. Emptiness gnawed at her. She was alone in the world. But then she'd really always been alone. She'd always been the strong one. The one Father and Uncle Jeffrey had relied on in a time of crisis. Just once, she'd like to be able to lean on someone else.

With a rueful shake of her head, she grimaced. It was time to stop crying into her milk. If Father and Uncle Jeffrey were here, they wouldn't let one man's anger prevent them from enjoying this moment. Her hands clenched at the pommel. Altair's feelings toward her didn't matter in the least. A small whisper in her head called her a liar.

She watched as Jane called out a question to Altair and he dropped back to ride at Jane's side. Why should she care that he was paying special attention to Jane? It wasn't as if she was even interested in the man. There was no doubt he was a beautiful male specimen. But that didn't mean she cared what he thought of her.

Of course, she cared. She gave an unladylike snort of disgust. It was foolish to try to deny she didn't want the man's approval. Trailing behind the two of them, she saw him turn and look back at her for a brief instant. Satisfied she was still drawing up the rear, he returned his attention to Jane. She gritted her teeth at the cavalier glance.

Well, approval or not, she definitely didn't like the way he was behaving. She'd done nothing wrong, and his erroneous assumption had simply served to show his faults. The man was quick to judge, inflexible and maddeningly arrogant.

Nodding her head to herself, she released another sound of disgust. And here she was worried about the man being angry at her. Ridiculous. That's what it was. Ridiculous. All she needed to do was keep her mind on her work. She had come to Egypt to find Per-Ramesses, nothing more. *So enjoy yourself, Alex.*

The internal command tugged a smile to her mouth. As they rode into the shadow of Khufu's Pyramid, the relief from the heat was immediate. Staring up at the colossal structure, she marveled at the engineering feat the Pharaoh Khufu had ordered built more than four thousand years ago.

Up ahead, the main entrance loomed like a dark hole in the side of the Pyramid. At Altair's signal, they all came to a halt. The moment her camel lumbered down onto its knees, Alex slid off the animal and down into the sand. The thickness of it pulled at her boots showing beneath her riding skirt.

Striding forward, she almost fell. The sand sucked at her boots like thick mud as she moved toward the tomb's entrance. She passed Altair helping Jane off her camel. His solicitous attitude toward her friend made her grit her teeth.

After the third time almost falling on her face, she climbed up several giant blocks of stones to reach the tomb's dark doorway. She paused at the entrance. Altair had one arm around Jane's waist as he helped her through the slippery sand. Biting her lip, she scowled. A rake and a scoundrel who wasn't to be trusted. Eager to push on, she peered down into the cavernous depths of the tunnel in front of her.

"Alex, wait for us."

Another command. When was he going to learn she didn't like it when he ordered her around? She didn't like it all. Ignoring his order, she stooped and entered the narrow corridor. The small confines of the passageway forced a breath of surprise from her. The size of the Pyramid had made her think the corridor would be just as awe-inspiring. This passage was anything but. It was narrow, tight and constricting. Not only that, the roof was so low she had to remain hunched over.

A lit torch rested in a metal sconce on the wall. Ahead of her, there was nothing but darkness. Several unlit rushes lay on the floor, and she scooped one up. It would be just like the time she'd gone spelunking with Uncle Jeffrey. She'd just have to take care with the torch. The last thing she needed was to be stuck in here without a light.

Still bent at the waist, she scooted forward. Father would have found the passage difficult. His height had been roughly the same as Altair's. But where Altair was lean and hard, her father had been a bit more rounded. He would have managed though. The last thing Professor Alexander Talbot had been was a quitter. And neither was she.

Beneath her fingers, the walls were cool and smooth. Amazing how these massive stones were all chiseled by hand.

Even more astonishing was how they made their weighty presence felt just in the denseness of the air. It smelled exactly like a four-thousand-year-old tomb should smell. Dank and musty. The floor angled downward, and she saw a torch mounted in another metal sconce on the wall. Lighting the torch, she moved on.

She continued to find torches along the way, lighting them as she moved deeper into the tomb. Ahead of her, a scurrying, scratching sound made her hesitate. Rats. She hated rats. Stopping, she stretched out her torch to illuminate more of the passage in front of her. She tipped her head to one side and listened. Nothing but silence. As usual, her imagination was working overtime.

In the distance, she heard Jane and Altair behind her, but she couldn't make out their words. Perhaps her impulsiveness had been foolhardy, given the attempt on her life yesterday. Scoffing at herself, she shook her head. There was only one way in and out of this part of the tomb.

A murderer wouldn't choose a place from which he couldn't escape. Not to mention how easy it would be to find any assailant. They'd be easily recognizable from the permanent stoop in their back. She grimaced at the ache in her spine. It wouldn't be any big surprise if she suffered a similar fate.

Continuing forward, she finally emerged into a narrow, high-ceilinged chamber. Thank goodness. Any more scrambling forward like a monkey would have been torturous. She took a moment to catch her breath and study the high ceiling. Torches lined each side of the wall, and she lit them as she moved forward. This could only be the Grand Gallery, and just beyond lay the King's Chamber. She stared at the smooth walls. Where were the hieroglyphs and depictions of life during Pharaoh's time covering the walls? These walls were free of markings. At the far end of the chamber, the scratching noise came again.

Caught off guard, she jumped before grimacing at her nervousness. The torch she carried sputtered, and she quickly traded it for a fresh torch hanging on the wall. Lifting the light high over her head, she peered into the darkness. The Grand Gallery seemed to stretch on endlessly. From where she stood, she could see no end in sight.

As she strode forward, the scratching got louder. A soft

whine accompanied the sound. Dear Lord, someone had left a dog inside the tomb. It had to have been deliberate. One didn't bring an animal into this place and just leave it here. Locked up in the dark, the poor thing must be crazed with terror.

It took her several minutes to reach the far end of the Grand Gallery. The high-ceilinged chamber ended at a medium-sized doorway beyond which was more darkness. The King's Chamber. Her father would have been beside himself with excitement. A low growl sounded in front of her, and she took a step back.

No sooner had she done so than an animal slunk its way out of the dark chamber and into the Grand Gallery. As it moved into the light, Alex's heart flew up into her mouth. She'd been expecting a dog. This was no dog looking to be rescued. This was a gaunt, half-starved hyena.

She watched it circle her. First a snake, now a hyena. Whoever was trying to kill her had an affinity for animals of the exotic variety. The bizarre concept would have been funny if she'd not been so terrified. The hyena's mouth furled back in a snarl. Instinct made her grip the torch with both hands.

When it leaped forward, Alex swung her torch. Flames met the animal's furry hide, and it yelped in pain as it tumbled backward. Getting up to its feet, the animal bared its teeth and lunged at her again. With all her strength she swung the torch. The flaming club crashed against the hyena's head with a loud crack. The noise reverberated in the chamber, and the animal flew sideways and bounced off the wall. It landed on the floor with a small whimper before growing silent.

Alex stared at the hyena, prepared to ward off another attack, but the animal remained where it had landed. From the far end of the gallery, she heard voices. About to call out, she saw the hyena move slightly. Without a second thought, she leaped forward and brought her fiery club down on the animal's head repeatedly until a strong arm pulled her away.

"Enough, Alex. It's dead."

She shuddered, her chest heaving with deep breaths of terror. Altair pulled the torch from her limp fingers, and she turned away from the dead animal. Jane stepped forward to embrace her, but Alex spurned the offer of comfort with her raised hand. God, she felt sick. She wasn't sure if it was from fear or the sight of the hyena's blood.

"I'm fine."

"Alex, maybe you should rethink going to Khatana-Qantir." Jane's quiet suggestion hung in the dank air as Alex scowled at her friend.

"Why?"

"Don't be obtuse, Alex. Someone's going to great lengths to try to stop you." Jane's brow furrowed with worry.

"Jane's right, Alex. It might be—"

She snapped her gaze to Altair's face, daring him to continue. If the two of them thought she was going to quit, they needed their heads examined. Yesterday she'd been ready to give up, but she'd come to her senses. She wasn't going to let a couple of unpleasant encounters with desert wildlife deter her. Straightening to her full height, she glared at the two of them.

"I'm going to Khatana-Qantir. And no one, and I do mean *no one*, is going to stop me."

Without another look at either of them, Alex headed toward the exit. She refused to let someone frighten her into going home. This was no longer her father's dream. It was hers now, and she was going to do everything in her power to fulfill that dream despite the dangers involved.

✧

The camel ride back from the Pyramids had been bearable only because she wasn't in close proximity to Altair. But even then, she could feel his disapproving gaze on her back. Now, in the close confines of the carriage taking them back to the hotel, his penetrating gaze was that much harder to ignore.

Every time the vehicle came to a halt because of traffic in the street, she wanted to leap out and run as far away from him as she could. As if aware of her distress, Jane touched her arm.

"Oh, Alex, look. It's a silk shop." Jane looked at the man seated opposite them. "Altair, would you mind if we did a small amount of shopping?"

Irritated that her friend had asked his permission, Alex sent Jane a dark look. But her friend was oblivious to the condemnation. A smile on his lips, Altair nodded his head and ordered the carriage driver to stop. Not even looking in her direction, Altair opened the low door of the landau and stepped out of the carriage. With a gallant gesture he extended his hand to Jane to help her out of the vehicle.

His entire demeanor infuriated Alex. Why did the man have to be so damn solicitous to Jane all the time? With her, he was anything but that. She slid across the seat and exited the vehicle on the opposite side. As she turned toward the landau to shut the door, her gaze met Altair's. His eyes narrowed in a speculative manner, he studied her in silence for a brief moment.

"The silk shop is on this side of the street, Alex," he said quietly.

Not bothering to respond, she swept around the back of the carriage and followed Jane into the small store. She half expected Altair to join them, but he remained outside.

In her element, Jane moved around the small shop examining the fabrics available for sale. Alex could do little more than trail in her friend's wake. When Jane had decided on the folds of silk she wanted, she had Alex translate the sale for her.

As was the custom, Alex negotiated with the man for the goods. She had almost achieved a final price when Jane released a sharp cry of pleasure.

"Alex, come look at this." Jane waved her over to where a beautiful silk costume was displayed on the wall. "Isn't it exquisite?"

"More like decadent, although it appears to be of an authentic design," Alex murmured as she watched Jane slide her hand through the almost transparent skirt. "You aren't seriously giving any consideration to buying it, are you?"

"Of course I am."

"Where on earth would you wear it? If you were ancient Egyptian royalty, I could understand wanting to buy it, but..."

"Alex Talbot, haven't you ever bought something simply because it was beautiful?"

"Well...yes, but not a dress, especially not one that's so...so..."

"Seductive?" Jane asked with a chuckle. With a mischievous grin, she waved her hand toward the shopkeeper. "Go on now, find out what I need to pay the man for the silks *and* the dress."

Shaking her head in amused disgust, Alex returned to her bargaining session with the shop owner. With their shopping completed, they left the small store and resumed their journey to the hotel. As they arrived at the *Billôr Sarâya*, Alex exhaled a sigh of relief. The sooner she could retreat to her room, the better it would be for her frayed nerves.

Before she could exit the door on her side, Altair moved quickly to intercept her. He stepped out of the vehicle and extended his hand to her. Unable to avoid accepting his assistance, her hand slid into his as he helped her from the carriage. A pulse of excitement shot up her arm at his touch. Flustered and agitated by the tactile sensation, she yanked her hand free.

She moved quickly toward the hotel entrance, not bothering to wait on Jane and Altair. As she entered the lobby, Hakim, the hotel manager, greeted her in his usual profuse manner.

"Greetings, my lady. Did you enjoy your visit to the Pyramids?"

"Yes, thank you." Not in the mood for idle conversation, she headed for the staircase.

"Forgive me, my lady, but you had a visitor while you were gone."

She stopped and whirled around to face the man. "A visitor?"

"Yes, my lady." Hakim nodded with a smile. "He said Sheikh Mazir had sent him to pick up your trunks. So I let him into your room."

"My trunks?" Alex turned her head to look up at Altair as he joined her and Hakim. "Did you ask someone to pick up my things?"

"No," he said with a grim expression on his face.

"Oh, dear God. My notes."

With a gasp, she spun around and raced for the stairs. She didn't get far before Altair pulled her to an abrupt halt.

"No, Alex. Stay here while I make sure it's safe."

Leaving her in the vestibule, he took the steps two at a time and disappeared around the bend in the stairwell. Jane joined her and gave her a reassuring hug.

"I'm certain everything's fine, Alex."

"You don't understand, Jane." A miserable sinking feeling settled in her stomach. "If someone takes my notes or destroys them, I can't find Per-Ramesses."

Impatient for news and unwilling to wait for Altair's return, she sprinted up the steps. Behind her, she ignored Jane's cry to stop. As she reached the second floor, she heard Jane's voice again, and looked over her shoulder. Her friend was following close on her heels.

"Blast it, Alex, will you please wait," her friend snapped.

Jane rarely raised her voice in anger, and it surprised Alex enough to make her stop where she was at the top of the stairs. In that same moment, she heard Altair commanding someone to halt. She turned toward the sound of his voice and saw a Bedouin running in her direction. His face was covered except for his eyes, and as he drew near, she swallowed hard at the flat look of contempt in his gaze.

She wanted to run, but her precarious position at the top of the stairs left her with nowhere to go. Instinct made her reach for the banister as the man shoved her aside and continued down the steps. Her fingers touched nothing but air before she toppled backward with a cry of fear.

Unable to stop her fall, she hit something softer than wood, yet just as solid. Horrified, she realized she had sent Jane toppling down the stairs with her. As they tumbled onto the landing she heard a sickening crack and Jane's scream of pain.

The carpet on the landing provided little cushioning, and her lungs expelled a powerful whoosh of air as she hit the floor. Stunned, she didn't move for a moment until she heard soft weeping. Jane never cried. Rolling onto her side, Alex crawled to where her friend lay.

"Where are you hurt, Jane?"

"M-my...leg."

Altair reached the landing an instant later, but she ignored him. With care, she pushed her friend's skirts aside to examine

Jane's legs. The sight of one limb bent at an awkward angle made her stomach lurch. With a glance at her friend's white face, remorse swelled up into her throat.

"Oh God, Jane. I'm so sorry." Alex pressed her friend's hand to her cheek. "I'm so very sorry."

His expression grim, Altair looked at someone over Alex's shoulder. "Hakim, send for Doctor Arnaud right away, then bring me two flat pieces of wood and some bandages. *Do it quickly.*"

It wasn't until Altair had issued his command that she even realized the hotel manager was behind her. Glancing over her shoulder, she saw him and another man hurrying down the steps. It briefly flashed through her head that it was the first time she'd not seen the man acting obsequious when it came to being in Altair's presence.

"Jane, do you hurt anywhere else other than your leg?"

"N-no."

Jane's eyes were squeezed shut but a teardrop escaped to slide down the side of her face. Her heart filled with regret, Alex gently brushed the tear away. Across from her, Altair squeezed Jane's shoulder.

"Jane, unfortunately your leg is broken. It may be some time before the doctor arrives, and we need to set the leg before we move you."

A whimper escaped Jane's lips at Altair's words, but she nodded her understanding. He patted her shoulder in a gesture of encouragement.

"I promise to be as quick about it as I can."

He'd barely finished speaking when one of the hotel's valets returned with two smooth slats of wood and several rolled up bandages. In silence, Altair accepted the items then murmured something in Arabic. The man immediately moved to kneel at Jane's head and placed his hands gently on her shoulders.

In a brief instant, Altair grasped Jane's leg and snapped it back into position. The unexpected action forced a loud scream from Jane before her head lolled to one side as she fainted. Alex closed her eyes in relief. Jane was free of pain for the moment, and for that she was grateful.

Chapter Ten

Alex balanced the tray she carried on her hip then opened the door to Jane's room. The sound of her friend's laughter caught her by surprise, and as the door swung open, she saw Altair seated beside Jane's bed. The sight sparked an unpleasant emotion inside her.

Ever since Jane's fall a week ago, Altair had been a constant visitor to her friend's room. But where Alex was concerned, he'd barely spoken two words to her. It was bad enough that she blamed herself for Jane's fall, but the weight of his disapproval was more painful than any scourge she might inflict on herself.

"Oh, Alex," Jane exclaimed as she stretched out her hands. "Altair has brought me the most wonderful news. Lord Tunbridge has offered me the hospitality of his home while he's in Luxor over the next several weeks."

Alex's heart sank at the words. For the past week she'd been able to push thoughts of Per-Ramesses out of her head. But now, Jane's news forced her to realize she wouldn't be able to leave for Khatana-Qantir for quite some time.

The selfish thought made her wince. She'd been the cause of Jane's accident, and it was wrong of her to even think about Per-Ramesses when her friend needed her. Setting the tray on a small table near Jane's bed, she went to her friend and clasped her outstretched hands.

"That's wonderful news. I'll see that our things are packed and ready by the end of the day."

"You'll do no such thing," Jane said firmly as she pulled her hands free of Alex's grasp. "His lordship has plenty of servants who'll see to my needs. You've delayed your plans for Per-Ramesses long enough."

"Plans are easily altered." Alex shook her head.

"Don't be ridiculous, Alex. I've already discussed it with Altair, and he's agreed to make all the arrangements for you to leave in the next day or so."

"I won't leave you here on your own."

She sent her friend a stubborn look and saw Jane's eyes narrow slightly with assessment. Her friend turned her head toward her visitor.

"Altair, would you mind leaving me and Alex alone for a moment?"

"Certainly."

He reached for Jane's hand and brushed his mouth over the edge of her knuckles. Alex immediately suppressed the sharp emotion pricking her heart. The man's solicitous behavior toward Jane was none of her concern. She met his gaze as he rose to his feet. She found it impossible to read his expression, and she offered him a sharp nod of acknowledgement.

When he had left the room, she turned her attention back to Jane. Before she could speak, her friend lifted her hand in a peremptory gesture.

"Don't say a word," Jane said with an autocratic note in her voice. "I've already discussed this matter with Altair, and he's agreed to take you to Khatana-Qantir without me."

"But when your leg is better, you—"

"Blast it, Alex. I can't go to Khatana-Qantir with you."

Startled, she stared at her friend in dismay. "Why ever not? We can wait—"

"That's just it, Alex, I don't want you to wait. It's going be several weeks before I'm capable of walking without any assistance. That means I won't be able to travel until the beginning of the summer." Jane waved her hand toward the open window. "Altair tells me that getting to Khatana-Qantir is dangerous enough without making the trip in the throes of summer."

"Then I'll wait until the fall. It's only a couple of months," Alex said stubbornly.

"Listen to yourself. What happens if the British Museum sends someone to look for Per-Ramesses?"

"They won't find anything." She kept her tone emphatic, but fear sent a shiver down her back.

"Are you so sure?" Jane sent her a piercing look. "I know you said nothing was missing from your room, but your notes were scattered everywhere. What if that man found something in your work that he could sell to the Museum?"

She grew still at Jane's words. Was it possible? She was reasonably certain her notes were all accounted for, but if the man had read them— Frowning, she shook her head.

"I still can't leave you here."

"I'll be fine. I can always join you in a couple of months once I'm completely recovered."

"But, it's not—"

"For heaven's sake, Alex. Did you or did you not come to Egypt to find Per-Ramesses?" Jane exclaimed with exasperation.

The sharpness of her friend's tone surprised her, and all she could do was respond with a simple nod. Scowling, Jane wagged her finger in a scolding manner.

"Then it's high time you were on your way."

Still hesitating, Alex frowned. "Are you sure you don't mind?"

"Mind what—being waited on hand and foot at Lord Tunbridge's house?" Jane laughed. "You should know the answer to that. I have never denied my love for the material things in life."

Bending forward, Alex gave her friend a grateful hug. "I don't know why, but I'm inclined to think you're almost relieved at not having to come with me."

"As I recall, you did say there were few conveniences to be had in the desert. And I do like my creature comforts."

"Something Lord Tunbridge's staff can offer you in great abundance?"

"And which I'll gladly accept." Jane nodded and smiled. "But you—you're about to find treasure beyond your wildest dreams, my dear Alex."

She arched an eyebrow at Jane's grandiose statement. "That's *if* I find the city."

"Oh, I'm certain you'll find Per-Ramesses. In fact, I'm convinced your search will unveil far more treasure than you ever imagined."

There was a twinkle of mischief in Jane's eyes, but it was impossible to fathom the reason for her amusement. She started to question her friend then immediately closed her mouth. Asking Jane a question invariably resulted in an answer she didn't want to hear. This time would be no different. Whatever amused her friend, it was doubtful she'd find it equally entertaining.

✧

Dawn had barely broken on the horizon as Altair checked the ropes holding one of Alex's trunks for a second time. All around him was the cacophony of noise always associated with a caravan. The drivers yelling at their animals, the grunts and groans of the camels, the shouts of porters needing help with their loads. Out of this chaos would emerge a quiet, peaceful train of camels. Soon the desert would ring with the sound of bells tinkling in the air and the soft singing of the drivers to their animals.

In the distance, he heard Medjuel shouting orders at one of the workers they'd hired for the expedition. Despite his best efforts, his eyes were continually glancing toward the front of the large caravan where Alex talked with the lead camel driver. The blast of jealousy stiffening his fingers as he worked with the ropes irritated him. Why should he care if the woman talked with another man?

When he'd seen her toss the coins to the camel driver's children more than a week ago, he'd wanted to shake her senseless. Her callous behavior had not only surprised him, it had set off an explosion inside him from which he was still feeling the effects. Even now, he found it difficult to comprehend her actions.

He'd been a fool to think her different from the rest of English society. At least he'd not made the mistake of developing feelings for her. He quickly silenced the mocking laugh that filled his head. Keeping his distance from Alex was the first step toward crushing this attraction he felt for the woman.

With a shake of his head, he returned his attention to the knots in the rope. It was difficult not to admire her mettle and persistence though. That day in the Pyramid, when he'd seen her defending herself against the hyena, it had been impossible not to admire her courage.

Not only that, but even though it was clear someone wanted her dead, she remained resolute in her quest. He was certain she realized someone was trying to kill her, but did she understand why?

He did. The Mazir had sought Nourbese's tomb for a very long time—but they weren't the only ones looking. A few water wells wouldn't satisfy the Hoggar. Ever since his mother had rejected Sheikh Tarih as a husband, the man had been set on destroying the Mazir.

The man had been searching for Nourbese's tomb since that time. If Tarih found Nourbese's treasure, the tribe might never recover from the loss. Losing such a prize to their enemy would cripple the Mazir tribe in a way nothing else could. It would destroy their spirit.

Was that the connection between the traitor Mohammed and the Hoggar? Was he providing Tarih with information about Alex and her quest? It wasn't unreasonable to think Mohammed was giving the Hoggar information about Khatana-Qantir. Despite the Sahara's size, news traveled quickly on the desert winds. Was that why the bastard was in league with those devils? Altair finished with the ropes and moved up the line to check the next camel.

Again, his gaze swept toward Alex. Hunger gnawed at him for one more taste of her. The vision of her pale skin against his darker complexion was as tantalizing in his head as it had been in her hotel room.

"*Damm gahannam*," he muttered as he shook the image from his mind.

A second later, a hand clapped him on the shoulder. Immediately, he wheeled around, his hands raised in a defensive posture. Medjuel stepped back with a surrendering gesture.

"What in God's name is the matter with you? You're acting more skittish than an Arabian mare."

Grimacing, Altair shook his head and turned back to the ropes he'd been examining. "I'm just a bit edgy about this expedition."

"I see. Then why don't we convince Miss Talbot not to go?"

The odd note in Medjuel's voice forced Altair to pause in his work. One hand braced on the animal's pack, he turned and rested his opposite hand on his waist. He studied his cousin's face for a long moment, puzzled by Medjuel's cryptic expression. He shrugged off the uneasy feeling trickling down his spine as his mouth twisted in a grim, humorless smile.

"Obviously you've never tried to convince Alex Talbot of anything before. Feel free to attempt to persuade her otherwise where Khatana-Qantir is concerned, but I'm willing to bet you three spring lambs and my mare, Desari, that you'll fail."

"You're that sure of her?"

"Yes." Altair turned away and resumed his work. Behind him, his cousin uttered a grunt of irritation before he moved away to continue oversight of the caravan. With a sidelong glance and a troubled heart, Altair watched Medjuel walk off. Something was bothering his cousin. Was he worried that Alex might bring the tribe to its knees unintentionally? It was a thought he'd already considered. If Alex found Nourbese's tomb, it was imperative a tribe member be present. Even a half-Mazir was better than no Mazir at all.

Nourbese defined the tribe's belief structure. Her marriage to Ramesses made her royalty, and her son had ensured her descendants were of Pharaoh's royal house. For someone other than a Mazir to find her tomb would devastate the tribe.

The tribe would view an outsider finding the tomb as a sign of disapproval from Nourbese and Pharaoh. The Mazir would lose their identity, and the desolation sweeping through the tribe would extract its toll in a way not even the deadliest *ghazous* could. A raid only killed people and animals. It didn't destroy beliefs.

Satisfied the camel packs were secure, he moved toward the front of the caravan. From behind him, he heard Medjuel cry out for the expedition to mount. Alex had heard the cry as well and moved toward her camel. He restrained himself from rushing forward to help her. Instead, he watched the lead driver assist her with the camel's reins.

With a low growl of irritation, he proceeded to his own animal. Just as he was about to take his seat, Zada poked her head out of the bag attached to the back of the saddle. Ruffling the fur of the mongoose's back, Altair sighed as the mammal ran up his arm and curled its body around his neck. Now was as good a time as any to let Alex get acquainted with her latest protector.

Moving quickly through the sand, he headed toward the front of the caravan where Alex's camel was struggling to its feet. As the camel steadied itself, he reached up and touched Alex's arm. She jumped with surprise as she looked down at him. The panic on her face quickly changed to guarded observation.

"I've brought you a gift." Removing a small cloth bag from his utility belt, he handed it up to her. "This is for Zada. Once you've fed her three or four times, she'll know you as a member of her pack."

"Zada?"

Altair clucked softly and stretched out his arm to rest against the front of Alex's saddle. The banded mongoose unwrapped itself from around his neck and scurried along his arm to rest on the saddle horn. At the animal's movement, Alex stiffened in fear.

"There's nothing to be afraid of. Zada is my pet, but she's also able to protect you."

Her eyebrows arched in disbelief. She shook her head as she warily eyed the mongoose. "Exactly how is something this small supposed to protect me?"

"Mongooses are capable of killing large snakes," he said softly. "They have been kept by the Mazir for centuries as pets and specifically as deterrents to poisonous serpents and other unwanted creatures."

The skepticism on her face faded some, and she nodded toward the creature eyeing her with curiosity. "Will she bite?"

"Not intentionally. Offer her the meat in the sack from the palm of your hand and she'll not draw blood. Never feed her from your fingers. She has razor sharp teeth and might think your finger is part of the meat being offered."

Alex shuddered at his words. The small creature seemed to understand her new mistress's fear and moved quickly forward to curl up in a small ball at Alex's stomach. Startled by the animal's actions, she looked first at him then back at the mongoose. He smiled. He'd known Zada would take easily to Alex.

Gently, he stroked the banded mongoose's brownish red-striped fur. The action caused the animal to rumble a soft growl of happiness. "She's quite affectionate and loves to be scratched."

Biting her lip, Alex tentatively reached out to stroke the mongoose. The small animal uttered another sound of delight. Alex's touch grew bolder until she was caressing the mongoose as she might a house cat. Satisfied she was now comfortable with the animal, Altair made to pull his hand away, but failed to do so quickly enough. In her gentle stroking, her soft hand glided over his fingers.

The tingling shock racing up his arm made him snatch a quick breath as his fingers entangled with hers. She didn't pull away from him, and as he searched her face for some sign of rejection, he saw none. Her hazel eyes darkened and the pink of her mouth parted slightly as she breathed in rapid breaths. Desire hardened him immediately. Beneath his *gambaz*, his cock stiffened and pressed outward, unrestrained by the constraints of European dress. He quickly released her hand and stepped away from the camel.

"Feed Zada a couple of meat morsels every four to five hours, and remember, let the meat rest in your palm."

The confusion in her expression made him grimace as he turned and walked away. What had he been thinking? He should have had Medjuel take Zada to Alex. All he'd done just now was torment his cock. Throwing himself onto the back of his camel, he urged the animal to its feet. It was going to be a long day. A very long day indeed.

✧

The heat of the day hung heavy to the ground, the atmosphere wavy in the distance from the refractions of light. Altair was only just now beginning to feel the heat. In a couple more hours, the sun would set and nighttime would bring a drastic drop in temperature. Over the past day and a half he'd watched Alex from a distance. Zada had taken well to her new mistress, and the small mongoose seemed to delight her owner as well.

Last night after the evening meal, he'd heard Alex laughing. Drawn to the infectious nature of her amusement, he'd shifted his seat at the fire to watch her and the mongoose at play. It had been an intoxicating sight, and he'd regretted showing any interest at all when several of his tribesmen teased him. He kept telling himself he didn't feel anything for Alex, but he recognized it for the lie it was. His body didn't hide behind lies either. It lusted after her every time she entered his sight.

She'd permanently set aside her fashionable gowns and corset for the fawn-colored trousers she favored. The white blouse she wore, she'd rolled up at the sleeves. The dark brown leather of her boots showed off a shapely calf, as she seemed fond of tucking the pants into the footwear. At the end of the day, her shirt lay plastered to her skin so that every delicious curve of her body beckoned to him. The utilitarian nature of her clothes was all the more seductive because she had no comprehension of how sensual she looked.

The gentle rocking motion of his camel suddenly changed as the animal broke out into a trot and tried to pass the mount in front of him. Tugging on the reins, Altair pulled the balking camel out of the caravan to study the horizon. The sky behind them was brownish gray, and his heart sank.

With a loud cry of warning, he caught Medjuel's attention and pointed to the horizon. Without waiting for a response, he swatted his crop against his camel's hindquarters and wheeled to race toward Alex. Behind him, he heard his cousin continuing to raise the alarm, and the caravan quickly halted. Reaching Alex's side, he dismounted from his animal before the camel had a chance to sink to the ground.

In two strides, he was at her mount's head. Over his shoulder, he saw the distinct, and all too familiar, sand cloud racing toward them. Yanking the reins from her hands, he forced the protesting camel to its knees.

"What's wrong? Why are we stopping?"

Ignoring her bewildered look, he roughly pulled her from

the saddle and forced her down to the ground. "Sandstorm."

"But the camels—"

"The camels have natural defenses for the *sirocco*. We don't." His fingers flew to his utility belt and undid the straps. The belt slid to the sand, and then he removed the top layer of his *gambaz*. Swinging the dark cloth off his shoulders, he knelt beside her and stared into her worried eyes. He forced a brief smile to his lips. "We'll be fine as long as we remain covered and keep our eyes closed."

He hoped they'd be fine. *Siroccos* could swallow up entire caravans, burying them in the sand with no hope of survival. The wind blew up sand around them. He had no need to glance over his shoulder to know the storm was almost on them. Pulling Alex close, he pressed her face into his chest. In a swift move, he threw the *gambaz* over their heads before guiding her down into a prone position beside him.

Eyes closed, he buried his face into her hair. Even despite the danger they were in, he found his desire for her stirring inside him. The citrus smell of the silky brown tresses filled his nostrils and senses. The soft curve of her face pressing through the thin linen of his shirt. Her body curled into his, fitting snugly against his limbs as if she were the second half of him. The thought made his throat tighten. He needed to remember there was no place in his life for any woman. Not even this woman.

Seconds later, the storm engulfed them. Although he'd wrapped the *gambaz* tightly around them, sand still blasted its way through even the smallest of openings. Grit filled his mouth quickly, and he did his best to keep his body positioned so the least amount of sand reached Alex.

With the storm raging around them, time seemed to stretch out endlessly, but the *sirocco* passed over the caravan in less than fifteen minutes. As the air grew still, Alex stirred against him. From the weight on his back, he could tell they were half buried in the sand. Carefully, he pushed the *gambaz* outward and away from his body. The sand and dust slid off the dark blue cloak to mound up in a small dune.

Sitting up, he pulled Alex with him. Coughing, she arched away from him, her face covered with dust. She looked like a beige-colored ghost and he chuckled. Hazel eyes sparking with irritation, she glared at him.

"What—" her coughing interrupted her exclamation, "—are you laughing at?"

He gently brushed off some of the dust layering her skin. "You look like you've been dredged in flour."

The anger sparking in her gaze vanished as she grinned. "And you look like you could use a bath."

"Perhaps you'd care to join me." The moment the words were out of his mouth, Altair wanted to bite off his tongue. Had he lost his mind? The haunting answer to the silent question made his jaw tighten. Alex blushed deeply, the rose in her cheeks blazing through the dust caking her skin.

Scrambling to his feet, he pulled her up and stepped away from her. A second later, she staggered toward her camel. "Oh my God! Zada, I left her alone."

The fear in her voice tugged at him, and he followed close on her heels. "I'm sure she's fine. Like the camels, she knows how to protect herself from nature."

No sooner had he spoken than Zada raised her head out of the large bag that rested behind Alex's saddle. Chattering like an irritated monkey, the mongoose reared up on her hindquarters and glared at him as if she understood everything he'd said.

Alex extended her palm, her voice soft and apologetic as she coaxed the animal to her. For moment Zada hesitated, then as if she understood Alex's remorse, the small mongoose ran up her mistress's arm to settle around her neck. A smile tugged at his lips, and he was about to speak when Medjuel called for him. Giving Alex a brief nod, he walked away to assist in the reorganization of the camel procession.

Although the storm delayed their journey for a short time, the caravan reached the last oasis between them and Khatana-Qantir just as the sun was beginning to set on the horizon. As they had the night before, the men moved quickly to set up camp. Alex's tent was one of the first to go up, and Altair ordered one of the men to erect the collapsible tub he'd brought for her. It had been an extravagant purchase, but he knew the harshness of life in the desert. She would miss the conveniences of civilization.

As he walked through the camp directing tasks needing

completion, he contemplated the damage they'd incurred from the sandstorm. They'd been lucky. Only one lamb lost, and aside from a few men suffering minor injuries from flying debris, they'd come through the storm with relative ease. It could have been much worse. People could have been buried alive in the sand, suffocating before they were found.

Pondering their good fortune, he offered up a prayer of gratitude that they'd escaped the wrath of nature. Tomorrow by midday, they would reach Khatana-Qantir. A blade of excitement sliced through him. It was impossible to repress the anticipation or hope that Alex might actually find Nourbese's tomb.

The sun was sinking below the horizon, and he arched his back to stretch his tired muscles. The image of sinking into a hot tub of water to soothe his limbs made his lips curl up at the corners. What would Alex Talbot do if he suddenly appeared to take advantage of her bathwater?

He turned his head toward her closed-off tent. The tantalizing images flooding his head made him growl with irritation. Behind him, one of the men called out to him to come eat. Heeding the cry, he moved toward the small fire over which a small chicken turned on a makeshift spit.

As he sat down to eat, he saw a familiar face. Stiffening, Altair watched the man walk past him in the direction of a nearby fire. Did Medjuel know the traitor was part of the caravan? At that moment, his cousin emerged from his own tent. Setting his meal aside, he sprang to his feet and went to Medjuel's side.

"Did you know Mohammed is a part of the caravan?" he asked with quiet concern.

Medjuel shot him a brief glance before looking away with a heavy sigh. "Yes. I invited him to come. It is better to keep your enemies close than too far away."

Remembering the last time he'd questioned the wisdom of his cousin's actions, Altair nodded then turned to move away. A strong hand delayed his departure.

"I know what I'm doing, cousin. Do not question my judgment now or in the future."

The cold look in the black eyes glaring up at him reminded Altair of a time when he'd seen Medjuel extract harsh

145

punishment from a tribal member who'd disobeyed orders. It was an unforgiving look, and it was the first time it had ever been bestowed on him. With a grim nod, he pulled away from his cousin and returned to his meal.

As he bit into the tender, juicy chicken spiced with coriander, he studied Medjuel from a distance. His cousin wasn't telling him something. He was also certain that it involved the traitor seated nearby. With a swig of his camel's milk, he casually glanced in Mohammed's direction.

He was just about to turn away when he saw the traitor nod at Medjuel. Instinct told him not to move and he forced himself to study the meat on his plate. The back of his spine crawled as he sensed Medjuel's eyes on him. Whatever was going on, his cousin refused to talk about it, and whatever secret Medjuel carried, Altair was certain he wouldn't like it. No, he was certain he wouldn't like it one bit.

Chapter Eleven

Walking quietly through the oasis's palm trees and foliage surrounding the camp, Alex glanced up at the night sky. The full moon made the landscape almost as bright as day, while the stars looked close enough to reach out and grasp.

She paused for a moment to study the night sky, wishing her father and Uncle Jeffrey were with her. They would have loved this country despite its harsh environment. For almost five years, they'd planned and studied how they would excavate Per-Ramesses. Uncle Jeffrey had always said he would finally be going home. He'd been so convinced he was the reincarnation of the Pharaoh Ramesses. She hoped that wherever he was now, he was happy and that Nourbese was with him.

The fragrant aroma of jasmine drifted beneath her nostrils, and she stopped to look at the white blooms on the climbing vine. The bloom-laden greenery wound its way around a tall palm. The petals were soft and fragile beneath her fingers. She leaned closer and inhaled a deep breath of the beautiful-smelling flower. Odd, she remembered smelling jasmine in Uncle Jeffrey's room the day he became ill.

For all his complaints of a painful insect bite, she'd done nothing but tease him about his need for attention. She cringed at the memory. Even with his sudden onset of influenza she hadn't connected his complaint with his illness. How could she? There'd been no mark on Uncle Jeffrey's neck where he'd insisted he'd been bitten.

With all that had happened over the past two weeks, she knew whoever was trying to kill her had most likely killed before. And whoever it was had a fondness for using deadly creatures. Uncle Jeffrey's and her father's deaths could easily fit the pattern of a killer who used nature to destroy an enemy.

Influenza deaths were not uncommon, and a scorpion's bite produced similar effects with the same deadly results. More importantly, a scorpion's bite didn't leave any mark. Their deaths had been viewed as accidental, not as murder, reducing the assailant's risk of being caught. There was no proof to substantiate the idea that someone had murdered her father and Uncle Jeffrey. But she knew in her heart it was true. The only thing she didn't understand was why. She bit back the grief that swelled her throat.

Up above, sparkling pinpoints of lights sprinkled the satiny black sky, refusing to offer up any affirmation to her unfounded convictions. She sniffed a soft noise of disgust at her fanciful musing. The underbrush rustled softly. Panic made her spin around sharply, her body tense with the expectation of some new terror.

Instead, she found Zada perched upright on the grassy trail, giving her a curious look. Relieved, she laughed and bent down to scratch the back of the animal's head. The mongoose rubbed against her hand for an instant before suddenly leaping away and back into the undergrowth. As her small pet returned to hunting, Alex proceeded along the trail.

Even Altair seemed to think someone was trying to kill her. He'd not come right out and said it, but she knew he thought it. She couldn't explain how she knew his thoughts. She just did. Intuition also said he knew the reason why too.

Things had become so complicated. With Jane recuperating in Cairo, she really didn't have anyone she could talk to, let alone trust. She'd thought she could trust Altair, but he had secrets, and he wasn't about to give them up to her. She was alone.

Alone and with no one to trust.

No, that wasn't true. She might be without friends or family, but there was one person on whom she could rely. Herself. She'd solve this mystery on her own if need be. If someone wanted her dead, all she had to do was figure out why. Uncle Jeffrey had warned they might encounter trouble in their search for the lost city, but his remarks had always been so cryptic. If only he'd told her more.

"Think, Alex. What is it you know that Uncle Jeffrey and Father knew too?"

Per-Ramesses? No. Other scholars had been looking for the lost city for years. Something in the city then? A treasure of some sort? There would be the usual artifacts and the like, but nothing like other sites. The only treasure that might— *Nourbese.* Of course, that had to be it. But why?

Why would someone want her dead simply because she knew about Nourbese? It didn't make sense. The moment she thought she had the answer to one question, it simply evolved into a new question. She wanted to ask Altair more about Nourbese, but was afraid to ask him anything. It was difficult to trust him, but something about the man said he wouldn't let anything happen to her. He'd been discreet, but she'd noticed how he was always close by to protect her. The sandstorm had been a good example. Then there was Zada.

The mongoose scurried along the ground beside her before disappearing into the underbrush one more time. The loveable creature had stolen her heart, and the fact that Altair had given her the small protector made Zada all the more special.

In front of her, the trees gave way to a small glade with a large pond in the middle. As she drew closer to the water's edge, she heard a small splash. Startled, her heart skipped a beat in first fear, then excitement as she saw Altair rise slowly up out of the water. With his eyes closed, he flung his head backwards and shoved his long hair out of his face.

Muscular arms extended from a broad chest, the sinews in his arms rippling like supple steel. They were a subtle reminder of his powerful embrace. The silvery light dancing across his bronze skin showed his body glistening with water droplets. It was a perfect moment, and she struggled to breathe as she absorbed the sheer splendor of his lean, hard figure.

Well accustomed to the male form due to her unorthodox education, she experienced no embarrassment. Instead, she wanted to stand there and admire him for hours. Admire the sculpted curves of his biceps, the way the dusting of hair on his chest converged at his waist to become a straight line diving toward his phallus. He was beautiful to look at. A splendid pharaoh in this exotic oasis.

Without thought, she looked down to where his staff rested in the dark hair at his thighs' apex. The sight of him aroused the wanton sensations she had experienced in her hotel room. It stirred a warmth inside her that spread its way down into the lower half of her body.

Suddenly coming to her senses, she realized she couldn't stay here. He'd think the worst if he caught her watching him. Just as she prepared to wheel about, Zada raced out of the underbrush. Rising up on her hindquarters, the mongoose chattered worse than a magpie. Altair's eyes flew open to trap her in his piercing gaze.

Horrified, she froze. How on earth could she explain what she was doing here, let alone justify her reasons for watching him? The slow, wicked curl of his firm lips set fire to her face, and her heart lurched inside her chest. *The rake!* He was enjoying this. Why hadn't he or someone else warned her about the pond?

She remained frozen as he slowly walked toward her. The closer he came, the harder it was to breathe. She wanted to run, but something deep and primitive rooted her feet to the spot. When he reached her, his hand brushed lightly across her throat. The caress pulled a muted sigh from her.

God, she wanted to touch him. Kiss him. Feel his hard, muscular skin beneath her fingertips. Stretching out her hand, she splayed her fingers across his chest. Beneath her palm the accelerated beat of his heart pounded wildly. Unable to help herself, she allowed her hands to slide over his wet skin. Hard and dangerous, his erection jutted out at her.

"Touch me, *emîra.*"

The commanding whisper sucked the air from her lungs. Her eyes locked with his as she slowly took him in her hand. He was full and solid in her palm. As her fingers encircled him, he jerked.

"Hold me tighter," he whispered hoarsely as his hand forced her fingers to tighten around him.

With a gentle thrust of his hips, he slid back and forth in her grip. As he did so, her thumb slid over the tip of his erection and a growl rumbled in his throat. "Tighter, *ana anide emîra.* Tighter."

A strong hand cupped the nape of her neck as he covered

her mouth with his while she held him in the palm of her hand. The sensation of him moving back and forth in her hand as he kissed her shot a bolt of need through her. The sharp pitch of it spiraled its way downward until she experienced a tiny shudder at the apex of her thighs. It radiated outward, and she realized her insides were creamy with wet heat.

She tightened her grip on him as his tongue mated with hers. Hot and sweet, the dance was an imitation of an act she knew she wanted to experience with him. The thought made her insides clench and her hand automatically tightened around him. He groaned deeply, and she knew her touch pleased him. Excited him. She slid her thumb around the tip of him, enjoying the way he shuddered with obvious pleasure at the touch. A small bead of fluid smeared the pad of her thumb, and his body flexed with a sharp tension.

Releasing her lips, he threw his head back, his eyes closed as he drove himself hard into the cup of her hand. Passion tensed his features, and her mouth went dry as she realized she wanted him inside her like this. She wanted to feel his hard length filling her, heating her until she couldn't bear it any further. A deep groan poured from his throat as he stiffened and rocked to a stop in her hand. Wrapped in her hand, he throbbed and surged beneath her fingers as he gave way to his release.

His gaze was languid with satisfaction, and she realized he'd climaxed by her hand. Frozen in place by the intimate act she'd just performed, she stared up at him in uncertainty. The fiery glow of desire in his eyes made her tremble as she realized she was still touching him.

Her breathing hitched. There was only one explanation for what had just transpired. Insanity. How could she have done something so wicked? So sinful. So delightful. The knowledge of what she'd done excited and alarmed her in the same breath.

The sudden sound of Zada chattering brought her out of her trance, and she leaped away from him. She had to be insane. It didn't matter how excited he made her feel, the man was dangerous, and she needed to remember that. She was simply borrowing more trouble becoming involved with him. Her heart thundering, she wheeled about and raced back toward camp.

As she reached the edge of the small open space behind her tent, she slid to a halt and closed her eyes in mortification. Only a wanton hussy would have done what she did. How could she have touched him so intimately without any sense of morality at all? Oh, but the pleasure it had given her to feel his arousal. To see the intense pleasure in his face as he found his release at the touch of her hand. The memory of it made her cheeks burn. Dear God, what he must think of her.

A noise in the underbrush made her start. Before she could turn, a hand clapped over her mouth while a strong arm wrapped around her waist and dragged her deep into the foliage. Her first thought was that Altair had caught up with her, but the pungent odor of sheep told her someone else held her prisoner.

Frightened, she clawed at the hand over her mouth as her assailant dragged her deeper into the trees. Her panicked attempts to escape made her captor mutter an angry Mazir curse, but he simply tightened his grip. Frantically, she grabbed at his forefinger and snapped it backwards. A low curse filled the air as the man snatched his hand away from her mouth. The moment he did so, Alex screamed as loud as she could. At her cry for help, a large hand connected harshly with the side of her head. The blow knocked her sideways over the arm holding her prisoner, and her ear rang from the force of the assault. Dazed, she struggled to regain her equilibrium.

Desperate to escape, she bent her arm and jabbed her elbow into the stomach of her assailant. The man grunted in pain, and as his grip loosened, she wrenched out of his hold. Without looking back, she stumbled through the trees and vegetation toward freedom. As she flew out into the area behind her tent, she charged straight into a wide chest. Thinking her attacker had circled round to stop her, she tried to break free of the arms that pulled her close.

"It's all right, Alex. It's me. You're safe." Recognizing Altair's voice, she shuddered before wrapping her arms about his waist and burying her face into his shoulder.

An instant later, several men raced around the side of her tent and slid to a halt. Knowing her attacker might well be among them, Alex lifted her head to study the faces of the men.

"It's all right. She thought she saw a jerboa. She's fine, a bit frightened is all," Altair said with a grin.

The men broke out into laughter, and she sent Altair a baleful look. He couldn't have come up with a better excuse? She didn't want the Mazir thinking she was a hysterical female. Someone wanted her dead, and that was all the reason she needed for screaming. Whoever wanted her dead no longer seemed interested in subtlety. This time she'd escaped, but what about the next time? Still laughing, the men slowly dispersed. Left alone with Altair, she tried to force the tension from her limbs. A tremor ran through her.

"Tell me what happened." Beneath the quiet demand was a calm resolve to have the truth from her.

"Someone grabbed me from behind and dragged me into the bushes."

"Did you get a look at his face?"

"No. But I know he was Mazir."

She watched his features harden into an implacable expression. He wasn't surprised. He'd known all along that someone from the Mazir tribe was trying to kill her. His eyes narrowed as he studied her closely.

"How do you know this?"

She hesitated. Why should she trust him? The answer whispered through her soft and firm. Because he'd done everything possible to keep her safe. That wasn't the mark of a killer. But he wasn't telling her everything either. Why didn't he trust her? Her eyes met his, and she swallowed hard at the determined glint in his dark gaze.

"He spoke the Mazir language."

"What else did you notice? Even the smallest thing might be important."

She tried to remember everything she could about the attack. She shook her head. "It all happened so fast. I can't remember anything else."

The tension in her muscles had slowly ebbed away, and the safety of his embrace made her feel warm and protected. She had no desire to leave his arms. Breathing in his scent, she relished the light fragrance of soap drifting off his skin. Just a hint of dampness clung to him, the clean freshness of it filling the air. Intense longing spread through her limbs as a shudder ripped through her.

"You're safe, Alex. I promise you that. If I have to sleep at the foot of your cot, no one is going to harm you."

Oh, this was absurd. She definitely feared for her life, but it was the last thing on her mind right now. Fear wasn't making her tremble—being so close to him was. All she could think about was how she'd touched him moments ago. How he'd filled her palm and the response of her own body.

She swallowed hard and nervously wet her lips. Brown eyes studied her with the sharpness of an eagle. He was aptly named. The intensity of his gaze sent her pulse racing out of control. She wanted to taste him again. Savor the male essence of him against her lips. It was a heady image. She didn't care that anyone could stumble upon them at any given moment. She'd faced death three times now in a little more than two weeks. It emphasized how short and precious life could be. It made her realize that all she wanted right now was to be as wild and wicked as possible. The thought made her suck in a sharp breath. His eyes narrowed at the sound, and he slowly lowered his head to kiss her.

From a distance, she heard someone call out for him. He stiffened and withdrew from her sharply. Deprived of his touch, she turned her head to find Sheikh el Mazir watching them with a strange look on his face.

His voice sharp, the Sheikh spoke to Altair in the Mazir tongue. She didn't understand the words, but she understood the tone of contempt. Beside her, Altair was still close enough for her to feel his tension. He didn't respond, but she saw his jaw clench in a hard, tight line of anger. The Sheikh suddenly spat on the ground and stalked away.

She reached out and touched his arm. He shook her hand off with a sharp gesture. Shocked, she stared at him in bewilderment. What had the Sheikh said to make him so aloof?

"Altair, what's wrong?"

"It's time you turned in. We'll get an early start in the morning so we can reach Khatana-Qantir before the noon hour. I'll post guards to ensure your safety."

He started to walk away from her, and she put herself in front of him. "You didn't answer me. What's wrong? What did Sheikh el Mazir say to you? I thought...I thought you...that we..."

"I overstepped my bounds tonight."

"What are you talking about?"

"You're our guest in this camp, under my protection."

For a moment, she didn't understand. Tension flowed between them in the silence. Dark, sensual and inviting. His desire for her still burned in his gaze, but he was refusing to act on it. With a grimace, he grasped her arm and pulled her toward her tent. The silence was heavy with unspoken heat as he shoved her past the tent flap. As the wool door whispered shut, she clenched her teeth. A gentleman. That's what Sheikh el Mazir had meant. He had accused Altair of not being a gentleman.

Consumed with unsatiated need, she suppressed a small groan. She'd been more than willing a few moments ago to forget everything but Altair's touch. Even Per-Ramesses. The thought chilled her. She was letting her attraction to the man interfere with everything she'd set out to do. Everything she and her father had worked for over the years. A shiver skated down her back. She couldn't let that happen. From now on, she had to stay as far away from Altair as possible. Something that was going to prove more difficult than she liked, because the truth was—she didn't want to.

✧

From his dromedary, Altair watched Alex force her mount into a trot. They were close to Khatana-Qantir, and she knew it. He wanted to go after her, see the excitement he knew would be on her face. No, it was best to stay as far away from her as he could. It made it difficult to protect her, but he could still monitor her movements from a distance.

Last night had been a mistake. A terrible mistake. His cousin had been right to berate him for treating a guest in such a dishonorable way. If Medjuel hadn't interrupted them when he had, there was no telling how far things would have progressed.

Ha. The outcome had never been in doubt. He would have bedded her. *Damnation.* What a fool he was. Desire didn't mean she cared for him. But her grip on him last night had sent him over the edge. Even now, he wanted her hand on him. No. Not her hand. He wanted her mouth sliding up and down on him until he exploded.

The enticing image made him wince. He needed to rein in his lust. At present, his main concern was ensuring Alex's safety. He turned around on his camel to see if he could catch sight of Mohammed herding the sheep behind the caravan. The man was a traitor, but was he a killer? If he was, why? Were the Hoggar plotting Alex's death using Mohammed as the assassin? Why would the Hoggar want her dead? If they were after Nourbese's treasure, they needed Alex to show them where it was. It didn't serve their interests to hurt her before the discovery of Nourbese's tomb.

From the front of the caravan, the lead camel driver let out a loud cry. The cry raced back through the long line of dromedaries until the Mazir shout of greeting filled the air. At the noise, the small village of Khatana-Qantir poured out of their stone houses to meet them.

Medjuel rode past him on his Arabian mare toward the front of the caravan. Alex had already dismounted, and he watched as his cousin stopped and spoke to her before returning his attention to the procession's encampment.

His camel lumbered closer to her, and he watched as she rested her hands against the small of her back and stretched her body in a backward arch. She had to be tired. The journey had been a grueling one, and yet not once had she complained. Professor Talbot would have been proud of her. Damn it, he was proud of her.

In spite of everything that had happened to her, she'd persevered. Now she could honor her father's last wish. She would discover Per-Ramesses and help Nourbese join her Pharaoh in the afterlife. He'd keep her from harm and see to it that she was able to succeed in her task.

The dromedary groaned loudly as he pulled the animal to a halt at Alex's side. Excitement made her face glow as she shaded her eyes and looked up at him. It was impossible to resist her smile of exhilaration. His own mouth curled upward in response to her happiness.

"I take it you're pleased to be in Khatana-Qantir?"

"Pleased? No, ecstatic is probably more accurate. It's been so long in coming. Father and Uncle Jeffrey would have been thrilled to be standing here."

Sadness lay just beneath the joyful sound of her voice. How was it he'd come to know her so well in little more than two weeks? "I'll see that the men set up your tent immediately. I take it you'll want your trunks?"

"Oh, yes." She bobbed her head. "I have a lot of work to do this afternoon so that tomorrow we can begin our search."

"Then I'll see to it immediately."

She stepped forward and rested her hand against his leg. The touch sent a jolt of pleasure through him. "Altair, I...I want...I want to thank you for helping me honor my father's last wish. I'm not sure I'd be here if it weren't for you."

The softness of her voice wrapped itself around him, and he swallowed the desire to tell her everything. No. Now, more than ever, he needed her to trust him. With someone out to kill her, the only way he could keep her safe was to have her complete trust. One day soon, she'd learn the truth, but until then he would continue to weave this damnable web of lies he'd built.

The last thing he wanted was for her to see how vulnerable he was where she was concerned. Vulnerable? *Damm gahannam.* If he was being truthful with himself, he was completely defenseless against her. He'd not been this smitten with a woman since Caroline. And he remembered all too well how that had turned out.

Fearing he might break his resolve not to confess everything, he merely nodded before riding away from her.

Chapter Twelve

Alex removed her wide-brimmed hat and dragged her arm across her sweaty forehead. Fanning herself, she stared gloomily at the rocky terrain in front of her. *Two weeks.* Two frustrating weeks with no sign of Per-Ramesses. Nothing. How could they have been so wrong in their calculations?

Everything pointed to the Pharaoh's lost city being here. She refused to believe all the work she and Father had done was for naught. The first day of exploration had revealed several pieces of pottery that dated back several centuries, but nothing as far back as Per-Ramesses. Almost three thousand years had passed since the existence of the city. If Ramesses' golden city had been at Khatana-Qantir, time had hidden it well. There was nothing here to show for it now. It was as if the desert had opened up its arms and swallowed the city in its entirety.

"Here, have some water." Altair's voice made her start with surprise.

Glancing up at him, she noted the look of commiseration in his eyes. She took the goatskin bag and drank thirstily from the flask. The water was cool and fresh as it filled her mouth. Finished, she capped off the flask and returned it to him.

"Thank you."

He looked just like a sun-drenched Bedouin in his *gambaz* and the utility belt that crisscrossed his robe. The henna markings on his cheeks made him look dangerous and exciting. The designs held more meaning than simple wards against evil. She remembered how he'd explained the dark symbols also reflected the sunlight away from his eyes to protect them from sun damage. Since arriving in the desert, he'd also taken to wearing the blue Mazir headdress to block the sun's rays. It only enhanced the edge of danger she found so attractive in him.

He followed her example and took a long draught from the bag. Watching him tip his head back to catch the liquid refreshment, she had the urge to run her hand down the side of his muscular neck. Done drinking from the bag, he dropped his head and she noted a water droplet glistening on his firm mouth.

She bit her bottom lip as he pressed the back of his hand to his mouth and erased the shiny bead. For an instant, she found herself wishing it were her hand caressing his beautiful, sensual mouth. Rattled by the image, she frowned and turned her head away. For the past two weeks, she'd focused all of her attention on finding Per-Ramesses, and she'd kept as much distance between her and Altair as possible. He kept his distance as well, although she was always aware of him watching her.

"You look discouraged."

"I am." She jammed her hat back onto her head and returned her gaze to the landscape in front of her.

"Don't be. Did you think you'd get to Khatana-Qantir and just walk into the lost city?" He took another swig from the goatskin flask. His bronze throat rippled in the sunlight as he drank. Was that it? Had she really expected it to be that easy? She grimaced. That's exactly what she'd thought. She really had believed it would be as easy as that.

An idealistic fool was what she was. Lord Merrick had been right. Whatever had made her think she could find a city dozen of scholars had been seeking for decades? She shook her head. No, she was definitely a fool.

"Well, did you?" His question pulled her out of her thoughts. She shot him a quick glance.

"Yes. I thought I'd be excavating parts of the city by now. But there's nothing here."

He grasped her shoulders and forced her to look at him. "Impatient and impulsive as always, aren't you? You'll find Per-Ramesses, Alex, and you'll do so soon. I'm sure of it."

"You say that with a confidence I don't feel."

"Believe in yourself, Alex. You'll find Per-Ramesses. It just might take longer than you thought."

She nodded and sighed as she walked away. The ground beneath her feet was hard. A thin layer of sand failed to cover the finite fissures in the dark clay's top layer. More than two thousand years ago, this had most likely been a riverbed, but time had turned it into just another parched piece of land. The banks of the dry channel rose up almost to her shoulders, and she marveled at how time and water had carved such a deep passage through the terrain. Continuing along the path, she noted how symmetrical the bedrock looked.

It always amazed her how nature could define such a smooth line over the centuries. A stone lay on the ground in front of her. Bending over she picked up the pebble. She frowned as her thumb grazed over the textured surface of the rock. Water polished stones smooth. So why was this stone so rough? Still puzzled, she tossed it into the air and caught it as it fell. She repeated the action, but this time missed the stone and it dropped behind her. As she bent to retrieve it, she looked at the side of the riverbed and froze.

"Oh my God," she whispered.

The smooth bank rose up to blend with the encroaching desert, but the bend in the dead river was what took her breath away. She'd walked the riverbed many times, but this was the first time she'd really looked at it. Now, as she stared back the way she'd come, a rush of excitement filled her. She wasn't standing in a riverbed. The way the terrain turned sharply around the bend behind her was her clue. It was far too sharp a turn to be natural. Time and nature had disguised it, but she was certain she was standing beside what must have been a wall.

She jerked her head around to look back in the direction she had been headed. The line of the wall stretched on beyond her sight. Bolting upright, she saw Altair leaning against the side of what she was now convinced was a fortification of Per-Ramesses. He stood a short distance from where the wall turned sharply off to the right. Excitement made her leap forward. As she raced toward him, she let out a loud whoop of delight.

"It's here! It's been here all along!" Flinging herself into his arms, she gave him a huge hug. "It's the city wall. I don't know how I missed it. Well, I know how I missed it. Nature's done her best to hide it. But it's here. I mean it's really here."

"Slow down, Alex. What wall are you talking about? This is a riverbed."

"No, no, no. It's Per-Ramesses. It's the city wall." She released him from her joyful embrace. Grabbing his hand, she pulled him toward the place where the wall turned sharply to the right. "Here, do you see it? It's the wall."

"I don't see anything, Alex."

"Look." She pulled out the small pick from her back pocket. With several quick strokes, she chipped away dirt from the wall's corner. The more dirt she removed, the sharper the line of the wall's turn became. She paused. "See! It's the city wall. Sandstorms must have buried the city too long ago for anyone to remember Per-Ramesses was here. But this is the city. I know it."

Amazement curved his mouth slightly as he reached out to touch the spot she'd cleared away. She watched him turn in first one direction then the other. It was like watching her own reaction to the discovery. The wonder, the disbelief and then the excitement. He suddenly reached for her and lifted her up in his arms. Whooping with a Mazir cry, he swung her around in a wide circle.

She laughed at his excitement, which was equal to her own. The city was here. She'd found Per-Ramesses. Their laughter didn't stop as he set her back down on her feet. Enthusiastically he bent his head and gave her a hard kiss.

Still laughing, he released her and grasped her shoulders. "And just a few minutes ago you doubted yourself."

Dazed by the excitement and the sweetness of his impulsive kiss, Alex stared up at him. Had he even realized he'd kissed her? Her mouth burned from his touch, and she swallowed the knot in her throat. For two weeks, she'd agonized over whether or not to act on her instincts. Sweet, tormenting dreams of Altair coming to her and making her his haunted her nights. Although she knew a liaison would probably never grow into something permanent, she didn't care. There had been opportunities in the past to settle down, but she'd chosen her work. Now, she wanted to experience passion. A passion only he could make her feel. He'd not hid his attraction in the past—the question was did he still feel the same way now?

With a quick movement, she grasped the sides of his head and tugged his head down to her lips. He stiffened for a moment before he pulled her into a tight embrace and returned her kiss. The caress seared and burned without any pain, only a blinding delight. She was in heaven, her mouth drinking in the sweet taste of him. Cedarwood drifted across her senses, the hot, masculine scent of him more potent because of his kiss.

His tongue swept into her mouth, teasing and probing until she responded with heated abandon. The way she sank into him made Altair's blood roar. God, he'd missed the feel of her in his arms. The past two weeks had been hell as he'd deliberately kept his distance from her. Gently his teeth tugged at her lower lip before moving across her chin and down her creamy throat. The smell of the desert lingered on her skin like exotic wine. A soft moan poured out of her as he tenderly scraped his teeth across her throat.

"Altair, please..."

The quiet plea bit into him like the sting of a scorpion. *Damm gahannam.* He couldn't do it. He couldn't make love to her with this lie between them. Pushing her away from him, he shook his head.

"No, Alex. It would be a mistake." A mistake she'd come to regret. Damnation, it was going to be hard as hell to tell her the truth. She'd hate him, but he'd despise himself if he made her his without explaining everything.

"A mistake?" Her eyes were wide with stunned disbelief.

"Damn it, Alex. That's not what I meant."

A stricken look darkened her gorgeous eyes, and he clenched his jaw in self-disgust. Christ, she thought he was rejecting her. God, if the woman only knew how much he wanted to throw everything to the wind just to claim her as his. The sound of her sucking in a deep breath tugged a grimace of regret from him. As he reached out to her, she slapped his hand away.

"You're right, my lord. It was a mistake—one I regret with all my heart."

Her voice was crisp and free of emotion, but she couldn't hide the bright red humiliation cresting in her cheeks. She whirled around and walked away with steps that were stiff and unnatural. God, he needed to explain. She needed to realize that he couldn't continue like this with a lie between them. Lunging forward, he grabbed her by the arm and halted her retreat.

"Alex, you don't under—"

"I don't *want* to understand." With a sharp tug of her arm, she pulled free of his grasp. "Stay away from me."

The sharp bite of her words made him flinch. Good. She wanted him to feel the same stinging pain she was feeling. Humiliated and bitterly regretting her behavior, she quickly scrambled up out of the ravine and set off for the Bedouin encampment.

Her legs pumped their way through the sand that rose to the edges of Per-Ramesses as she tried to put as much distance between them as she could. How could she have done something so stupid? Once again, her impulsive nature had brought her nothing but grief. When was she going to learn to think before acting? She didn't even want to think about the next time she came face to face with him.

And she wouldn't. Immersing herself in her work would be a soothing balm to the wound she was nursing in her heart. After all, she'd just found Per-Ramesses. She was making headway in her determination to prove herself as a competent Egyptologist. Work was the one thing that would never betray her. It would always be there for her. A steadfast companion without the pain of remorse. Then why did the thought of not being able to share that with someone make her feel so miserable?

✧

Furious with himself, Altair turned and slammed his clenched fist into the hard, sandy wall behind him. Telling her the truth was the only thing he'd needed to do, and he'd managed to botch it as he had with every opportunity over the past month.

He damn well could have made her listen to him, but he hadn't forced the issue. Instead, he'd managed to make her think he didn't want her. If the woman only knew how difficult it was for him to keep his hands off her.

"*Damn gahannam*," he muttered fiercely.

It was impossible to put off the inevitable any longer. He would let her cool down, and later this evening he'd explain everything. His jaw tensed as he grimaced. She was going to tear him limb from limb when he explained about his connection with her father and his true identity. Attending a social engagement as Lord Blakeney held more appeal for him right now than the image of Alex's fury.

Blast, he was worse than an old nanny goat. What did it matter if she was angry? He needed to stop letting his lust for her control his head. Confessing his lies later as opposed to now wouldn't change things. The outcome would still be the same. Either she would scorn him or she wouldn't. He would simply have to wait and see what was real and what was a mirage where Alex was concerned.

Still disgusted with his behavior, he followed Alex back toward the encampment. She was the most complex, complicated woman he'd ever met. Intelligent, courageous and feisty, she would make some man a wonderful wife. His body tensed at the idea of her with another man. He didn't like that thought at all.

Shoving the notion aside, he scrambled up the ravine trail and stood at the top of the ridge. From the rise above the Mazir camp, he watched Alex walking quickly across the sand. The straight line of her back clearly showed her anger hadn't dissipated. Somehow, he didn't think it was all anger in that furious pace she maintained.

His ill-spoken words had hurt her. That was the last thing he'd wanted to do. She was strong and spirited, but in the past two weeks, he'd seen how vulnerable she really was. Although she hid it well, he'd seen the fear and self-doubt in those beautiful eyes of hers. At least she'd found Per-Ramesses. It would bolster her spirits.

With Alex occupied with her new discovery, it would free him continue the search for the assassin. Since their arrival in Khatana-Qantir, he'd kept a close eye on Mohammed. Despite being a traitor, the man had done nothing to reveal himself as the possible murderer. The only odd thing he'd noted was that

Mohammed visited Medjuel's tent from time to time. His cousin seemed to have the situation well in hand, but it made him feel better to continue watching the traitor closely.

From where he stood, he studied the small valley's landscape. The oasis that supported life in Khatana-Qantir was quite large, and the lush vegetation splashed vivid color against the background of the desert. The Mazir tents, spread out across the valley, gave the impression a small army was encamped at the oasis.

The sight comforted him. The life of a Bedouin was simple, yet fulfilling. He should have never promised his grandfather he'd spend so much time in England. He would be far happier here, among his mother's people. His people. They'd always accepted him for what he was. A movement off to his right pulled his gaze in that direction. Squinting against the bright sun, he held his hand up to shade his eyes. A caravan. Had someone from the British Museum sponsored an expedition to Khatana-Qantir? No, Merrick had declared Alex's expedition a fool's errand. The man wouldn't do anything unless he thought it worth the expenditure.

The caravan drew closer and he caught his breath as he saw a white horse race to the front of the procession, followed by two black Arabians. The tribe was here. It didn't make sense. They were supposed to go west to the tribal heartland. Why were they here?

Mother.

With another oath of disgust, he kicked the dry, sandy soil. She'd convinced the elders to come to Khatana-Qantir. Her presence could mean only one of two things. She was here to witness the discovery of Nourbese's tomb or she'd come to evaluate Alex's suitability as a wife. Since his mother didn't put much stock in folk tales, that left Alex.

God help him. Things were difficult enough without having his mother here, playing matchmaker. If he knew his mother, either she'd send someone to Alex inviting her to dine, or she might even visit Alex herself. The thought made him set out for camp at a quick pace. He needed to reach Alex before someone else did. He'd wanted to wait until her anger had abated, but he had little choice in the matter now.

He reached the outer rim of the encampment at almost the

same time the tribal caravan did. Most of the men from the expedition gathered on the edge of camp, anxiously awaiting the arrival of their families. Debating his own course of action, he looked toward Alex's tent. Yellow, brown and green stripes wrapped the walls of her tent. Contrasted against the striped walls was a dark brown roof. As customary, one wall was rolled up to allow fresh air to circulate, and Alex stood just inside the colorful tent.

The earthy quality of her beauty brought him to a halt as desire sped through him. His hands flexed involuntarily at the sight of her. He wanted to charge across the compound and bed her. Mesmerized, he noted the fullness of her breasts and the way the linen blouse she wore revealed her creamy throat. Her light-colored trousers clung to her softly rounded hips, emphasizing her sensuous figure. She placed her hands behind her and arched her back in a stretch. The movement jutted her breasts out in a provocative movement.

Merciful God. He swallowed hard and reminded himself that she needed to hear the truth from him and no one else. But damn if he didn't want to just stand here and watch her. Almost as if she'd heard his thoughts, she turned her head in his direction. For the first time he wasn't able to read her expression. She'd closed herself off to him. Her gaze skimmed over him with a derisive glare. With a deliberate movement, she unlashed the cord holding the tent wall in place. She turned away from him as the wall flap fell closed behind her. *Damm gahannam.* She'd just cut him. Cut him as nicely as any English noblewoman could have.

What had he expected? A warm reception after the way he'd rejected her earlier? He snorted with exasperation. Seldom one to indulge in alcohol, he knew tonight would most likely be an exception given what he was about to tell Alex. Intent on confronting her with the truth, he started for her tent.

"Altair! Altair!" Kahlil's voice rang out through the air.

Frustration clenched his jaw as he turned to face his stepbrother riding toward him on a beautiful black Arabian. Hiding his impatience with a smile, he grabbed the mare's halter as his brother stopped in front of him.

"Well, little brother, how did my mare take to the journey?"

Laughing, Kahlil swatted Altair's headdress from where he

sat in his saddle. "She did wonderful, and Nawar's not your mare any more. You gave her to me, remember."

"Did I, hmmm, well I suppose I did." He laughed in spite of his preoccupation with Alex. "So let me guess, you sought me out to avoid doing your chores."

"I know better than to try that with Mother. Actually, I'm following her orders. She sent me to find Miss Talbot."

He stiffened at Kahlil's statement. "Exactly *what* does Mother want with Miss Talbot?"

"I'm to invite her to take the evening meal with us."

So he'd been right, his mother had come to Khatana-Qantir to inspect Alex. Well, not if he had anything to say about it. And definitely not until he'd had a moment to talk with her. "Well, little brother. I hate to tell you this, but you're not going to ask Miss Talbot anything."

"Mother will be madder than a horned viper if I don't, Altair."

"Perhaps, but I'll see to it that she's mad at me, not you." His hand still on Nawar's halter, he led the mare back toward the newly arrived caravan.

"How is it you can get away with not doing what Mother wants, but I can't?"

"I don't get away with anything. I simply make her think it was *her idea* for me not to do something."

"In other words you sweet-talk her." Kahlil snorted.

"You're learning, little brother." He gave a playful punch to the boy's thigh. "Go on and see to Nawar. I'll see to Mother."

With a nod, Kahlil urged his horse forward and disappeared into the thick of the chaos spreading its way around the oasis. Camels groaned and squawked as they sank down to have their load removed from their backs. Instructions and shouts surrounded him as men, women and children set up their tents. Off in the distance, the bleating of sheep caught his ear.

Damn, he didn't know which was worse, facing Alex's anger or his mother's determination. Knowing he couldn't put it off any longer, he sighed. Alex would have to wait. It was time to face the lioness in her den.

Despite its mobility, the tribe always set up camp the same way wherever they went. His mother's tent would be easy to find amidst the organized chaos. Dodging a camel lumbering to its feet, he made his way through a small group of pack animals. As he emerged into an open area, he caught sight of his mother's tent. In the next instant, Alex's warm curves plowed into him.

"I'm sorry, I—you!" She jumped away from him with a violent twist of her body. The glare she sent him tugged a grimace to his mouth.

"What are you doing here, Alex?"

"The Sheikh told me his aunt wanted to meet me."

Altair stiffened. Damnation. His mother had sent two messengers in the event the first one failed. She would have made a brilliant general. Hesitating, he tried to come up with an explanation for why she needed to return to her tent.

"Actually, now isn't a good time. I think—"

Out of nowhere, Kahlil charged forward and tugged on his arm. "I thought you were going to talk to Mother. She ordered me to make sure Medjuel invited Miss Talbot back to the tent."

Thrown off balance by his brother's interruption, Altair glanced toward Kahlil then back to Alex. As he'd feared, horror and repugnance filled her features. Chilled by the look, his stomach twisted into a tight, unforgiving knot. He'd expected this reaction. But why was it so painful? The coldness of her gaze threatened to freeze him where he stood.

"You're *married?*" Alex choked out the words with restrained fury. For a moment, he didn't think he'd heard correctly. Married—why the devil would she think he was married?

"What?"

"How could you?" she snapped. "What type of man are you?"

"Alex—"

"Don't you dare try to justify your actions. I can't believe I let you kiss me. That we—"

He grasped her by the shoulders and gave her a small shake. "Alex, listen to me. I'm not married."

"But I just heard this boy use the word Mother. I might not be fluent in Mazir, but I've learned enough over the past two weeks. He distinctly said Mother. How do you explain that?"

The challenging expression on her face tensed his muscles. "Because Kahlil is my brother."

"*What?*" Puzzlement was slowly replacing her anger.

"Kahlil is my stepbrother. Our mother is Gameela Mazir."

"But that's...the Sheikh's aunt...which makes..." Her voice trailed off as she raised a hand to her brow.

"Medjuel is my cousin."

Her hand fell from her forehead to her cheek as she stared at him in stark confusion. The extent of her bemusement tugged at his heart. "I should have told you, Alex. I tried—"

"You're damn right you should have told me. Why would you hide something like this?" The harsh accusation in her voice was like the sting of a whip against his skin.

"I had my reasons," he ground out between his clenched teeth. This was not going the way he'd hoped it would.

"What reasons? Were you afraid I might scorn you because you have Bedouin blood?" She froze with surprise. "That's it. You thought I wouldn't want anything to do with you if I knew about your background, didn't you?"

The raw disappointment in her words bit into him with painful clarity. He'd misjudged her. She glared up at him, waiting for him to explain. *Damn gahannam*, this was more of a mess than he'd ever thought possible.

"Alex, I had no idea when I wrote your father that last time that you'd be coming in his place."

"When you wrote my father?" she whispered.

"Yes." His cheek twitched from the tension in his jaw. "Your father and I have corresponded with each other over the past three to four years on a regular basis."

"You...and father...corresponded."

"I'm sorry he died before I got a chance to meet him."

"But you said you'd just translated the letters for the Sheikh." Bewilderment clouded her face as he watched her struggle with his confession.

"In a manner of speaking, I did translate the letters." He frowned. This wasn't going well at all. Determined to keep her close until they sorted this mess out, he grasped her shoulders. The tension flowing through her body throbbed against his fingertips. He could almost see the wheels of comprehension churning in her head as she narrowed her gaze at him.

"Then..."

"As head of the entire tribe, Medjuel is Sheikh el Mazir. I serve as my cousin's advisor and hold the title of Sheikh Mazir."

Anger brightened her hazel eyes and she went rigid beneath his hand. As he reached out to caress her cheek with his index finger, she knocked his hand away from her with a vicious slap.

"You lied."

"No. I merely skirted the truth."

"You lied. You lied about everything."

Breaking free of his grasp, she turned and proceeded to walk away. Caught off guard, he stared after her for a moment in disbelief. Then in four quick strides, he grabbed her arm and dragged her to a halt.

"Alex, wait. We need to talk about this."

She whipped around to face him. For the first time he noticed their argument had become of avid interest to nearby tribe members. His attention distracted, he was too late to stop her hand from reaching his face. The loud crack rent the air and the area surrounding them grew deathly quiet. His hand fell away from her arm as he faced her fury in silence.

"Stay away from me. You're despicable, and you can't be trusted." She sent him a scorching look of disgust before she turned and stalked away.

Chapter Thirteen

The ground shifted beneath her feet as Alex stumbled away from Altair. She could barely keep from throwing up as she struggled to remain upright. He'd lied. He'd been lying to her all along. Why hadn't he said something in Lord Merrick's office, on the ship or in Cairo? There had been plenty of opportunities for him to explain who he was.

The late afternoon heat pressed against her, and she tripped over her own feet. Ahead of her was the open flap of her tent. Cool darkness enveloped her as she plunged into the tent, dragging the flap closed behind her. Clinging to the tent's center pole for support, she swallowed the bile threatening to rise in her throat.

First he'd rejected her, and now this. The pole's surface gave way slightly as her fingers dug into the wood. He could have told her about his correspondence with her father. She would have trusted him if he'd told her that. Instead, he'd made her think his cousin, the Sheikh el Mazir, was whom Father had been dealing with. Why hadn't he told her the truth?

She inhaled a sharp breath of angry dismay. Per-Ramesses. He'd lied to cover up the real reason he'd been helping her. He worked for the British Museum, it made sense that they would send him. They could easily say that their representative helped to find the lost city and that she'd assisted. Oh, the bastard. He'd deliberately manipulated her every step of the way. His pretense at the museum regarding her welfare, the way he'd expressed concern for her safety in London, the way he'd arranged for her to board the *Moroccan Wind*.

A sound of furious disgust broke past her lips. Outside the

sun was close to setting, and the light was almost gone in the tent, forcing her to light a lantern. He was despicable. If she were a man, she'd...she'd...challenge him to a fight. Oooh, it would feel so good to pound him with her fists.

Well, she had news for the man. She wasn't letting him get close to the excavation if she could help it. She'd found Per-Ramesses without his help, and she'd continue the dig without his help. Striding to the makeshift desk set up in one corner of the tent, she sank down into the folding chair and stared at the papers on the small table in front of her.

A tear slid down her cheek, and she angrily brushed it away. It was useless to cry. The man certainly wasn't worth shedding any tears over. But it hurt. The lies, his rejection, all of it hurt. She wished Jane were here to offer advice or at the very least comfort. If her father had been here, none of this would have happened. Another teardrop landed on her hand. Never had she felt so alone in her life.

With a determined swipe of her hand, she sniffed back her tears. Enough. She wasn't going to give in to homesickness or anything else, least of all Sheikh Altair Mazir. The excavation would start tomorrow on top of the plateau the city wall encircled. And God help him if he tried to do anything else to stop her. Flipping open her notebook, she pored over her notes as she fanned herself with a sheaf of papers.

After more than an hour, she released a sound of disgust. She was feeling too miserable and sorry for herself to work. What she needed was a long soak in the cool water of the tub Altair had brought for her use. The thought of him twisted her insides. If he'd only been honest with her.

Pulling her robe from out of her trunk, her gaze fell upon the square white box Jane had given her when they parted ways at the hotel in Cairo. Since leaving for Per-Ramesses, she'd been tempted so many times to open the present. But she'd promised Jane she would save it until the day she found Per-Ramesses. Well, that day had arrived, and a present would go a long way in lifting her spirits.

She sat down next to the trunk and pulled the box into her lap. The blue silk ribbon tied around the box slid easily off the package, and she lifted the lid. Silks of different shades of turquoise and green layered the inside of the box. On top of the material was an envelope. Lifting the flap, she pulled out the card.

Dearest Alex,

If you're reading this, your dream has come true. You've found Per-Ramesses. I knew you could do it. I never doubted it for a minute, although I know you did. Here's something to wear that will make you feel like Nourbese did when she was with her Pharaoh. I hope you like it.

Love, Jane

Laying the card aside, Alex lifted the silky material from the box. It was the gown Jane had bought the day they stopped at the silk shop in the Cairo market. She rose to her feet and shook out the soft, fluid gown. The craftsmanship of the garment was exquisite. Based on an ancient Egyptian pattern, the silk gown shimmered in the lantern's light, and she bit back a grin of delight at the wickedness of the dress. She should have known Jane had meant for her to have the gown.

She had to try it on. But not until she'd bathed. The heat of the day still clung to her with a cloying dampness that threatened to suffocate her skin. As she ducked past the wool drape cordoning off her bathing area from her main living area, the rough material lightly brushed against her cheek. For being in the desert, she had more creature comforts than she'd ever dreamed possible in such a rustic setting. Alex set the gown aside and prepared the water in her tub with some oil she'd bought in Cairo.

The seductive smell of jasmine surrounded her as the oil's fragrance scented the air. The aroma soothed her senses as she slid into the tepid water, and the floral scent sluiced its way over her skin as her pores absorbed the fragrance. Her gaze shifted to where her present lay. Eager to try it on, she proceeded to rush through her bath.

A large wool towel soaked up the droplets from her bath, leaving only the soft, fragrant smell of jasmine on her skin. Refreshed, she slid the Egyptian garment over her head. The sheer lightness of the fabric made her sigh with pleasure as the silk caressed her body.

The remaining heat from the day no longer pressed against her skin as the vented dress allowed the air to flow around her. She could understand why ancient Egyptian women had chosen to wear such garments. The air sighed over her skin instead of clinging to her.

Narrow bands of silk rested on her shoulders as the diaphanous material plunged downward to the bodice, criss-crossing over her bosom. Despite its transparency, the folds of the gown discreetly covered her breasts and the apex at her thighs. From her waist, narrow panels of turquoise and green silk presented the illusion of a skirt that reached to her ankles.

However, the moment she took a step forward, the illusion disappeared and the panels fluttered about her, revealing the entire length of her leg. Stretching out her bare arms, she twirled around in a circle with the material flowing and whispering about her legs. The gown was wicked, decadent and provocative. She loved it.

Forgetting her woes for the moment, she allowed herself to enjoy the beauty of her present. She swept past the wool drape into her main living quarters, dancing her way lightly across the carpet. No, hardly suitable behavior for Pharaoh's wife. She assumed a regal stance and paraded across the tent's plush floor, trying not to laugh at herself as she did so.

The small bell hanging outside her tent rang sharply. She froze. She couldn't possibly receive anyone in this gown. It was far too revealing. If she ignored the bell and remained quiet, whoever it was would go away.

The bell sounded again. This time with vicious force.

Altair.

She frowned. The man was impossible. Well, she refused to let him spoil her enjoyment of Jane's gift. She'd pretend the bell hadn't rung and he'd go away.

"Alex, I know you're in there. We need to talk."

"No, we don't." Blast, why hadn't she kept her mouth shut? He would have gone away. No, he wouldn't. She knew better than that.

"Damn it, Alex. I need to talk to you."

"Well, I don't want to talk to you. *Go away.*"

"Alex," he growled softly. "I'm in no mood for games."

Games. Had he actually said games? This wasn't a game to her. She'd invested the last ten years of her life to finding Per-Ramesses. Whatever Sheikh Altair Mazir wanted wasn't any concern of hers. He was the one playing games. Not her. If he thought she was going to let the British Museum just waltz right in and take over her dig, he'd better think again.

"Alex, I'm warning you."

She paced the carpet before stopping in front of the tent flap. "Don't you dare threaten me. I'm not the one who's the liar."

"Bloody hell, I want to explain."

"I don't want your explanations. I want you to leave me alone."

She glared at the tent flap then turned and walked away. Pausing at the pillows strewn about the floor, she heard his angry growl of disgust followed by the crack of the tent flap as he pulled it aside and entered her tent. Who the hell did he think he was? She spun around and glared at him.

"Get out."

"Not until I—" His words ground to an abrupt halt as he stared at her. Ignoring his stunned expression, she braced her hands on her hips and scowled at him.

"I told you—we have nothing to say to each other."

He didn't say a word. He just stood there and stared. Infuriated, she wanted to throw something at him. How dare he come into her tent uninvited? The man was unbelievable, standing there like a king, fists jammed into his waist, his feet set apart in an aggressive stance. Had he lost his tongue?

"What are you looking at?"

"You." The hoarse word brushed over her skin causing her hair to stand on end. She saw his eyes gleaming with a disturbing emotion.

No. Oh, no. Absolutely not.

She refused to let this man manipulate her again, even if his eyes glowed with a tempting invitation. With determination, she fought to hold onto her anger.

"I want you to leave."

"And if I don't want to?"

The question startled her. What was he up to? She eyed him suspiciously. "What you want is irrelevant, my lord."

"Oh, I don't think it's irrelevant, Alex. You see, for the first time in a very long time, I have complete clarity as to what I want."

"How comforting for you. And precisely what is it you want?"

"You." The single word whispered its way across the space between them. She clutched at her throat. With just one small utterance, the man had reduced her legs to jelly. Damn him. She refused to let that seductive voice of his lull her into surrendering.

"Well, you can't have me," she said belligerently.

His gaze narrowed and his mouth tightened in a thin line of determination. "You challenge me, *emîra?*"

There was a dangerous edge to his voice. Lord, but the man had the most disquieting ability to throw her off balance. His unyielding temperament made her feel as though she were standing in the direct path of a massive flood. Even more alarming was her desire simply to let the deluge sweep her forward and into his arms.

"I'm doing no such thing."

"I think you are, and I *never* avoid a confrontation."

She had to end this. There was no telling what might happen if she didn't make him leave. That wasn't true. She knew exactly what he wanted, and she hated to admit that she wanted it too. He stepped forward slowly, and she took a quick step back. If she let him near her, she'd be lost. Something in his face said he'd thought the same thing.

As he advanced once more, she took another shaky step in retreat, and stumbled over a stray pillow. Seconds later, she tumbled backwards into the plump cushions strewn about one corner of her tent. Sprawled on top of the jewel-toned amber, emerald and ruby pillows, the skirt panels of her gown parted to reveal her bent leg.

Altair sucked in a sharp breath. He'd come here to talk some sense into her. It was important to make her understand why he'd lied to her. Instead, the sight of her in this imitation of an ancient Egyptian garment had him teetering on the edge of a powerful carnal need.

The pale color of her lushly curved thigh melted into a soft calf down to a narrow foot with toes that looked delicious enough to nibble. She looked delectable. An exotic fruit that promised intense pleasure. Heat pounded through his body. The moment he'd entered the tent, his cock had grown hard at the sight of her.

Where the devil had she found such a provocative gown? A base need tugged painfully between his thighs, and he knew he wouldn't leave until she gave herself to him. Even then, he wasn't sure he'd be capable of leaving her. Somehow, he'd make her understand he was trustworthy. But all he could think about at the moment was bedding her until they were both spent.

He towered over her as he watched the emotions flashing across her face. Anger no longer darkened her full features—instead, a bewildered look furrowed her brow as she bit her lip.

"This afternoon, you...you didn't...want..." Layered underneath her words was the pain he'd caused her.

"No, *emîra*. I wanted you then as much as I do now."

"Then why—?"

"I didn't want any lies between us."

A flash of doubt crossed her face, and he slowly knelt down in front of her. The top of her bent leg almost brushed his lips, and he leaned forward just a hair and kissed the inside of her leg. The sharp hiss of air she dragged into her lungs assured him she liked what he was doing.

"Tonight, *emîra,* I'm going to show you how my body craves you."

With one finger, he traced a path from her knee down to the top of her foot. She drew in another throaty breath. He smiled as he drank in the floral scent of her. God, she smelled good. Exotic and rich to his senses. The silky skin of her foot slid smoothly beneath his palm as he massaged the top of her foot.

Watching her face, he saw her eyes flutter halfway shut as he lifted her foot to nibble on her toes. A tiny mewl of pleasure escaped her. His cock throbbed between his legs at the sound. Damnation, no woman had ever made his body respond with such acute need just from a simple cry. With a feathery touch of his mouth to the inside of her foot, his hand stroked the back of her silky calf.

She jumped at the caress. Satisfaction sailed through him as he lowered her leg and leaned back to study her. Reclined among the vividly colored cushions, her skin was flushed with a rosy hue. He'd been right. The glow he'd witnessed that morning in Cairo covered her now. Her pink mouth parted slightly, and he wanted to have those delicate lips encircling him, sucking on him until he exploded. The image tugged at him with tense expectation.

As he pressed his lips to the inside of her knee again, his hands kneaded the soft flesh of her thigh. The gentle stroke pulled a breathy gasp from her, and her breathing became erratic as he stared down at her. The possessive glint in his eyes sent her heart racing. It was a look of stark desire, and heaven help her, it excited her. Her gaze slid down to where his bronzed fingers stroked her leg.

Her mouth went dry as she realized she wanted his hands to caress all of her. She should be putting a halt to this, but she couldn't think straight with him touching her so intimately. Pleasure exploded inside her, and the blood in her veins grew thick and sluggish. Mesmerized by him, she watched his hand slide up her leg to curve around her hip. Dear Lord, the man's touch was hypnotic. There were no other words to describe it.

Desire coiled in her stomach until it moved downward and ignited a familiar ache between her legs. As he kissed the inside of her lower thigh, she couldn't contain the low moan that broke past her lips. God, if she didn't stop this now, there would be no turning back. Fighting to overcome the sinful delight of his touch, she scrambled backwards, her hand outstretched in a gesture telling him to stop.

He reached out and clasped her upraised hand in his. Brushing his mouth across the tips of her fingers, he turned her hand over and pressed his mouth to her palm. The scent of him wafted its way up to her. Potent and spicy, it teased her senses in the same way his touch teased her skin. He continued to caress her fingers until they were entwined with his. All the while, his gaze never left hers.

"Do you really want me to stop, *emîra?*"

She was mad. Insane. But she couldn't deny his touch made her ache with longing. Inhaling a quick breath, she shook her head slowly. His brown eyes darkened as he kissed the tips of her fingers once again. An instant later, his lips encircled her index finger, gently sucking on her as his eyes locked with hers. The caress blasted a wave of heat down her throat past her belly and into the apex of her thighs.

From there it became a tight ache that clenched her insides until decadent pleasure took hold in her brain. As his tongue swirled around her finger, she gasped at the wicked thoughts the sinful caress sent spiraling through her head.

Pleasure filled his body as he breathed in the jasmine that cloaked her skin. There was a new scent there as well, musk, the sign of her arousal. God he wanted her. She was a rich wine that had gone to his head. He slid one hand over her smooth, supple hip. Raising his head, his gaze met hers, and he took in the glazed expression of desire in her hazel eyes.

She was beautiful. Colorful silk layers whispered across her thighs as she shifted her hips amongst the pillows. Through the fluttering fabric, he caught sight of a golden-brown thatch of curls. He inhaled a sharp breath and his cock throbbed its demand for satisfaction.

Leaning forward, he reached behind her head and removed the pins holding her hair in place. The thick locks tumbled down over her pale shoulders like a luxuriant silk cloth. Fascinated, he watched the tendrils frame her hard nipples jutting through the silk of her gown. His groin tightened at the sight. God help him, but the woman was the most enticing creature he'd ever seen. Gently he pushed aside a lock of hair as his thumbs rubbed against the stiff peaks.

A soft moan escaped her, and he lowered his head to capture the sound with his mouth. Heat rushed through his body at her eager response. She tasted of warm nectar as she parted her lips, and her tongue mated with his in a furious dance. Her hips thrust upward to brush against him, and he growled at her eagerness. God, he wanted to dip his cock into her the way his tongue was doing now. Feel her around him, squeezing and gripping him until he erupted inside. Her cunny would be tight around him. Tight and hot.

Need drove his hand downward and with a light touch, he swept aside the silk at her legs, seeking the curls at the apex of her thighs. It excited him to feel her shudder beneath him as his fingers parted the slick, velvety folds of her sex. He barely grazed the small nub inside her folds with his finger, and she bucked against his hand.

Cream coated his fingers as he stroked her snug passage. The way her body clutched at him with fierce abandon sent desire barreling through him with the force of a *sirocco*. She wasn't just hot with need—her body was demanding the satisfaction he wanted to give her. Needed to give her. As he pulled his hand away from her, she whimpered her protest against his lips.

To his delight, she grabbed his hand and tried to guide him back to her lovely hot core. No, before he satisfied either one of them, he wanted to see the fullness of her beauty. He wanted to see all of her. Pulling away, he smiled at her quiet objection. He rose up on his knees, and gently slid her dress up to her waist. Although she sucked in a quick breath, she didn't protest. Instead, she reached down and tugged the silk gown up and over her head.

He swallowed hard at the sight of her. The voluptuous curves of her body tightened the desire burning out of control inside him. She was a feast for his eyes. Her creamy skin contrasted with the brown thatch of curls at her legs. Like a large fan, her hair spread out on the pillows. She was an odalisque fit for a pharaoh. No, she was for him. No one else. A needy hunger clutched at him as he removed his clothing with a sharp tug. His erection jutted outward and he swallowed hard as she reached out to touch him.

"I want to please you like I did that night at the oasis."

Her soft words sent a bolt of disbelief streaking through him. She wanted to please him. She was putting him first. No other woman coming to his bed had ever done that before. Stunned, he simply stared down at her. A rose-colored stain crested up over her cheeks as she turned her head away. He caught her chin with his hand and forced her to look at him.

"And I want to please you, *emira*."

"I thought my forward behavior had shocked you."

He shook his head. "Never. In fact, I find it quite stimulating." He couldn't help teasing her as he glanced down at his arousal.

With a breathy laugh, she reached out to brush her fingertips over his stiff cock. His mouth went dry as her hand encircled him, stroking him like a silky glove. Hazel eyes sparkling with a new found confidence, she stared up at him as her thumb rubbed a small bead of desire over the tip of him. A second later she stroked the sensitive vein along his hard length. She seemed to instinctively know what would please him. And God knew she was doing just that. With just a few strokes from her hand, he was throbbing in the heat of her palm.

"God yes, *emîra.*"

His breath quickened as he stared at her white hand wrapped around the dark stiffness of his cock. Christ Jesus, that felt good. Her hand slid back and forth over his rigid erection, creating a friction that tugged his ballocks up against his cock. No not yet. He needed to feel her hot silky core clutching him.

Grabbing her hands, he gently pinned them above her head and kissed her. At the same time, he positioned his cock at her wet, narrow opening. He inched into her, and she lifted her hips to accept him. With each slow thrust forward, her body took in more of him. God, she was so tight. The muscles inside her hot, slick passage clenched at him with fierce intensity, and he struggled to keep from exploding inside her.

The palms of her hands warmed his chest, and she ran her thumbs over his nipples. The pleasurable sensation tugged a groan from him. She was wonderful. His cock pressed deeper into her before he eased back. Hot cream smoothed its way over him as he thrust deeper into her. Buried inside her like this, she felt so good. No, better than good, incredible. Her eyes were closed, and her expression showed she was close to a climax. Lowering his head, he flicked his tongue over the stiff peak of one breast. Her response was to arch her back and thrust her hips upward. The movement heightened the intensity of his pleasure as she tightened around him like a hot vise.

"Look at me," he rasped. Her eyes flew open to meet his gaze. "Tonight, *ana anide emîra,* you are mine."

With a low cry, he plunged deep into her. With increasing speed, he created a friction that was about to push him over the edge. Her body rippled and constricted around him. It was the most exquisite pleasure he'd ever experienced. Her buttery core melted over his cock as he drove into her one last time. Need

Chapter Fourteen

A feathery touch on her skin stirred Alex from sleep. Brushing at her cheek, she snuggled deeper into the warm pillows. The touch came again, only this time it was the distinct sensation of a finger trailing across her cheek. She opened her eyes to find Altair looking down at her as he brushed her hair off her face.

The low light of the lantern cast its soft glow around them. The sinewy muscles in his chest flexed as he curled her into the warmth of his long bronzed body. His eyes held a possessive glint as he stared down at her.

"It will be morning soon."

She ran her hand across his hard chest, skimming his breastbone then trailing her fingers down to below his waist. When her thumb rubbed over the sensitive edge of his cock, he inhaled sharply. She smiled at him.

"Do not tease, *emîra,* unless you are prepared to follow up on your boldness." His hand glided over her stomach until his fingers slipped between her curls. The stroke of his thumb against her sensitive nub pulled a moan from her.

The world slipped away at his touch until the only thing filling her head was him. They'd made love all through the night, and still he could drive her beyond reasonable thought. Her hand fully enclosed him in her grasp, and she rubbed her thumb under the thick cap to stroke the turgid vein there. She'd learned last night how much he liked that. Already he was throbbing in her hand. A low growl of pleasure rumbled in his throat.

Rolling over on his back, he pulled her with him. Hands

braced against his shoulders, she tugged in a sharp breath as his hard phallus pressed against the sensitive spot beneath her curls. A moment later, he lifted her up and slid her down on top of him. As he filled her, she emitted a small gasp of delight at the pleasure it gave her. He rested deep inside her and her body quivered.

"Ride me, *ana gamâl.*" The raw need in his voice startled her.

He'd called her his beauty. It amazed her, and she tenderly touched his cheek. He immediately turned his head, and his lips sought the palm of her hand. His fingers gripped her hips firmly as he urged her to rock her body over his. The earthy rawness of the act sent excitement streaking through her as she met the glowing passion in his eyes. Arching backward, she braced her hands on his hard, muscular thighs, taking in more of him.

The sleek feel of his hard legs beneath her palms heated her blood to a simmering boil. With each stroke of her body against his, pleasure radiated its way through every nerve ending in her body. Tremors of delight cascaded over her as she tipped her head back until her hair brushed against her buttocks. Not even last night had she felt so wicked or wanton. And she loved every moment of it. His touch was sweeter than honey, and she trembled as his thumb pressed between her wet folds to stroke the firm button of her sex. The sensation of having him inside her while his fingers played with her dragged a cry of pleasure from her lungs.

Sweet heaven, how could each time be better than the last? A tingle edged its way over her skin as his touch sent first one shudder and then another lacing through her. The faster he stroked her with his thumb, the faster she moved against his hard erection. A firm hand caressed her stomach and pressed her back further. The change in position increased her delight, and for a moment she was blinded to anything but the rising pitch inside her body.

With a small cry, she instinctively fell forward, her hips gyrating against his at a frenzied pace. Dear Lord, was this wanton body really hers? Something about this man drew out her most wicked desires. He tempted her, thrilled her. Each time he surged upward her body clung to him, trying to keep him buried deep inside her.

The intensity of it all made her whimper with a need that demanded fulfillment. The familiar tension spiraled through her limbs once more, and suddenly, the muscles below her stomach shuddered wildly. Her body clung to him as he throbbed deep inside her. Spasms of pleasure rolled through her, and the ferocity of her response left her weak, but satisfied. Lowering her weight down onto his, she continued to throb against him, her body trembling with the aftershocks of their lovemaking.

Satiated, she let her fingers drift over his hard, muscular shoulders. The faint aroma of cedarwood tickled her nose. He smelled wonderfully male as she nuzzled his neck, the light sheen of sweat on his skin salting her lips.

She lifted her head to stare down into his eyes. With one hand, he lightly stroked her cheek, brushing away a stray lock of hair. He rolled them over onto their sides, his mouth seeking hers in a deep kiss. The hard muscles of his arm tensed as her fingers ran downward to his hand. He entwined his fingers in hers, raising them to his mouth.

"I should return to my tent."

"Must you?" Was that low, sultry voice really hers?

"Yes. I may not practice the tribe's faith, but I respect their beliefs. Many would frown darkly on my presence here."

The warmth of his mouth caressed hers again before he reached for his clothing. Troubled, she watched as he dressed. So much had happened in the past few hours. She'd given herself so easily to him and now he was leaving because he didn't want anyone to know they'd spent the night together. His explanation made perfect sense, but what if it was another lie?

Fear cooled her skin, and she pulled a blanket over her. The warmth didn't keep her from shivering. When he was ready to leave, he knelt beside her, and she forced a smile to her lips. He cupped her face.

"I'll see you later this morning, *ana gamâl.*"

She nodded, stubbornly keeping her smile on her face. Altair bent his head and gave her a quick kiss before leaving the tent. The wool flap whispered his departure, and she buried her face into a pillow. What had she done? Last night she'd allowed him to beguile her with his seductive words and touch.

The sudden brush of fur against her neck made her jump. Zada. The little mongoose pushed her warm, soft body up against Alex's chin. She absently rubbed the animal as it nuzzled her cheek. If she didn't know better, she'd swear the affectionate little creature was trying to ease her fears.

She'd given in so easily last night. How could she have forgotten he'd lied to her? He couldn't be trusted. No, that wasn't the problem. The real problem was she couldn't be trusted around him. Every time he came near her, her knees turned to water, and she was willing to do whatever he asked. Tonight had been incredible beyond words, but she was afraid to let it happen again.

Tomorrow she would have to find a way to put distance between them. She couldn't afford to lose her heart to a man she couldn't trust. Worst of all, she didn't trust herself to say no to him. She buried her face in her blanket, fighting back tears. Today would be better. Today she could focus on Per-Ramesses and forget the pleasure she'd found in Altair's arms. She uttered a soft moan of despair. Now who was the one lying?

✧

Elbows resting on the top of her folding desk, Alex rubbed her tired eyes. Sitting beneath her work tent at the excavation site, she had a clear view of the dig area. She just wished her eyes would stop drooping. After Altair had left her early this morning, she'd not been able to sleep. The memory of his touch had been far too disturbing.

A light breeze riffled the papers in front of her. With a quick move, she slapped the papers down in place until the delicate wind danced away. It wasn't just the way she'd responded to his caresses that troubled her, but the fact she'd given in to him so quickly.

She was far too impulsive for her own good. He'd deliberately lied about knowing her father and about who he was. But it was the ease with which he'd deceived her that was so frightening. Then there was his connection to the Museum. He'd given his word not to tell the British Museum about Per-Ramesses, and while the code of honor among the Bedouin was legendary, he wasn't a full-blooded Mazir. He was half English.

Per-Ramesses was almost as important to Altair as it was to her. The lost city represented a part of the Mazir culture and

186

legend. Now the threat to her dream of excavating Per-Ramesses was greater than ever. If Lord Merrick learned of her find, it would only be a matter of weeks before his minions arrived to take control of the dig. Even worse, how could she have forgotten Altair's lies so quickly that she'd eagerly welcomed the pleasure she'd found in his arms? It had been a grievous error on her part.

Quivering at the thought, she leaned back into her chair. No, not a mistake. Nothing so magical and sensual could ever be labeled that way. When she'd emerged from her tent this morning, his tall figure had been easy to see among the workers he'd chosen for the day's excavation work. The moment his eyes had met hers across the encampment this morning had been enough to set her heart skittering along at an outlandish pace.

That dark gaze of his had held a possessive glow, and she hadn't been able to resist enjoying the way he looked at her. Closing her eyes, she sat in the heated silence, listening to the desert wind as it played gently with the roof of her work tent.

The sound and smell of the restless air was hot. Hot and sensual. As hot as Altair's hands on her skin last night. Even now, the memory of his touch made her belly grow taut with desire. She sucked in a sharp breath of air as her eyes flew open. He could be lying about that too. What if his lovemaking was simply a way to lull her into a false sense of security?

Her nails bit into the palms of her hands at the thought. No, surely he wouldn't do something as vile as that. It went against everything her heart was trying to tell her. Brutally, she crushed the fierce cry of denial and reminded herself of every lie he'd told her. From their first meeting he'd hidden the truth from her. It would always be there between them. A vine that choked the life out of everything in its path, including her trust. And yet she'd given in to his seductive words, his hedonistic caresses. She winced at the thought.

From the work tent's elevated vantage point, she could see the workers measuring off the city wall. She tried to find Altair's tall figure, but the distance was too far to recognize any one individual. Her frustrated gaze scanned the terrain underneath which Per-Ramesses was buried. Rocky and covered with gritty sand, the landscape reminded her of paintings she'd seen of the American West.

Odd how she'd traveled through a seemingly endless expanse of sand to find an oasis surrounded by an almost mountainous terrain. Thousands of years ago, this area had been an abundantly fertile land. Time had shrunk it to the small oasis that housed the village of Khatana-Qantir.

With a tiny noise of disgust, she stood up and paced the sandy floor beneath her black boots. Until now, she'd managed to avoid being alone with Altair, but it hadn't been easy. Soon she'd have to face him, and she dreaded the thought. For most of the day, she'd allowed her thoughts to drift along like this— anything to avoid thinking about how she was going to tell him there would be no repeat of last night.

Another light breeze drifted through the tent, stirring up more of her papers. She was unprepared for the gentle wind, and her fingers slipped as she tried to keep the documents from scattering off the desk. Grabbing her sextant box, she buried a stack of notes under the narrow case then retrieved the papers that had landed on the sand-covered ground.

Seated once more at her desk, she glanced down at the materials she held. Uncle Jeffrey's drawings of Per-Ramesses and Nourbese's tomb. With a critical eye, she scanned the Coptic symbols drawn with such confident strokes. About to return the pages to the table, she stopped as she eyed the warning Uncle Jeffrey had seen in his vision. With her index finger, she traced the line of text.

"Trust not the Mazir who lies for he intends only death and destruction to those in his path." She pondered the sentence for a moment. The first time she'd read it out loud to her father, they'd both puzzled over the meaning. Even now, the warning still perplexed her. Why would Nourbese's tomb markings contain a warning about a Mazir tribesman? The Mazir were Nourbese's people.

Shaking her head, Alex leaned forward and laid the paper on her table. As she looked up from her notes, her stomach curled into a tight knot. Altair was moving up the incline toward the work tent. A hot wind stirred the blue hem of his *gambaz* until it flowed out behind him as he strode quickly up the hill. The intricately embroidered Mazir robe emphasized the exotic darkness of his skin. Gray goatskin boots dug through the sand as he moved toward her, the powerful muscles in his legs taut beneath the snug fawn trousers he wore.

The raw power of his stride and the lean strength of his body made her limbs tighten with desire. Last night's pleasures hovered on the edge of her senses, the hair on her arms standing on end at the memory of their lovemaking. No, his lies were what she needed to remember. She had to end this today.

Her fingers nervously tapped the worktable. With another glance at the paper, she sighed. *Trust not the Mazir who—* She jerked upright in her chair and read the warning again. Oh God. Was it possible? Was Altair the Mazir in the warning? He'd lied to her time and again, and every time her life had been in danger, he'd been in close proximity to her.

Fear chilled her hands, and she shivered in spite of the heat. It made perfect sense, and yet it didn't make sense at all. She didn't believe in curses. But Uncle Jeffrey had warned of something or someone trying to stop them. Any other time, she would have scoffed at the caveat, but this was different.

No matter how eccentric Uncle Jeffrey might have been, he'd written this warning as if he'd known how to read and write Coptic all his life. That was something she could believe in, even if it didn't make any sense at all. The real question demanding an answer was whether Altair was the Mazir referred to in the warning. Despite all his lies, she couldn't bring herself to believe it.

Damn, she was so confused. Last night had been a terrible miscalculation on her part. She'd lost sight of why she was here in Khatana-Qantir. It was something she couldn't forget again if she intended to keep her vow to her father and realize her own dream. All she'd done last night was muddy the waters. Fingertips pinching the bridge of her nose, she tried to balance what her heart was telling her against what her head was telling her.

"Are you all right, *ana gamâl?*"

Every muscle in her body tensed at the sound of his deep, sensual voice. Her head snapped up as she watched him enter the tent. Still confused by her mixed emotions, she immediately ducked her head again to avoid meeting his probing gaze. Her hand casually buried her uncle's warning under a pile of notes.

"Yes, I'm fine." Inside she cringed. The stormy emotions brewing inside her were making her feel far from fine. "How close are they to finishing the measurements of the west wall?"

"They should be finished marking it off shortly, then they can proceed with the south side of the perimeter."

God, even now, the sound of his voice was an erotic stroke to her senses. Desperate to suppress the sudden stirring of desire burning through her, she clenched her teeth. She needed to remember he'd been lying to her from the start. His deception about the correspondence with her father. Hiding who he really was. But he'd had good reasons for doing so, hadn't he? Bile threatened to rise in her throat. Sweet Lord, how had she come to be so under his spell that she wanted to excuse his lies?

Avoiding his gaze, she looked out over the site. "How far have they measured to this point?"

"Almost a seven mile stretch. I rode toward the east wall, and I think the adjoining ramparts will measure close to five miles."

"Well that at least gives me some approximations to compare with my notes. I think the first place to start digging is somewhere in the vicinity of where Ramesses' palace would have been." Leaning forward, she reached for a blank pad of paper. She tensed as he stepped around the worktable. The edge of his knuckles grazed her cheek.

"You've been avoiding me."

Thrown off balance by his accurate observation, she sucked in a quick breath and kept her eyes focused on the papers in front of her. "I've been busy."

"So busy you dart away every time I come near you?" There was just a hint of puzzlement in his voice as he braced one hand on the back of her chair and the other on the table. "I've missed you since the moment I left you this morning."

The scent of cedarwood drifted beneath her nose, and she closed her eyes for a brief moment as his mouth brushed against the nape of her neck. Dear Lord, the man's words were as seductive as his touch. She swallowed the desire to turn her head and seek his mouth for a kiss she knew he'd be more than willing to give.

Quickly twisting away from him, she stood up and walked around the worktable to stare out at the view before her. Per-Ramesses. Her dream. She couldn't give that up. There could be no distractions of any kind, not even pleasurable ones with a man she found difficult to trust. The white linen of her shirt clung to her like a second skin in the heat, and she tugged at the front of it to pull it away from her.

"What's wrong, Alex?"

Ignoring his question, she moved back to the table and pointed a spot on the grid she'd drawn. "I...I think we should look for the palace here. From all my notes, I'm certain it's in this general vicinity."

Sun-drenched fingers stroked the back of her hand, and before she could stop herself, she yanked her hand away. It was self-preservation. If she allowed him to touch her again, it would be impossible to resist him.

"Damn it, tell me what's wrong." The taut vibration in his voice made her wince. Avoiding his gaze, she shook her head as she pretended to peruse her notes and the map.

"Nothing's wrong, I'm just—"

From across the worktable, a strong hand wrapped around her wrist as he forced her to look at him. "Don't lie to me, Alex."

The words set her teeth on edge. He had the gall to say such a thing to her, after all the lies he'd told her. With a sharp tug, she yanked her arm free of his grip. "No. That's your forte," she said with quiet outrage.

"It didn't seem to be a problem for you last night." Dark eyes narrowed as he studied her from across the worktable.

Her body tugged with emotion, gravitating toward him just like a magnet. She wanted to throw herself into his arms and forget everything but his touch. Her heart was telling her to forgive him, while her head screamed at her to reject him. Crushing the thoughts, she hardened her heart against him. He'd lied to her. He wasn't to be trusted.

"Last night I wasn't thinking clearly. I am now."

"I see." He folded his arms across his chest and watched her with a forbidding expression on his regal features. "And exactly what are you thinking at this moment?"

The harsh, chiseled line of his jaw illustrated the tension in him. It reflected his suppressed anger. She stiffened at the affronted look on his face. Who was *he* to assume the look of an injured party? *He* was the liar—not her.

"Last night was a pleasurable experience, but—"

"A pleasurable experience," he snarled. His anger was

almost a tangible force between them. Alarm skated down her back as she kept her eyes averted. "Take care with your words, Alex."

The menacing words hung in the hot air between them. The stony look on his face cut into her like sharp granite. Turning away, she walked to the edge of the tent and stared out at the unending sea of desert. Why did his anger bother her so much? He'd done nothing to earn her trust, only destroy it. She refused to let him see how torn she was over her decision.

"I...I can't be with you again—like that."

"Explain." The solitary command lifted the hair on the back of her neck.

She didn't like someone ordering her around, least of all a man who'd manipulated her since their first meeting. In the past, he'd always been able to convince her to do things his way, but today he was going to fail. She was here to work, not to indulge in an affair with a man she couldn't trust. Turning around, she glared at him.

"I came here to find Per-Ramesses, not to have an illicit liaison with someone like you."

"*Damm gahannam*," he growled. The fierce anger in his voice made her stiffen. "And last night—"

"Last night was a mistake I want to forget."

Even to her ears, the words sounded cold and harsh as she rushed to interrupt him. God, she hadn't meant it to come out like that. She trembled at the cruelty of it. It had been a mistake, yes, but only because she couldn't trust him. She would never forget their night together. What she wanted to forget was this miserable twisting in her stomach.

Statues reflected more emotion in their faces than his did at this very moment, and she flinched at his glacial expression. The icy fury darkening his eyes sent a shiver racing down her spine. She'd only seen him this furious once before. But this time it frightened her.

"A mistake you want to forget?" The icy staccato of the question chilled her hot skin.

"I'm sorry, I didn't mean for it to sound that way." She stumbled over her words. "I lost my head last night. I won't—can't let it happen again."

"Exactly when did you decide this, Alex—before or after you rode me with all the skill of a Cyprian?"

The taunt made her jerk as her cheeks burned at the memory. He made it sound as if last night had been her idea. He was the one who'd entered her tent uninvited. Seduction had been his goal, and she'd not stood a chance of resisting him. Glaring at him, she tightened her lips.

"Since we're throwing out insults, perhaps you need to consider the barbaric manner in which you charged into my tent yesterday evening. Not to mention your refusal to leave when I ordered you out. Tell me, my lord, do English ladies find your savage nature as unappealing as I do?"

A dark hand slammed down on the worktable in fury. His livid expression frightened her, and she jumped back as he rounded the table. Grabbing her by the shoulders, he pulled her toward him. The sun-hot cartridges on his utility belt stung her hands as she tried to push away from him.

"Trust me, *yâ 'aini*," The tone he used as he said *my dear* was filled with scathing derision. "I was quite restrained in my savagery last night. At the moment, however, I am close to losing what little restraint I possess."

"If that's your way of saying you expect a repeat of last night, then you're certain to be disappointed, my lord." With a sharp twist, she almost broke free of his grasp, but he was too quick for her. He wrapped his strong arms around her, pinning her against his hard, hot body.

"And *you* overestimate the appeal of your charms, *yâ 'aini*. While last night was pleasurable, you've confirmed one thing for me."

"Oh, please, don't keep me in suspense, tell me, my lord." As she glared up at him, his eyes became narrow slits. Heaven help her, the man looked like he wanted to kill her. Panic sent her stomach lurching wildly inside her. The warning had to be correct. Altair was the one not to trust.

"American women whore just as easily as English women do."

Her skin grew clammy as the brutality of his words sent a numbing chill through her body. With one swift stroke he had demeaned the night they'd spent together. Cheapened it into a sordid moment. Desperate to conceal her pain, she turned her head away from him. She didn't want him to see how deep his words had sliced through her.

She'd told him their night together was one she wanted to forget, but that was impossible. Even now she craved his touch. Every fiber and nerve in her body was attuned to the lean hardness of him, his spicy male scent. Her body would never forget anything about him.

Swallowing hard, she knew none of that mattered. She couldn't trust him. He'd lied to her from the beginning, and last night he'd beguiled her with his seductive words and touch. Trusting him came at price she wasn't willing to pay either with her heart or her work.

"Now that you've made your opinion of me quite clear, I would appreciate your releasing me, my lord." The quiet dignity in her voice gave her a small measure of satisfaction. She hadn't revealed the depth of the pain his words had caused her.

"*Damm gahannam*," he exclaimed as he thrust her away from him.

Free of his arms, she stumbled backwards a few steps until she regained her balance. She mustn't look up. If she saw the same contempt in his eyes that she'd heard in his voice, she'd burst into tears. And that she refused to do. She wouldn't let him see how badly he'd hurt her. Without looking in his direction, she seated herself at her worktable and proceeded to straighten her notes as if nothing had happened.

A foul expletive escaped him. Wheeling about, he stormed out of the tent. Only when she was certain he was gone did she release the pent-up tears swelling her throat. Oh God, what had she done? She'd fallen in love with him—a man she couldn't trust. Her sobs shuddered through her, and she lifted her head to watch Altair's retreating figure blur behind her watery eyes.

✧

Damn her. God damn her to hell. The little bitch had played him for a fool. She'd been eager enough for him to bed her last night, but suddenly the light of day had brought her to her senses. What was it she'd said? An illicit liaison with someone like him. Yes, that was it. He was a Bedouin half-breed. A savage. A barbarian. Obviously, she'd had a change of heart when it came to taking a lover whose heritage was far from pure.

He'd lowered his guard and been tricked again. When it came to women with hearts of stone, he should have known nationality didn't differentiate. She was no different from Caroline. No doubt, it had been an adventure to her. A tale she could share with her friends. But if that were true, why had her face gone stark white, her hazel eyes dark with pained horror, when he'd called her a whore? Could there have been another reason for her rejection of him?

The toe of his boot scuffed viciously at a small mound of sand, sending the pulverized stone flying into the air in a small knee-high cloud. Bloody hell, what a mess. Was he wrong? Alex was always easy to read, her emotions clearly visible in her expressive face. When he'd entered the work tent, she'd definitely been disturbed by something. Had it been her distaste of what was to come or had it been something else?

Hands on his waist, he stared at the ground as his fingers dug through the wool of his *gambaz* to bite into his skin. And last night. God help him, but last night had been the closest thing to heaven he'd ever imagined or experienced. The feel of her, the scent of her. It had been a humbling experience for him.

No other woman had offered herself to him so sweetly or with such willing enthusiasm. Beautiful and sensual, she had given pleasure as well as taken it. That's what made all of this so difficult to understand.

He looked over his shoulder toward the work tent. She stood leaning over the table, apparently studying her notes. The sight of her bent over the table with her head down wreaked havoc with his insides. God, he wanted to be standing behind her right now, driving into her, his hands gripping the soft curves of her hips. What the hell was wrong with him? The woman had just scorned him, and all he could think about was how much he wanted to make love to her again. He pulled his gaze away from her and continued walking toward the walled city. Unwillingly, his mind raced to offer up an explanation for her behavior.

Something else was at the heart of this about-face. He

couldn't believe she was like Caroline or any of the other women he'd known in London. A small voice inside his head mocked him. No, what he really meant was that he didn't want to believe it of her. He didn't want to think that he'd been wrong about her. That would signal she'd come to mean more to him than he was willing to admit.

Out the corner of his eye, he saw a horse and rider approaching. Medjuel. He came to a halt, watching his cousin ride up in a dashing display of Bedouin horsemanship. When he'd dismounted, the Sheikh rubbed the animal's jowl fondly as he moved past the horse's head. Surprised by his cousin's visit, Altair gave him a nod of greeting.

"You're a long way from camp. Are you bringing me news about Mohammed?"

"No. I think he knows I'm watching him. He's been an exemplary shepherd to the flock. Eventually, I'll learn what he's up to, and when I do I'll address the man's betrayal." There was a quiet edge to Medjuel's voice that hid a deep anger. The sound of it reassured Altair that his cousin wasn't neglecting the tribe's interest in the matter.

"So if there's nothing new to share about Mohammed, what brings you so far out?"

One hand stroking his beard, Medjuel glanced up toward Alex's work tent. "I wanted to talk to you about your Miss Talbot."

"She's not my Miss Talbot," he said in a tight voice. At least not any longer she wasn't. He watched the expression on Medjuel's dark face hover between curiosity and one other emotion Altair couldn't quite pinpoint.

"Miss Talbot then." His cousin shrugged. "I hear she's found the city wall and that it's only a matter of time before Nourbese's tomb is discovered."

"We've yet to confirm that she's actually found Per-Ramesses, but I'd be willing to wager money she's found the city."

Medjuel nodded as he turned his head once more to study Alex working beneath the shade of the tent. "I must admit that I'm worried about her finding it."

"What? The city?" Altair stared at his cousin in surprise. "Why?"

"Not the city, but the tomb. I'm concerned about the effect on our people. Already they're talking about Nourbese's treasure and who will benefit from this newfound wealth."

"Of course, they're excited. The prophecy is more than two thousand years old, and they're seeing it happen right before their eyes. Why is that so terrible?"

His gaze still on Alex, the Sheikh shook his head. "And what if she finds the tomb, but there's nothing there? What will we do then?"

Altair stiffened. He'd never considered that possibility before. Medjuel was right. If Alex did find Nourbese's tomb, but found nothing inside, it could rip through the very fabric of the tribe's existence. For generations, they had listened to tales of Pharaoh's love for Nourbese. It had fed their culture, their belief structure. If Nourbese's tomb was empty, it could easily destroy the tribe's belief system.

"I see by your face, you agree with me." Medjuel frowned. "You must convince Miss Talbot to give up this search for Nourbese."

Unable to help himself, he burst out into bitter laughter. "What makes you think I have any control over Alex? The woman does as she pleases."

"I realize she's a *Ferengi*, and a woman at that, but doesn't she understand the danger she's in with this undertaking?"

"What the hell is that suppose to mean?"

The fierce expression on Medjuel's face immediately lightened, and he raised a placating hand. "You know how foreigners are when it comes to living in the desert. I only meant that the woman might do something during the excavation to endanger her life or that of the workers. We both know digs like this can be dangerous."

"True, but you've never shown this much concern for a *Ferengi* before."

"And you appear quite sensitive about the woman whenever I mention her." Medjuel sent him a probing look. "What does she mean to you?"

"I made a commitment to Alex's father, and I agreed to honor that commitment with her. It's my responsibility to see to her safety."

"Then see to it she doesn't get herself or anyone else hurt while she continues with this excavation."

Altair studied him for a long moment before nodding. His cousin seemed satisfied with the response as he gathered up the reins of his horse. "I should return to camp—I have a dispute to settle between two mothers and their children."

"The work of Sheikh el Mazir is never done."

Medjuel mounted his horse. A tight smile that resembled more of a grimace curved his lips. "So it would seem."

Watching his cousin ride off, Altair frowned. In all the years he'd known Medjuel, there had never been this cold distance between them. His cousin said all the right things, but something lay just beneath the surface to create a tension between them. Had he unknowingly done something to incur Medjuel's wrath? Why didn't his cousin confront him about it? Whatever was causing the tension between them, it was becoming more evident with each passing day. Something told him it was only going to get worse, but even more chilling was the idea that Alex's presence might somehow be part of the discord between him and Medjuel.

Chapter Fifteen

With a vicious swipe of her hand, Alex wiped the worktable clean of her notebooks and tools. What an arrogant fool she was. Three more weeks lost because she'd miscalculated. She'd thought for certain Ramesses Palace would be where they'd been digging. But she'd been wrong. Just like she'd been wrong about everything else on this excavation. Two months of searching and they were still empty-handed.

She wanted to scream—break something. It was hopeless. No matter what she did, it was always the wrong choice. If there was anything of value buried at Khatana-Qantir, it was doubtful they'd find it with a woman in charge. That's what Merrick and his cronies would be thinking if they were here. They'd be right. She couldn't find an open barn door to save her life. Not that she really cared anymore. She hadn't really cared about anything since the day she'd fought with Altair.

Dejected, she sank down into her chair and stared at the mess she'd made of the work tent. It resembled her life. Since their fight, Altair only spoke to her when necessary and in a voice that always lowered the temperature around her considerably. She kept telling herself it didn't matter, but it was a lie. It did matter.

The days following their argument had been emotionally draining. His cold, impassive attitude toward her had deepened the wounds he'd inflicted during their fight. Perhaps his chilly behavior would have been easier to bear if she didn't care for him. She didn't want to, but she did. How was it possible she loved a man she didn't trust? Not even logic could answer that question. She loved him. Simply and completely.

Even his mother had unknowingly added to her pain. The tribe's second evening at Khatana-Qantir had brought Altair's mother to her tent. Gameela had been gracious about Alex's failure to visit the first night, but had demanded penance in the form of eating dinner with them at least once a week.

Part of her had hoped Altair would eat with his family, but he was always absent on the evenings she came to dinner. She told herself it was a relief not to see him in his mother's tent; but it was easy to lie to herself. What wasn't easy to ignore was the way she listened for the sound of his voice in hopes he would join them.

Rising from her chair, she began the task of cleaning up the mess she'd made. If only it were as simple to straighten out her own life. She shook her head. No, she'd made a mess of things with her inability to trust Altair. Instead of thinking through the problem, she'd impulsively leapt to the conclusion that his lies meant he would break his word to her. And she'd allowed that ridiculous warning from Uncle Jeffrey to add to her fear.

And for what? The Museum had yet to appear on the horizon and Altair hadn't tried to hurt her. If anything, he stayed as far away from her as he could. He'd made his disgust for her perfectly clear. It was something she felt keenly every time he was near.

One knee pressed into the sand, she gathered several sheets of paper from the ground and shuffled them into a neat stack. Pausing in her chore, she closed her eyes and wished she were home. At least there, only her memories of Father and Uncle Jeffrey would haunt her. Here, everywhere she turned there was something to remind her of Altair. A light breeze stirred the damp curls at her neck as she stood up and arched her sore back.

"What happened here?" Altair's deep voice washed over her. The coldness she was accustomed to had changed to concern. Without looking at him, she returned to picking up the papers strewn all over the sandy floor.

"I had a temper tantrum."

"I see."

For the first time in weeks, she heard a thread of humor lacing his voice. Slowly she turned to look up at him. His sensual mouth held the beginnings of a smile, but as his eyes met hers, it died. Turning away from her, he bent and retrieved several notebooks from the ground. Together they worked in silence, and as the last piece of paper settled on the desk, Altair sent her a penetrating look.

"I understand your frustration, Alex, but excavating a site requires great patience and time."

"Do you think I don't know that?"

"Sometimes I wonder. It's as if you think it's going to be as easy as marking off so many paces to the spot where you think something is buried."

The truth in his statement made her wince. He was right. Patience had never been one of her virtues. Father had warned her the excavation would be time-consuming and tedious. But she wanted to see results. She wanted to see them this very minute.

She'd found the city in honor of her father. Now, she wanted to find something specific and concrete to show those stodgy, conservative jackasses at the British Museum. The look on their faces when she showed up with her ancient treasure trove would be worth every ounce of heartache she was suffering right now.

But would it really? Ignoring the internal question, she darted a glance in Altair's direction. For a brief instant, she could have sworn there was warmth in his gaze. It disappeared the moment their eyes met. Unable to keep from flinching at the inscrutable expression on his face, she grimaced.

"I guess I did think it would be as easy as walking off distances from the city's wall. I just feel like I'm wasting my time."

"That I don't believe. In all honesty, you've achieved a great deal in a relatively short time." The gentle note in his voice nearly undid her. Once again she shot him a glance. She was afraid to believe it, but it seemed as though there was a thawing in the icy look he normally bestowed on her. Was he actually offering her encouragement? Had he experienced a change of heart where she was concerned? No, that was simply wishful thinking on her part. She shrugged.

"I suppose. It doesn't really matter anymore."

"This lack of determination is something I've not seen in

you before." He fiddled with the stack of papers he'd returned to her desk.

Biting her lip, she didn't answer. Instead, she relished the opportunity to drink in the strength of his jaw line and the way his dark brown hair brushed his shoulders. The need to thread her fingers through the silky waves made her tremble. That train of thought was a dangerous one. She shifted her attention down to his sun-drenched hand. As her gaze lingered on his tapered fingers, she watched them draw up into a tight fist.

"What the hell is this?" he growled.

Startled by the fierce question, she shook her head. "What?"

"This." His fingers scrunched one edge of the paper he waved at her. "Trust not the Mazir who lies?"

Tense with anger, he turned the paper around so she could see the Coptic writing. He wanted to throttle her. She'd kept a vital piece of information from him. Did she think the danger had passed just because there had been no other attempts on her life in the past few weeks?

"My uncle wrote that after his vision of Nourbese."

"You've known about it all this time, and you didn't think it important enough to tell me about it?"

"No, I didn't," she snapped.

"Damn it, Alex, when are you going to start trusting me?"

The stubborn set of her mouth made him clench his fist. *Damm Gahannam*, the woman had to be the most exasperating creature he'd ever met. One minute he wanted to shake some sense into her and the next he wanted to bed her.

Instead of answering his question, she turned to begin sorting and reordering her notes. It was easy to see she didn't intend to discuss the topic. Inhaling a deep breath of frustration, he watched her work. Over the past three weeks, he'd seen flashes of her vulnerability. With each small setback in her search for Ramesses' palace, the fire in her eyes had dimmed just a little bit more.

Seeing her disappointment and fear of failure, he'd wanted to comfort her, but he was certain she wouldn't welcome his consolations. He'd kept his distance from her, but it had been difficult. The nights had been agonizing without her warmth curled into his side. Now he was beginning to realize how wide the chasm was between them because of his deception.

He'd been a fool to lie to her. For the first time, he'd met a woman who was more than capable of surviving the harshness of the desert. If she could do that, she could most certainly survive the rigors of London society. As always the voice in his head mocked him. She might have the ability to survive his nomadic lifestyle, but she was like all the other women he'd met. Unwilling to see beyond his Bedouin blood to the man he truly was.

No. He couldn't believe that. That one night of passion they'd shared had been too intense an experience. She'd given herself to him and held nothing back. That wasn't the sign of a woman who wanted only one night with a Bedouin sheikh. Something else had driven this wedge between them.

The paper in his hand crackled as he clenched his fist tighter. Glancing down at the note once more, he read it again. It didn't make sense. Why hadn't she told him about the warning? Hadn't she recognized the importance of it?

"You should have told me about this, Alex."

"Tell me why I should have?"

Damn her stubbornness. If it took the rest of the afternoon, he was going to find out why she didn't trust him with information that could keep her safe from harm. He glared at her, determined to wring the truth out of her if he had to shake some sense into her. With a grunt of frustration he shoved his fingers through his hair.

"You want me to tell you why?" he growled. "Let me think, at least three attempts on your life that we're aware of, and who knows how many others. It says right here death and destruction to those in his—"

The paper in his grasp scorched his palm. *Trust not the Mazir who lies.* Narrowing his eyes, he studied her closely. The silence stretched taut between them, and he watched her try to suppress a shudder.

With a deliberate movement, he replaced the paper on the desk. He smoothed out the wrinkles with his hands, his head bent as if reading the words again. Then with the speed of a leopard, his hand lashed out and captured her wrist. Yanking her toward him, he glared down at her.

"Explain why you didn't tell me about the warning."

"Because I didn't want to," she snapped.

Despite her crisp retort, her eyes were wide in her face. She was lying. It glimmered in the fear darkening her hazel eyes. An icy calm washed over him as he glared at her.

"You think I'm the Mazir in this warning, don't you?" When she didn't answer him, he suppressed the urge to shake her. "Answer me, Alex."

She jumped at the sharp command and glared up at him. "Yes!" she exclaimed angrily. "What else am I suppose to think? You've done nothing but lie to me since we first met, and every time someone's tried to kill me, you've been close by. Do you expect me to take your word as the gospel?"

The sharp reminder of his duplicity made him shove her aside. Moving to the edge of the work tent, he wrapped his hand around a wood pole.

"I should have told you from the beginning who I was. It's a mistake I've paid for ten times over." He gritted his teeth as he realized how harsh that payment had been.

"Why didn't you?"

Her quiet question made him turn around to face her. "I couldn't afford to lose your trust once we set out for Khatana-Qantir. I had to keep you safe."

"But don't you see? It's your lies that made me *not* trust you." Disappointment glimmered in her hazel eyes, and the sight of it sent tension streaking through him. He was responsible for her disillusion, and it twisted his insides with regret.

"And is that the *only* reason why you've refused to have anything to do with me for these past several weeks?"

"Yes."

For a moment, he wasn't certain he'd heard her correctly. He simply stood there and absorbed the significance of her response. His Bedouin ancestry didn't matter to her. She hadn't rejected him for that reason. Slowly, he moved to stand directly in front of her. Jasmine.

The scent she'd taken to using since their arrival in Khatana-Qantir. He breathed in the fragrance, his body already attuned to hers.

"Do you trust me now?"

"No...yes...I don't know." She sighed with confusion.

His mouth curled slightly as he brushed a strand of brown hair behind her ear. She trembled at the touch, but didn't resist as he pulled her into his arms. As he folded her into his embrace, she fought to control the emotions raging inside her. It was impossible to do.

Hard, sinewy muscles pressed pleasurably into her back, while beneath her fingers she could feel the strength of his heart beating against his solid chest. The sensation made her pulse rate double in speed, making it difficult to breathe.

"Answer me this, *ana anide emîra*. What Mazir has done everything in his power to protect you? Keep you safe?" His husky voice rasped over her skin, and the intoxicating sound made her drag in a ragged breath.

"Y...you have."

"And who has done everything he could to help you grant your father's last wish?" The pad of his thumb rubbed across her bottom lip. It made her want to plead with him for a kiss.

"You."

"Correct, and I'm the last Mazir who would ever think to harm you. Do you want to know why?"

She swallowed quickly and nodded.

The corners of his mouth tipped upward slightly, and his brown eyes glowed with a possessive gleam. "Because my body craves you like the desert craves water. I can't forget the feel of you, your scent or the intense pleasure I experience when I'm buried deep inside you. Because if something happened to you, my body would find existing unbearable."

Her legs wobbled under her. Dear Lord, with just a few softly spoken words the man had made her slick with desire. She wet her lips with the tip of her tongue, and he sucked in a quick breath. A second later, his mouth captured hers.

The heat of his kiss parted her lips in a small gasp, and his tongue swept into her mouth, swirling around hers. Desire simmered in her veins as she slid her hands into his thick hair. Oh God, how she'd missed the taste of him.

He smelled wonderful. The spicy masculine scent of him pitched her desire to a new level of intensity. God she wanted him. She'd missed his touch, the hardness of his body beneath her hands.

Arms wrapped around his neck, she clung to him in a wanton state of arousal. Hunger crashed through her, and she thrust her hips against him, pressing into him with a gentle swivel of her body. His phallus hardened beneath the seductive move. The groan rumbling in his throat sent a shudder through her, and she slid her hands to his chest, then downward to where her fingers could lightly brush over the hard length of him.

Another groan ripped through him as his mouth frantically sought hers in a kiss that burned her lips. Beyond thought or care, she stroked him again with a demanding touch. His lips broke away from hers to sear fire across her cheek and then neck.

"I want you." The moment her words whispered between them, he froze. Lifting his head, he cupped her face in his hands, his eyes dark with need.

"And you shall have me, *emîra*, but not now. Tonight, when I can take my time with your beautiful body." His hot gaze swept over her, and she clung to him for fear of falling. "For now, I need to get back to the men. I only came to find out if you wanted them to begin digging in another section since they've not had any luck where they are at the moment."

Brushing his lips across hers in a quick kiss, he pushed her away from him. She struggled to keep from swaying as his strong arms left her bereft of support. The logical part of her brain was screaming in outrage at her traitorous body's desire to throw herself back into his arms. It demanded to know how she could let a few heady kisses erase the lies he'd told her.

She shut off the protests in her head. For once she was going to let her heart rule her head. She loved him. His reaction to Uncle Jeffrey's warning told her enough. He'd been angry because she'd kept the note from him. Concern for her safety had driven his anger, not deception. She darted a glance up at him, flushing at the tender amusement on his face. He stroked her cheek with one finger.

"Where shall we look now, *emîra*?"

"Umm, yes. Let me look at my chart." Cursing her earlier temper tantrum, she sifted through paperwork, looking for her excavation grid. As she pulled the meticulously prepared drawing out from under one of the paper stacks, a faint cry went up behind them.

Altair turned toward the sound and walked to the edge of the tent. Below them on the plateau, under which Per-Ramesses lay, a man stood waving his arms madly. Stepping out into the sunlight, Altair answered the man with a wave of his own.

"Come, *emîra*. They've found something." His hand grasping hers, he picked up her wide-brimmed hat and jammed it onto her head. With a gentle tug, he pulled her out into the sunshine and down the hill toward his horse.

"How do you know? What if someone's hurt or sick?"

"If it was an emergency, they would have shot off a round as a general distress call. They've found something. I'm sure of it."

Not daring to hope, Alex tried to keep her balance as he dragged her down the sandy hill at a fast pace. Reaching the ravine that separated the city from the rest of the land, they scrambled into the shady section of the gully. A beautiful black Arabian mare waited quietly in the shade, and with a quick jump, Altair was seated in the saddle. He offered her his hand, and the touch of his strong fingers gripping hers warmed her entire body. Pulling herself up behind him, she wrapped her arms around his waist. With her cheek resting against his back they galloped off through the gully toward the rear of the city.

"Why are you going this way?"

"If we take the west trail to the plateau, it will take longer. I found another path that runs up to where the men are. It's narrow, but Desari won't have any problem getting up there."

Deep affection for the animal echoed in his voice. In the past two months, she'd seen how passionate Bedouins were about their animals. Every night after dinner, the family rolled up one side of the tent to visit with their horses. The animals were a part of the family, and love between owner and horses was always evident.

Now she found herself wishing she could invoke a similar emotion in Altair. Although his desire for her was more than obvious, it didn't mean he loved her. That was something she could only hope would come with time.

As Desari charged up the narrow trail to the top of the plateau, rocks slipped underneath the animal's hooves and tumbled down into the gully. One glance over the edge of the incline made her stomach lurch before she turned her head away. When they were topside, she breathed a sigh of relief. It took only a few more moments for them to reach the men gathered around a hole in the side of a large mountainous section of the plateau. As they slid to a stop, the men broke out into a wild cacophony of excited shouts.

Without waiting on Altair, she jumped to the ground and hurried forward. What had they found? From their excitement, she could tell the men thought it important. Pushing through their thin ranks, she stopped in front of the hole.

The air whooshed out of her lungs at the sight in front of her. Stunned, she slowly sank to her knees and stared at the exposed portions of two wide columns bordering a yawning black hole. Leaning forward, she pulled a small brush from her pants pocket. With a light touch, she dusted away the sand still obliterating her view of the columns' symbols.

The hieroglyphics were not difficult to read and she tried to breathe. She'd found it. It was the palace. Her hand trembled as she retraced the markings to make sure it was real. A tremor shot through her as she closed her eyes. She bent her head as a shuddering sob of joy whipped through her. She'd done it. She'd done what no other *man* had been able to do. She'd found Ramesses' palace, and next she would find Nourbese's tomb.

Dragging in a deep breath, she rose to her feet, stumbling as she did so. The magnitude of it washed over her. The sweet joy of accomplishment, the validation of ten years' worth of work and study. Still, it was bittersweet. Her father and uncle were not here to share in the moment. A tear trailed down her cheek. She tried desperately to stem the tide of her release but couldn't. Strong arms drew her into a warm, protective embrace, and she pressed her forehead against his chest.

"You did it, Alex. You beat them all. Your father and uncle would have been very proud of you." His fingers caught her chin and lifted her head so she was looking up into his eyes. A gleam of tenderness warmed her heart. "I'm proud of you, *emîra*."

She gulped at the heartwarming compliment. "Thank you."

"Now then, what do you want to do?"

"Celebrate!" She choked out a laugh.

He grinned down at her before turning his head toward the waiting men. "*iHtafal, iSHâb, iHtafal.*"

A loud cry of excitement welled out of the men, and Alex laughed again through a renewed onset of tears. Happiness had never seemed so sweet. For the first time in her life, she felt lucky. She'd found Per-Ramesses and the palace, she was in the arms of the man she loved and tonight—tonight she would taste heaven once more.

Chapter Sixteen

The cool night air caressed her skin as Alex sipped warm camel's milk from her wooden cup. It was interesting how the women ate their meal on one side of the fire circle, while the men sat opposite them. Earlier, when she'd said they should celebrate, she'd had no idea the Mazir would put on such a wonderful party. The sound of music filled the air, and she found her foot tapping in time to the fascinating rhythm of the instruments the musicians were using. The stringed harmonies of the *al'ud* and the rhythmic drumbeat of the *tablah* were sounds as ancient as the palace that lay buried not too far away.

Beside her, Altair's mother, Gameela, clapped her hands as they watched several tribesmen spring up from their seats to dance to the infectious music of the *al'ud* and *tablah.* The celebration was in full swing, and she watched as one of the men left the dancers to pull Altair to his feet.

Laughter curved his mouth, and her heart skipped a beat at the beautiful sight. She couldn't take her eyes off him as he danced with his people. His raw sensual nature made the hair on her arms stand up on end. He was magnificent to watch.

"My son is as handsome as his father." Gameela's voice made Alex jump.

"How did you meet Altair's father?"

A wistful smile curved Gameela's mouth. "I was in Cairo with my father. A runaway horse almost ran us down, but Peter saved us. My father was impressed with him right away."

"And you?"

"I was lost from the first moment he smiled at me. Except

210

for Nourbese, it was unheard of for a Mazir to marry outside the tribe, but my father knew how much I loved Peter. When he gave his permission, I thought I would live a thousand lifetimes of happiness, but I was wrong."

Gameela's face twisted in pain as she looked into the blazing fire. Alex touched her on the arm in a gesture of sympathy. The grief on the older woman's face was something she understood so well.

"If it troubles you, we needn't speak of it any more."

With a nod of her head, Gameela patted Alex's hand. "I'm fine. Although it was many years ago, to me it feels like yesterday. Altair was only two when Peter went to visit his father. He pleaded with me to come, but I had no wish to leave the desert. His ship sank off the coast of Spain."

"Oh, Gameela, I'm so sorry."

"Thank you. My hardest moments are when I wish Peter were here to see what a wonderful son we have." The Bedouin woman blinked quickly. "But this is a night for rejoicing, not sad memories."

Accepting the woman's silent request to end the discussion, Alex returned her attention to the fire and the dancers. From where she sat, she watched the intricate steps the dancers made as they circled the campfire.

"I am pleased you have resolved your differences with Altair."

"I...I'm not sure I know what you mean." Alex's hand trembled as she took another sip of the sweet milk in her cup.

"Don't you?" The older woman smiled serenely at her. "I am pleased my son has found a woman who loves the man and not his background."

Coughing on the drink she'd taken, Alex stared at the woman for a long moment then looked away. Gameela's eyes were far too observant. Was her love for Altair so blatant? Did he know she was in love with him? Oh God, she wouldn't be able to bear it if he knew and didn't love her in return. She looked back at Gameela as the woman heaved a sigh.

"You are as stubborn as Altair. Listen to me, *zuRaiyar waHda*—since childhood Altair has struggled to find his place in the world. There have been times when I despaired for the pain he's suffered. A pain I've inflicted on him."

"Oh, surely not."

"No, it is true. My blood runs in his veins, and for that he is ridiculed and treated with disdain in England." Gameela waved a hand as Alex started to protest. "I have my sources, and I've seen the pain in his eyes each time he knows he must leave the warmth of our family and return to that cold island."

"But if he's unhappy there, why does he go back?"

"Because he is an honorable man." The beautiful Bedouin woman turned her gaze back to her son. "He gave an oath to his English grandfather that he would remain in England at least six months a year to tend to his title and holdings."

Alex breathed in a breath of surprise. "He never told me."

"None of that matters now. He has found a woman who sees his heart and nothing else. That is a love worth keeping. I believe he has feelings for you, but as I said, he is quite stubborn. He won't admit he cares for you until he is certain of your love."

Alex nodded, uncertain how to reply. Could she really risk opening her heart to him, not knowing whether he loved her or not? If Gameela was wrong, the devastation such a confession would wreak could possibly destroy her. She stared out at the dancers. A group of women had replaced the dancing men; and across the fire's flames, her eyes met Altair's.

He sat on the sand with one arm resting on a bent knee. It was the pose of a man born to command, born to rule. The possessive spark in his deep brown eyes sent a shiver of anticipation through her. His look said she was his. A thrill of delight cascaded through her, and she wet her dry lips. As she did so, his bronzed face took on a look of dark desire. Her breathing came fast and furious as he caressed her with his gaze across the blue and yellow flames of the campfire.

Suddenly, someone grasped her wrist and pulled her to her feet. Startled, she recognized one of the female dancers. The woman motioned for Alex to join them. Embarrassed, she shook her head no and tried to pull away. Laughing, Gameela encouraged her.

"Go on, Alex. Tonight is a celebration of your accomplishments. Follow Jasmin's steps, she will help you."

Several of the men let out a loud cry, and her gaze found Altair's again. Amusement curved his mouth, and he arched a challenging eyebrow at her. He didn't think she was game enough to do it. Well, the man was in for a surprise. She'd vaguely been watching the women as their long dark tresses flew through the air or served as a curtain to cover the faces of a man they chose.

It was a dance of seduction, and she intended to turn Altair's look of challenge into one of complete and total need. She answered the unspoken dare with a look of audacious determination. Slowly she removed the pins holding her hair in place. As her hair tumbled down past her shoulders, a loud cheer went up around the campfire amid a large amount of laughter.

Altair, however, wasn't laughing. If anything, he seemed stunned by her actions. She smiled. He'd thought she'd refuse. The knowledge made her laugh as she looked at Jasmin and imitated the other girl's steps. Another girl danced into place on the other side of her, and the three of them joined hands, their arms lifted over their heads.

For a brief moment, she wished she had on one of the colorful robes Jasmin and the other girl wore. Then her eyes locked with Altair's again, and she saw him swallow hard as they danced closer toward his side of the fire. Following Jasmin's lead, Alex threw her head forward, her hair just touching the sand before she rolled her head in a circular motion so her hair twirled in front of her. She snapped herself upright, brown hair flying back, and sought out Altair's face once more.

He was completely enthralled. His expression glazed with desire. Smiling, she continued to mimic the steps Jasmin and the other girl made as the three of them danced around the fire. Arms extended, they swayed their bodies and hips in a slow, seductive manner. Their dance steps holding them in place where they were, Alex watched the girl beside her. The dancer leaned forward and draped her long black hair over the head of the man facing her.

Alex hesitated as she looked down at the handsome young Bedouin grinning up at her shamelessly. Glancing toward Jasmin again, she watched the other girl shimmy forward to drape her hair over the man she'd chosen. A loud roar of

213

approving laughter tugged her attention back to the young man in front of her. She missed a step as she saw Altair taking the young man's place.

Dancing forward, she flung her hair over his shoulders. A wild storm of desire flared in his eyes as she smiled down at him. Deliberately, she wet her lips. The action pulled a rough growl from his throat, and she laughed as she started to pull away.

He quickly reached up and wrapped several locks of hair around his wrist to hold her in place. "Tonight, *emîra*. Tonight, I'll make you understand that you're mine, and no other man shall have you."

Astonished, she could only stare at him. As he released her hair, she straightened and danced away from him. Following Jasmin's lead, she danced back to her seat. As the music changed, another group of dancers sprang to life, and Alex sank down onto the blanket covering the sand. Laughing, Gameela leaned toward her.

"He has claimed you as his, *zuRaiyar waHda*. That is a start."

She bit back a smile as Gameela called her *little one* once more, then shook her head in confusion. "What do you mean?"

"He pushed another man aside to claim the honor of being covered with your tresses. By his actions, he has told the tribe you belong to him."

Alex shifted her gaze in the direction of Altair. A slow smile curled his mouth as he studied her. It was a smile of seductive triumph, and it made her heart hammer against her chest at a furious pace as she anticipated what was to come.

Beside her, Gameela rose to her feet. "I am tired. Come—walk with me to my tent."

Unable to keep from grinning at the command, Alex stood up and followed the older woman as they left the campfire. There was no doubting where Altair got his authoritarian manner. Walking side by side, they moved through the camp, and Gameela turned her head toward Alex.

"You smile as though greatly amused by something."

"Actually I was thinking how much you and Altair are alike." Alex ducked her head as the woman arched her brow in a manner reminiscent of her son.

"I think I am afraid to ask which traits you think we share."

"Oh, they're not bad traits, just very similar, that's all."

"I see." Gameela halted outside her tent, turning to face Alex. The woman stared at her for a long moment before brushing a hand across her cheek. "I understand what my son sees in you, Alexandra Talbot. You are a strong woman. Strong enough to face whatever storms life may fill your path. Love him well, *zuRaiyar waHda.*"

With a gentle smile, Gameela turned and entered her tent. Left alone under the starry sky, Alex turned and walked back toward her humble dwelling. Was Altair's mother right? Did he love her? Hope lightened her heart at the possibility.

Ahead of her, a tall figure emerged from the darkness, and Alex inhaled a sharp breath of fear. Coming to an abrupt halt, she wasn't sure whether to scream or run.

"It's just me, Alex." The deep notes of Altair's voice filled her with relief.

"You frightened me," she said as she pressed her hand to where her heart pounded against her breast. "I thought..."

As he stepped out of the shadows into the moonlight, her stomach clenched at the fire blazing in his eyes. "You thought what, *emîra?*"

"I thought I was going to be attacked again."

"I've promised to keep you safe. You have to trust me," he said in a tight voice.

Despite the dim shadows she could see the frustration that crossed his face. His expression tugged at her heart. Trusting him to keep her safe was easy compared to trusting him with her heart. Heat enveloped her as he moved to stand in front of her, his hand capturing her chin.

Lethargy seeped into every muscle in her body as his thumb slid across her lower lip. As always, the deliciously spicy scent of him caressed her senses. The sound of her heartbeat thrummed in her head as a familiar pair of strong hands pulled her toward him. The strength of his arms reminded her that a Pharaoh's blood flowed through his veins.

Even if she'd wanted to, resisting him would be as impossible as asking the sands not to shift with time. The moment his mouth took hers in a heated kiss, she melted into him. All the pent-up yearning over the past several weeks filled her response to his kiss. Wrapped tightly in his arms, she knew there was no other place she wanted to be.

Lifting his head, he cupped her face in his large hands. "Tell me, *emîra*, what would you have done if I'd not taken Yusuf's place at the fireside?" There was a rough edge to his voice.

"I don't know. Did I do something wrong?" Puzzled, she blinked up at him.

"Do you mean to tell me you don't know the significance of the hair dance?"

"No, your mother encouraged me to dance, so I did."

A low growl escaped him, and with the smooth grace of a leopard, he swept her up into his arms and carried her toward her tent.

"My mother interferes where she shouldn't," he said gruffly. "It's a mating dance. Young women drape their hair over the man of their choice, and the man in turn knows the woman will not reject his suit."

"Oh." His words pulled the wind right out of her. She'd almost given another man the right to court her. But Altair had deliberately taken the man's place. The memory of his possessive action thrilled her. He cared. But how deep were his feelings for her? Would he trust her with his heart?

"So tell me, *emîra*. Were you trying to tell me something tonight?"

"Yes." She nuzzled the side of his neck.

"And are you going to tell me what?" He bent slightly as he pushed his way past the flap of her tent. She tipped her head back to study his handsome face. There was an imperial tilt to his sensual mouth, and she smiled. The small lantern she always used had been lit, and the regal lines of his dark features were softened in the low light.

"I've already told you once."

Setting her down on her feet, he brushed his mouth across hers in a soft kiss. When he moved away, her body ached with disappointment. Removing his utility belt, he tossed it aside then turned to face her. Hands on his hips, he arched an eyebrow in her direction.

"And what was it you told me?"

"That I want you." Her words rushed out of her, and the heat flooding her cheeks told her they were bright red. Silence filled the tent, and she looked down at the carpet as she waited for him to say something.

"I want you too, *emîra*." The deep richness of his voice enveloped her, and she jerked up her head to find him watching her with the same look of desire she'd seen on his face at the campfire. She took a step toward him, but he raised his hand. Halting immediately, she marveled at how easily he could control her. Whatever he asked her to do, she would, if only to please him.

"Undress for me, *emîra*."

That hadn't been quite what she expected. Swallowing her embarrassment, her fingers trembled as she reached for the buttons of her shirt. His eyes watched her like a hawk as first one button and then another came undone. A gentle heat suffused her skin, and she dropped her gaze beneath his passionate stare. Slowly she removed her shirt and it fell out of her hand to flutter to the floor.

Her chemise clung to her skin, and she knew her nipples were hard with desire. They tingled with the frisson hanging in the air. She raised her gaze to his. Bending over, she removed her boots. As she tugged off her sturdy socks, she grimaced. These were far from sensuous or alluring.

Upright once more, her fingers fumbled nervously with the buttons of the male trousers she wore. Grasping the cotton material along with the silk of her drawers, she slid the garments past her hips. As she stepped out of them and straightened, she heard him inhale a sharp breath. Her chemise fell just past her stomach, leaving her fully exposed to his eyes.

"The chemise, *ana anide emîra*. Let me look at all of you." The hoarseness of his voice made her quiver. Crossing her arms, she pulled the silk undergarment over her head and stood naked in front of him. Her eyes studied the pattern in the carpet, afraid to meet his gaze.

"Do you have any idea how beautiful you are, *emîra*?"

His words surprised her. Looking up, she watched as he removed his clothing. The muscles in his arms and chest

217

rippled as he stood before her. Sleek and powerful, he was a pharaoh come to life. Her gaze roamed over his bronzed muscular chest then down to where his hard arousal jutted out from the apex of his thighs. Her heart skipped a beat as he watched her with his eagle-eyed gaze.

"You haven't answered me, *ana gamâl*. Do you not know how beautiful you are?"

She shook her head. Again, he'd called her his beauty. How could he possibly find her beautiful? She thought herself passably attractive, but beautiful, no. Her lips were too full, her hair and eyes were ordinary, while her figure was much fuller than the women society always held up as ideal.

"Well, *ana gamâl*, don't you believe me?"

"No."

Surprise darkened his face. "*No?*"

"No."

He moved toward her, and she trembled as his hand slid down her cheek to cup her chin and his thumb caressed her lower lip.

"Since you don't believe me, it seems I have no choice but to demonstrate how beautiful you are, *emîra*."

Gently, he pulled her toward the red, green, gold and blue pillows strewn about the woven carpeted floor. As he guided her down into the silk cushions, he kissed the palm of her hand before trailing his mouth along the inside of her wrist. It was a blissful sensation.

"Your skin is lovely, *ana gamâl*. Softer than silk." The husky note in his voice ignited a flame in her middle. It eased its way into her limbs, and a lethargic pleasure took hold of her. She wanted to stay like this forever. Listening to his beguiling words, enjoying the delight of his mouth against her skin.

With the back of his hand, he traced the outer line of her breasts. The feather-light caress teased her senses. Dear Lord, she wanted his mouth on her again. As he cupped one breast, he leaned forward. Delicious expectation rose in her throat.

The spicy scent of him teased her senses as she slid her hands up over his muscular arms. His mouth came closer, and she held her breath. Waiting for his mouth to close over her. God, she wanted his touch. She needed him so desperately.

Eyes fluttering shut, she inhaled a quick breath of anticipation. An instant later he blew a warm breath over her taut nipples. Startled, her eyes flew open to meet a brown gaze dark with mischief.

"These are beautiful breasts, *emîra*. And I love watching you while I suck on you."

The seductive words fired her cheeks with color. He smiled broadly. Still watching her, he lowered his mouth and suckled her nipple. His touch made her arch upward as her nipples tightened with intense need. The caress sent desire spiraling through her limbs and into the lower half of her body. Oh God, she never wanted this to end.

His mouth had the ability to render her senseless with pleasure, and the more he touched her the more she wanted. Her fingers stroked through his silky brown hair, pulling him closer as his tongue teased and flicked its way around her nipple in a wicked dance of seduction. The touch of his hands on her belly tugged a moan from her as his mouth followed the caress of his hands.

"You smell like jasmine and the sultry heat of the desert, *ana gamâl*. How could I not find you beautiful?" His mouth seared its way over her skin as he feathered her stomach with kisses. Sweet heaven, she was already wet, and her body craved more of his touch. She shivered as his mouth trailed down the side of her hip. Did he know what delicious torment this was? She wanted to feel him inside her again—filling her, expanding her until she shuddered with the same mind-numbing pleasure he'd given her before.

"Your hips are tempting curves that hint of the treasures below." His mouth nibbled on the inside of her thigh, and she moaned. Now. She needed him now. Her hands grabbed his broad shoulders, and she pulled on him to show him she needed him inside her. A laugh tickled her inner thigh.

"Not yet, *emîra*. I haven't yet finished telling you how beautiful you are." His teeth gently nipped at her thigh again. "Here, do you feel this, *ana gamâl*? Do you feel the beauty I can see?"

She could barely nod her head as his finger parted her slick folds and stroked her. Her eyes fluttered shut in delight. A moment later, his mouth settled on her sex. Stunned, she bucked beneath the touch, her hands clutching at his shoulders.

"Oh. My. God."

She'd never experienced anything so wildly wicked in her entire life. If this was sin, then she'd gladly go to hell if only he wouldn't stop. As his lips parted her wet slit, his tongue swirled around the sensitive nub between her folds. Her hips arched upward at the incredible sensations enfolding her skin.

Vibrant colors crashed against her closed eyelids as each nip or stroke of his tongue tightened the coil of need inside her. The intimate touch of his mouth melted her insides as her fingertips dug into his shoulders.

"Oh God, *yes!*"

Shudder after shudder assailed her body as she succumbed to his sinful caresses. She spiked her hands through his hair as she trembled with a release that left her limp. As her tremors eased, his mouth shifted from her sex to the inside of her thigh, lightly nipping her flesh.

"Do you believe me now, *ana gamâl?* You're a beautiful woman."

Unable to speak, she simply nodded. He slid up the length of her, his lips trailing heat across her skin as he did so. As his mouth brushed across her shoulder, he stroked one of her nipples with his thumb. The touch made her sigh softly. Everywhere he touched her pleased her beyond belief. She wanted to please him too.

She remembered how much he enjoyed her touching him. Her fingers caressed the hard muscles of his hip, before they edged their way to his inner thigh. The ragged sound of his breathing increased as her fingers brushed over his erection.

Enclosing him in her hand, she smiled. Her touch excited him. She could hear it in the way his breathing hitched as the pad of her thumb circled the rim of his erection. A slick bead of desire smeared against her skin. So powerful and strong in her hand, and yet smooth, almost velvety against her fingers.

She slid her thumb over the cap and down to the heavy lip of his phallus. Gently she rubbed the ridge just below the cap. He inhaled a sharp breath at the touch. Pleasure skidded through her as she realized how much he liked the way she was touching him. She wanted to explore every inch of him, touch him, kiss him, just as she'd read in the Erotic Papyrus of Turin.

Again, she repeated the caress, and he groaned. Closing her hand around him more tightly, she stroked him slowly at first, then with increasing speed. A deep growl of pleasure rumbled in his chest as he rolled onto his back, giving her free access to his hard length.

God, but the woman had no idea what she did to him. His cock continued to jump with every stroke of her hand and each flick of her thumb against his sensitive flesh. Eyes closed, his muscles tightened with intense pleasure as she slid her hand up and down his erection.

The friction from the palm of her hand burned him with a fire that threatened to engulf him. He wanted her. He wanted her in every possible position he could imagine. Even then, it wouldn't be enough. She was a part of him. The scent and taste of her forever embedded inside him.

Ready to spring up and drive himself into her, he froze as her hot tongue swirled around his staff. The shock and pleasure of her touch held him rigid. A second later as her lips closed around him, he arched upward into her mouth with a guttural cry of delight. God, she was incredible. Her teeth edged over him as she sucked on him.

"Yes, *ana gamâl.* Christ Jesus. Suck me."

Her tongue flicked over him in quick, intense movements as she eased him in and out of her mouth at a quick pace. The intensity of the pleasure her mouth generated in him made his ballocks tighten. God help him, he was going to spill his seed if she didn't stop. His hands stroked her hair, and he struggled to speak as she continued the maddening caresses of her tongue.

Did she know what she was doing to him, or was she simply moving on instinct? He didn't care. Her beautiful mouth had thrown him into a state of unadulterated pleasure, and he didn't want it to end. Once more, her tongue probed the tip of him, and he groaned. She had to stop. He wouldn't last much longer at this rate. His hands reached for her when her mouth tightened on him and she plunged down to his ballocks. The resulting friction etched its way sharply through his body, and his hands slammed down into the pillows at his side as he cried out. God Almighty. No woman had ever sucked on him like this. With increasing speed, her mouth rocked over him. Tension filled his body as he struggled to keep from coming in her mouth.

"*Damm gahannam.* Alex, you have to stop," he said hoarsely as he reached out to touch her head. Instead of releasing him, she increased the pressure around him, her teeth grazing over the sensitive vein of his cock. The pressure building inside him was quickly reaching a breaking point. With great effort he struggled up out of the fog blinding him. Christ Jesus, he was going to come.

"For the love of God, Alex. I—" As her lips clutched him tightly, he came in her mouth. White heat surged out of him as his cock erupted between her lips. Stunned he pulsed in her mouth as the pleasurable sensation of her swallowing his seed sent his senses reeling. With each throbbing beat, she drank every drop. He shuddered. How in the hell had she known such an act would please him? She slowly released him from her mouth. All the while, her tongue lapped at him, licking and swirling around him.

She pressed a kiss to his stomach as she sat up and stared down at him. There was a look of satisfaction on her face, and he blew out a breath of awed disbelief. Spent from the depth of his pleasure, he brushed his hand over her breasts. The warmth of her curves melted into him as she lay down beside him. Incredible. That's what she was. Absolutely incredible. She'd pleasured him unlike any other woman before her. His fingers played with her golden-brown hair. The tresses were like a young hawk's feathers. The warmth of her curls caressed the back of his hand like the finest silk.

"Did I please you?" she whispered.

He expelled another breath of disbelief. "Beyond words, *emîra.* Beyond words."

A sigh of relief escaped her as she pressed a kiss against the top of his shoulder. "I thought you might think it wicked of me to please you in that way."

"I like it when you're wicked." He chuckled, relaxing into the balmy heat of her. "Although I must confess to finding your knowledge a bit surprising."

"I've read the Erotic Papyrus of Turin." A slight hint of guilt filled her voice.

Turning his head, he stared at her in amazement. "Where

the devil did you get your hands on that document?"

"Father had a copy of it hidden in his library. I shared it with Jane who explained the things I didn't understand."

"I might have known." Beneath her hand, his chest rumbled as he released a soft laugh. "You're incorrigible, *emîra*, but I cannot deny how much pleasure you gave me a few moments ago."

Dark fingers stroked her cheek as his gaze met hers. In the dark depths of his eyes there was great tenderness. Glimpsing the emotion, she rested her fingers against his cheek.

"Altair, why did you think your Bedouin heritage would revolt me?"

The question made him stiffen, and he looked away from her. She'd raised painful memories for him. She could see it in the taut line of his sensual mouth. Remorse made her feather a kiss against his shoulder. Silence hung between them for a long time, and she nestled her head in the dip of his shoulder. His unwillingness to discuss the matter disappointed her, but she knew better than to persist with her questioning. Cradled against his side, she contented herself with simply being in his arms.

"When I was much younger, I fell in love with a woman named Caroline." The quiet confession surprised her as she watched his chest drag in a deep breath. "I asked her to marry me and she accepted."

Silence filled the air again and she waited patiently. She could tell it was difficult for him to talk about the matter.

"Against her parents' objections, we announced our engagement. At first, little changed, but then the social cuts and snubs started. Soon the numerous invitations Caroline was accustomed to dwindled away until none came at all."

He stopped speaking, and she watched the muscle in his cheek twitch as he clenched his jaw into a tense line.

"One evening, in an effort to lift her spirits, I surprised her with a trip to the theater. From the moment we arrived, the snide comments directed at her were overt and vicious. I was accustomed to the slurs, but it devastated Caroline. It pushed her over the edge, and she denounced me then and there, breaking our engagement."

The harsh rasp of his voice made it clear how deep Caroline's betrayal had been. Society's scorn must have been difficult enough for him, but to have the woman he loved denounce him in public could only have been devastating.

Such a terrible betrayal would most certainly have made him leery of trusting anyone. Especially women. She could now understand why he'd not told her who he really was. All the reasons for hiding the truth from her had been motivated by a lack of trust and a fear of scorn. Misleading her about who he was and his connection to her father had been a self-preservation measure. He'd had no reason to trust her. With a gentle touch, she stroked the side of his cheek.

"I'm sorry I thought you were the Mazir in my uncle's warning. I should have known better."

Tenderness flitted across his face as he stared down at her. The expression made her heart leap with happiness. Time would tell whether he would come to trust her enough to share his heart with her. She caressed his face as a sleepy yawn parted her lips. Brushing her hair away from her forehead, he kissed her brow as she snuggled against him and another yawn escaped her.

The quiet apology was a balm to the wounds he seldom allowed himself to feel. It thawed a part of him that he'd never expected to feel again. She yawned for a third time, and he smiled at the sound.

"Sleep, *emîra*." Gently, he rolled them over so they faced each other. Her hazel eyes drooped and another yawn rounded her mouth.

"You promise to wake me?"

"Wake you for what?" He grinned as her hand punched at him in a sleepy move, and she protested with an inaudible response. "Sleep, *emîra*. For I have every intention of waking you."

He watched as her breathing slowed and she drifted off to sleep. After more than two months, she was once again in his arms. But would she stay here?

She'd read that Coptic warning and thought it was him. She'd thought him capable of hurting her. Could he really blame her? He'd lied to her, and he'd seen the look of fear on her face when he'd gotten angry.

The sound of her soft breathing made him tighten his arms around her. She was so precious to him. If something happened to her—he didn't want to think about it. Nothing was going to happen to her. He'd see to that.

Tomorrow he would tell Alex about Mohammed. She needed to know all of his suspicions about the man. He couldn't wait for Medjuel to do something about the traitor. While no one had tried to harm her since that night in the oasis, it didn't mean the danger no longer existed.

He didn't know how or why, but something told him the discovery of the palace had raised the odds of someone trying to hurt her. Closing his eyes, he tightened his arms around her. Whatever it took, he'd keep her safe. He wasn't going to let anything happen to her. He couldn't. Without her—life was meaningless.

Chapter Seventeen

He was blind. Not even a thin line of light punctured the darkness. He waited. For what he didn't know, but he waited. Then it came—a rush of sound that engulfed him like a huge wave. The stone. It was moving. He had to stop it. He couldn't let it close. He leapt forward, but the stone settled into place with a deadly thud.

"Altair."

Jerking upright, he stared around the dimly lit tent in confusion. Where was he? A gentle hand touched his arm. Alex. He was in Alex's tent. He dropped back into the pillows with an inward sigh of relief. It had been a dream. Only a dream.

"You were talking in your sleep." She snuggled into his side, one arm wrapped around him as if to ward off evil.

"Was I?" He didn't want to think about the nightmare. Fear wasn't something he was accustomed to, but dread slithered through him at the finality of the dream.

Overhead, a small slit in the tent roof told him it was almost dawn. He needed to go, but Alex's warm body made him linger. He wasn't going to leave until he had some reassurance she wouldn't retreat from him as she had the last time.

"Alex." He tipped her chin up so he could look into her sleepy eyes. "I don't want to go, but I must."

She opened her eyes wide and studied him for a moment. "Why?"

"I've told you before. I don't wish to offend the tribe."

"No, I mean why don't you want to leave me?"

The question stole his breath. What could he say without

making a commitment he wasn't ready to offer yet? The way her eyes watched him clenched his heart. Her expression asked for nothing, but he could read the hope in her gaze. Unable to give her what she wanted, he lightly stroked his finger down the length of her nose.

"Because leaving you is like kissing the moon goodbye at the break of dawn. And you are the moon to me, *emira.*"

A faint blush crested her cheeks at his words, and he winced at the disappointment he saw reflected in her eyes before she lowered her gaze. When she didn't comment, he kissed her brow then scrambled to his feet. As he pulled his gambaz on over his head, he heard her utter a cry of fear.

Startled by the sound, he tugged his clothing away from his face and looked in her direction. The horror glazing her eyes as she stared at something behind him chilled his blood. His first thought was another snake, but Zada was sitting on top of the pillows as if she hadn't a care in the world. Still, he turned his head slowly, prepared for the worst. The sight of a dark hand and arm pushed under the flap of the tent made him leap toward his utility belt and the pistol he always carried.

"Get dressed, Alex. *Now.*" The low-pitched violence in his command sent her scurrying as he stepped toward the tent exit. Stretching out his hand, he cocked his weapon as he slowly pulled aside the wool flap. A low groan echoed nearby. With a quick gesture, he threw aside the cloth doorway and flinched as he saw Medjuel lying on the ground beside Mohammed's bloodied body.

"*Damm gahannam.*" Kneeling to check the pulse of the man at his feet, he knew Mohammed was dead before his fingers touched the traitor's bloodied neck. Swiftly, he moved to his cousin's side. The Sheikh pushed himself up into a sitting position, his hand pressed against his arm. "How badly are you hurt?"

"It's a flesh wound. Nothing more." Medjuel waved him aside. "I'm only grateful I saw Mohammed when I did. He was ready to enter Miss Talbot's tent when I stopped him."

Altair frowned. Any other time he would have heard a noise. Something—anything—telling him there was trouble. Even Zada hadn't stirred. "I should have been more vigilant. I never heard a sound."

"Why would you?" Medjuel paused as if guarding his words. "Mohammed moved with great speed and stealth. I am fortunate I was able to stop him."

He'd misjudged his cousin. Medjuel had been watching Mohammed all this time. Now the man was dead. He wouldn't be able to hurt Alex anymore. He laid his hand on his cousin's shoulder.

"Thank you. Once again, you've saved Alex's life. I'm in your debt, cousin."

"I did what I had to. He was a threat to all I hold dear." Medjuel gave an abrupt toss of his head toward the dead man. Altair glanced back at the body lying in front of Alex's tent and frowned. There was a distinct edge of bitterness in his cousin's response.

That wasn't unexpected given Mohammed's betrayal, but there was something else layered in his cousin's voice. Something darker that he didn't understand. There was no time to ponder his cousin's thoughts as Alex stepped out into the early dawn air.

"Oh my God." The color drained from her face as she saw Mohammed's *gambaz* covered with blood.

"*Gahannam, damm gahannam.*" Dropping his pistol, he sprang toward her, catching her as she slid into a faint. Behind him, Medjuel groaned again as he stumbled to his feet.

"So the *shagi emīra* has a weakness after all."

"What the hell does that mean?" He threw his cousin a blistering look. Had the whole world gone mad? A man had been killed right outside of Alex's tent, and he'd not heard a sound. And all Medjuel could do was comment on Alex's tendency to faint at the sight of blood. *Why hadn't he heard anything?* And where in the hell were the guards who had been assigned to watch Alex's tent?

"It means nothing. Nothing at all." Medjuel sighed heavily. "I suggest you take Miss Talbot back into her tent. I'll have one of the men tend to Mohammed's body."

"Where are the guards I ordered for Alex's tent?"

"I'm sorry, Altair." Medjuel shook his head with regret. "I pulled the guards three nights ago. Jemal and the others have lost several sheep to the hyenas. I needed the men to guard the flock."

"You did what?" He stared at his cousin, dumbfounded. How could Medjuel have just pulled the guards without telling him? "Why didn't you tell me? I would have stood guard myself."

"I'm sorry. I meant to, it simply slipped my mind. I truly thought Miss Talbot was no longer in danger."

"Your apologies would have been meaningless if Mohammed had gotten to Alex." Furious, he swung Alex up into his arms and glared at his cousin.

Medjuel stiffened. Glancing away, he nodded his head. "I'll see that Mohammed's body is moved quickly."

"Make sure you have my mother look at that cut." Without waiting for his cousin's response, Altair reentered Alex's tent and laid her on the cushions.

On the other side of the tent wall, he heard Medjuel calling out for help. With a glance over his shoulder, he saw Mohammed's hand disappear. Thank God, his cousin had stopped the man. His gratitude wouldn't stop him from asking questions though.

His cousin had a lot to answer for. Alex was paying the tribe well for assistance with her excavation as well as protection. Returning his attention to Alex, he saw her eyes flutter. He gently stroked her brow as he met her troubled gaze.

"Altair, was that man...was he..."

"Yes, *emîra*, he's dead. Medjuel stopped him before he could enter your tent."

Another shudder ripped through her. "I...I've seen him before."

"I'm not surprised. He herded sheep with my stepfather."

"No." She shook her head. "He followed me in London."

"*What?* Why the hell haven't you mentioned this before?"

"I thought it was my imagination. I haven't seen him in the camp before."

"Damn it, Alex. When are you going to learn to trust me?" He growled with suppressed worry. Her hand trembled as she cupped his cheek, a smile of relief on her lips.

"I'm sorry, but at least the danger is past."

"Perhaps, but I don't want to take any chances. I'm going to follow your every move, *emîra*."

"That sounds like a delicious threat." The soft light in her eyes entranced him as he leaned forward.

"I never threaten, *ana anide emîra*. I only promise." He kissed her hard. Raising his head, he smiled at the soft sigh she released. "I'm sure you're eager to explore the palace, but I want you to wait here until I come back. I want to talk to Medjuel about what happened and make sure he's all right."

When she frowned, he kissed her again. "I promise I won't be long."

✧

Alex emerged from her tent more than an hour later just as the sun made its full presence known in the sky. As Zada scurried past her feet, she looked down at the ground. Both the dead man and the blood she'd seen earlier were gone, which pulled a deep sigh of relief from her. Despite Altair's strict orders to stay put, she couldn't wait. Waiting wasn't something she did well.

Besides the danger was gone, and it wasn't as if she was really disobeying him. He'd just told her to stay put; he didn't say she couldn't go somewhere else and stay put. There'd be hell to pay when she used that argument. She shrugged, and a smile tugged at her lips. The making up would be wickedly delicious.

Would things always be this wonderful between them? What if Altair tired of her? Her heart skipped a beat at the thought. She would never weary of him. In fact, she could easily become domesticated. The notion shocked her. Until she'd met Altair, she'd viewed marriage as a prison to avoid at all costs.

Well, marriage wasn't necessarily in the picture. Perhaps she was thoroughly wicked for thinking that way, but she'd come to realize that life was too short not to enjoy its pleasures. Altair hadn't said he loved her, and he'd not mentioned anything about how long their relationship might last. She wanted it to last a lifetime. But even if it didn't, she would treasure every minute of the time she shared with him.

Slinging the knapsack that held her tools and notebooks over her shoulder, she reached for the water bag hanging on the tent pole. The weight told her it was a full bag as she slipped the strap over the top of her knapsack. Altair must have filled it for her. She grinned. He'd known she wouldn't be able to wait on him to explore the palace interior.

Eagerly, she hurried to the edge of the camp, where she found the dromedary she'd been using to go back and forth to the excavation site. She smiled at the young man tending the animals as she mounted the camel. Zada sprang up into the saddle with her, curling around the pommel as Alex urged the dromedary to its feet.

Eager to reach the palace, she rode across the sand, the morning sun beginning its blazing trail up into the sky. The molten hue of purples, blues and pinks had given way to a bright yellow that already held the promise of a scorching day. As she headed toward the ravine, Zada scrambled up her arm and wrapped herself around Alex's neck. She scratched the animal's small head as they traveled.

Last night had been even more incredible than the first time she and Altair had made love. Several times through the night she'd come close to speaking her heart. But each time the idea popped into her head, she'd held back. She was still so unsure of him.

He'd made no commitments, nor had he professed anything other than desire for her. Did he really care for her in the remotest sense? Gameela was convinced that he cared for her. And what if he did love her? What then? She had no wish for a marriage that would result in her loss of freedom to pursue her studies and explorations. But somehow she didn't think Altair would expect that from her.

He was very much like her father. Not once had Altair treated her with condescension or ridicule. In fact, he'd been wonderfully supportive. The idea of being his wife filled her with pleasure. There would be long nights of passion without his leaving before the break of dawn. And children. Would he want children?

Oh, this was ridiculous. The man hadn't even expressed his feelings for her. She needed to concentrate on reaching the city. The closer she got to the city wall, the more Alex hated to think about the time it would take the camel to reach the trail down into the ravine. It meant riding at least six miles out of the way, then another mile beyond that to get to the trail Altair had used yesterday to reach the plateau. From where she sat on the dromedary, she could see the large, rock formation where the men had found the palace entrance. It was only about a mile away from here.

She hesitated for a moment before making her decision. A mile hike would be easy enough, the heat hadn't reached an intolerable level yet, and she had plenty of water. Besides, the thought of riding up the narrow path Altair had used the day before made her stomach lurch.

When those rocks had rolled off the side of the narrow path, she'd been certain his horse was going to fall. No, walking was *much* safer. Dismounting, she pulled her things off the camel's back and made her way down into the ravine. Zada chattered angrily as Alex reached the hard floor of the trench.

"All right, all right. I'll let you down."

She bent over and allowed the mongoose to scurry down her arm. After a quick survey of the wall in front of her, she found a spot that offered her a foothold. As if aware of what she was about to do, Zada scrambled up her leg onto her back then leaped up to the flat ground over Alex's head. Climbing the wall, she heard Zada chattering with what she could have sworn was encouragement. With a grunt, she pulled herself up onto the flat plateau.

Not moving for a moment, she lay still on the ground. Zada ran across her stomach to rise up on her hind legs. The quizzical look in the mongoose's eyes made her laugh, which made the animal scamper away. Standing upright, she dusted off her clothes, and took in the wide expanse before her. Ahead of her, the rocky terrain under which the palace lay rose up into the sky.

Excitement made her strike out at a quick pace, and she quickly grew hot, despite the early hour. Reaching for the water bag, she opened the goatskin flask and drank a large portion of the liquid. If she became dehydrated, it would only give Altair another reason to restrict her movements. She winced at the slightly bitter taste sliding over her tongue. Whoever thought a goatskin would keep water fresh and tasty needed their head examined. She recapped the flask, and continued toward the entrance to the palace.

She'd walked more than half a mile, when she realized she was thirsty again. Putting the goatskin flask to her lips, she took another swig, ignoring the peculiar taste of the liquid. Water was one's lifeblood in the desert, and to avoid drinking simply because she found the taste odd was courting disaster. As the sun filled the sky, the sharp rise in temperature had a lethargic effect on her.

Brushing off the sensation, she frowned. It wasn't much farther to reach the palace, and the interior would be sufficiently cool enough to help her body rehydrate. With the thought of the cool, palace interior as added incentive, she pushed on, making good time toward the palace entrance. A short time later, she stood in front of the columns she'd seen yesterday. Her hand lovingly rested against the stone pillars. They were warm from the sunlight.

Removing her wide-brimmed hat, she rubbed her temples and winced. Her head had been throbbing for the past ten minutes, and it seemed to be getting worse. A thin wave of nausea tumbled through her stomach. Damn, she needed to get out of the heat. She wasn't used to it, and she'd just hiked more than a mile in the sun-drenched desert. The way she felt she'd probably already developed a small case of heatstroke. She took a quick drink of water then pulled her candle lantern from her knapsack.

Lighting the lantern, she held it out in front of her and peered down into the hole. Satisfied she wasn't going to fall into a bottomless pit; she scooted over the edge of the hole and dropped down onto the floor. From the edge of the entrance, Zada chattered at her. Reaching up, Alex pulled the little mongoose into her arms. She ruffled the animal's fur.

"No need to get upset, I wasn't going to leave you behind. I could use the company." She set Zada on the floor as she retrieved the lit lantern and raised it over her head. The room she stood in was enormous. Pillars lined each side of the room, supporting slabs of rock that served as a roof.

Ahead of her, the darkness yawned on into cavernous depths. Icy chills of excitement curled down her spine as she moved forward. She was walking across the floor Ramesses II had trod. Her stomach lurched suddenly, but she ignored the uncomfortable sensation. Curiosity tugged her deeper into the dark depths of the palace.

Passing through the large room, she could see the numerous markings on the columns. It would take her months, years even, to decipher them all. But she had plenty of time. She walked into a wide corridor, her lantern high over her head to spread the light further.

Behind her, the entrance to the outside seemed small. The last thing she needed was to get lost inside the palace. Who knew how many passageways or dead ends there were in here? Quickly, she pulled a piece of chalk from her bag and marked her progress with a large X. She tucked the dusty marking tool into her pocket and reached into her bag for her notebook and pencil.

Marking her progress would help her find her way back more easily, but she would also save time later, if she sketched a map as she explored the palace. As she moved deeper into the interior of Ramesses' great house, she continued to ignore the protests her stomach was making.

There was far too much to look at to take a rest. She ran her hand over a wall filled with markings, but she didn't try to analyze them. There would be time for that later. Right now, all she wanted was to get a layout of the palace.

She traveled through several hallways and rooms, marking her way on the walls and in her notebook. At the end of a large corridor, she entered an enormous room, which contained what could only have served as a terrace before whatever cataclysmic disaster had buried this archeological treasure.

Even the balustrade of the patio was visible in spots against the rock and sand. Underneath her feet were giant slabs of stone. On one slab, directly inside the room's doorway, there were numerous hieroglyphs. As she knelt on the floor, Zada scurried over to her and sniffed at her hand. Absently, she petted the mongoose, then pulled out her brush and dusted away the light layer of sand covering the symbols. Her finger traced the edges of the hieroglyphs as she read the inscription.

"Let those who enter the chamber of Pharaoh serve their God with humility." Stunned, she sank back onto her heels. "Pharaoh's chamber."

Her words whispered through the darkness surrounding her. Was she in Ramesses' bedchamber or his throne room? Holding her lantern high, she studied the room and its entrances. Aside from the wide doorway she'd passed through and the terrace, there was only one other doorway.

It was Ramesses' bedchamber. She knew it. Her stomach gave a fierce lurch. Excitement, that's what it was. Excitement. Closing her eyes, she ordered her body to grow still, but the churning only grew worse. She was going to throw up. Oh, Lord, not here, not on the markings.

A corner, she needed to find a corner.

She scurried toward the nearest recess and gagged. Bile rose in her throat and she wretched violently. When she'd finished, she rinsed her mouth out and took a small sip of her water. What if she'd picked up a virus from something she'd eaten? Sanitary conditions here were not what they were at home, and so far, she'd actually been lucky not to become ill since her arrival in Egypt. Damn, she couldn't be sick, not now. There was so much to be done.

Leaning against the stone wall, she pressed her cheek into the coolness of the manmade structure. The cool stone soothed her warm skin. She'd rest a bit, let her stomach settle, then she could go back to exploring the palace. Seated in front of her, Zada clicked softly to herself, watching Alex.

"Well, what are you looking at? Haven't you ever seen someone get sick before?" The mongoose scurried forward and rubbed her back against Alex's leg. She stroked the creature's fur. "Thanks, but there's nothing you can do at the moment."

Comforted by the animal's presence, she waited for the churning to ease. Several minutes later, the nausea was still present. She didn't want to go back, but maybe it was for the best. A sharp pain flashed across her midsection, and she doubled over in response. Unable to stop herself, she threw up again. As the heaving stopped, her insides twisted painfully. Damn, of all the times to get sick she had to choose now. It could be anything.

It was all right, she could come back. No, it wasn't all right. She wanted to stay and find out more. Logic won out over her impulsive nature. She needed to go back to camp. There was quinine in her trunk for just this sort of thing.

Grunting her displeasure, she washed away the horrid taste in her mouth, then gathered her things. Grateful for the small mongoose's presence, she sighed. "Come on, Zada. We're going home."

The animal scurried along in front of her as Alex dragged herself back toward the entrance. She'd never been this sick before in her life. Another pain twisted through her, and she clutched at her stomach as if doing so would stave off the agony. Doggedly, she continued forward.

She stumbled along for quite some distance before exhaustion settled into her legs. Slowly she sank down onto the ground and rested her head against the stone wall. She needed to rest, just for a minute. Altair was going to have her head for disobeying his orders. Her stomach cramped again. The idea of putting anything into her stomach at the moment was daunting, but she was so thirsty. She took another swig from her goatskin flask. Her fingers reached into her rucksack and pulled out her notebook. When she tried to read the map she'd sketched, the drawings and words kept jumping around on the page. Shoving the thin volume back into her bag, she pushed herself to her feet.

Keep moving. She had to keep moving.

Stumbling her way back through the corridors, her hand brushed over each X she'd drawn on the walls. Wearily she congratulated herself on the forethought to mark her path through the palace. For once, she'd done something right despite her impulsive nature. Ahead of her, she saw sunlight pouring into the darkness of the palace interior.

It took her several tries to pull herself up out of the palace, but when she finally did, Zada waited for her. Weak and exhausted, she lay still in the sand, her arm covering her eyes. She must have dozed off for a moment, because Zada's chattering in her ear jarred her awake. Sitting up, she unplugged her water bag and took a sip.

The sun was high in the sky, and already the heat had made her thirsty. Damn, she was going to have to trudge back to camp in the mid-day heat. *Not very smart, Alex.* Not very smart at all. She should have gone the long way. At least then, she wouldn't have a mile walk ahead of her to where she'd left the camel. The thought of it made her stomach lurch again.

She drank deeply from the water bag. Climbing to her feet, she suddenly realized how quiet it was. Where was everyone? Maybe they were moving her work tent down here to the palace. Her stomach twisted again, and she retched where she stood, the heaves draining her energy.

When she finished, she remained bent over trying to catch her breath. She felt horrible. Why on earth hadn't she had the common sense to get sick while she was still in her tent? Already her head throbbed from the heat, and she even considered retreating into the coolness of the palace. No, she needed to get back to the camp. There was quinine there, and it would hopefully settle her stomach.

Off in the distance, she thought she saw some of the Mazir spread out in front of her in a line. Odd, why were they spread out across the sand like that? She started forward, trying to ignore the heat, her aching head and the pain in her stomach. As she walked, she drank some more water. Dehydration was the last thing she needed on top of a stomach bug. The familiar lurching started again.

When she'd finished retching, she stumbled forward, dragging one foot after another. God, she was miserable. Every inch of her ached, her head hurt, she was exhausted and all she wanted to do was lie down and go to sleep.

The heat of the sun had now grown almost unbearable. Rest. She had to rest for a moment. Sinking down into the sand, she released a mirthless sound that she recognized as an attempt at laughter. Lord Merrick had been right. The desert was no place for a woman.

Zada climbed into her lap and chattered softly. Her fingers ruffled the animal's fur as she watched the wavy line of Mazir in the distance. Wearily, she took another sip of water. The bitter taste seemed stronger, and she shuddered. Scooting the mongoose off her lap, she got to her feet. It wasn't that far to go. When she reached the men, they'd be able to help her get back to camp.

Ahead of her, the heat rose up off the surface of the sand in a shimmering wave. Through it, she saw a horse and rider racing in her direction. Sinking to her knees, she waited. Beside her, Zada chattered wildly as the horse approached them.

The thunder of hooves was a soft echo in her ears as the

world spun dizzily around her. With a detached sense of reality, she watched the black animal careen to a halt while she struggled to remain conscious. The sight of Altair's leather boots crossing the sand toward her filtered through the pain in her head. A moment later, she was engulfed in his arms.

"You little fool. What the hell did you think you were doing?" The deep note of worry in his voice softened the sharpness of his words.

He reached for her water bag and offered it to her. Pushing it away, she shook her head. She refused to drink another drop. "No."

"Damn it, Alex. You have to drink or you'll die."

Exhausted, she closed her eyes against the harsh determination in his face. She murmured a protest, but was too weak to fight him as he forced the water down her. Lying quietly in his arms, she thought her queasiness had passed.

Then in the next moment, her stomach twisted painfully inside her, the nausea overwhelming her. She feebly rolled away to retch again. The touch of his hand on her back was one of tenderness, and she could hear the concern in his voice.

"It will be all right, *ana anide emîra.* You'll feel better once we return to camp."

He lifted the water to her lips again. She gave a weak shove at the goatskin flask, but failed to stop him as he poured more of the liquid down her throat. With the last bit of strength she possessed, she pushed away from him and rejected the water he'd just given her.

"*Damm gahannam.*"

Back in his arms once more, she turned her head into his shoulder. She was so tired. All she wanted to do was sleep. If she slept, her headache might go away and maybe her stomach would stop this horrible churning.

"Don't go to sleep, *emîra.*" His hand gently patted first one cheek then the other.

She couldn't open her eyes.

"Alex, do you hear me? I want you to stay awake."

She couldn't. Not even for him could she stay awake.

Chapter Eighteen

Altair flinched when she didn't open her eyes. Perspiration layered her upper lip in a thin line, and she looked exhausted. He swallowed the knot of fear swelling his throat as he stroked her cheek with the back of his hand.

Her breathing was rapid, and fear tensed his hand at the way her pulse beat furiously against the pad of his fingers. Zada watched from a short distance away, alternating between quiet looks and soft clicking noises of what he knew could only be worry.

Once more, he lifted the water bag to her lips and trickled the liquid into her mouth. She gagged on the water, but he gently stroked her throat to help her swallow. If he didn't keep water in her, she'd be worse off than she was now. He had to get her back to camp, quickly or she might— No, he wouldn't let that happen.

He wasn't about to let her go. Once more, he eased some water into her mouth. This time she swallowed it more easily. He relaxed a small fraction, until a soft moan poured out of her. She turned her head as her stomach rejected the water he'd just poured down her. What the hell was wrong with her? The last person he'd seen this sick had died of malaria.

Ice filled his veins. With a vicious tug at his *gambaz*, he ripped off a piece of cloth and dampened it with the water. His touch light, he wiped the spittle off her lips. God, it was killing him to see her like this. He'd never felt so helpless in his entire life.

Gathering her up into his arms, he carried her back to where Desari waited quietly. Why hadn't she done as she was told? He'd specifically told her to stay in the tent until he returned for her. He should have known better. Ramesses' palace had called to her as strongly as the Sahara called to him when he was in England.

The Arabian mare blew out a warm breath of air against his cheek as he awkwardly reached for the reins and looped first one, and then the other around the pommel. When Alex was well, he was going to give her a lecture she'd never forget.

He'd warned her not to disobey him in the desert, and she'd committed a cardinal sin. She'd left camp alone and without telling anyone where she'd gone. Half the camp was looking for her at the moment. When he'd seen her dromedary sitting at the edge of the ravine, he'd feared the worst. What had made her walk to the palace instead of riding the camel?

With a low whistle, he waited as the small mare bent one leg in a deep bow. Zada didn't wait for an order, but leapt up onto the saddle and settled on the mare's rump. The horse didn't move as he threw his leg over the animal's back and settled into the saddle. At his low command, Desari's ears quivered and she lurched to her feet.

Alex murmured a protest, and he kissed her forehead. Her hat hung over his arm, the strings under her chin preventing it from falling off. Gently, he shaded her face again then picked up Desari's reins and urged the mare into a canter. He wanted to send the mare racing across the hard-packed sand, but he knew better. In this heat, the mare would drop dead from the strain. His fear escalated. What would he do if Alex died? He tightened his mouth into a grim line. She wouldn't. He wouldn't let her.

It took only a few minutes to reach the Mazir who had been scouring the sand for signs of Alex. He pulled Desari to a halt, noting her labored breathing. With a quick word, he ordered his men to return to camp. As they followed his orders, he debated whether to continue on toward the ravine or follow the men. No. Desari would be able to clear the gap, saving him the time it would take to use the paths leading in and out of the ravine. *Bloody hell!* Impulsive as usual, she'd thought to save time; that's why she'd walked. It was the only explanation that made sense. She moaned again, her tongue licking her lips in search of water. Reaching for the flask, he gave Alex a few drops of water then took a swig to ease his own parched mouth.

No sooner had the bitter taste entered his mouth than he spat it out. *Damm gahannam.* Seconds later, Alex choked up the small amount of liquid he'd given her. Lifting her water flask, he took a whiff of the liquid inside. The sickly sweet smell was faint, but it was enough to send fear slithering through his limbs. *Damn it.* Why hadn't he thought to check her water before now? Another quick swig of the water spread more of the bitter, oily taste over his tongue before he spat out the vile liquid. Ipecac.

Someone had poisoned her water with ipecac. He immediately flung the flask away from him. With a tug at the water bag attached to his saddle, he tore another strip of cloth from his *gambaz* and drenched the material with water. Gently he squeezed several drops into her mouth.

If she died, it would be his fault. Not only had he failed to keep her safe, he was the one responsible for giving someone in the tribe access to the ipecac. He'd introduced the drug to the Mazir more than two years ago when a severe case of dysentery had infected the tribe. It had saved lives, but he'd given explicit instructions on its use.

Too much was deadly. He tightened his mouth in a firm line. The cloth he held was still damp, and he wet her mouth again. She parted her lips as he squeezed water from the cloth.

"That's it, *emîra.* Just a little at a time."

With a nudge of his heel, he urged Desari into a canter. As the small mare rapidly closed the distance between them and the ravine, Altair continued to glance down at Alex. Each time he did so, he feared she might have stopped breathing. As they came to the gap they needed to cross, the mare pranced to a halt. Clucking softly to Desari, he rode the edge of the gap for several hundred yards, but the gap didn't narrow.

Damn, he hadn't realized how wide the gap really was. He was asking too much of the little mare. He came to a halt, his heart wrenching in his chest as he tried to focus and make a decision. It was quite possible Desari wouldn't clear the jump. The horse had more heart than any animal he'd ever owned, but with two riders on her back she might not clear the ravine. There wasn't time to go around now. Alex needed medical attention right away. If she died— He would have to trust that Desari's heart was big enough to carry the three of them over the gap. Wheeling the mare away from the edge of the wall, he cantered her back several hundred yards before turning around. The Arabian snorted and tossed her head, then leaped forward as he nudged her side with a light touch of his heel.

They pounded across the desert floor directly toward the gap. Just as they reached the edge of the drop off, the horse gave a tremendous leap and sailed through the air. Seconds later, she landed on the opposite side.

As she landed, the mare lurched to one side, her left front leg taking the full impact of the large jump. He heard a loud snap splinter through the air, and the noise sent a lash of pain ripping through him. The hard landing jerked him forward, but by some miracle, he managed to remain in the saddle.

Most animals would have immediately rolled after such a landing, but Desari sank to her knees, her head tossing wildly. With Alex held tight against his chest he slid off the horse and stumbled away to a safe distance.

Sinking to his knees, he stared in stunned horror as the animal struggled and thrashed about in an effort to stand. After several attempts she collapsed back to the desert floor. How was he going to explain this to his brother? The two of them had raised Desari from birth. Kahlil would be heartbroken. Hearing a loud cry behind him, he looked over his shoulder. Kahlil and Medjuel rode toward him, and a moment later, Medjuel was at his side. The Sheikh nodded toward his horse.

"Ride Maysa back to camp, Altair. I'll take care of Desari."

The words broke through his stupor. God help him. He'd destroyed her. Swallowing a huge knot of pain in his throat, he shook his head.

"No. She's mine, I should do it." His throat ached from the hoarseness of his words. "Take Alex to my mother. Her water's been poisoned with ipecac. Mother will know what to do."

Medjuel frowned, but did not argue. Together, they walked to Maysa, and he passed Alex up into his cousin's arms. Zada chattered loudly at the action, and he scooped the little mongoose up, setting her in Alex's lap. With a twist of his reins, the Sheikh wheeled around and galloped back to camp.

The sight of his brother holding the mare's head in his lap, stroking her nose, wrapped a band of pain around his chest. He struggled to control the dark grief welling up inside him.

Arabians were beloved members of a Bedouin's family, and in his tent, Desari had always been a favorite.

He touched Kahlil's shoulder, and the boy lifted a tear-stained face to him. Closing his eyes against his brother's sadness, he swallowed his own grief. "Say goodbye, Kahlil. I can't continue to let her suffer like this."

The youth nodded and released another sob. Not looking at his brother, he drew his rifle from the saddle. His hand shook as he loaded the rounds and snapped the gun closed. The sharp click scraped at the nerves along his spine. Turning, he knelt by the animal's head and stroked her jowl.

"You saved her, Desari. I thank you for that *yâ 'aini SâHib.*" The animal snorted loudly, her eyes rolling with pain. With a quiet order, he told Kahlil to step away from the horse. He gave Desari one last caress before rising to his feet.

Stepping back, he aimed at the mare's forehead. His vision blurred, and he closed his eyes for a moment. The animal floundered again in agony. God give him strength. He took aim once more and waited for his finger to stop trembling on the rifle's trigger. He couldn't afford to miscalculate otherwise Desari would suffer more. A moment later, the rifle's gunfire exploded in his ear and the mare went still. Sinking to his knees, he pressed his forehead against the hot barrel of the rifle, reeling from the grief at losing the beloved animal.

✧

Altair came to a halt outside Alex's tent. The sides of the tent wall were rolled up to allow what little breeze there was to pass through the dwelling. Alex lay on a pallet inside, while several women hovered over her, fanning her with small towels and cooling her body with damp cloths.

Gripping one of the poles that supported the tent, he inhaled a deep breath to suppress the fear coursing through him. From where he stood, he watched his mother brush her hand across Alex's brow. He cleared his throat, and she looked up.

The grimness of her expression marred the beauty of her creamy, caramel-colored skin. His heart sank as she approached him.

"How is she?"

"Time will tell, but I think she will live."

The words shuddered through him. He closed his eyes as relief washed over him. Thank God. She was going to be all right. He released the breath he'd been holding in preparation for the worst.

Guilt seared him again. If he'd been more vigilant, she wouldn't be lying in her tent having narrowly escaped death. He should have known she wouldn't be able to resist going to the palace without him. If he hadn't been so determined to talk to Medjuel this morning, she wouldn't have been alone.

The vivid blue of his mother's headdress contrasted with her silver-lined black hair as she covered her head before stepping out from under the tent's shadow. Gameela sighed.

"You love her very much, don't you?"

The question swirled a knot of tension in his stomach. He wasn't even ready to reveal the extent of his feelings to Alex, let alone anyone else. All he could do was evade answering the question.

"I swore to protect her and I failed." He'd failed miserably.

"Nothing you could have done would have prevented this."

"Perhaps." Averting his gaze from the spark of curiosity in his mother's observant eyes, he cleared his throat. "But her safety was my responsibility."

"And are you responsible for Mohammed's actions or traitorous thoughts?"

"What do you know about Mohammed?" He watched the anger and disgust flashing in her cerulean eyes.

"The whole tribe knows about his fight with Medjuel this morning. And we can be grateful that you found Alex in time to save her from the man's attempt to kill her with poison as well."

He stared at her. "How do you know it was Mohammed?"

"Medjuel told me he'd found an empty bottle of ipecac in Mohammed's tent. He believes Mohammed had already poisoned Alex's water bag before they fought this morning."

"And he didn't think to mention that to me when we were trying to find Alex earlier?" Anger warmed him like a hot fire.

"Even if he had, would it have helped you find Alex sooner?"

"No," he said with great reluctance. He stared into the tent, his gaze falling on Alex's ashen features. He'd almost lost her. It wouldn't happen again. A gentle hand squeezed his arm.

"Medjuel was right, my son. She is truly worthy of you. Now go to her." Tenderness brightened her eyes, and she kissed his cheek before walking away.

He entered the tent quietly and knelt at Alex's side. A damp blanket covered her body from her neck to her ankles. One arm lay on top of the cool covering, and he enclosed her hand in his. The temperature of her body had cooled, but she was still too warm.

A young woman dipped a cloth into a bowl of water then dribbled water into Alex's mouth. With a gentle touch, he stopped the girl and took the damp rag from her. This he could do. Caring for her was something he needed to do. It would ease his sense of helplessness.

The cool water skimmed over his fingers as he squeezed all but a small amount of fluid from the rag. Gently he dabbed her mouth with the damp cloth before parting her lips with his finger and sprinkling water into her mouth.

The sudden sensation of Alex's lips moving against his fingers startled him. With gentle strokes, he brushed wet strands of hair off her face. She didn't open her eyes, but again her lips moved. Her murmur was unintelligible. Elated, he bent his head so he could make out her words. "Tell me again, *emîra*. I didn't hear you."

"Wa...ter."

With an impatient wave of his hand, he motioned for the woman closest to the water flask to pass it to him. The goatskin bag in hand, he slid his arm under her head and lifted her slightly. He gave her a sip then laid her back down.

"Mo...re."

"Slowly, Alex, slowly." Soaking the cloth he'd been using, he moistened her mouth then squeezed a few drops of water past her lips. "When this is dry, I'll soak it again."

Her eyes still closed, she barely nodded before drifting back to sleep. Frowning, he brushed his fingertips across her brow.

He needed to talk to Medjuel again. This morning, his cousin had been almost evasive in his explanations about what had happened between him and Mohammed. At the time he'd attributed Medjuel's responses to the heat of the moment, but now he wanted to know everything his cousin did about Mohammed and the man's activities.

As Sheikh el Mazir, Medjuel was obligated to protect Alex by virtue of her presence in his camp. Although his cousin had done his best this morning, he wasn't convinced Medjuel had done everything possible. He still couldn't understand why there'd been no sound of a struggle. Then there was the vast amount of blood on Mohammed's *aba* and *gambaz*. It was as if there had been no struggle at all. But then Medjuel had been injured.

He needed more information about Mohammed's actions. The man's treachery with the Hoggar had made him the most likely suspect for poisoning Alex, but there were still too many unanswered questions. If the Hoggar wanted Nourbese's treasure, why would they kill Alex before she found the tomb? None of it made any sense.

Satisfied that Alex was sleeping peacefully, he left her in the care of the women and headed toward Medjuel's tent. Whatever discord lay between them, it was time to settle it. He wanted answers, and as his cousin's trusted advisor, he was entitled to them. Striding through the camp, he ignored the calls of several people.

Medjuel's large, luxuriant tent was set off from the rest of the tribe. The main entrance flap was rolled up, and Altair respectfully waited for his cousin to ask him to enter. Almost as if he had expected him, Medjuel looked up from the collapsible desk he sat at. With a regal wave of his hand, the Sheikh beckoned him to enter.

"Altair. Come in, cousin, come in."

Rising from his seat, Medjuel approached him and guided him toward the sumptuous bed of pillows that filled one part of the tent. "How is the *shagi emîra?*"

"She'll recover."

"Excellent, excellent." Medjuel gestured for him to take a seat on the pillows then sat as well. Slim, dark fingers forming a temple, the Sheikh's face took on a sorrowful expression. "I'm deeply sorry about Desari, cousin. She was a beautiful animal."

The reminder made Altair's jaw tense as he silently acknowledged his role in the death of his horse. It wasn't a pleasant thought. His head bobbed in a sharp nod. Medjuel eyed him carefully for a moment before he heaved a sigh.

"It seems your suspicions were right about Mohammed. I should have listened to you. I'm sorry. I found an empty bottle of ipecac in his personal belongings shortly after you discovered Miss Talbot missing."

"Why didn't you tell me?"

Medjuel shrugged. "I had no idea what he'd used it for until Kahlil and I found you."

It made sense. His mother was right, there was no way anyone could have known about the poisoned water.

"I'm sorry I questioned you. I shouldn't have."

"It is forgotten."

Altair frowned at his cousin. Something about the way Medjuel was looking at him set him on edge. It was obvious his cousin wanted to say something else, but he hesitated. This wavering was unlike Medjuel.

"How is your arm?"

"A flesh wound. Your mother is a fine healer. I doubt there will even be a scar."

"You were in no mood this morning to discuss how Mohammed died. But, I'd like to know what happened."

Medjuel shrugged. "There is little to tell beyond what I told you this morning. I noticed Mohammed lurking by Miss Talbot's tent. When I approached him, he attacked me with his knife. We fought. Fortunately, I survived."

He nodded at Medjuel's explanation. It was neat and concise, almost painfully so. He'd seen the knife wounds on Mohammed's chest. Surely, such a struggle would have resulted in enough noise to wake the dead. And yet, there hadn't been any sounds at all.

Fear coiled in his stomach. Could Medjuel be lying to him? No. Impossible. They were of the same blood. They were brothers. But still he couldn't silence the doubt.

"It's fortunate you were up and about early."

Medjuel rose from his seat to pace the plush woven carpet beneath his feet. The flowing *gambaz* he wore whispered against the colorful and intricately patterned rug. Why did he look so uneasy? Could he possibly be lying about his struggle with Mohammed?

"Most fortunate, but I'm afraid there's something else, Altair. I erred in thinking Mohammed wasn't a threat to the *shagi emîra*. Now I have reason to believe he had an accomplice."

"An accomplice?" His blood chilled his limbs as it slid through his veins. Alex was still in danger.

"Yes. When I searched Mohammed's tent, I found not only the ipecac bottle, but this." Medjuel pulled out a crumpled piece of paper from inside his *gambaz* and stretched out his hand. Taking the note from him, Altair looked down at the writing.

We cannot wait any longer. She is too close to finding the tomb. She must die quickly. Meet me tonight in the village square.

The drum of his heartbeat echoed in his ears as he stared at the words. There was someone else trying to kill Alex. He raised his head to meet Medjuel's worried gaze.

"Do you have any idea who it might be?"

Stroking his beard, Medjuel shook his head. "No. I wish I did. But I think you should seriously consider convincing the *shagi emîra* to stop this pursuit for Nourbese until we can find Mohammed's accomplice."

The statement pulled a mirthless laugh from him. He shook his head at his cousin. "That is the one thing I'm not able to do. Where this excavation is concerned, Alex would no more listen to me than she would the British Museum."

"Well, we'd better do something; and quickly. With Mohammed dead, the danger to her is even greater than before, because we have no idea who's trying to kill her."

Altair closed his eyes as he tried to formulate a plan. What could he say to Alex that would convince her to stop her explorations for a while? He released a small noise of disgust. Getting her to stay away from Per-Ramesses was like asking a fish to stay out of water.

No, he needed something drastic, something that would keep her safe. He needed to draw the killer's attention away from Alex somehow. The obvious solution was right in front of him, but he ignored it. No, he couldn't do that to her.

He'd given his word.

Logic continued to press at him. He shoved the thought aside, but it returned with reasons he couldn't ignore. There was safety in numbers, and no matter how hard he tried to ignore it, they would come sooner or later.

The British Museum.

They had more resources than he did. They were better equipped to protect not only Alex, but the excavation as well. No, she'd never agree to it. But what other option was there? What would she do when she found out? There wasn't even any point asking himself that question. He already knew the answer. The moment Alex discovered he'd contacted the Museum she'd be ready to skin him alive.

He had no choice. Protecting her was his only concern. Her fury he could live with, but he couldn't live without her. Opening his eyes, he saw Medjuel eyeing him with a questioning look.

"I'll talk to her, and I intend to guard her night and day. She's not going to leave my sight."

An odd look flared in Medjuel's eyes before it died a quick death, and for a brief instant, Altair thought he saw fear in his cousin's expression. But Medjuel had nothing to fear. It was Alex who was in danger.

Chapter Nineteen

The setting sun hovered over the horizon as Altair strode through the Mazir camp. Reaching his mother's tent, he paused at the open side of her dwelling. She was sitting on the carpet preparing the evening meal as his shadow fell across her face. Her brow furrowed with concern as she met his gaze.

"What is it? What has happened?"

"I need someone I can trust to take a message back to Cairo. I want to send Kahlil."

"No," Gameela protested as she scrambled to her feet. "No. He's just a boy."

"I'm sixteen, Mother."

Altair turned around to see his stepbrother watching them closely from the edge of the tent. There was an assuredness in the young man's posture that told him Kahlil was more than equal to the task he needed done. As a pure-blood descendant of Nourbese, the boy was direct in line to eventually take the reins of leadership from Medjuel. A day that might come sooner than either of them expected. Clenching his jaw, he didn't allow himself to consider the origin of that particular thought.

"I won't have it," Gameela snapped. "I won't."

"You know I wouldn't ask if it weren't important." Altair tightened his jaw at his mother's reluctance. Didn't she realize if there were another way, he'd have chosen it rather than asking Kahlil to deliver the message?

"What could be so important that you find it necessary to send your brother back to Cairo alone?"

"I wouldn't send him alone. I'd have Omar go with him. But

I need Kahlil to go because he's the only one I trust with my message."

"What is this message that is so important?" Gameela said in a tight voice.

"I need to get a wire to the British Museum. I need them to send an expedition team to Khatana-Qantir as soon as possible."

"But I thought the excavation was under Miss Talbot's direction," Kahlil exclaimed.

The statement sliced through him. Kahlil was right. The credit for Per-Ramesses belonged to Alex, but she'd be far safer if the British Museum were here working under her supervision.

"It is her project, but someone is trying to stop her from finding Nourbese's tomb."

Gameela stared at him confusion. "Mohammed is dead. How can he hurt her now?"

"He has an accomplice." The astonishment on their faces made a muscle in his cheek twitch as he tried to keep his fear at bay. His gaze settled on his mother's disturbed expression. "I can't leave her to go myself. Her safety during the day wouldn't be an issue, but I won't leave her alone at night."

"But why Kahlil? Why not someone else?"

"Kahlil is the only one, aside from Jemal, who I trust. And we both know Jemal's absence will be noticed more quickly than Kahlil's."

His brother stepped forward and touched her shoulder. "Let me go, Mother. I've enjoyed Miss Talbot's company at dinner over the past several weeks. I'd like to help."

"How does asking the British Museum to come here protect Alex?" Gameela ignored Kahlil's plea as she arched her eyebrows at Altair.

He heaved a sigh and turned away from his mother. Moving to the center tent pole that supported the abode's roof, his hand rubbed the smooth wood as he contemplated the question. The answer was elusive. It could very well not be of any help at all. The only thing he was certain of was that Alex would be furious with him.

"I don't know that their presence will be any help at all. I just hope that whoever wants to stop Alex will give up once

251

they're faced with a number of people seeking Nourbese's tomb."

"Safety in numbers," Kahlil murmured.

"Precisely." Altair sent his brother a look of approval, pleased at the youth's quick thinking. He turned his gaze back to his mother. "What do you think Jemal would say to my request?"

Gameela shot him a frigid look. "You know very well what he would say."

"Then let Kahlil go. Omar will look after him." Indecision caused her to bite her lip, and he pushed the advantage. "Alex's life is at stake, Mother."

She sighed and turned away from him and Kahlil. Her soft words barely crossed the small space between them. "Very well."

The hushed words sent relief coursing through him. He turned to his brother and quietly ordered him to find Omar. He watched Kahlil dart off before turning to see his mother wipe at her cheek.

Aware of her fears, he stepped forward and hugged her close. "He'll be all right, Mother. Omar will watch out for him."

"I know." She frowned. "And what of Alex?"

Releasing her, he shook his head as he studied her worried features. "I'll protect her."

"You must realize that despite all your efforts to protect Alex, you may still fail. Not because you don't try, but because whoever is trying to kill her must be very desperate."

"You say that as if you know who's trying to kill her."

"No, but I think Alex is a threat to whoever is trying to kill her."

"A threat? Why would Alex be a threat to anyone?"

"Because of the prophecy."

His jaw sagged. His mother had never believed in the Mazir prophecy, why would she start now? He shook his head as she faced him again, touching his cheek. The black embroidery edging the light blue material of her *labbas* reminded him of his childhood when he'd watched her stitch intricate patterns on all her dresses.

"Don't look so surprised, Altair. I married your father because I loved him, but I did not give up all the old ways because of it. I simply chose to let you form your own beliefs without my interference. Why do you think I allowed the old Viscount to take you from me when you were still a boy?"

Raking a hand through his hair, he frowned. "I thought it was because you'd promised Father."

"Yes, I gave him my promise, but I also knew I had to let you find your way in the world. That meant sending you to England to secure the birthright you received from your father."

"I wanted no part of that. I was content to remain here."

"Experiences are the spectacles of intellect. If you had stayed here, your view of the world would have been limited. To find one's place in life, one must experience all manner of things. It is the only way to know your true self and your destiny."

"As I recall, you've never left the desert," he said with a touch of bitterness.

"The love I experienced with your father was my destiny, and as short as our time was together, I regret not one moment of it. Jemal is a good husband and I love him, but he accepts that the love I shared with your father is a rare thing. Now you face your own destiny."

"You're talking in riddles, Mother."

"Then let me make myself quite clear. I believe your destiny is tied to Alex, and she may very well be the one mentioned in the prophecy. If that's true, then she may be in even greater danger than you realize."

"That's ridiculous."

Even as he spoke the words, he knew Alex was the one the Mazir had been waiting for. She would set Nourbese free and the Mazir would be blessed with Nourbese's treasure. Denying it was pointless. He'd seen her find the city—fulfilling the prophecy was simply a matter of time.

"Then ask yourself this. Who stands to gain if Alex doesn't find Nourbese's tomb? Answer that question and you'll find the person trying to hurt her."

Thunderstruck, he stared at his mother. All along, he'd been trying to figure out why people who wanted to find the tomb would want Alex dead. He'd never considered the possibility that someone might not want her to find the tomb. He'd been a fool.

The weight of her words rested uneasily on his shoulders. Still reeling from the realization that he'd been asking the wrong questions, he turned as Kahlil and Omar entered the tent.

Short and stout, his old friend might look harmless, but he knew how handy Omar was in a fight. It had been one of the reasons he'd selected him for the task at hand. If Kahlil came to harm, it wouldn't be due to his friend's lack of skill as a fighter.

"Greetings, Gameela. I trust you are well?" Omar bowed respectfully.

"I am, thank you," she said quietly.

His mother returned to her seat and continued with her dinner preparations. To anyone who didn't know her it would seem she had little care about the conversation occurring in her home. Altair knew differently. He could see the small furrow on her forehead that indicated how closely she was listening to the conversation.

"Altair." Omar grasped his arm in an ancient form of greeting. "Your brother says he needs to go to Cairo, and that you wish me to go with him."

"Yes. I know I can trust you to keep an eye on him. I don't want him getting into any trouble." A trusted friend from childhood, Omar smiled at him with cheerful openness. There was nothing suspicious in Omar's gaze, and yet Altair hesitated. No, he couldn't trust even his oldest friend. Alex was too important to him.

"You'll need to leave at dawn."

Omar chuckled and clasped Kahlil's shoulder in an affectionate gesture. "Then we should pack our supplies and turn in."

"I need you to reach Cairo in two days."

"Two days?" Omar rubbed the back of his neck as he considered the request. "It will be difficult, but it can be done."

"Good. Once you reach Cairo, Kahlil will know what to do." He hesitated. How far could he trust his old friend? "And one more thing. You are to tell no one that you are leaving, not the elders, not Medjuel, no one."

Omar furrowed his brow. "No one?"

"Your lives and that of others depend on your remaining silent about this journey. Trust no one."

"It will be as you order."

Relieved by the loyalty threading his friend's voice, Altair shook his head. Hands resting on Omar's shoulders, he saw the gleam of determination in the black eyes studying him so quietly.

"Not an order, my old friend, but a request that you have care with both your lives."

"I've never doubted your words before, Altair. I'll not do so now." Bowing toward Gameela, the stocky man left the tent.

Kahlil watched the Bedouin walk away then turned to Altair. "Do you think him trustworthy, Altair?"

"I do." He pulled his gaze away from Omar's receding figure. "But to be safe, you're not to tell him why you're going to Cairo. If he asks, simply tell him it's family business."

"All right. And when we reach the city?"

"You're to go straight to the British Electric Telegraph office. I want you to send a wire to Lord Merrick at the British Museum with this message. Per-Ramesses is in Khatana-Qantir. Have found palace. Send team immediately. Reply with date of arrival."

"That's all?"

He flinched at the sickening lurch his stomach made. "Yes. He'll act as soon as he gets the message. It might be three weeks before anyone arrives, but have supplies and transport ready so you can guide them here as soon as they arrive."

"Are you sure you want to do this, brother?" Touching his arm, Kahlil eyed him carefully. "Is there no other way to protect her?"

The maturity in his brother's voice surprised him. In the past eight months, Kahlil had developed perceptive faculties beyond his years. The boy would be a great leader. He turned his gaze back to his mother's troubled expression. No, there was no other way to keep Alex safe. He wouldn't breathe easy until the Museum's team arrived.

"There's no other way."

"Then I'll do as you ask."

Gratitude flowed through him at his brother's support. One hand on Kahlil's shoulder, he studied the youth's face for a moment before embracing him in a brotherly hug. Releasing him, he sent Kahlil a stern look. "And you're to be careful. Do everything Omar tells you. He'll ensure you come to no harm."

His brother moved toward Gameela and knelt at her side. "I'll be careful, Mother."

For a moment, she didn't move. With an abrupt movement, she climbed to her feet and pulled her youngest son into her arms. She spoke no words, but Altair could read every emotion on her face as she met his gaze over Kahlil's shoulder. The fear on her face made him bite the inside of his mouth. If anything happened to his little brother, she might never forgive him.

The muscles in his body ached from the tension flowing through him. Not only was Alex's life at stake, but so were the lives of his brother and friend. And for what? What was so important about Nourbese's tomb that it endangered those he loved? Where did one start to search for an elusive enemy?

Watching Kahlil rise to his feet, he flexed his jaw. "I need to see to Alex. Take care, little brother. And remember, tell no one about the message. God speed."

He swallowed the tight ball in his throat and strode quickly out of his mother's tent. As he moved through the camp, he barely noticed the hum of early evening activity surrounding him. Should he tell Alex what he'd done? No, she was too ill for him to do that now. Later, he'd tell her later. But when?

For the first time in his life, he lacked the courage to do something. How was he going to explain his actions to her? He'd only done what he believed necessary to protect her. What could be so difficult in making her understand that? She wouldn't see it that way. He'd given her his word and then broken it. That's what she would remember first and foremost.

Her tent loomed in front of him, and he saw the sides had been dropped to seal in the day's heat as a guard against the night's chill. He gave a sharp tug to the small bell outside her tent before pushing the tent flap aside.

Only one young woman was in the dwelling with Alex. He recognized her as Jasmin. She'd been the one to encourage Alex to dance at the campfire the night before.

"Good evening, Sheikh Mazir," Jasmin said with a quiet smile.

"How is she?"

"Much improved. The *shagi emîra* has amazing recuperative powers. Nourbese walks with her."

Relief warmed his blood at the response. Returning the woman's smile, he joined her on the floor, putting Alex between them. Jasmin's venerating tone and her reference to Alex as a princess told him the woman believed Nourbese's prophecy. It shouldn't have surprised him, but it did.

"Why don't you go and get some dinner. I'll watch her through the night."

"And you, Excellency. Do you not wish to eat?"

Amazingly, he realized he'd not eaten since breakfast, but he still wasn't hungry. He shook his head. "I'm fine for the moment, thank you."

"As you wish, but if you need refreshment, there are fruit and nuts in the bowl here." Jasmin waved her hand toward the container sitting behind her. Rising to her feet, she bowed and left the tent.

Alone with Alex, he brushed a hand across her brow. She was still warm to the touch, but her temperature wasn't as unnatural as it had been earlier. Her features were no longer ashen as a touch of color crested over her cheekbone.

He lifted her hand and studied her long fingers. She'd broken a nail. He kissed the bruised finger then laid her hand back down on the blanket that covered her. A soft murmur parted her mouth, and he turned his head to see her staring at him with a dazed expression. Smiling, he leaned forward and kissed her cheek.

"How do you feel, *emîra*?"

"Not very good. Am I going to die?"

The question startled him. With a firm shake of his head, he brushed the hair at her forehead back. "No. You're not going to die. I refuse to let that happen."

When she licked at her dry lips, he reached for the water bag. Uncapping the goatskin, he lifted her head, but she pushed the bag away.

"No."

"Alex, I can tell you're thirsty. You must drink."

With a weak shake of her head, she licked her lips again. "No, it tastes bad."

"Not this water, *emîra*." Her hazel eyes studied him warily, and he opened the waterskin and took a large swallow from it. "See, there's nothing wrong with it."

The flicker of relief in her gaze tore at his heart. Gently, he offered her the water, and she drank thirstily from the water bag. After a moment, he pulled the water away from her lips.

"I think that's enough for right now. You can have more when we're certain you can keep this down."

"Thank you." She closed her eyes.

He stroked her cheek with the back of his hand. "I won't leave you, *emîra*. You're going to be fine."

Her only answer was a quiet sigh as she drifted off to sleep once more. Silently, he studied her. She'd never looked more beautiful to him than she did now. The memory of how close he'd come to losing her chilled him. He shoved the thought away. The future was what he needed to consider now. Their future.

Stunned, he shook his head as if a heavy blow had struck him. It was the first time he'd considered a life with Alex beyond Per-Ramesses. Was it possible? If she did care for him, would her love be strong enough? She would have to bear not only the harsh existence of a desert life, but the malicious backbiting of English society as well. None of those concerns mattered until he knew how she would react when she discovered he'd invited the British Museum to Per-Ramesses.

She'd be furious. But would she forgive him? Would he be able to earn his way back into her good graces? Surely when he explained why he'd summoned the Museum, she would understand. Her safety was too important to him. Somehow he'd make her see that.

Lying down on the carpet beside Alex's pallet, he cupped the back of his head with his hands and studied the tent ceiling. All he needed to do was find the appropriate moment to tell her what he'd done. Timing was critical. He closed his eyes, wishing he could find Mohammed's accomplice.

Was his mother right? Had he been approaching the

problem from the wrong angle? Who would benefit if Alex didn't find Nourbese's tomb? Could that be the aim of Sheikh Tarih of the Hoggar? No, Tarih was far too greedy to give up treasure in an attempt to destroy the Mazir cultural beliefs. The man didn't possess the political shrewdness for that.

Then if not Tarih, who else? He didn't like the answer. No, there must be another option or something he was missing. Medjuel had consistently saved Alex's life. There wasn't any way he could be involved in a plot to kill her. Not to mention how important finding Nourbese was to the Mazir. Medjuel wouldn't do anything to jeopardize the tribe.

His cousin had been right about one thing. If Alex did find the tomb and there was nothing inside, then the cultural fabric of the Mazir tribe would disintegrate over time. He winced at the thought. It wasn't a pleasant image.

Well, Alex would find Nourbese's tomb, and it would happen soon. Of that, he was certain. What he wasn't so sure of was how difficult the killer was going to make her task.

Chapter Twenty

Daylight flooded Alex's tent as she rolled up the tent wall and secured it to the roof. It was her first day of freedom since Altair had found her in the desert. She'd been confined to her tent for the past three days until Gameela had finally declared her fit for duty again. Still Altair insisted on dogging her every movement.

It was as if the man feared she would vanish if she wasn't at his side. She smiled. His constant concern for her well-being pleased her. Perhaps Gameela was right. Maybe he really did care for her. But if that was true, why hadn't he said something? Talked about a future together?

Falling in love with Altair had changed her in so many ways. The idea of being his wife grew more appealing every day, and the thought of bearing his child filled her with a joyful expectation. The irony of the situation tugged a smile of chagrin to her mouth. She'd refused to conform to the standards other men had tried to enforce on her, and here she was contemplating hearth and home. It wasn't just amazing. It was amusing as well.

Of course, all of this hinged on whether or not Altair loved her. His behavior made her think he cared deeply for her, but how could she be certain if he didn't express his feelings? Perhaps he wanted nothing more than a brief affair. She grimaced. No. She wouldn't think that way. It was too painful to think what they shared was little more than a brief liaison.

She turned back to where her tool bag lay on the floor. Retrieving it, she turned to leave her tent only to find a large figure barring her path. The sight of Altair's tense expression made her smile.

"Don't you look cheerful this morning." She arched an eyebrow with amusement at the scowl on his face as he folded his arms.

"Where do you think you're going?"

"Oh, I don't know. Ride out into the desert, walk through the village." She shrugged and sent him a wry smile. "Where do you think I'm going? I've lost three days of work, and I'm not about to lose anymore."

A muscle in his tense jaw line twitched, and she frowned. What on earth was wrong with him? He was acting as if she'd decided to march into hell itself. His head tipped to one side in a brief nod.

"If you plan on going to the palace, then I'll be going with you."

His response didn't surprise her. Smiling, she stepped close to him and rested one hand on his arm. "Then you'd better bring some tools because I intend to put you to work."

A reluctant smile curled his mouth. "As you wish, but for my peace of mind, you'll walk with me to my tent. I want to make certain you don't go off on your own again."

"You worry too much." She didn't protest as he cupped her elbow with his hand and guided her through the camp.

"No, I'm simply being cautious where you're concerned."

"Why?"

"Why what?" Although his grip didn't change on her elbow, she could still feel his fingers stiffen against her skin.

"Never mind." Disheartened by his evasive answer, she shook her head. Even gentle prodding failed to move him to speak his heart.

They halted in front of a beautifully colored tent. The dwelling's dark, rich burgundy looked soft as velvet, and the gold fringe lining the edges gave the tent an air of luxury. He pulled back one side of the tent and lashed it to the roofline. As he entered the dwelling, she hovered on the edge of the opening, her eyes drinking in the space he called home.

Three large metal prickets holding fat candles rose majestically up from the floor to offer lighting at night. Plump red and gold pillows lined a wide pallet that she knew had to be his bed. A small round table sat in the middle of the tent, surrounded by cantles that served as something to lean on during a meal or just a conversation.

Covering the cantles were sheepskin rugs, while three leather trunks stood near the far wall of the tent. On top of the trunks were elaborately woven blankets layered with wide, colorful, fringed tassels. Despite its simplicity, the tent's interior was decidedly male. It suited him well.

She watched as Altair opened one of the trunks and retrieved several items, stuffing them into a knapsack. When he'd finished, he returned to her side at the tent's entrance. The look of disquiet on his face troubled her, and she frowned as he looked away from her.

"Alex, I have something to tell you," he said.

The tension in his body was palpable in its intensity. Suddenly wary of him, she struggled to keep from taking a step back. What had he done? Oh God, he'd contacted the British Museum. How could he? He'd given his word. A wave of fury welled inside her as she tried to calm her fears.

"What is it?"

If possible, his posture grew even more rigid, and she noted the way the muscle in his cheek twitched as he clenched his jaw. He glanced away from her, then back again. After what seemed like an eternity, he heaved a sigh. "While you were ill, I went back to the palace to do some exploring. I found another room adjoining Pharaoh's chamber. It's a shrine to Nourbese."

Relief washed away her tension in a huge wave. He'd not betrayed her. He'd not broken his word. Giddy with joy, she shook her head with a laugh. "Heavens, I thought you were going to tell me you had contacted the British Museum."

He flinched at the remark. "And if I had?"

"Well, you didn't, so that's a moot question."

For a brief moment, she thought she saw anguish flicker in his gaze before it vanished. With a brusque nod, he cupped her elbow, and they walked toward the holding area for the camels.

Silence fell between them, but Alex didn't mind. She was with the man she loved, and they were going to explore Ramesses' palace. Soon, she'd find Nourbese's tomb. That final achievement would solidify her credibility as an archeologist despite the misguided beliefs about her gender.

The ride to the palace was longer than she'd have liked, but Altair had insisted on taking the long route. She'd started to protest his decision, but the disaster of her last visit to the palace was enough to make her remain silent.

As they approached the entrance, she noticed Altair had been busy over the last three days. Although he'd never left her side at night, he'd entrusted her care to Gameela during the day. Now, as the camels lumbered toward the palace, she could see he'd had her work tent and materials transferred to the plateau. Her heart warmed at the thought.

His thoughtfulness and regard for her could not have been clearer. As they dismounted, she stood in his tall shadow. Looking up at him, she smiled. "Thank you for moving my work tent down here. It will make things much easier."

He smiled and ran his index finger along her jaw line. A flame sparked in his dark eyes, and she trembled at his touch. "You can thank me later, *emîra*. Right now, Ramesses' palace and Nourbese await you."

Nodding, she moved toward the dark entryway of the palace with Altair close on her heels. At the entrance, she realized someone had built steps down into the buried palace. She hesitated and turned her head to meet his watchful gaze. He arched an arrogant eyebrow.

"I was getting tired of pulling myself up out of that hole. I thought steps would make it easier on all concerned."

With a smile, she gave a slight nod of her head, but remained silent. Carefully, she made her way down the wooden steps to the palace floor. The inside of the palace was well lit from a large number of torches, and she knew these were Altair's doing as well. It was amazing what he'd accomplished during her short recovery period.

Glancing around the main chamber, she had to force herself to restrain her laugh of excitement. Behind her, Altair descended the stairs. As he halted next to her, she looked up to see a small smile on his lips. She smiled back.

"Well, *emîra*, where shall we start?"

Her fingers trembled as she pulled her notebook from her knapsack. She wanted to go back to Pharaoh's chamber. Altair had said he'd found a shrine to Nourbese there. Excitement and tension charged the air as she looked at the map she'd made during her last visit. She glanced at the corridor almost directly in front of her.

"Are there torches throughout the palace?"

Altair shook his head. "I instructed the men to place torches only along the path you marked on the walls. I instructed them not to do any exploring in areas you'd not visited. However, as I told you, I found the shrine to Nourbese off Pharaoh's bedchamber."

There was a hint of regret in his voice, which made her smile. Quickly, she pressed a kiss to his cheek. Over the past few days, he'd done everything in his power to ensure her every wish was granted. She didn't begrudge him the curiosity. Pulling back from him, she caught the brief flash of anxiety in his gaze.

He'd been on edge ever since he'd rescued her. A terrible burden rested on his shoulders, but he was unwilling to share it with her. Every time she tried pressing him for an explanation, it only resulted in his complete withdrawal from her. She could only hope that he would reveal his thoughts in the near future. He arched an eyebrow at her in the manner she loved, and she grinned. "Let's go look at Pharaoh's chamber."

Without waiting for him, she followed the torch-lined path until she reached Ramesses' personal quarters. Kneeling in front of the stone slab that declared the room belonged to Pharaoh, Alex ran her fingertips over the hieroglyphs carved into the stone. Altair entered the room and knelt at her side.

"I didn't see these markings before. Did you notice them the last time?" He pointed to another set of symbols two slabs further into the room.

"No, I was too sick to do anything but try to return to camp at this point."

He scooted forward and pulled a brush from his *gambaz*. Quickly he dusted off the stone, his fingers splayed across the yellowish surface. Joining him, she listened as he translated the markings.

"From the west she comes to aid Pharaoh and his beloved."

Alex sank back onto her heels. Puzzled, she studied the odd expression of amazement on Altair's face. "Do you know what it means?"

"Yes, it's a reference to the prophecy."

"Prophecy? What prophecy?"

"The Mazir prophecy about Nourbese." His fingers traced the hieroglyphics. "It's been handed down for generations."

Intrigued, she stared at him in puzzlement. "Why haven't you told me this before? Tell me what the prophecy says."

"I thought you already knew it." The surprise in his voice made her laugh.

"No." She laughed again. "Would I be asking if I did?"

The foreboding look on his face made her grow silent. He studied her face for a moment, then turned back to stare at the hieroglyphics on the slab. "The prophecy has been handed down from one generation of Mazir to the next since the time of Ramesses and Nourbese."

"And?"

"It says that from the new world, a woman crowned in hawk feathers will come to find Pharaoh's wife. She will return the jars of life to Nourbese, enabling her spirit to join Ramesses in the afterlife. In return, Pharaoh's beloved will bestow a wealth of ancient knowledge and treasure on her deliverer, which will benefit all the Mazir."

Alex arched her eyebrow at him. "Do you believe it?"

"Yes."

"Why would you believe a folk tale? Isn't it part of your work with the Museum to deal in facts, not superstitions?"

"This isn't about my position with the Museum. It's about you and what I've seen."

"Me!" She shot up both her eyebrows as she studied him. Had the man gone daft on her? Why would he think the prophecy had anything to do with her? What was it he'd said— from the new world, a woman crowned in hawk—

Many Europeans still referred to America as the New World. And a hawk's feathers were brown just like her hair. Staring at him, she shook her head in amazement.

"You think I'm the one in the prophecy."

"I know you are."

"But it's just a legend. How can you put any stock in it?"

Altair scrambled to his feet to pace the stone floor.

Watching him prowl the room like one of the leopards the ancient Egyptians prized so highly, she frowned. How could he believe such an outlandish folk tale?

She immediately chastised herself. Uncle Jeffrey had believed there was a curse. She'd even thought it that afternoon in the Museum when she'd almost been crushed by that large sandstone masonry. But logically, she knew there wasn't a curse. Someone didn't want her to find Nourbese's tomb, and they were using superstition to their advantage. Altair came to an abrupt halt and bent down to capture her face in his hands.

"I believe the prophecy because of what I've seen over the past two months. I've witnessed the ease with which you found first the city wall, and then the palace. Tell me, how long do you think it really should have taken you to find Per-Ramesses?"

His hands slid down her arms. Grasping her hands, he pulled her to her feet. She shook her head at the question.

"I don't know. A couple more weeks?"

"At least that many, if not more. And the palace. It should have taken a hell of a lot longer than it did for you to find this place."

The words smarted. He thought she'd found Per-Ramesses and the palace by sheer luck. Pulling herself free of his grasp, she glared up at him.

"In other words, you think I just stumbled onto it by accident."

"No," he growled. "I'm just saying that providence is at work here."

"Providence? Hardly." She released an abrupt sound of disgust. "I worked at my father's side from the time I was fifteen years old, studying everything I could about Ramesses and his city. I'm an expert on the subject, and you have the presumption to suggest providence was the reason I found Per-Ramesses!"

"Damn it, Alex. I'm not saying that. I merely—"

"I think you've said quite enough all ready."

She couldn't believe it. He doubted her. He doubted her ability. He put her discovery of the palace down to sheer luck. Time and again she'd proven herself as capable as any man. Yet he couldn't bring himself to believe it was her knowledge and not some prophecy that had helped her find Per-Ramesses.

Disgusted, she turned to walk away from him, and he caught her by the shoulders, giving her a slight shake.

"Listen to me. I'm simply trying to explain why I think you're the one the prophecy foretold."

"I don't want to listen to you." She glared at him.

He must take her for a complete fool. She'd worked hard to get here. To have him attribute her knowledge and work to providence cut deep. It was the same thing as saying she wasn't as capable as him or any other man. She glanced at the large hands resting on her shoulders before sending him a cold glance.

"Let me go."

The quiet request filled the chamber with icy silence. Altair's features became a stone mask hiding his thoughts from her. But his eyes blazed with anger and another emotion she couldn't define. Slowly his hands released her and he took a step backward. He bowed slightly.

"As you wish, but know this, Alex. This conversation is far from over."

She refused even to acknowledge his statement. Her movements deliberate, she picked up her knapsack and removed her notebook from it. As if she hadn't a care in the world, she knelt at the stone slab and recorded the hieroglyphic message. Over her head, she heard his exclamation of anger before the sharp click of his boot heels against the stone floor echoed his departure.

Shoulders sagging, she closed her eyes. The disappointment wrapping itself around her heart was a physical pain. For the first time he had questioned her abilities. Not directly, but he'd attributed her success to an ancient prophecy. She grimaced. Even if what he said was true, it was clear she still didn't trust him.

Oh, she'd thought she did, but would she have jumped to conclusions so easily just now if she had complete faith in him? How could they have a life together without trust? She would never agree to give up her work. It meant too much to her. She'd rather live a lonely life without Altair than come to resent him for forcing her to choose between him and her passion. It was an impossible situation.

With a small sound of agitation, she snapped her notebook closed. Work, she needed to focus on her work. She'd once told Jane that she'd rather have a statue of Anubis or Ramesses over the affections of a man. She should have listened to her own advice. Then she'd still have a heart and some of her pride left.

Rising to her feet, she blinked away the tears threatening to course down her cheeks. Enough of this. There was work to do. Across from the balustrade buried in the stone was the doorway leading into what Altair had called Ramesses' shrine to Nourbese. From where she stood, she could see a soft glow of light coming from the doorway. Briskly she headed toward the room.

The chamber was small and narrow, not much bigger than a closet. Light filled the room from four different sconces hanging on the wall. Slowly, she circled the room, noting the numerous hieroglyphs covering the stone walls. At one end of the alcove, the wall dipped inward into a small shrine.

An empty ledge jutted out into the room from the indentation. Resting on the ledge and carved directly into the stone was a sculpture of a beautiful woman seated on a throne. She stared out at Alex, the lovely proportions of her face haunting in its beauty. At the foot of the sculpture rested a small creature that reminded Alex of a mongoose. One thing was clear—the woman didn't resemble any Goddess worshipped by Ramesses. It could only be Nourbese.

Excitement hitched her breath as she studied the carving. With a quick movement, she pulled out her brush and dusted debris from around the sculpture. Peering closely at the carving and the way it melded into the wall, she bit her lip in concentration. Fingers drifting over the stone surface behind the sculpture, she encountered two small indentations on the wall behind the carving. She frowned. Quickly she dusted away the debris off the small, finger-size holes.

She stepped back and stared at the sculpture. Was this really Nourbese? It made sense that Ramesses would have a small shrine to honor his lost love, but this translation didn't make much sense. Leaning closer to the hieroglyphs, she tilted her head to read the words as they rose toward the ceiling then turned to crest the statue's small inset before resuming their course back down to the shrine's ledge. She shook her head as she read the translation aloud.

"Nourbese, Pharaoh's beloved, awaits the woman from the west. Ramesses' rib will give the woman with hawk feathers that which the Mazir seek."

The back of her neck tingled. Blast, Altair had her half believing this prophecy of his. She sent the statue a fierce glare. No, she wasn't the woman in the prophecy. Still, it was difficult not to consider the prediction and the coincidental aspects of the hieroglyphs. She had brown hair, she was seeking Nourbese's tomb and she needed Ramesses' rib to do that.

Blowing out a breath of air in disgust, she re-examined the stone surface behind the statue. The two finger holes were spaced far enough apart to allow someone to insert their index and middle fingers. Impulsively, she started to insert her fingers then stopped. No, that might not be a good idea.

If it were some type of trap, escape might be impossible if her fingers were caught. Best to use her pencils instead. Pulling two from her knapsack, she carefully angled them into the holes. Nothing happened.

Gently, she pushed on the pencils again. This time a loud click echoed through the room. Jumping away from the wall and statue, she watched as a stone beneath the figure of Nourbese slid back to reveal a medium-sized compartment. Excited, she retrieved one of the torches to shine the light into the dark hole.

From where she stood, she could see a golden chest. She sucked in a sharp breath of exhilaration. Nourbese's canopic jars. She'd found them. Excitement pulsed through her as she reached into the compartment. The sound of footsteps made her realize the chest would have to wait. Quickly she straightened and used the pencils to close the secret cache.

As the stone slowly ground its way closed, Alex moved toward the doorway. Altair met her at the threshold. She narrowed her gaze at him, but his expression remained impassive beneath her stare.

"Done so soon?"

She shook her head. "No, I just thought I'd leave the chamber for tomorrow."

"*Tomorrow?*"

"Yes, I want to finish mapping out the palace before I delve into the translation of all the markings in here."

When he didn't move aside, she frowned and tried to slide past him. A steely arm shot across her path to grip the doorjamb and block her escape. "Alex, I upset you earlier. It wasn't my intention to do that."

"It doesn't matter." She recognized his attempt at an apology, but she wanted no part of it. "Now if you don't mind, I've work to do."

With a quick movement, she ducked beneath his arm and darted away. As she scurried down the hall toward the palace entrance, she waited to hear his footsteps following her. When all she heard was the sound of her own boots echoing in the corridor, she suppressed a sob.

No, she wouldn't cry. If he were to follow her and find her weeping, he'd only use it to his advantage. That she couldn't allow. She wouldn't give him the satisfaction of knowing her heart was breaking. He couldn't accept her for who she was, and she wasn't about to change for him or anyone else.

Chapter Twenty-One

"Damn."

Alex hit her fist against the wall. She turned around and pressed her back against the cold stone bearing the frustrating group of hieroglyphs she'd been deciphering. Slowly she sank down onto the floor. There wasn't a single hint of what or where Ramesses' rib was in any of the symbols she'd translated over the past three days.

The only thing she'd been able to determine was that she was supposed to look at the stars for inspiration. Whatever that meant. Ramesses seemed to have a gift for being obscure and it was irritating. Arms resting on her knees, she lowered her head against her forearms. The dank smell inside Ramesses' shrine to Nourbese registered with her for the first time since she'd entered the room almost a week ago. She wrinkled her nose at the unpleasant aroma.

Closing her eyes, she reclined against the wall. She was tired. No, exhausted was a more accurate statement. What little sleep she'd gotten over the past two nights had been rife with wild dreams and nightmares. Filled with elusive pharaohs and shadowy figures, they made little sense and only made her slumber all the more restless.

With a deep sigh, she rolled her neck in a slow circle. The tension of the past three days had twisted her shoulder muscles into knots. The image of Altair's fingers kneading out the bunched muscles made her bite her lip. She missed him.

He'd obeyed her silent command to leave her alone, but he never strayed far from her side. Every time her gaze met his, it was a reminder of every moment she'd spent in his arms. The flash of emotion in his dark eyes alarmed her because she knew her resistance to him was fragile at best.

Even now, she was making excuses for him. He'd claimed a belief in providence, and perhaps he was right. Look how easily she'd found Nourbese's canopic jars. She'd not shared her find with anyone. But when she did, she knew the Mazir would celebrate with even greater verve than when she discovered the palace. The jars meant she was close to finding Nourbese's tomb. One step closer to helping Pharaoh's wife join him in the afterlife.

She stared at the hieroglyphics on the wall across from her. If Altair's people believed she was the one from the prophecy, could she expect him to dismiss the stories he'd heard all his life? Perhaps she'd been too harsh on him. He'd never doubted her abilities in the past. In fact, his encouragement and support had equaled that of her father and Uncle Jeffrey. Had she been too quick to judge as usual?

Tipping her head back again, she looked up at the ceiling with a blank stare. It was so difficult to trust Altair. His lies and manipulation were not exactly a strong foundation on which to build a relationship. And yet there had been good reasons for his deceit. She understood his need for acceptance.

That was all she wanted. Acceptance for who she was. Her gaze scanned the ceiling, vaguely noting the pictures painted over her head. The priests in Thebes had never accepted Nourbese either. It was why they'd murdered her. She'd been a threat to them and their power in Ramesses' court.

She frowned as her attention focused more clearly on the ceiling. Why would Ramesses have the ceiling of Nourbese's shrine painted? Shifting her body away from the wall, she tipped her head back for a better view. This was artwork unlike anything she'd seen in her studies. It was simple and seemed to contain no significance whatsoever.

The scene depicted Pharaoh and Nourbese walking through a garden. Ramesses' left arm was around his wife's waist in a loving gesture that was atypical of the standard symbols and artwork of the period. Their animated features were also quite odd. It was extremely unusual to find anything but stoic expressions on the faces of Egyptian artifacts. Scooting across the floor, she stretched out on the stone to study the painting without developing a crick in her neck.

It was the strangest thing she'd discovered in the palace to date. While Pharaoh looked adoringly at the face of his queen, his right hand pointed to something in the sky. Nourbese was looking up to the sky in the direction he indicated. Alex did the same as the queen, her gaze coming to rest on a depiction of the Field of Reeds, the Egyptian afterlife. Frowning again, she closed her eyes trying to comprehend what the picture might mean.

"*Damm gahannam!* Alex!"

Jerking upright, she found her face inches away from Altair's worried features. "*What?* What's wrong?"

Relief eased the pallor beneath his darkened skin. "I thought you were—"

A whoosh of air escaped his lungs as he sank back onto one heel, his arm resting atop his bent knee. The fear in his dark gaze warmed her heart. He cared what happened to her, even if he might doubt her abilities. She stretched her hand out to him, and he captured it in a rough grasp, pulling her to him.

His mouth slanted against hers, the fire of his kiss scorching her lips. She didn't pull back. She'd missed him. Missed his touch, the way he made her feel. His hand slid up to cup her breast, and she moaned as his thumb rubbed over the taut nipple. The last few nights had been agony without him.

Her arms wrapped around his neck as his fingers raced to undo her shirt buttons. A moment later he lifted her higher against him, his mouth settling over her hard nipple. She released a small cry of pleasure at his touch.

Need settled deep in her center, dancing its way downward until she was slick with desire. Eager to feel his skin against hers, she pushed his *gambaz* apart. He switched his attention from her breast to her mouth as he shrugged out of the flowing garment.

The incendiary nature of his kiss sucked her breath from her, and she tugged his shirt open to skim her fingers over his bronzed skin. God, she wanted him. Now. She needed him filling her, expanding inside her until the ache only he could soothe dissipated.

Feverishly, she mated her tongue with his. Fingers shaking from the need spiraling through her, she tugged at the belt of her trousers. Sliding her hand downward, she could feel his arousal beneath his own trousers and she slid her hands past the tapes that served as a closure for his Bedouin clothing.

The hardness of his phallus was a direct contradiction to the velvety softness of his skin. The pad of her thumb skimmed over the sensitive ridge just below the tip of him. A deep groan rumbled in his throat. She couldn't wait anymore. She'd been too long without him. Pulling at her shirt, she tugged it off. With a shaky movement, she half stood, half knelt in front of him and removed her trousers.

He growled with excitement and leaned forward as if preparing to mount her. Instead, she stopped him by pressing her hand against his chest. Need, hot and heavy, sank into her limbs as she shifted her body and nestled her curls on the tip of his shaft. A second later, she sank down on him. The guttural noise he made pulled goose bumps up on her flesh. Driven with desire, she moved over him. Filled with him, she arched backward and the molten pleasure heating her body intensified.

Strong arms grasped her waist and a moment later, he was commanding her to move more quickly as he thrust up into her. The intense, raw nature of the act was exhilarating. The primitive, delightfully wicked sensation of it all drove a soft cry from her lips. A wanton creature had taken over her body, demanding he assuage her desire. He filled her completely. Driving deep into her hot slickness. Dear Lord, but she would never grow tired of this sinful pleasure. With each thrust, he offered her an exquisite lesson in need and fulfillment.

The strength of him surrounded her, filled her. Her body stretched toward the ultimate pitch. Arching away from him, she cried out with pleasure, and his deep voice answered as he shuddered and throbbed inside her.

Coming forward, she rested her forehead against his, her breathing erratic. The heat of their lovemaking flushed her skin, and she trembled against his hard body. She wanted to stay in his arms forever. He shifted his body slightly so he could look into her face. The abating passion in his expression mixed with another emotion, but she didn't dare label it. She quivered with the wish for him to speak his heart, but he didn't.

Instead, he lifted her off him and handed her the clothes she'd torn off in her haste to love him. An awkward silence settled between them as they dressed. It was as if speaking after such a frantic joining might somehow shatter the tenuous bond between them. She finished fastening her belt, while Altair watched.

"What the hell were you doing lying on the floor?" The rough edge of his voice told her how badly she'd frightened him.

"Because of this." Tipping her head back, she pointed up at the ceiling.

His head fell back against his shoulders as he looked upward. Puzzlement made his eyes narrow as he studied the painting. "What do you make of it?"

Shaking her head at the quiet question, she continued to stare up at the ceiling. "I don't know. What I don't understand is why Ramesses would put a painting like this where no one would even think to look. It doesn't make any sense."

Lithely, Altair stood up and moved to stand beneath the spot where Ramesses held Nourbese. "Did you notice this odd protrusion here?"

As he pointed toward the spot where Nourbese's side joined that of her husband Alex stood to join him. The sound of voices coming toward them made her stop. She'd grown accustomed to the sound of the lyrical Mazir language, and other than her conversations with Altair, she hadn't heard another English voice in more than two months. Now, the distinct sound of a British accent sent a chill through her.

Altair had grown still as well. She cut him a quick glance, her gaze taking in his impassive features. Footsteps accompanied the voices, and she started toward the chamber door. Altair's hand shot out to grasp her arm.

"Alex, I want—"

"Blakeney, are you in here? Merrick said you'd be in the thick of things." A cheerful voice echoed in Ramesses' bedchamber and a second later, a lean, scholarly-looking man stood in the doorway.

The sight of him made Alex's throat close with panic, and Altair's fingers bit into her arm. It wasn't possible. He wouldn't betray her so cruelly. She'd misunderstood the man's words. Stunned, she stared at the stranger as he stepped deeper into the shrine.

"Ah, there you are. I say, you look like one of the natives, old chap. So, this is the great discovery the little lady made. Merrick is going to be extremely pleased."

Unable to move, she tried to keep breathing. The reality of what Altair had done washed over her. He'd contacted the British Museum. Her stomach swirled with nausea, and she swayed on her feet as she violently tugged herself free of Altair's hold.

A tremor shook through her, and she bit the inside of her cheek until it bled to keep from crying out with anguish. He'd betrayed her. He'd given his word, and he'd broken it. What a fool she'd been. She'd led him and his precious British Museum right to Per-Ramesses.

The depth of his betrayal was a sharp sword that sliced through her with each breath she took. A wave of heat flushed her skin as anger, bitter and fierce, engulfed her. Ignoring the stranger, she turned her head toward Altair. "You bastard."

"Alex, I know what this looks like, but I can explain—"

"Explain what?" she bit out between clenched teeth. "You lied. You gave me your word, and you broke it. You've lied and manipulated me since the day we first met. God help me, I even let you seduce me. Blind me to what you really are—a malicious, self-serving liar, who's only interested in furthering his own ambition."

She watched his face twist with harsh anger at her words. "That's enough, Alex. I know you're upset, but if you'd—"

"Upset? Don't you dare try to patronize me. You have no idea what I'm feeling right now." She wanted to hit him. Hurt him as much as she was hurting now. "God, you're as despicable and vile as Merrick is. *No!* You're worse. Merrick never pretended to believe in my abilities. At least he was honest about his bigotry."

"I've always believed in your skills and abilities," Altair snapped, his eyes flashing with anger. Grabbing her by the arms, he shook her. "And if you'd give me a chance to explain why Caldwell is here, you'd think twice about what you're saying."

Fury wrapped her body in a cloak of fire, and she jerked free of his grasp. She struck out at him with all the cruelty she could muster. "*Keep your filthy Saracen hands off me.*"

Shocked rage held him rigid as she turned away from him. In a daze, she walked toward the chamber doorway, a lead weight resting in her breast where her heart was. It pressed against her chest, making it difficult to breathe. In the space of a few minutes, the air in the shrine had become a cloying scent of betrayal and corruption.

"Come now, Alex. Surely you can do better than that." His voice chilled the air around her. "Why not speak in Coptic to impress Caldwell here. Perhaps he'll find your charms pleasant enough not to mind taking soiled goods."

A clammy coldness slid over her skin at his words. Her gaze swept over Caldwell's embarrassed face, and he had the grace to avert his eyes. Slowly she turned to face the man she loved, her body crying out in protest at his betrayal. Why had he saved her life only to destroy her like this? He was toying with her as one might a mouse. It was cruel and sadistic.

"I never thought I'd ever hate anyone, Lord Blakeney, but you've made the impossible, possible." She amazed herself at how calm and collected she sounded, even though it felt as if she were dying with each word she uttered. Caught up in her own angst, she didn't even wonder at the way his dark skin turned gray at her words. "Stay away from me, my lord. If I never see or talk to you again, it won't be long enough."

Without waiting for his response, she raced from the room.

✧

Ice clogged his veins at the sight of Alex flying from Nourbese's shrine as if every demon in the world were chasing her. He stepped forward to go after her, then changed his mind. No, she wouldn't listen to him right now. She needed time to think.

God, he'd been cruel beyond belief to suggest Caldwell might be interested in her favors. As if he'd let the man near her. She was his, and he wasn't about to give her up without a fight. He should have told her what he'd done. Where Alex was concerned, he never seemed to learn his lesson. Where she demanded honesty, he erred on the side of deception.

He'd known she'd be furious, but he'd never thought to

hear her say she hated him. Fresh and vicious, the memory tormented him with its vividness. His body ached at the remembrance of her dispassionate words. Not even when Caroline had humiliated him in front of the peerage had he felt this much anguish.

Now, Alex had retreated behind a thick wall of fury, and he wasn't sure how he was going to reach her. He'd already bungled things by telling her he believed the prophecy. Certain he was questioning her skills, she'd kept her distance from him over these past few days.

Still, he could have gone to her and explained why he'd contacted the Museum. But each time he'd lost the courage to do so. Thinking time was on his side, he'd put off telling her what he'd done. The last thing he'd expected was someone arriving so soon after he'd sent Kahlil to Cairo.

Across from him, Caldwell cleared his throat. "I take it my arrival was unexpected."

"Quite," Altair bit out. "How did you get here so quickly?"

"I was in Cairo shipping some antiquities back to London, when Merrick wired me you needed assistance out here. Amazing thing, a woman finding Per-Ramesses."

The astonishment in Caldwell's voice made Altair grimace. Not just any woman, but the woman he loved. The simplicity of the thought crashed down on him with the strength of a sandstorm. He loved her, and now he'd lost her. He didn't know what to do.

She hated him for betraying her, but he'd had little choice. Her safety was all that mattered. Surely, he'd be able to make her see that. Doubt flickered inside him. Time. He'd give her time and then he'd set things right between them.

"I say, Blakeney. Have you heard a word I said?"

"What?" Altair looked at the other man. "Sorry, what did you say?"

"I said that Sheikh Medjuel seems beside himself with worry over this dig. The last thing we need is for the natives to balk at helping with the excavation."

"When did you talk with Medjuel?"

"The man met me as my entourage entered the camp. If his skin wasn't so dark, I could have sworn he went white as a

278

sheet when I told him the Museum's team would be arriving in two weeks."

"What did he do then?" Altair's muscles ached with the tension flooding his body.

"He walked away as if I'd hit him. Damnedest thing I've ever seen. Didn't speak another word, just walked away."

Caldwell's comments didn't really surprise him. Instead, he struggled to fight off the suspicions rearing up in his head. He needed to talk to Medjuel. If his cousin was somehow involved in the attempts on Alex's life, he intended to find out.

"I need to return to camp to speak with Sheikh el Mazir. In the meantime, I suggest you find Alex and explain to her that she's in charge, not the Museum."

"I say! A woman in charge of a dig? Have you gone daft, Blakeney?"

"Alex Talbot is one of the best archeologists I've ever worked with." The leashed fury tightening his body made him step quickly toward the other man. "She knows more about Per-Ramesses and Nourbese than anyone the British Museum might care to send. So unless you want to go back to Cairo, I suggest you get used to the idea that she's in charge. Is that clear?"

He'd not meant to make his words appear like a physical threat, but it was apparent Caldwell was worried about his safety. Caring little what the other man thought, he didn't wait for the scholar's answer. Instead, he stalked out of the shrine.

With each step he took toward the palace exit, a sense of doom hung like a dark cloud over his head. If Medjuel was involved in the plot to kill Alex, he didn't know what he'd do. No, he was reading too much into his cousin's behavior. For all he knew, Caldwell had misinterpreted Medjuel's reaction.

Reaching the exit, he charged up the steps and burst out into the sunlight. The sun hovered high above his head, and he glanced over at the work tent. Alex, seated at her table, looked up as he watched her from where he stood. Contempt curled her mouth downward, and he clenched his fists at the scorn in her gaze.

With a final glare of disdain, she returned her attention to the work spread out in front of her. Altair tightened his jaw. He had his work cut out for him when it came to healing the breach between them. But first, he needed to talk to Medjuel. He could only hope his suspicions were wrong.

For the past three days, he'd never left the work site unless Alex did. He'd remained on hand in the event of an emergency, and now he hesitated to leave her unprotected. At that moment, Caldwell emerged from the palace, a wary expression on his face as he circled Altair. Although the scholar wasn't the most rugged of men, he'd at least be able to keep Alex safe until he could return.

"Caldwell, I want you to stay close to Miss Talbot. I won't be gone long. Do you think you can do that?"

"Of course." The man nodded his head.

Satisfied that Alex would be safe until he returned, Altair strode toward his horse and rode toward the Mazir encampment. The ride seemed interminable, but in less than a half-hour, he stood outside Medjuel's tent.

From where he stood, he could see his cousin reading one of the ancient texts reserved only for the Sheikh el Mazir. Without looking at him, Medjuel waved him into the tent.

"Come in, cousin."

Altair stepped into the opulently decorated abode. His cousin's tastes ran to more ostentatious decorations, and there were fringes, beaded throws and expensive furs throughout the vast tent. Uncertain how to begin his questioning, he just stood inside the tent's door.

Medjuel closed the book he held with a snap, then looked up at him. "I've been reading up on the prophecy. It seems your Miss Talbot is very close to finding Nourbese's tomb."

"You sound as if that troubles you." Tension coiled like a snake in his belly, waiting to strike. Something about Medjuel's expression troubled him.

"Not at all." The Sheikh shook his head, his expression a picture of pleasantry. "I simply fear for the *shagi emira's* well-being. However, there is another issue I'd like to discuss with you."

"And that is?"

Medjuel paused as if weighing his words carefully. "I've spoken with the elders, and it's been agreed that you're to step down as my advisor."

Altair stared at his cousin. He'd not been certain what to expect when he entered Medjuel's home—certainly not this. His title of Sheikh had been an honorary one. Losing it was of little consequence to him, but it was his cousin's decision to relieve him of his responsibilities that stung. Even more bruising was the notion Medjuel found him untrustworthy. A man he considered to be a brother. Loyalty had always been his first consideration when it came to the tribe and to Medjuel's leadership. What had he done to make his cousin distrust him?

"Why?"

His cousin reached up to stroke his beard, his black eyes cold and emotionless as he studied him. "Because you've dishonored the family."

Taken aback, Altair glared at Medjuel. "What the hell are you talking about?"

"You bedded the *Ferengi*, Altair." The Sheikh raised a hand in a placating manner. "I can understand that, she's lovely to look at. But you dishonored me and your family by bedding this woman without the vow of marriage."

Altair went cold. When had his cousin become so conservative in his way of thinking? There had always been room for an exchange of different ideas and cultures between them. What had changed that? Not once had anyone ever questioned his actions before.

He'd always acted as his own conscience decreed while respecting the tribe's right to their beliefs. The Mazir had never disapproved of his actions before. What was different now? He bit the inside of his cheek to keep from lashing out at his cousin. With a level stare, he controlled his anger.

"Even if what you say is true, my ways are not your ways, Medjuel. You know that."

"Your ways might not be ours, Altair. Nonetheless your dishonor forces me to strip you of the duties as my advisor and the title of Sheikh." Medjuel sighed heavily. "Altair, this has been a long time coming. I need someone here all the time. Half the year you're in London, and the other you're with us. Each time you come home, you've drifted that much farther away from our ways."

The minor rebuff cut deep. Never before had his English heritage been a subject of criticism or displeasure. "I've done everything in my power to support you and the family. Whenever you've asked something of me, I've done it. You're the Sheikh el Mazir, and not once have I failed to do as you asked."

"That is beside the point. The elders agree with my decision."

For the past two months, his cousin had excluded him from decisions and pushed him out onto the fringes of the tribe's governing system. Now, Medjuel was removing him from his advisory position. It stung. Not because he cared about the title or position, but because Medjuel was a stranger to him. The decision to relieve him of his duties also fanned the flames of suspicion.

His sojourns to England had never been an issue in the past. None of this had been a problem until he'd brought Alex out into the desert. From the very beginning, Medjuel had subtly tried to convince him to stop Alex in her quest. If anything, he should be anxious for Alex to find Nourbese's tomb. The prophecy predicted wonderful rewards for the tribe. Why would Medjuel not want that for his people? Only a man with something to hide would act as his cousin was doing. But how to get Medjuel to reveal his secrets?

"What are you afraid of, Medjuel?"

Black eyes narrowing, the Sheikh shook his head. "I don't know what you're talking about, Altair. I've explained my reasons for relieving you of your duties."

"I see. And what am I to make of all the other strange happenings since my return from England?"

"I've always wondered where Kahlil got his vivid imagination from. It must be your mother's side of the family." Although his cousin's tone was light and his lips curved upward, Altair caught a glimpse of fear in Medjuel's eyes.

"And is it my imagination that you ignored my warnings about Mohammed and the Hoggar?"

"I didn't ignore your warnings, I followed the situation closely."

"And is it my imagination that you never wanted Alex to find Per-Ramesses?"

"That's an exaggeration. I simply indicated concern for her well-being."

"Ah, yes. Her well-being." Altair folded his arms across his chest and watched his cousin closely. "So how do you explain Mohammed?"

"Mohammed? I don't understand the question." This time the fear in Medjuel's eyes was plain to see, and Altair inhaled a deep breath of disappointment and betrayal.

"You didn't fight Mohammed outside Alex's tent, did you? I never could figure out why I'd not heard anything, until this very minute. You made it look like the two of you had fought, but you killed the man in cold blood."

"You forget yourself, cousin."

"No, you've forgotten yourself, *cousin.*" Altair glared at Medjuel. "Did you kill him before or after the ipecac was added to Alex's drinking water?"

Silence filled the tent, and Medjuel stared at him for a long moment. Sharply turning away from him, the Sheikh strode toward a trunk in the far corner of the tent. Throwing the lid open, he rifled through the contents. "Come here, Altair. I want to show you something."

Wary of Medjuel's conciliatory tone, he moved toward his cousin. He'd almost reached the trunk, when Medjuel yanked a rifle out of the trunk and swung it at Altair like a club. His cousin moved far too quickly for Altair to block the weapon's metal barrel. As the rifle connected with the side of his head, his body exploded with pain. Unable to remain standing, his knees gave way as he slid to the floor. His eyes met Medjuel's cold, flat gaze as his cousin raised the rifle again. Before the blow reached him, Altair pitched forward into a dark pit. The last thought flitting through his mind was of Alex. He'd failed to keep her safe again.

Chapter Twenty-Two

Damp with perspiration, the linen shirt Alex wore clung to her skin with the annoying persistence of a wet leaf. Even sitting in the shade of her work tent, the heat made it difficult to concentrate. No, that wasn't true.

Altair's betrayal was what made it difficult. Despite all the warnings her head had screamed, she'd allowed her heart to guide her when it came to listening to his lies. Now she was paying a price beyond measure. She was in love with a man who thought nothing of using her to achieve his own goals.

The memory of his cruel words inside Nourbese's shrine tore at her heart. How could she love a man who lied to her time and time again? A man who'd betrayed her. A fat teardrop landed on the page of notes in front of her. With an angry swipe of her hand, she dashed the tear away. No. She refused to cry over a mess she'd created. She was responsible for letting Altair into her heart.

Still, the pain of that moment in Nourbese's shrine twisted her heart in ways she'd never experienced before. The physical sensation was acute. It jolted her body with every breath she took. Not even the deaths of her father and uncle had prepared her for such torment. Another tear followed the first one.

Her body ached with the memory of his brutal words. Their burning cruelty singed her heart once more. What was she going to do? Per-Ramesses was hers, and he'd handed it over to Merrick on a silver platter. It was her find. Her work.

A bull kicking her in the teeth would be less painful to deal with than watching the British Museum come in and simply take over her father's life work. No, it was her life's work. Worse yet, she didn't know how to fight it. She had more than enough money to see her through the expedition, but she didn't have the power to keep the Museum out.

"Excuse me, Miss Talbot?"

Alex lifted her head to see the lanky figure of the man who'd revealed Altair's betrayal. She pressed her fingers against the bridge of her nose at the sight of him. Her heartache had expanded into a headache, and she grimaced at seeing the man's bookish features. A typical British Museum scholar.

"What do you want?" She returned her attention to her notes. If the bastard thought she'd hand over her notes along with Per-Ramesses, he could think again. Hell would freeze over before she helped this man, or any other for that matter, take over her dig.

"Lord Blakeney indicated that I should see you about what was needed in terms of helping with the excavation. I'm quite skilled in hieroglyphic translation."

"I'm sure you are." She raised her head and glared at the man. "So have at it. There are thousands of markings requiring notation."

"Actually—" the man cleared his throat with a nervous twitch of his cheek, "—I think it would be better if you instructed me where to start."

"Look—what did you say your name was?"

"Reggie Caldwell."

Narrowing her eyes at him, she gave him an abrupt nod of her head. "Right. Now then, Mr. Caldwell, what makes you think I'm going to give you or the British Museum any help whatsoever with my find? Merrick refused to assist me in my search for Per-Ramesses, but now that I've found it, the Museum wants to take it over. How convenient for them and you. So if it's cheerful cooperation you're expecting, you better think again."

"I don't think you understand, Miss Talbot. Lord Blakeney ordered me to get my instructions—"

"Lord Blakeney can go hang for all I care."

"Please, Miss Talbot; I don't think I'm explaining myself very well at all. Lord Blakeney was quite clear in his instructions. I'm to follow your directives in all matters with regard to the dig. He said in no uncertain terms that you were in charge."

The words echoed in her ears, but Alex didn't really comprehend them. Staring at the man, she sank back in her chair in disbelief. What was Altair up to? Befuddled, she shook her head in confusion. What was he planning? Did he think to gain her help for the Museum? Her headache pounded against her temples. She didn't want to think about any of this. She simply wanted everyone to leave her alone.

"Mr. Caldwell, I'm not sure what Lord Blakeney meant by his directions, and until I do know, I'm afraid I can't help you. Now, forgive my rudeness, but I'd like to be left alone."

With a sharp movement, Alex flipped open another notebook and bent her head over the detailed writing. Across from her, Caldwell remained still for a moment before he quietly walked away. As he retreated, she leaned back in her chair and heaved a sigh. Why would Altair tell the man she was in charge of the expedition if he'd been the one to contact the Museum? It didn't make sense.

She breathed in the hot, dusty air and suddenly longed for the cool dampness of the Palace interior. Working always helped ease her heartache. She'd discovered that fact when she'd lost Uncle Jeffrey and her father. Quickly, she gathered up her notes and tools before heading toward the palace entrance. She noticed Caldwell hovering nearby and stopped. Her mind made up, she strode over to him.

"Mr. Caldwell, I think you need to go into the village and make sleeping arrangements. Unless, of course, you've brought your own accommodations."

The man stared at her as if she were breathing fire, and Alex bit back a bitter smile. He fit the description of one of Merrick's minions well. Unlike Altair. She pushed the thought away. Without waiting for the man to speak, she headed back into the palace. The moment she entered the dark interior, the cool temperature acted like a soothing balm to her body and senses.

Inside, she didn't even need to think where she was going. Nourbese's shrine was the key to everything, and she was determined to find Pharaoh's wife before anyone else did. That, they wouldn't be able to take away from her.

As she entered the shrine, she moved to the center of the room and looked up at the ceiling where Altair had pointed out the odd protrusion. Something about where this bulge was positioned in the painting made her think it was deliberate. It rested in the exact spot where the Pharaoh's ribs were. Stretching up her hand, she tried to touch the protrusion, but she wasn't tall enough. Determined to examine the spot more closely, she remembered the step stool she'd been using to reach the wall border that edged the ceiling. She dragged the stool across the rough floor and placed it squarely under Ramesses and Nourbese.

With the stool in place, she could easily reach the long narrow bump that curved its way around half of Ramesses' chest. A rib. Ramesses' rib. Excitement skipped its way through her until her stomach jumped with nervous anticipation. Surely, it couldn't be that easy.

But then what better way to protect Nourbese's remains than right under everyone's nose. In plain view. Her fingers trembled as she gently brushed over the narrow ridge of stone. A sprinkling of dust floated down as she stroked the curved protrusion. Beneath her touch, the painting gave way. It crumbled down onto her face and clothing. Sputtering slightly from the debris, she pulled out her tool brush and began to clear away the material that surrounded what looked like a metal bar.

Her breath hitched in her throat as pigment dust floated downward. With each stroke of her tool brush, it became evident there was a bar beneath the paint. Her fingers trembling with excitement, she brushed away the last bit of pigment dust that had covered the short lever curving around Ramesses' chest.

Hesitating for only an instant, she reached out to touch the bar. Her fingers wrapped around the lever, she gave it a gentle tug. It didn't move. She tried again and still nothing happened. Disgusted, she frowned up at the bar before glaring at Ramesses' expressive face. Irritated, she slammed her fist into the flat edge of the metal bar.

"Damn it! Give her up, you old goat!"

The lever moved slightly. Had she been trying to make it go in the wrong direction? She pushed at the thin, but solid, metal strip one more time. This time it definitely moved. With all of her strength, she pushed on the lever. On the wall opposite Nourbese's statue a large stone slowly shifted to one side revealing a black hole. Her stomach flipped at the sight.

"Excellent, *shagi emîra*. Excellent."

Startled by the Sheikh's unexpected appearance, she lost her footing and slipped off the stool. As her shoulder slammed into the floor's stone slab, she cried out in pain. Instead of bending to her aid, Altair's cousin remained where he stood just inside the doorway of Nourbese's shrine.

"Am I correct in thinking you've found the entrance to Nourbese's tomb?"

Bewildered by his strange behavior, she sat up and nursed her throbbing shoulder.

"I think so. I won't know for certain until I follow the passage." Her eyes searched his face as he quirked an eyebrow at her.

"You're surprised to see me," he said in a cool voice.

"Puzzled would be a more apt description. I've never known you to visit the ruins before."

"True, I have no desire to uncover the past."

"Even a past that will bring wealth to your people?"

The Sheikh folded his arms across his chest before he reached up to stroke his beard. Completely baffled by his odd manner, Alex got to her feet with a grimace.

"I doubt the wealth you mention is there, Miss Talbot. But we shall see." He pulled a torch from one of the wall sconces and moved toward the dark passage.

As he disappeared into the low tunnel, Alex tightened her lips. She damn well wasn't going to let someone else enter Nourbese's tomb without her. Grabbing another torch, she followed the Sheikh into the passageway. Ahead of her she could see his hunched-over figure as he moved forward.

A moment later, she saw his torch disappear as he reached the tunnel's exit. Light filtered its way back into the dense crawl space from where the Sheikh was, and Alex hurried forward to reach the chamber. As she reached the end of the tunnel, she stared in amazement at the sight before her.

Sheikh el Mazir stood in front of a sarcophagus situated in

the center of the room. Aside from the stone coffin, there was nothing else in the chamber. Hopping down into the crypt, she looked around her in disappointment. If this was Nourbese's tomb, where was the treasure? Suddenly throwing his head back, the Sheikh laughed. The maniacal sound lifted the hair on Alex's arms.

Something was definitely wrong. She'd made a mistake following the Sheikh into the tomb. Slowly, she took a step back toward the tunnel. His laughter dying off, the Bedouin leader rested one hand on the stone coffin. "Tell me, *shagi emîra*. Do you love my cousin?"

The extraordinary question caught her off guard and ill prepared to provide a guarded response. "I... How did...yes."

"I see. And would you sacrifice yourself to save him?" The quiet words echoed in the tomb with an insidious air that made her skin crawl. What was wrong with the man? He'd never acted like this with her before. In fact, he'd always been polite and charming. The man had even saved her life on more than one occasion, for heaven's sake.

"I don't understand."

"No, I don't suppose you would. But then you didn't understand about your uncle or your father either."

Fear encased her skin with ice. How could this man know about her family? She'd rarely spoken with him throughout her entire stay in Egypt. "What do you know of my father and uncle?"

"I know they were infidels who wanted to steal what is mine."

"My father and uncle would never have stolen from you."

"I saw to that, *shagi emîra*. I ensured they wouldn't come here, but I didn't account for you and your tenacious will."

A tremor shot through her, and she tried to swallow the lump in her throat, but her mouth was completely dry. "What...how did you keep my...?"

She couldn't continue for the answer was already in front of her. For the first time he turned his head to look at her. The cold, flat look in his eyes terrified her.

"Scorpions are small, but deadly, *shagi emîra*. They died quickly and fairly painlessly, did they not?"

Mute with horror, she could only nod her head. She had to get out of here. He was close, but if she moved quickly enough, she could hop up into the tunnel and scramble back into Nourbese's shrine. Once there she'd have a better chance of escape. She knew the palace layout by heart, and there were several places she could hide if necessary.

"You have not been so easy to get rid of, *shagi emîra.* Nourbese has definitely walked with you since you arrived in Egypt."

"I don't understand. Why would you want me dead?" She stumbled over the last word, her mind trying to concentrate on escaping this madman. A draft of air from the tunnel stirred the hair on her neck, and she shivered. She could only hope it was the tunnel causing the chill against her skin, because the Sheikh was doing an excellent job keeping all the hair on her body standing on end. With the speed of a cobra, he leaped for her and yanked her away from the room's only exit.

"Come now, Miss Talbot. I can't possibly let you stay so close to that tunnel, you might escape your destiny."

Dread spiraling through her veins, Alex tried to twist out of his tight hold. "Let me go!"

"Ah, but if I did that you wouldn't hear the answer to your question. It's quite simple, really. I can't let you live because if you free Nourbese, I lose everything, and that I cannot allow."

"You'll forgive me if I say you're mad."

"Mad? No, *shagi emîra.* I see all too well the results of the prophecy."

"Prophecy?" Alex ground her teeth as anger mixed with her fear. She'd had more than her fill of Mazir fortunetelling. "The prophecy is only a legend. It doesn't mean anything. You and Altair are reading far too much into it."

"Are we? I don't think so. In fact, my cousin was putting the puzzle together when we last spoke, although I must admit I left him a bit—how shall I put it—stunned."

A new fear wrapped its way around her heart, squeezing her chest with a painful tightness. "Is he all right?"

The Sheikh laughed, and she knew her nonchalant tone had failed to conceal her fear. His dark gaze scanned her features with a scornful glance. "He will live, *shagi emîra,* but

I'm curious as to what you're willing to do for him."

"Anything." She spoke the single word with all the strength and purpose of everything she'd ever believed in. There was nothing she wouldn't do for the man she loved.

"Excellent. Then here is my offer. I will spare Altair's life in exchange for yours."

The sinister words were not unexpected, but they still pulled a whoosh of air from her lungs. Staring up at him, she tried to keep breathing as she met his emotionless gaze.

"How do I know you'll not harm him?"

"You don't, but I give you my word as Sheikh el Mazir."

"How do I know you'll keep your word?"

For the first time, fury crossed his controlled features. "I am of the Bedouin tribe the Mazir. We do not go back on our word."

Strangely enough, she believed him. Shaking her head, she sent him a hard look. "I want to know why. I want to know why you want me dead. I deserve that much at least."

"Agreed." He sent her a sharp nod. "The prophecy is everything to the Mazir, and you are about to fulfill that prophecy. But there is a piece of the prophecy that only the reigning Sheikh el Mazir knows about. It has been handed down in the ancient text since the time of Nourbese."

"Let me guess. This missing refrain means something bad is going to happen to you." Alex surprised herself by the sarcastic tone she used. Inside she was a mass of jelly, but it made her feel better to hide her fear behind a façade of angry sarcasm.

"Disrespect is something I won't tolerate, *shagi emîra*." He twisted her wrist sharply, and she gasped at the pain slicing up into her injured shoulder.

"Now then, where was I? Ah yes, the prophecy. From the new world, a woman crowned in hawk feathers will come to find Pharaoh's wife. She will return the jars of life to Nourbese enabling her spirit to join Ramesses in the afterlife.

"In return, Pharaoh's beloved will bestow a wealth of ancient knowledge and treasure on her deliverer, which will benefit all the Mazir. With Nourbese's blessing, the infidel will lead the tribe until the anointed one comes of age and takes his place at the head of the Mazir."

As the Sheikh recited the prophecy, Alex stiffened at the line the man had added. The infidel. It could mean only one thing. Altair. If she lived, then Altair would lead the Mazir. She met the Sheikh's narrowed gaze.

"I see you understand now, *shagi emîra*. I will not surrender my people to an infidel leader."

"But he's your cousin. He loves you like a brother."

"True. It is most unfortunate, but he is after all an infidel. I'm not certain exactly how I'll explain your death, but I shall—"

"There won't be anything to explain, Medjuel, because I'm not going to let you harm her."

Altair's words pierced Alex's heart with first joy then fear. God, the sound of his voice was the most beautiful music she'd ever heard. A second later, a wave of dread rolled over her. Why had he come? The Sheikh would kill him. She couldn't let that happen.

With a quick twist of her wrist, she tried to break free from the Sheikh's firm grip but failed. Furious, the Sheikh jerked her toward him and as her back slammed into his chest, he pulled a curved blade from the front of his robe. Resting the sharp edge against her throat, he glared at Altair.

"So, cousin, was she worth it? Was this *Ferengi* worth losing your family, your position, possibly even your life? Was she?"

The words sailed into Altair like a sledgehammer. There was only one answer he could give. "Yes."

He watched the emotions flash across Alex's face. First shock, joy and then fear cascaded over her features. He should have trusted her. If he'd not been such a stubborn fool, she might be safe at this moment. His eyes met hers, and he marveled at the trust he saw shining back at him. She believed in him and his ability to save them.

Grimly, he returned his gaze to Medjuel's stony expression. The man he knew no longer existed. "Let her go, Medjuel."

"You know I can't do that."

"Why not? She's not the one you fear. I am. Kill me instead. Then it won't matter what Alex finds in Nourbese's tomb."

"*No!*" Alex twisted in Medjuel's arms and a drop of blood

glistened on the blade resting against her throat. His mouth dry with fear, Altair leveled his gaze at her.

"For God's sake, Alex. Stay still."

"Yes, *shagi emîra*. Don't make me cut your throat just yet. I've not tormented my cousin quite enough."

The words sent his heart colliding against his chest wall with a wild beat as he acknowledged the all too real possibility that he might lose Alex. He stared into her hazel eyes. The fear he saw there ebbed slightly. Overwhelming the fear was an expression of love he never thought to claim as his. It strengthened him as he faced off with his cousin.

"If you want me to beg for her life, Medjuel, I will."

"No, I only want you dead."

"Then kill me now. I grow weary of this game you're playing."

"Patience, cousin, patience." Medjuel clucked his tongue inside his cheek. "You never were one to savor the kill were you? Your English blood makes you weak. Even Mohammed in his limited intelligence could see that. Unfortunately, for him, I do not tolerate people who fail me. I have no problem killing to protect what is mine. That's the difference between us, Altair. You've never really been worthy of the Mazir name, nor the title Grandfather bestowed on you."

Medjuel spat out the words at him viciously. The loathing in his cousin's voice and face cut into his soul. He'd always been accustomed to the English taunting him about his Bedouin blood. Now, his English heritage had aroused the same hatred in the man he'd always considered a brother. His body ached from the tension stretching his limbs taut.

He'd never felt so lost in his entire life. The one haven he'd always called home no longer existed. Medjuel had destroyed that oasis with his message of scorn and loathing. The only thing left to lose was Alex, and at this moment, he didn't know how to save her. He was condemned. Condemned by his birthright.

His eyes met Alex's, and the sorrow in her hazel eyes nearly undid him. They mirrored all the agony and sadness racing through his veins. As he stared into her eyes, he stiffened as he recognized the determined glint he'd seen so often. Before he could move or cry out, she reached for the knife at her neck.

In horror, he watched as she grabbed Medjuel's arm and bit into his hand savagely. Enraged, Medjuel cried out in fury, the knife slicing across Alex's arm as she tried to twist free of the Sheikh's grip. Blood soaked her shirtsleeve as she screamed with pain.

Leaping forward, Altair caught his cousin's arm, allowing Alex to stumble away. Now eye-to-eye with his cousin, he allowed his fury to take hold. This man had tried to kill Alex, but he would make damn sure Medjuel wouldn't get the opportunity to succeed.

As they faced off against each other, Altair remembered how as children they'd struggled with each other. Medjuel had won many of their wrestling matches. A sly, vindictive smile curled his cousin's lips. He had remembered too, Altair was certain of it.

"Come now, cousin," Medjuel panted. "We both know I've always been the better wrestler, and your lovely Miss Talbot is of no use to you. No doubt, she's fainted since the sight of blood distresses her so."

"You're *wrong*, you arrogant jackass, I'm too damn mad to let a little blood get the best of me!" Alex cried out as she swung her torch against the Sheikh's head.

As fire and embers crashed upside Medjuel's head, he screamed in pain and fury. For a split second, the man eased his struggle as his hand lashed back and landed a vicious blow to the side of Alex's face. It was enough time for Altair to knock the knife from his cousin's hand. As he stared into the demented gleam in Medjuel's eyes, he knew his cousin would do whatever it took to kill him and Alex.

"Alex, get the hell out of here."

When he didn't hear an answer, he allowed his attention to stray. Fearing for Alex's safety, he glanced in the direction he'd seen her last. The brief flash of distraction was all Medjuel needed. With a quick twist of his body, the Sheikh ducked under Altair's raised arm. A sharp pain snagged up into his shoulder as Medjuel twisted his arm behind his back.

Grunting with pain, he saw Alex on her knees, stunned by the blow his cousin had landed on her cheek. He fully expected to die at that moment. It would be nothing for his cousin to snap his neck with a single twist. Instead, Medjuel shoved him toward Alex.

As he tumbled to the floor, he struggled to keep from landing completely on top of her. Beneath him, she moaned in pain, and turning his head, he watched Medjuel disappear into the tunnel. He almost ignored his cousin's retreat before he realized the consequences of doing so.

"*Damm gahannam.* He's going to seal us inside the tomb." Leaping to his feet, he threw himself into the dark tunnel. He had to reach Medjuel before his cousin closed the sepulcher. If he didn't they'd die of suffocation or worse. The confines of the tunnel closed in on him as he scrambled toward the shrine room.

Ahead of him, the passage grew brighter as Medjuel reached Nourbese's shrine. Increasing his pace, Altair scurried forward in time to see his cousin tug on the bar set in the ceiling. Before he could reach the exit, the stone slab started scraping slowly back into place.

"Medjuel, *stop.*" The opening was closing fast, but he could see his cousin standing in the middle of the shrine, continuing to pull on the mechanism that served to close the tomb. The only answer he received was his cousin's insane laughter followed by a low rumble and the sound of the stone thundering back into place.

Chapter Twenty-Three

The dark closed around him, and he lay prone against the cold stone, a wave of fury sweeping over him. He slammed the side of his fist into the solid wall of stone. He should have known what Medjuel was up to. Why hadn't he moved more quickly? Damn the bastard. Damn him to hell. When he got out of here, he was going to give his cousin a real reason to hate and fear him.

He needed a plan. No one except Medjuel knew where they were. He backed out of the tunnel bit by bit. When he reached the tomb, he dropped lightly to the ground. Turning around, he saw Alex reclined against the sarcophagus. Even in the dim light, he could tell she was pale.

God, this was all his fault. He should have mentioned his suspicions to her. Kneeling at her side, he gently pushed a lock of hair off her cheek. Her eyes fluttered open at the movement and she smiled.

Heaven help him. How could she look so happy when things were so grim? He shook his head. "I'm sorry, *emîra*. I wasn't able to stop him. He closed the tomb."

Her fingers stroked his cheek. "It doesn't matter. We're together. And even if things look bleak at the moment, I wouldn't want to be anywhere else but here, because I love you."

The soft words wrapped themselves around his heart, and he caught her hand in his, burying his lips in her palm. *Yâ maHabba*, that's what she was. His love. Bringing her hand down to rest against his chest, he swallowed the knot in his throat. Even now, it was difficult to put his feelings into words.

"The heart beating in this chest is yours, *yâ maHabba.* I love you is far too simple a phrase to describe how much you mean to me, but I love you with every part of my being."

Leaning forward, he kissed her gently. His mouth pledged his devotion to her in a way words never could. Loving her fulfilled him. Made him whole. Even more amazing was the fact that she loved him simply for himself and no other reason. Her hand clutched his arm as she groaned softly against his mouth. Immediately, he pulled away.

"Damnation, I'm a beast," he rebuked himself in a harsh voice. "Let me see your arm."

"It's nothing. A scratch." She shook her head as he carefully tore her shirtsleeve open to examine her wound. The deep cut made him draw in a sharp breath. It needed suturing. Throwing off his *gambaz*, he tore several strips of cloth from the linen shirt he wore. With a tender touch, he proceeded to bandage her arm. A sigh blew past her pink lips as one of the torches sputtered against the stone floor.

"Why didn't you tell me about the Museum?" The question caught him off guard, and he stopped what he was doing. He had no time to answer as she burst into speech again. "I'm sorry. It seems pointless to be asking that question considering our current predicament."

"You have every right to ask me why, *ana gamâl.* I should have explained before Caldwell arrived." He grazed her forehead with his mouth. The problem was he didn't know how to justify his actions in a way she would understand.

"But you didn't. Why?"

"I was afraid to tell you. I knew it would be difficult making you understand my reasons were based solely on keeping you safe from harm."

"How could giving the Museum my work protect me?"

"Because I knew Merrick would send a large team of archeologists, and the more people there were on the dig, the fewer opportunities there would be for someone to hurt you."

He watched her mull over this explanation for a moment, comprehension dawning slowly on her face. Her eyes met his again. Direct, yet filled with love.

"How long had you known about Medjuel?"

"I've suspected for some time now, but I could never make myself believe it." He tried to suppress the note of anguish in his voice, but she heard it nonetheless. With her good arm, she reached up to brush her fingers across his cheek.

"I know how betrayed you must feel."

He heaved a sigh. "Because I betrayed you by contacting the Museum."

"Yes."

"I only had your safety in mind, *yâ maHabba*. I only wanted their presence here as a protective measure. It was always my intent to use my position as liaison to ensure you were in charge of the excavation."

"So that's why you instructed Caldwell to get his orders from me."

"Yes." He lifted her chin to look directly into her eyes. "I love you, Alex. No matter what happens, I'll always love you."

Tears welled in her eyes, and he swallowed his deep misgivings about their chances for escaping the tomb Medjuel had condemned them to.

"We aren't going to get out of here, are we?" When he ignored her question and busied himself with dressing her wound, she grimaced. "Okay, I guess that answers that question."

"I haven't given up yet, *yâ maHabba*."

When he finished with her bandage, he got to his feet to run his hands against the walls of the small chamber. There often was a second passage into Pharonic tombs, and perhaps Nourbese's crypt possessed one as well.

Bas-relief figures lined the walls of the tomb, creating scenes from Nourbese's life. One showed a child with a Mazir tribesman, another of a young girl and a boy with a pharaoh's crown hovering over his head. The scenes continued around the walls, creating a panorama of important periods in the queen's life.

A familiar tension tugged at him, tightening his muscles like a taut bowstring. It was the way his body always reacted whenever she was near. Turning around, he frowned. She looked weak as a newborn babe. "Sit down, before you fall down, *ana anide emîra*."

She ignored him and nodded at the wall. "Have you ever seen anything like this in a tomb before?

"No, and I can't study them if I'm worried about whether or not you're about to faint."

A feverish light gleamed in her hazel eyes. Was it her injury or renewed excitement about Nourbese? It didn't matter, she needed to stay still or she was going to soak her bandage a lot sooner than he'd like.

Grasping her shoulders, he forced her back toward the sarcophagus. As he made her sit down on the stone floor, his eyes caught a scene carved into the heavy stone coffin. He studied the oddly familiar view for a moment, before dismissing it and returning his attention to Alex. She was still pale, but excitement gave her skin a healthier glow than she'd shown just a few moments earlier.

"Altair, look, the relief on the wall over there." She bobbed her head in the direction of a diorama depicting the wedding of Nourbese and Ramesses. "It's on the sarcophagus. See?"

She raised her good arm and pointed at the head of the coffin. Following her gaze, he compared the two scenes. He sprang to his feet and examined one wall after another. Every image he studied was repeated on the sarcophagus.

The only scene not repeated on the walls was that of the Pharaoh and his queen walking together under the stars. Carved into the head of the stone coffin, the picture was virtually identical to the painting on the shrine's ceiling. Kneeling in front of the carving, he ran his fingers over the sharp lines of the detailed picture.

The workmanship was exquisite. Ramesses again pointed to the sky, but this time Nourbese's hand rested just beneath a round medallion at her throat. Something about the medallion struck him as odd. It looked almost like a plug of sorts. He pulled in a sharp breath of air. "Alex, I need you to get away from the sarcophagus."

"What's wrong?" The weary note in her voice troubled him. Not waiting on her to obey his command, he moved to where she sat and scooped her up off the floor. Gently he set her down against the far wall.

"I'm not sure what I've found, but I think the sarcophagus is a sham. I doubt it's real."

"I don't understand."

"Watch."

Satisfied that she wasn't going to get up and follow him, he returned to the relief carved into the head of Nourbese's coffin. With his fingers, he tried to pry away at the medallion. When nothing happened, he pushed against the round decoration. Beneath his fingertips, the carving gave way slightly.

As he pushed against the relief with more force, the jewelry slowly sank into the throat of Nourbese's figure. As the medallion disappeared deeper into the carving, a loud click, followed by the familiar sound of stone scraping stone, filled the chamber.

Jubilant, he grinned with satisfaction. Ramesses' reputation for being wily had not been off the mark. Standing up, he saw the lid of the sarcophagus sliding slowly to the right and then left until it came to rest horizontally across the vertical line of the coffin.

He peered inside. The darkness yawning up at him was not a surprise. The torch on the floor had almost spluttered out, and as fast as he could, he picked it up and dropped it down into the open coffin. It didn't go far, and as the torch fell, he could see the steps leading to the passage beneath the chamber.

A soft sigh reached his ears, and he glanced over at Alex. She was watching him with such a look of trust and love he grimaced. He wasn't worthy of her. "I need to go down and see where this leads. Will you be all right for a few minutes?"

"If you think I'm going to let you go exploring without me, you can forget it. I'm coming with you."

"No, it might be dangerous, and you're in no shape to go scurrying about ancient tunnels."

"I refuse to argue with you." Her eyes fired a look of irritation in his direction. Slowly getting to her feet, she carefully stalked over to where he stood. "If you think I'm going to sit here in the dark while you go off to God knows where, you'd better rethink that idea. Either I come with you, or I'll follow you in the dark."

Resigned to her tenacity, he shook his head. She was far too stubborn and bull-headed for her own good. "Just once, I'd like to hear you say, *Yes, Altair, I'll do as you ask.*"

"And if I did, then I wouldn't be the woman you fell in love with, would I?"

"No," he said as she grinned up at him. "You wouldn't."

Unable to help himself, he lowered his head and kissed her. She tasted spicy and warm, exactly like the heat that rose up off the sand in the waning hours of a sunset. He suppressed the urge to clutch her close. The last thing he wanted to do was hurt her or make her arm bleed again.

Instead, he clasped her face in his hands and crushed her mouth beneath his in a demanding kiss. He breathed in her scent, and his groin stirred at the heady taste of her. God help him. It was insane to want her at a moment like this. With a groan of frustration, he set her back from him.

"You go to my head, *ana gamâl*, and now isn't the time for me to indulge in the delights of your delectable body. I intend to find a way out of here, marry you as soon as possible, and then I'll spend the rest of my days exploring every temptation you offer me."

Love sparkled in her eyes, and she smiled. "Hmm, I don't recall anyone asking me if I wanted to get married."

For only a brief flicker of time did fear wrap itself around his heart, and a wry smile tugged at his mouth. "Do you wish for me to propose now or later, *emîra*? However, I must warn you the torch will only last for a while longer."

"Then I suppose I'll have to wait, but I intend to hold you to your word."

With another hard kiss on her lips, he retrieved the torch from the metal ring buried into the sepulcher wall and climbed into the stone coffin. Descending a few steps, he offered his hand to her, and she followed him. Together they slowly walked down the stone staircase.

At the foot of the steps, they had a choice of going left or right. He frowned. Which way to go? The torch would only last so long, and then they'd be helpless. As if sensing his indecision, she touched his arm.

"We go left, I think."

"Why?"

"Because Pharaoh always keeps Nourbese on his right to protect her."

He had no idea if she was guessing or not. It didn't matter. The decision made, he held her hand as they went to the left. As they walked, the tunnel slanted upward until he estimated they were a little higher than the tomb they'd just left. The passage leveled off, extending beyond the light of the torch. The sputtering hiss of the flame told him it wouldn't last much longer.

"Can you move faster, *ana gamâl?* There's not much time."

She was breathless, but she gave him a weary nod. Satisfied that she would be able to keep up, he increased the pace. They'd gone about thirty yards, when the passage turned left at a sharp angle. As they rounded the turn, the torch flashed as if it had inhaled a sudden breath of air. The flame flared brightly and he drew in a quick breath. Air. Fresh air. His hand squeezing Alex's, he pulled her along the corridor at a fast pace. The dank smell of the buried tomb slowly gave way to the heated aroma of the desert. Excitement sent a tremor of relief through him at the small stream of light he could see up ahead. They were only a few feet away from the crack through which the light invaded the darkness when the torch died a quick death. Behind him, Alex gasped in dismay. Her hand still in his, he squeezed her fingers in a reassuring manner.

"It's all right, *emîra.* Daylight is just beyond this stone. We simply need to find a way to get through it. I need both hands to work, but I'm right here."

"I'm not going anywhere. But I do think I'll sit down," she said in her usual feisty manner.

The corners of his mouth tugged upward. He couldn't see her face, but his senses told him she had lost her fear. Still the quiet edge to her voice confirmed her exhaustion. Not once had she complained about her arm, but it obviously pained her.

When he got his hands on Medjuel, he'd make the bastard pay for hurting her. Never would he have thought his cousin capable of such treachery. Of such betrayal. Betrayal. The word dried his mouth with bitterness. Who else in the Mazir tribe viewed him with such bitter hatred?

Wincing at the thought, he pressed his hands against the smoothness of the cool wall. Ramesses had been a cunning ruler. Outwitting his political enemies and avoiding assassination had sustained his long reign. A man of that caliber always planned for contingencies. There had to be a way out of here.

He continued his exploration of the wall, looking for a lever, a hole in the wall, something—anything that would release them from this darkness. Behind him, Alex scrambled to her feet with a strangled cry. He reached out for her and pulled her to him.

"What is it, *yâ maHabba*?"

"Something just ran over my foot."

"Then that means there's definitely a way out of this bloody prison."

"Well, if we don't find it soon, I'm not going to be responsible for what I intend to do to that maliciously arrogant cousin of yours."

"I'll deal with Medjuel."

"You're going to have to stand in line, darling. I'm going to make him rue the day he ever heard the Talbot name."

The fire in her voice made him laugh for the first time since their troubles began. It was only a brief instant before she was laughing with him. With her warm body snuggled against him, it was easy to forget that he'd ever been alone in the world. Not for anything would he give up the precious gift of her love. He pressed a kiss against her forehead.

"Come, I need to find the mechanism that will open this tunnel. Ramesses would have designed it so he had a way to escape if someone tried to seal him up in Nourbese's tomb."

"But it wasn't her tomb."

"We know that now, but it's doubtful his political enemies knew that."

"Then, let's get to work. I can check the wall on the right. And don't you dare suggest I sit down. I'm in no mood to find out what went across my foot."

There was just a thread of terror in her voice, and he knew better than to argue. She needed to do something to take her mind off their troubles. If helping him kept her mind from imagining the worst, she'd be far better off.

"I wouldn't dream of interfering with Alexandra Talbot's quest to defeat the mighty Ramesses."

"Beast."

He laughed. The lighthearted note in her voice neutralized the insult. They resumed work and after more than an hour, neither of them had experienced success. For the first time, he succumbed to the possibility they wouldn't find an exit. He didn't voice his negative thoughts. Let her keep her optimism a little longer.

The sudden sound of her sharply indrawn breath made him reach for her in the darkness. His hand on her shoulder, he followed her outstretched arm to where her fingers had wrapped around a solid iron lever.

"Shall I pull or do you want to?"

The breathless quality of her voice confirmed a hope he didn't want to crush. "You found it, you have the honor."

With a spurt of energy, she tugged on the lever. He could tell from her grunt of irritation that the lever was being difficult. Gently, he searched for her hand in the dark and wrapped his fingers around hers. Together, they yanked the lever toward them. For the third time that day, the ominous sound of heavy stone moving against stone echoed in his ears. Only this time the noise was a welcome one. As the wall slowly slid back, sunlight poured into the once fathomless darkness of the passageway.

Pulling Alex into the light, he relished the heat of the late afternoon sun. She stepped into his side and buried her face into his shoulder. With a shudder, she burst into tears. In silence, he held her, allowing her to cry for both of them. Several long moments passed before her crying evolved into soft hiccups.

His fingers nudged her chin upward so he could look into her glistening gaze. "You're safe now, my love. I won't let anything else hurt you."

"The only promise I care about is your promise to love me for the rest of our lives and into the afterlife."

He kissed her gently. Lifting his head, he smiled. "That's a vow I can easily keep. I can also guarantee you happy days and wicked nights of pleasure."

"I can think of no one else I'd want to be sinful with other than you, my love."

"Say that again."

"What?"

"That endearment. Say it again," he demanded.

The sultry smile curving her lips stirred his desire until his body was taut with hunger. She knew her power over him, but she didn't covet that power. She only wanted him. It was plainly evident in her loving gaze.

"*Yā maHabba.* My love," she whispered.

He lowered his head again, determined to reiterate over and over the depth of his love. She didn't protest. Instead, she clung to him in a display of passion that gladdened his heart and enflamed his desire. She was his, and he would never let her go.

Epilogue

"Gameela Alexandra Montgomery! You get down from there this instant." Hands braced on her hips, Alex glared at her seven-year-old daughter standing on a scaffold against one of the walls of Hathor's temple. It was their latest find in the Per-Ramesses complex.

"But, Mama, I think I've found something."

"I'm warning you, young lady. If you don't get down here right now, there'll be the devil to pay."

"Oh, all right."

"Where's your brother?" Alex stood ready to catch the slender child at the first misstep during her descent.

"Cam's racing camels with Uncle Kahlil."

"Good." Helping Gameela down off the last rung of the scaffold, Alex jerked upright. "What do you mean he's racing camels with your uncle?"

"Uncle Kahlil is teaching him how to race." Shrugging, the child looked up at her with a mischievous twinkle in her dark eyes.

"God in heaven! A five-year-old doesn't need to be racing camels." Alex grasped her daughter's brown arm and started to pull her toward the temple entrance.

"It's all right, *yâ maHabba*. Cameron is with my mother."

"Altair!"

"Papa!"

Gameela broke free of Alex's grasp and raced toward the tall figure filling the temple doorway. With a laugh, Altair swung

306

his daughter up into his arms and kissed her cheek.

"Oh, Papa, we missed you. Mama especially. She's been very grouchy for the last few weeks."

"Has she now?" Altair smiled as he quirked an eyebrow at Alex and stepped forward to give her a quick kiss. Her heart skipped a beat before it accelerated to twice its usual pace. Altair sat down on a nearby workbench and perched Gameela on his knee.

"Yes, please don't go away again, Papa. I don't like it when Mama is so unhappy."

Arms firmly locked around her father's neck, Gameela pressed her cheek against his face. The sight made Alex's heart ache. The children had missed Altair as much as she had, and she'd failed to realize it. She smiled at her daughter.

"Why don't you tell Papa what you found in the temple last week."

Gameela's face lit up with excitement as she nodded at her mother. Turning her head, she proceeded to share the tale of how she'd found three small statues buried in the rubble outside Hathor's temple. For the next quarter of an hour, Gameela kept her father laughing as she regaled him with tales of her escapades during his absence.

As Alex watched her husband and daughter get reacquainted, she experienced an overwhelming sense of joy. She had everything she could ever want. A wonderful man who loved her, two beautiful children and her work. There wasn't anything else she needed for her happiness. Although it saddened her that her father and uncle had never lived to see Per-Ramesses, she believed with all her heart that they had been watching over her all these years.

"Mama said we'd go to Cairo to see the Pyramids when you came home. Didn't you, Mama?" Gameela's voice pulled Alex's attention back to the conversation at hand.

"Cairo?" Alex sent her only daughter an ironic smile. "Yes, I seem to recall you wheedling that promise out of me."

Altair laughed. "I think that can easily be arranged. Your mother will want to go when I tell her who I saw there."

"Who? Who did you see?" Gameela eyed him with expectation.

"Your godmother."

"Aunt Jane," the child squealed with glee.

"Jane! Why didn't you bring her with you?" Alex demanded. "Surely she could have come for a short visit."

She frowned at her husband. It had been almost a year since her friend's last visit, and they had a great deal of catching up to do.

A slow grin curved his mouth as he sent her a devilish look. "She sent her regrets as she's been rather busy since her husband's recent appointment as Viceroy to Egypt."

"Viceroy!" She gaped at Altair.

She couldn't remember the last time she'd been so surprised. Jane would be perfect in the role of vicereine. A talented hostess, her friend would excel at entertaining dignitaries. She smiled broadly.

It would be wonderful having her dear friend so close. This new position meant Jane would be living in Cairo full time now, not just a few months out of the year. She would have to make time in her schedule to go for a visit as soon as she could. Altair smiled at her before he winked at their daughter.

"I tell you what, *ana emîra,* why don't we kidnap your mother and carry her off to Cairo next week? We'll visit the Pyramids *and* your Aunt Jane. Would that make you happy?"

"Oh, yes, Papa. Yes." Gameela flung her arms around Altair's neck and kissed his cheek.

"Then it's settled," he said in a loud whisper. "But we'll have to keep her guessing as to when."

Gameela giggled as Altair set her on her feet. "May I tell Cameron we're going to see the Pyramids and Aunt Jane?"

"If you like, you can run back to camp and tell him now." Altair kissed her forehead. "Your mother and I will be along shortly."

Gameela squeezed her arms around his neck one last time before she scurried out of the temple. As their daughter disappeared, Altair rose to his feet and pulled Alex into his arms. Her hands cradling his head, she pulled his mouth down to hers. She wanted to devour him. It had been so long since he'd left for England.

Heat slid across her skin as her blood grew hot and spread

its warmth throughout her body. Her fingers burrowed into his thick, brown hair as her mouth opened beneath his. Their tongues mated in a familiar dance, and her belly grew taut at the sensual touch. God, she'd missed him. From now on they were going to London together. She breathed in the deliciously familiar scent of cedarwood and sweet fennel.

With a bold move, her hands slid inside his gambaz, and she opened his shirt to trace her fingers over his hard chest. The touch pulled a deep groan from him, and his mouth increased its pressure. Already she could feel the familiar ache between her thighs, and she wanted it now. She didn't want to wait for tonight.

Pushing away from him, she took several steps back. The surprise on his face made her smile. The man had no idea what she was up to. With each step backwards, she undid a button on her shirt. Desire glowed in his eyes as he came after her, stalking her with the grace of a large cat. A breathless laugh parted her lips, before she wheeled about and darted into a dead-end corridor. Turning to face him, she pressed her back into the wall and waited for him to draw near.

"You know the penalty for teasing, *yâ maHabba.*"

She guided his hands to her breasts. "Oh, yes, my love. I'm counting on it."

A deep growl echoed in his throat as he dipped his head and swirled his tongue around a hard nipple. Moaning her delight, Alex struggled to slide her feet out of her boots. One boot off, she reached inside his gambaz, past his trousers to find his hard length. God, she was so wet for him. If she waited any longer, she'd surely die from the craving that assaulted her body. His mouth still suckling her breast, his large hands quickly unlatched her trousers until his fingers stroked the sensitive nub at her core.

"Please, my love. I need you. I want to feel you inside me, now." She shuddered at his touch, a rush of liquid heat flowing over his fingers.

Raising his dark head, he stared down at her. Passion and desire filled his eyes, but there was great love there as well. His gaze never leaving her face, he roughly pushed aside his clothing, followed by her trousers. She gasped as his large hands cupped her buttocks as he pressed himself against her curls. Seconds later, he lifted her high against his chest so he could thrust inside her.

Damn, she felt good around his cock. Even after almost nine years of marriage, he could never get enough of her. The hot, silky folds of her gripped him fiercely as her legs wrapped around his waist. One hand braced against the smooth temple wall, he thrust into her with a fury that drove home his need. She answered with a thrust of her own. The heat of her created a pleasurable friction as his cock filled her then retreated, one stroke after another. Her fingers bit into his shoulders, and the first tremors of her climax ran through her.

The spasms rippling along the length of him tugged a deep groan out his throat. If possible her insides clenched around him tighter as she kissed him, her tongue sweeping into the warmth of his mouth. There was the lingering taste of citrus on her tongue. Need whipped through him, and he surged up into her. A low cry escaped her as her body shuddered around his hard cock. Burying his own cry of release in her neck, he spilled his seed and throbbed inside her.

He threw back his head a moment later and a sigh of pleasure eased out of her. "Now that, my lord, is the proper way to say hello to your wife."

A deep chuckle rolled up out of his throat. "Heaven help me. Sometimes I think you're randier than I am."

"Only with you, my love. Only with you."

The tender words made him rest his head against her forehead, and he sighed. "I missed you terribly, *emira*. Never again will I go to London without you."

"You won't get any argument from me on that score, darling."

As he released her, she gathered her clothes and proceeded to make herself presentable. Moments later, they walked back out into the temple's main shrine, their arms around each other's waists. Alex rested her hand against his chest, and she took a deep breath. The question hovering in the back of her mind for the past two months was about to be answered.

"Well?"

"Well, what?" There was a distinct trace of amusement in his husky voice, and Alex scowled up at him.

"You're as deliberately vague as your daughter."

He laughed. "The answer is yes. The Museum is going to open up an office in Cairo."

With a whoop of excitement, Alex danced away from his side to grasp his hands and stretch out his arms. "So, Mr. Director, how does it feel to be running the British Museum's Egyptian Office of Antiquities in Cairo?"

"Actually, I wasn't given the post."

"What! Who the hell do they think they are?"

"Alex—"

"You're perfect for that job, and no one else knows this area like you do."

"*Alex—*"

"I thought once Merrick retired, things would—"

With a quick, forceful tug, he pulled her into his arms, and his mouth covered hers in a deep kiss. As he lifted his head, she sighed. "All right, I'll be quiet. But I still think they're fools!"

"Will it help if I tell you I was named Assistant Director?"

She snorted in disgust. "Assistant Director! Ha! So what bumbling idiot is the Director?"

"Someone by the name of Lady Blakeney."

"Blakeney! Who the hell—?" She stared up at him in stunned disbelief. It couldn't be. Dazed, she saw the pride gleaming in his eyes as he smiled down at her.

"Yes, *yâ maHabba.* Viscountess Blakeney, otherwise known as Alexandra Talbot Montgomery."

"Oh my God. You can't be serious? But how?"

"Your work here says it all, *emîra.* In fact, the temple here in the complex has been the talk of the Museum for months. One new member of the department was especially enthusiastic about your work. Mr. Budge is his name. He was particularly interested in the transcripts you've made."

Alex inhaled a deep breath and closed her eyes to seal in the tears. For so long she'd fought for acceptance in the archeology community, and now that it had arrived, she realized it wasn't as important as she once thought. She had everything she could have ever wanted—a man who adored her and two beautiful children. It was simply icing on the cake.

"Alex?"

She looked up at him and smiled. "I'm fine. Just a bit shocked."

"I'd thought you'd be thrilled." He shook his head in confusion, and she snuggled against him.

"I am, but I've learned that you and the children are far more important to me than anything else. This is simply dessert. And speaking of dessert, I want to show you something. Come on."

With a tug of his hand, she pulled him out of the temple and across the heavily excavated complex of Per-Ramesses. When they reached the palace, she led the way into the completely open site. The centuries of earth that had once buried the palace was now gone, revealing the beauty of Ramesses' home. As Altair stared around him, he marveled at what his wife had accomplished over the past eight years.

Her father would have been proud of her. Damn it, he was proud of her. As they entered Ramesses' bedchamber, his jaw tightened. He'd not been in here since the day Medjuel had tried to seal them in what they'd thought was Nourbese's tomb. When they'd escaped and returned to the shrine, they'd found Medjuel buried beneath the shrine's collapsed ceiling.

Despite his relief that Alex was safe, the anger and pain of his cousin's betrayal had not made it easy for him to accept the possibility of happiness with the woman he loved. But Alex had refused to let him retreat from her.

Ruefully, he admitted that whatever his wife set out to accomplish, she did just that. Now as he entered the shrine behind Alex, he looked up at the ceiling. When the edifice had collapsed on top of his cousin, it had revealed the mechanism that opened and closed Nourbese's false tomb, along with the trigger that caused the ceiling to collapse. It had also uncovered a strange inscription. He read the words again.

When the evil one condemns his brother to a cruel fate, so shall he seal his own destiny under the weight of his treachery.

How could Ramesses have known? It was as if the ancient ruler had foreseen everything and planned for it. There could be no other explanation. Somehow, Pharaoh had known what would happen and designed the ceiling to collapse when someone used the lever to seal the tomb. The theory would explain why he'd built the escape tunnels from the false tomb.

But if all that were true, why couldn't they find Nourbese's real tomb? For almost eight years, they'd been searching the complex in hopes of finding the burial place of his Mazir ancestor. And no matter where they looked, they found nothing. It was puzzling to him, frustrating to Alex, but for the Mazir it had become a painful reminder of Medjuel's dishonor.

"Are you all right, darling?"

"What?" He looked down into Alex's worried expression. "Hmm, yes, I'm fine."

"Are you sure? This room holds painful memories for you, and I wouldn't have brought you here if it weren't important."

He pressed his lips against her furrowed brow before smiling at her. "I'm fine. So tell me, what is this important discovery you want to show me?"

"We'll need to go into the tomb itself."

With a nod, he watched as Alex slid into the opening that led to Nourbese's empty tomb. Following close behind, he grimaced at the memories flooding through him. The sound of the tomb rumbling shut was something he'd never forget. He blocked it from his mind as he jumped down onto the floor of the burial chamber.

"All right, Lady Blakeney. What exactly are we doing here?"

"Do you remember my showing you Nourbese's canopic jars shortly after Medjuel's death?" Folding his arms across his chest, he nodded at her question, waiting for her to continue.

"Well, two weeks ago, I felt this need to come back here. I don't know why, but the tomb drew me back in here, and that's when I noticed it."

"What?"

"The indentations. Look." Tugging on his hand, she pulled him into one corner of the room and pointed to a shallow dent in the floor. "Do you see it?"

"Yes, but what's so important about an anomaly on the floor?"

"Because there's one in each corner of the room. One for each canopic jar."

He froze. Slowly he scanned each corner, trying to see the

curved indentations before he noticed the canopic jars sitting at the foot of the sarcophagus. She thought she'd found Nourbese's tomb at last. It was why she'd brought the canopic jars in here. He met her excited gaze.

"So you've finally come to grips with the prophecy?"

"Yes. I've never really been comfortable with it, but there's not much I can do about it. Now, are you going to help me set these jars in place or not?"

With a wry smile, he picked up a jar and moved to one corner to set the container in place. As he did so, he noticed the faint, circular outline in the floor. The indentation was so faint, it was amazing she'd even been able to see it at all. The canopic jar settled inside the concave indentation, he watched Alex set her funereal container in place. A moment later, he retrieved another jar and proceeded to place it in the corner farthest from him.

When he finished, he turned to see her waiting for him at the final indentation with the last jar. She truly did believe in the prophecy now. She knew his presence as a Mazir would fulfill the tribe's destiny. Taking the jar from her, he set it in place. Straightening, he waited for something to happen. When nothing did, Alex expelled a noise of furious frustration.

"Damn it! I could have sworn this was it."

"It's all right, *emîra*. I'm sure—"

The sudden scraping of stone against stone filled the tomb. Wheeling about, he stared in wonder as the entire sarcophagus slid back until the foot of the heavy container touched the far wall. With the sarcophagus moved back, two descending passages were made visible. The first was the escape route they'd used to save themselves. The other staircase descended in the opposite direction. It could only lead to Nourbese's tomb.

Alex let out a whoop of joy and launched herself into his arms. "I was right! I was right!"

He pulled her close, his heart swelling with love and pride. This glorious woman had given herself to him with everything she possessed. And now, she was about to offer his people the treasure promised to them more than three thousand years ago.

"I love you, Alex."

"Come on, you have to go first."

He nodded and taking a torch from one of the wall sconces, he descended the staircase. Behind him, he heard her rapid breathing. Surprisingly, he was breathing hard with excitement himself. At the foot of the stairs, a small passage opened up into a large room.

As the torch lit the room, he could only stare in amazement at the interior of the chamber. Beside him, Alex drew in a sharp breath. "Oh my God."

Everywhere he looked gold glittered in the torchlight. The sarcophagus in the middle of the tomb was one of the most elaborate he'd ever seen. Scrolls of papyrus lined the walls, while chests and furniture filled the chamber.

"We did it, Altair. We finally did it. The Mazir will have Nourbese's treasure and knowledge."

"No." He shook his head and pulled her into his arms. "No, I did nothing except have the extremely good fortune to find a woman crowned in hawk feathers. Without her, I'd still be a man without a home to call his own."

"And when Kahlil becomes Sheikh el Mazir next year and you turn over the reins of leadership—will you still feel that way? Will you still feel like you have a home?"

Staring down into her hazel eyes, he remembered the first time they'd met, and how she'd buried her vulnerability beneath a calm exterior, but her eyes had revealed her trepidation. She possessed that same look now. He tightened his embrace and smiled at her.

"Home is where the heart is, *yâ maHabba*, and my heart is wherever you are."

A sigh of happiness eased past her pink lips, and desire and love welled up inside him. Lowering his head, he kissed her deeply. Never again would he feel caught between two worlds. His *anide emîra* had shown him that love wasn't a mirage, but a tangible force of the heart with which to celebrate life. He'd finally come home.

About the Author

A multi-published author of erotic romance, Monica Burns penned her first short romance story at the age of nine when she selected the pseudonym she uses today. Even then she knew that Burns was a great last name for an erotic romance writer who writes burning hot stories. A workaholic wife and mother, Monica is a 2005 Golden Heart Finalist, 2008 double EPPIE finalist, and a recipient of JERR's Silver Star award.

To learn more about Monica Burns, please visit www.monicaburns.com. Send an email to Monica at monicaburns@monicaburns.com or join her on her Bulletin Board at www.monicaburns.com/bulletinboard to join in the fun with other readers as well as Monica! For her announcements only Yahoo group, visit http://groups.yahoo.com/group/MonicaBurnsAnnouncements.

Behind the mask lies love—a dangerous and deadly emotion.

Dangerous
© *2008 Monica Burns*

Constance Athelson, Viscountess Westbury, has a gift she can't reveal. She sees things others can't, including the dead. The only thing she can't see is into the heart of Lucien Blakemore, Earl of Lyndham. After one blissful night in his arms, she knows if she's ever to win his heart, she must free him from his tortured past.

Lucien Blakemore met the Egyptian goddess Isis at a masked ball, but she vanished into the night before he could learn her real name. It's just as well, since the Blakemore Curse makes love a dangerous and deadly emotion for him. But the erotic night he spent with his mysterious lover makes him want to throw caution aside—if only for one more night with his masked goddess.

Warning, this title contains the following: explicit sex with a hero whose torment equals that of Jane Eyre's Mr. Rochester.

Available now in ebook and print from Samhain Publishing.

Enjoy the following excerpt from Dangerous...

At the foot of the main staircase, Constance hesitated as she thought she heard a sound coming from the library. When there was no repetition of the noise, she entered the salon and closed the door behind her. Seconds later, she picked up the violin off the top of the baby grand piano.

The wood of the instrument heated her hand with the same warmth Lucien's caress had aroused in her. The memory of his hand on her skin sent a sweet tremor through her. If she was to be held hostage to her passion then she'd play out the emotions in her music. With a deft movement, she tucked the violin under her chin.

The familiar curve of the chin rest warmed and soothed her skin as she grasped the bow's frog in her fingers. Eyes closed, she slowly caressed the instrument's strings with the bow. It was a musical imitation of Lucien's hands sliding across her skin. The heat of his imagined touch expanded and tingled across every inch of her body as she feathered the bow back across the strings. The violin's haunting notes heightened the slow, teasing image of his dark hands stroking her body until her senses hummed with awareness.

Her nipples grew hard at the erotic images flying through her mind, and in desperation she focused all her attention on the difficult sonata she was playing. It was a useless attempt. The memory of Lucien licking her nipples until she was writhing beneath him was too delicious to clear from her head. With each note her bow pulled from the strings, it reminded her of the passion she'd shared with Lucien.

The memory of watching the two of them in the mirror over his bed sent her heart and fingers racing. What had begun as a slow arc of sensual notes quickly erupted into a flurry of sound that echoed the heat flooding her body. The bow danced across the strings of the instrument, and her breathing grew ragged as the pace of the music increased.

She had always loved this particular piece, and had played it many times with Sebastian accompanying her on the piano. But tonight she understood the meaning of the sonata. It was a cry of desperation. It represented the need and hunger of two lovers. And in her mind, her hands caressed Lucien, touching him, arousing him until he groaned with need. Need for her...

"Most impressive, my dear lady."

With a jerk, Constance opened her eyes to see Nigel watching her from the darkened corner of the room. Setting her violin and bow down on the piano, she glared at the ghost.

"Must you do that?" she snapped. "It's disconcerting when you simply appear out of nowhere like that."

"My apologies. I'm afraid I have little control over my comings and goings."

"Just like you have no control over knowing where I can find the statue, I suppose."

"Not exactly, but I do remember where one of the entrances to the labyrinth is, although I doubt you'll be pleased."

"Where is it?" Trepidation hitched her breath as she saw the rueful expression on the ghost's features.

"My brother's bedroom," he muttered.

"What?" She starred at him in disbelief. "Of all possible locations, that's the *only* one you can remember?"

"I am sorry. If I could remember where another entrance was, I would tell you, but at the moment, this is the best I can offer."

"And exactly how am I supposed to search his bedroom?" she snapped.

Nigel bent his head as he cleared his throat. Rigid with horror, she shook her head vehemently. "*No.* Not again. You can't ask it of me. I don't think I could bear it."

"Exactly *what* couldn't you bear, my lady?"

The familiar low growl in her ear made her cry out in surprise. Wheeling around she took two quick steps backward as she looked up into Lucien's dark features. His gaze scraped over her with contempt as he moved forward to search the area where Nigel was standing. When he found nothing, he whirled around to face her, a cold rage tightening the muscles of his jaw.

"Where is he?"

GREAT
CHEAP
FUN

Discover eBooks!

THE FASTEST WAY TO GET THE HOTTEST NAMES

Get your favorite authors on your favorite reader, long before they're
out in print! Ebooks from Samhain go wherever you go, and work with
whatever you carry—Palm, PDF, Mobi, and more.